Michael S[...]
Hartsville, SC
December 4ᵀᴴ 2011

This book was given to me
by my friend and
colleague, Judge Bubba
Gunterton.

River Road

River Road

Gordon "Bubber" Jenkinson

To my good friend and brother on the Bench Michael Holt
Bubber Jenkinson

PELICAN PUBLISHING COMPANY
Gretna 2011

Copyright © 2011
By Gordon Jenkinson
All rights reserved

---

*The word "Pelican" and the depiction of a pelican
are trademarks of Pelican Publishing Company, Inc.,
and are registered in the U.S. Patent and Trademark Office.*

Library of Congress Cataloging-in-Publication Data

Jenkinson, Gordon B.
  River Road / Gordon "Bubber" Jenkinson.
    p. cm.
  ISBN 978-1-58980-963-5 (alk. paper) — ISBN 978-1-4556-1477-6 (e-Book) 1. South Carolina—Fiction. I. Title.
  PS3610.E695R58 2011
  813'.6—dc23
                               2011038740

Printed in the United States of America
Published by Pelican Publishing Company, Inc.
1000 Burmaster Street, Gretna, Louisiana 70053

To my wife, Peggy, who has always been the wind beneath my wings!

Right's right and wrong's wrong.
—Old African-American proverb

PSALM 1

Blessed is the man that walketh not in the counsel of the ungodly, nor standeth in the way of sinners, nor sitteth in the seat of the scournful.

But his delight is in the law of the Lord; and in his law doth he meditate day and night.

And he shall be like a tree planted by the rivers of water, that bringeth forth his fruit in his season; his leaf also shall not wither; and whatsoever he doeth shall prosper.

The ungodly are not so: but are like the chaff which the wind driveth away.

Therefore the ungodly shall not stand in the judgment, nor sinners in the congregation of the righteous.

For the Lord knoweth the way of the righteous: but the way of the ungodly shall perish.

ACKNOWLEDGMENTS

With special thanks to the following:

LINDA BROWN and MARTHA CARR, for their wonderful editorial advice.

ANDREA KELLY and PAM MUSICK, for their tireless efforts in getting the manuscript in shape for the publisher.

WELLS DICKSON, a good friend, for providing me with a number of newspaper articles about the murder of Ovid Gilbert in 1926.

BEAUFORT MABRY, who patiently answered all of my questions about law enforcement's wire technology and the use of informants in 1978.

LEE GORDON BROCKINGTON, my dear cousin, for her encouragement and help in finding a publisher.

BETH COTTINGHAM, my beloved high-school teacher, who continues to inspire and teach me even though I haven't been in her classroom in over forty years.

River Road

CHAPTER 1

Elizabeth Chase didn't know what was more offensive about her client, his constant pawing at her legs under the counsel table or his bad breath. He was like so many of her clients in the public defender's office, repeat offenders who were the poorest imaginable specimens of the human race. Joe Rizzo was even more despicable because he had been indicted for selling cocaine. The Commonwealth of Massachusetts was about halfway through its case on this June day in 1978, and Elizabeth hoped that her client would stick to his earlier decision not to testify. He had no witnesses to support his murky alibi, so the case would not last much longer if he didn't take the stand.

"Your Honor, I object," Elizabeth said as she rose from her chair. "The officer is referring to this white substance as cocaine. The Commonwealth has offered no expert testimony establishing that this substance is in fact cocaine."

"Sustained," Judge Hobgood replied gruffly, glaring at the assistant district attorney and then at the vice sergeant. "You know the rules, Sergeant. Don't forget them again."

"Yes sir, Your Honor," the sergeant replied, sitting up straighter in the witness chair.

Elizabeth looked at her client and the smirk on his face. Why is it they always think they can beat every charge? she wondered. Rizzo had sold the dope to an undercover agent, and the police recovered some of the marked money from him when he was arrested the next day.

The assistant DA had the officer correct his statement and the witness soon finished his testimony. Elizabeth tried to hammer him and the Commonwealth's other witnesses on cross-examination, but she could only bring out minor inconsistencies in their case. Each time she sat down, Rizzo would grab her arm and whisper encouragement, but he was the only person in the courtroom who was optimistic about his chances for an acquittal. The blue-collar jurors occasionally gave both of them contemptuous looks throughout the presentation of the Commonwealth's case.

Thankfully, the Commonwealth rested at quarter to five, and after Judge Hobgood denied Elizabeth's motion for a directed verdict, he recessed for the day. As Elizabeth began gathering her file together, she felt a hand grip her forearm. A deputy had Rizzo's other arm, ready to lead him back to his jail cell for the night.

"You're doing real good, pretty lady. After you get me out of this mess, me and you might just have to have ourselves a party."

"I'll see you in the morning, Mr. Rizzo," Elizabeth replied, looking at the deputy. The officer caught her signal, and with a tug, Rizzo headed back to his cell.

Upon her return, the public defender's office was vacant except for several overworked lawyers. Just about everyone else left at five. Elizabeth had recently been promoted to deputy chief public defender, and she was proud of what she had accomplished in her six years with the office. She had tried over a hundred cases, involving every conceivable offense from petit larceny to murder, and had won several high-profile felony cases. The burnout that always comes with the job was accelerating now, but she wanted to stay on as deputy for at least another year before she went into private practice.

Elizabeth grabbed her phone messages from her secretary and looked through them as she walked to her office. She recognized all of the names except one as either clients or ADAs calling about files. Slumping into her desk chair, she started massaging her temples and decided to wait until the next morning to return her calls. No matter how many cases she tried, she always felt numb at the end of a day in court.

Elizabeth felt better the next morning, knowing this would be the last day she would have to deal with Joe Rizzo. If convicted, he would go to prison for a long time, and if acquitted, he would be out of her hair.

"There's a Robert Hamilton on line three," her secretary shouted as Elizabeth passed her doorway.

"Hello?"

"Miss Chase?"

"Yes, this is Elizabeth Chase."

"Elizabeth, this is Robert Hamilton." The thick Southern accent was faintly familiar, and she was silent as she tried to place the name. "You don't remember me, do you?"

"No, I am sorry. I don't."

"I'm calling from Weenee, South Carolina. I'm your grandfather's law partner. I mean, I was. I'm sorry to have to tell you this, but your grandfather passed away yesterday. I've been trying to reach you."

"Yes, I was in court. I didn't get back to the office until late." Elizabeth felt a surge of guilt. She hadn't seen her grandfather in years although he was faithful in writing to her and calling on holidays. She hadn't been as faithful, and she could feel a certain emptiness now. Her mother, an only child, had died years ago, and Elizabeth had drifted away from her South Carolina roots.

"I'm sorry," Hamilton said softly. "He went quietly in his sleep. Rebecca found him when she went in yesterday morning."

"Thank you for calling, Mr. Hamilton."

"Do you want me to make the funeral arrangements, or wait until you get down here?"

"No, you make the arrangements, please." Then she stopped, trying to think of the right words so she wouldn't sound callous. "Mr. Hamilton, I'm afraid I'm in the middle of a trial, and I don't know if I'm going to be able to attend the funeral."

"We can wait a few days. When do you think your case will be over?"

"Soon, but this is a three-week term. This is a very bad time for me."

"I know what you mean. I used to be a criminal lawyer myself a while back. I do think it's very important for you to come down here, though. You are the executor and sole beneficiary of your grandfather's estate. Your grandfather owned a large amount of property, and it's going to take a considerable amount of work to settle the estate."

"How can I do that, even if I'm there for the funeral?"

"We just need to get you qualified as executor in the Probate Court and file the will. I'll be glad to help you with it. That's the least I can do for John. After that, I believe we can do almost everything else by mail."

"Let me talk to my boss. I'll get back to you this afternoon, Mr. Hamilton. I know it sounds as if I'm uncaring, but I did love my grandfather very much. It's just that this is so sudden, and it's a very bad time for me. I'll see what I can do."

As Elizabeth hung up the phone, she felt guilt seep through her body like an early-morning fog, and she knew she had to go.

Harry Hirsch leaned back in his chair and locked his hands behind his head. Elizabeth had just finished filling him in on the details of her phone conversation with her grandfather's law partner.

"What do you think I should do? I sent one of the clerks over to BU to do some research on South Carolina probate law. I can renounce my appointment as executor, and I'm sure Mr. Hamilton would consent to serve."

"But if it's a big estate, he can get some pretty sizable commissions, you know. Just how big is the estate?"

"I don't have any idea. But it's not the money."

"Oh, I am well aware of that, Miss Silver Spoon," Hirsch said with a grin. Everyone in the office was familiar with Elizabeth's Boston Brahmin background on her father's side of the family and the trust that went with it. She was so financially secure that she didn't have to work another day for the rest of her life, but that was not Elizabeth's nature. Her activist days started with the Vietnam War protests at Wellesley, and after graduation, she worked tirelessly for the McGovern campaign for almost a year. She had been strongly influenced by her father, who also enjoyed the privilege of not having to punch a clock. Unlike his daughter, however, he chose not to work but instead traveled from Johannesburg to Belfast to Saigon with various agencies, seeking an end to the world's problems.

Elizabeth gave her boss a contemptuous look.

Hirsch held up his hands, not wanting to take this particular discussion any further. "I think you need to go, Elizabeth. This is the last of your family down there, isn't it?"

Elizabeth nodded.

"You better go and check everything out. There's no telling what your grandfather's law partner may do if you don't. He'll probably clean out the estate—claim it was all partnership property or something like that. You'll be in pretty good shape after the Rizzo trial, won't you?"

"Yeah. They're going to call Woody's murder case next, and that'll take a week or ten days, according to him."

"Go on, then. We can cover for you for that long."

"I guess you're right. I was trying to use my caseload as an excuse, but my conscience kept getting the best of me. Thanks," she said as she stood up. "I'll check in with you once I get to South Carolina."

As Elizabeth looked at the New Jersey coastline from 20,000 feet up, she tried to get Joe Rizzo off her mind. He had been convicted, as she had expected, and sentenced to ten years. He would be out of Walpole in less than three, so she didn't feel too bad. He had angrily demanded an appeal, which he would get, but Hobgood had a clean record, and the conviction would more than likely stick.

She tried to focus on what she could remember about her mother's hometown in South Carolina. As a young girl, she had spent many summers there with her mother and had some fine, but hazy, memories. After her grandmother died, the trips became less frequent. She hadn't been back since her mother died during her sophomore year in college, and her father discouraged any contact with his ex-in-laws. He considered the Snowdens to be beneath him after the divorce.

There was one thing, however, she could remember vividly—the wide front porch of her grandparents' home. Even on the hottest South Carolina afternoons, it would be cool where she and her grandmother sat and sipped iced tea or lemonade. Slowly, events that had been stored in her mind's vault for decades came into focus, simple childhood experiences such as birthday parties and feeding the trout-sized goldfish in the lily-filled pool in the backyard.

Her reverie was broken by the pilot's announcement that the plane had been cleared for landing in Charleston. It was almost seven o'clock when she descended the steps to the tarmac. She was glad she had decided to stay in Charleston for the night, because she was bone tired. The jury had returned its verdict just before noon, and she had to race to make her flight at Logan.

Even though the sun was low now in the June sky, the heat hit her like a blast furnace. As she walked toward the World War II-era terminal, the tarmac felt like a skillet beneath her thin-soled shoes.

Once Elizabeth found the historic district in which her hotel was located, it took another twenty minutes of wrong turns to find the hotel. She was pleasantly surprised when she finally walked into the lobby that was as stately as any hotel in Boston. After a couple of scotches in her room, she ordered dinner from room service and was asleep before ten.

Elizabeth awoke at her customary 6:30 the next morning, and it took her a few seconds to realize where she was. When she opened the draperies, however, she was not prepared for the view. Her room was on the eighth floor, and for an instant she felt as if she were a twentieth-century Gulliver, looking down on a miniature city. Except for several tall buildings and a number of spectacular church steeples, all the other structures, many of which were dwellings, were not more than three stories high. She could see clear down to the Battery, where proud mansions oversaw the confluence of the Ashley and Cooper rivers. The sky was cloudless and cobalt, and the sun's rays were already filtering through the live oaks in the park across the street, creating a kaleidoscope of light on the weathered brick walks. Far out in the harbor, Fort Sumter held its ground defiantly, a grim reminder of one of the nation's darkest hours.

I've got to take some time to see this city some day, she said to herself as she surveyed the peninsula one final time. She made that promise again over shrimp and grits in the hotel dining room that overlooked a magnificent courtyard garden through Palladian windows. She remembered grits from her grandmother's kitchen, and her waiter cajoled her into ordering it when she mentioned that she hadn't had this Southern staple since she was a teenager.

Elizabeth allowed herself a thirty-minute drive through the historic district. Several times she was tempted to stop and walk so she could take in the beauty of the magnificent homes. Finally, from the seat beside her, she picked up the concierge's directions to the highway that would take her to Weenee.

She had to stop and ask for directions before she found the ramp to the Cooper River Bridge that would lead her north to Weenee. Once she reached the bridge's zenith, she stole a final glance over her shoulder at the old city, once again in miniature, like some architect's scale model of a proposed city. She followed the coast for about ten miles and then turned northwest, and the strip malls and fast-food restaurants disappeared immediately. They were replaced by forests of pines, palmettos, and winding salt creeks rimmed by brownish-green marsh grass. Once Elizabeth crossed the Wando River, the salt creeks and palmettos soon disappeared, and she now passed only foreboding pines and an occasional swamp.

About thirty miles from Charleston, she realized that she hadn't passed a car or a house for some time. All the landmarks on her directions had been correct, but she still couldn't suppress the fear that she might be lost. She gripped the wheel tightly when she remembered what had happened to those white freedom riders in Mississippi just a few years ago. After a few more miles, she passed through a small crossroads community, and her fears disappeared as quickly as they had appeared.

After crossing the wide and swiftly moving Santee River, she turned west and saw fields of tobacco, corn, and soybeans sharing the countryside with the pine forests and cypress swamps. After another twenty miles, she was relieved to notice the houses getting much closer together, and in another ten minutes she saw the Weenee town-limits sign. Elizabeth quickly got her bearings when she saw a street sign that indicated she was on Lee Street.

Elizabeth saw the courthouse on her left and remembered Hamilton telling her that his office backed up to the courthouse yard, so she took a left and immediately spotted the office down the street on the right. She pulled up to the curb and looked at the old office, once a private home. It had been built before the Civil War, and, like every residence built in Weenee during that period, it had a porch running the width of the house. It was well maintained and had recently been painted.

Walking up the wooden steps, she couldn't decide if she should knock or just enter. When she couldn't locate a doorbell, she turned the handle on the box lock and pushed the door open. There was a receptionist's desk in the entrance hall, but no one was in sight.

"Hello," a voice called out from one of the back offices. In a few seconds, Robert Hamilton himself stepped into the hall and walked briskly toward her. He was a tall man, and what hair he had left was combed straight back in a gray mane. He was impeccably dressed in a charcoal suit, white shirt, and burgundy-striped tie. Elizabeth started to extend her hand when Hamilton reached out both arms and hugged her.

"It's wonderful to see you again, even under these circumstances," he said as he took a step back to look at her. "You have grown into a lovely young lady. Did you have a good trip down?"

"Yes, I did, thank you. Charleston was interesting," she replied, taking a good look around the office for the first time. The walls were paneled in wide pine boards that had never been painted, giving the office a dreary, depressing appearance.

"I think I have everything worked out with the funeral home. The service will be tomorrow at three at the Methodist Church."

"Thank you. I appreciate your handling that for me. I really do."

"We have made arrangements for you to receive everybody from seven to nine tonight at your grandfather's house."

"What are you talking about, Mr. Hamilton?"

"You are the only family left. People will want to come by and pay their respects. Your grandfather left specific instructions."

Elizabeth swallowed hard. She had been trying not to think about the funeral, which she dreaded, but this was an unexpected and unwelcome chore. What could she say to these people she didn't know and with whom she had absolutely nothing in common?

"What sort of instructions?" she asked.

"He wanted his wake to be a happy occasion."

"What exactly do you mean, Mr. Hamilton?"

"Your grandfather wanted to make sure there was plenty of Craven County barbeque on hand, with plenty of liquor to wash it down with."

"Barbeque? Liquor? Sounds more like a party than a wake."

"It's a pretty good combination. I've got to go to the bank for a meeting. I'm sorry, but I'm chairman of the board, and I can't miss it. I'll be back after lunch sometime. Can I get you anything?"

"No, I'm fine. Could I see my grandfather's office?"

"Certainly, follow me." Hamilton led her to the first office on the left and turned on the light. "Inez, your grandfather's secretary, took the day off. She's really taking it hard," he added.

Elizabeth surveyed the room and looked back at Hamilton. "You go to your meeting. I'll be fine. I'll see you at seven."

"You sure you're okay?" Hamilton asked over his shoulder as he headed down the hall toward the front door.

"I'm sure," she said, almost to herself.

Looking around, Elizabeth could feel her grandfather in the room where he'd spent years counseling his clients about murder, mayhem, and much less serious disputes.

He had a fondness for old maps, and they covered the walls, some accompanied by early eighteenth-century land grants. The huge desk was walnut and appeared to have been locally made. She eased into the brown leather chair, creased by decades of wear, and gazed out the same window she knew her grandfather had looked out of thousands of times. After a few minutes, Elizabeth decided to leave a note for Hamilton and headed for her grandfather's house to get settled before the wake.

The house was only four blocks away on Beauregard Street, and she found it easily. As the two-story white house came into focus, she could almost see her grandparents sitting on the front porch. She slowly got out of her car and headed up the walk, noticing for the first time that the bricks were laid in a beautiful herringbone pattern. Several trips abroad and an architectural course at Wellesley had refined her eye considerably since her last visit. As she climbed the front steps, she noticed that the door was open, the entrance blocked only by a screen door. She rapped three times loudly and, after hearing nothing, called out a hello. Once again, there was only silence. Carefully she pulled on the screen until it opened. She stepped into the wide entrance hall bisecting the house and looked into the living room to her right. Not one thing had been moved in the years since she had last visited. Only the draperies had faded a little more, and the Serapi rug was wearing a little thin.

"May I help you, miss?"

Elizabeth jumped, turning quickly. She had not heard the person come up behind her. The question came from a tall, bony black woman in her sixties. She had on a blue cotton uniform, and her gray hair was pulled back in a bun.

As Elizabeth looked at her, the inquisitive look drained from the woman's face. Her mouth dropped open, and she quickly covered it with her hand. "Miss Elizabeth!" she screamed, throwing her arms around Elizabeth's neck. When Elizabeth didn't return the embrace, she pulled back, surveying Elizabeth's face.

"It's me—Rebecca. You haven't forgotten your old Rebecca, have you?"

"Rebecca?" Elizabeth asked, placing her hands on the woman's shoulders. Quickly she pulled the woman back to her, and the hug was mutual this time as hundreds of memories seemed to pour from the recesses of Elizabeth's mind.

"Oh, Rebecca, how many years has it been?"

"Too many, child," she replied, pulling away to get a better look at Elizabeth. "My, look at you. You are a beautiful woman now," she said, stroking Elizabeth's cheek with the back of her hand.

"How have you been, Rebecca?"

"Fine, just fine."

"No, really. I know the last few years have been tough on you and your people." Elizabeth had spent many summer afternoons playing with Rebecca's daughter out behind the house while Rebecca worked inside. She hadn't realized what the segregated South was all about until she went off to college. "How is Princess? Where is she now?"

"She's in Rochester, New York. She's got three children, and her husband has a good job in the Kodak plant up there. Alfreda and Cleve are up there, too. It gets kinda lonely in my old house now since I lost Henry."

"I'm so sorry, Rebecca. I hadn't heard."

"That's all right, child. He was a good man, and he lived a good life. When he died, he was senior deacon in the church. I ain't worried about him, not one bit, 'cause I know he's up in heaven."

Elizabeth smiled and nodded.

"Come on, Miss Elizabeth, let me take you to your room," Rebecca said, grabbing her hand as she headed up the wide staircase. "I already got your bed made up."

CHAPTER 2

VISITATION

The wake was not nearly as somber or sober as Elizabeth thought it would be. The mourners started arriving a few minutes before seven, and most got themselves drinks before they introduced themselves to her. The bar was set up in her grandfather's library, and behind a beautiful arrangement of magnolia blossoms stood a pecan-colored man in a white starched coat. He had a gold earring and long dark hair pulled back into a ponytail, and he spoke with a Hispanic accent. Boy, I'd love to hear how he got to Weenee, South Carolina, Elizabeth thought as she asked him for a scotch on the rocks.

A bald man of about sixty turned, looked at her, and arched his eyebrows. "Love that recipe," he said and introduced himself. They chatted a few minutes before he wandered off. The room filled up quickly, and Elizabeth was able to sip the scotch and collect her thoughts as her eyes wandered over the hundreds of books lining the mahogany shelves. She reflected that her grandfather was very well read for an old country lawyer.

"Nice room, isn't it?"

She turned and saw a man about her own age.

"Yes, it's lovely. It's always been my favorite room in the house," Elizabeth replied.

"Oh, then you must be Elizabeth."

"Yes, I'm Elizabeth Chase," she said, extending her hand.

"Jim Howard, Elizabeth, it's nice to meet you."

"Same here," Elizabeth replied, studying his face, which was long, angular, and handsome. His hair was dark and slicked back. Like the bartender, he didn't look as if he belonged in Weenee.

"I am so sorry about your grandfather," he said softly. "He was one of my patients, you know."

"No, I didn't know. You're a doctor, then?"

"Yes, I've been here in private practice for several years. It may not be much consolation, but your grandfather knew his heart was worn out and that he was living on borrowed time. Like most everyone here, I'd grown to respect him a great deal."

"Thank you, that means a lot to me," Elizabeth said as she took a sip of her drink. "Are you from here?"

"Born and raised right here. About two blocks away. My office is a long six blocks away, though," he said with a smile.

"Wow, tough commute."

"Yeah, but somebody's got to do it."

They smiled at each other before he asked, "Where's home for you?"

"Boston."

"Boston? I did my residency there. Boston General."

"Oh yeah? It's not far from my office."

"What kind of office, if you don't mind me asking?"

"Suffolk County Public Defender's Office."

"You're a lawyer?"

"Yes, why? You seem surprised."

"It's just that you don't look like a lawyer, that's all."

"What's a lawyer supposed to look like?"

"Like a man. No, that doesn't sound right," he said, holding his arms out in front of him. "It's just that we don't have very many women lawyers around here. In fact we don't have any. And besides, if we had any, I don't think they'd look like you."

"I'll give you the benefit of the doubt on that one," she replied, smiling with her eyes.

"You know what I mean, I think. What kind of cases do you handle in the public defender's office? Shoplifting, those kinds of things?"

"No, I'm in the felony division—mainly murders, rapes, those kinds of things."

"No kidding?"

"No kidding."

"Excuse me." A woman tapped Elizabeth's shoulder gently to get her attention. "You must be Elizabeth," she said, extending her hand and almost spilling her drink on the oriental rug.

"Yes, I am," Elizabeth replied, taking her hand.

"I'm Ida Pearl Middleton," the woman said.

"I'm pleased to meet you, Mrs. Middleton," Elizabeth replied.

It was difficult for Elizabeth to estimate her age due to the many layers of pancake makeup that did nothing to hide the hundreds of wrinkles on her face. She had ended the cosmetic application on the sides of her face abruptly, which made her look as though she were wearing a mask. Her bright-red lipstick, also generously applied, produced the effect of an elderly clown. Her suit was vivid yellow and well tailored. Her hand clutched a small, gold-sequined purse.

"And this is my daughter, Estelle," Ida Pearl said, turning to put her arm on the shoulder of a middle-aged woman standing just behind her.

"How do you do?" Elizabeth asked, shaking the extended hand. The daughter, in her fifties, Elizabeth guessed, had been an attractive woman, but she wasn't aging well. She also invested heavily in cosmetics, but the effect wasn't nearly as grotesque on her as on her mother.

"She's fine," her mother said, answering for her daughter. "We were both dear, dear friends of your grandfather's, child. Dear, dear friends," she repeated, shaking her head as her eyes filled with tears. Elizabeth wondered what Mrs. Middleton's makeup would look like if it was creased by tears.

"We're so sorry," Estelle added.

"How long will you be down here?" Mrs. Middleton asked.

"Just a few days. I have to get back to work."

"Work?" Mrs. Middleton said the word like it was an incurable, communicable disease. "Your daddy's got plenty of money, child. What are you doing working?"

"I want to work, and, besides, I enjoy it." Elizabeth was getting a little annoyed at this cross-examination from a pushy woman. She anticipated the next question. "I'm a criminal lawyer."

"A criminal lawyer," Mrs. Middleton said the words slowly, almost in a whisper. "Well, I never," she murmured as she shook her head. "Seeing how you are John Snowden's granddaughter, though, I bet you're a good one," she added, smiling broadly at Elizabeth. The warmth of her smile melted Elizabeth's annoyance immediately. This was clearly a woman who spoke her mind.

"We'll see you at the service tomorrow," Mrs. Middleton said, reaching for her daughter's arm. "See you, Jim, and don't forget the medicine you promised to send me in the morning."

"Pleased to meet you," Elizabeth called out as the two headed toward the dining room.

Jim smiled at Elizabeth and shook his head slowly.

"Why are you shaking your head that way?" Elizabeth asked.

"It never ceases to amaze me what comes out of Ida Pearl's mouth."

"I'd like to hear the story on those two before I leave."

"It'll take hours," he said, laughing. "But I'd be happy to tell you."

Before she could say anything else an elderly couple introduced themselves, and for the next hour and a half she was deluged by mourners, most of them contemporaries of her grandfather.

Finally, she made her way back to the bar, and the second scotch relaxed her a bit. She was glad to see that the crowd had thinned considerably and there were only four people left in the dining room. The long Sheraton mahogany table was still covered with food. There must not be a chicken left living in Craven County, she thought as she surveyed the platters of fried chicken. There were also casseroles, deviled eggs, and three kinds of aspics. In the center of the table were two platters that contained a brown, strange-looking meat.

"Miss Elizabeth, you look tired." She turned and saw Rebecca standing behind her. "Let me fix you a plate." She leaned over and whispered in her ear, "Go sit down in the kitchen. I'll bring it to you."

Elizabeth turned and surveyed the dining room. Those who remained were engrossed in the latest gossip, so she decided she wouldn't offend anyone by taking Rebecca up on her offer. She also realized she was starving.

She walked into the kitchen and pulled a Windsor chair up to the old heart-pine table with its lazy susan, and again childhood memories came flooding back. The room even smelled the same to her, but it still loomed large, the tall painted cabinets reaching to the twelve-foot ceilings. She had spent many hours sitting at this same table as she listened to her grandmother, talking and singing as she worked.

Her reverie was broken when Rebecca slipped a heaping plate in front of her. "I know you's hungry and it's best to get something in your stomach when you're drinking that stuff," Rebecca said, giving the scotch a disapproving look.

Elizabeth smiled and thanked her. The last thing she wanted to do was get in a temperance debate with Rebecca. "What did you fix for me? You're right, I'm starved."

"Just a little bit of everything. Including your favorite."

Elizabeth saw the strange-looking meat that had been so prominently displayed on the dining-room table. It now occupied a position of similar prominence on her plate. "What is this?" Elizabeth asked, pointing her fork at the meat.

"Barbeque, child, you done forgot? That was your favorite when you was a little girl. You been gone longer than I thought."

"Barbequed what?" Elizabeth asked, inspecting the greasy-looking meat as she turned it with her fork.

"Barbeque hog."

"And this was my favorite?" Elizabeth asked, shaking her head in disbelief.

"You couldn't get enough of it, child. Go ahead, eat it. Best thing for soaking up liquor I know." Elizabeth could tell by her tone that it was a command, not a request.

She picked out a small piece, slipped it into her mouth, and chewed slowly. The taste was wonderful, but she couldn't describe it. If she had been a food critic, she would have had a mountainous writer's block.

Rebecca grinned and crossed her arms knowingly. "Now you remember, Miss Elizabeth, don't you?"

Elizabeth answered her by shoving a much larger piece into her mouth. She ate heartily for several minutes before she realized that Rebecca was still standing over her, studying her closely.

"Rebecca, sit down a minute, I know you must be dead tired by now."

"Yeah, I sho am, Miss Elizabeth, but they's a lot of cleaning up that's got to be done before these old bones can rest," she said, looking around the kitchen.

"Sit just a minute," Elizabeth pleaded.

"Miss Elizabeth, you know I can't do that," Rebecca said, looking as though she had just been asked to handle a rattlesnake.

"Why not?" Elizabeth demanded, holding her hands out to her sides.

"We don't sit at no table when white folks is eating, that's why. I better go check the food in the dining room." She was gone before Elizabeth could say anything else.

Thankfully, the remaining guests were gone within half an hour. As Elizabeth fixed a nightcap, she realized there was probably some correlation between all the empty liquor bottles and the departure of the last guests. She said goodnight to Rebecca and was under the covers of a four-poster mahogany bed within ten minutes.

CHAPTER 3

Elizabeth slept a hard, dreamless sleep, and she could tell that it was late when she awoke to sunlight flooding her room. She hadn't paid much attention to the room the night before because she was exhausted, but she realized that she was in the upstairs guest bedroom, one she had slept in many times before as a child. The furniture was dark, mostly mahogany, and in one corner was a beautiful inlaid linen press. Her eyes met the eyes of a long-dead ancestor, staring down at her from a full-length portrait that hung over the mantel, and she instinctively pulled the covers up to her chin. She smiled at her folly and threw back the covers.

"Go ahead and get your eyes full, old man," she said with a laugh and climbed out of bed.

Rebecca had her breakfast on the stove when she walked downstairs in her bathrobe.

"My gracious, Rebecca, don't you ever go home?"

"Morning, Miss Elizabeth."

"Good morning. How are you?"

Rebecca was dressed from head to toe in white. Her uniform was stiffly starched, and even her hose were white. "I'm okay," she said as she raked scrambled eggs onto a plate. "You want grits? Or you forgot about them, too?"

"No, I didn't forget about grits, and, yes, I'll take some, but not too much, thank you."

"Funeral's at three, you know?"

"Yes, I know. After I get dressed I'm going down to Granddaddy's office." Elizabeth realized she hadn't said that name in many years.

"Don't worry, child, I'll have your dinner ready when you get back. You take care of your lawyering and I'll get everything ready here."

"Ready for what?" Elizabeth asked, puzzled.

"The people."

"What people?"

"You ain't seen nothing yet. Last night was quiet compared to what this house will be like after the funeral."

It looks like it is going to be another long day, Elizabeth thought as she sipped her coffee.

There was a wreath on the law office's door with a note saying the office was closed due to the death of Mr. John Snowden. The door was unlocked, but there was no one in the waiting area. Elizabeth called out for Mr. Hamilton, and after a few seconds he ambled out of his office.

"Good morning, Elizabeth."

"Good morning, Mr. Hamilton."

"I put your grandfather's will on his desk with some extra copies for your file. I also went ahead and made an appointment for you with the Judge of Probate for eleven on Tuesday. I hope that's all right. I know you want to get qualified and get things going as soon as possible."

"Yes, I do. Thank you very much."

"Your grandfather prepared an inventory and updated things on almost a monthly basis. He was a very meticulous man, so I think handling the estate is going to be fairly easy for you. It's also on his desk, as are all of his deeds and mortgages. Let me know if you have any questions. I'll be in my office. Inez isn't coming in today, but she can start on the petition to prove the will first thing in the morning. She can have everything ready by eleven." Hamilton nodded when he finished and turned and headed back to his office.

"Thanks again," Elizabeth said to his back and followed him down the hall toward her grandfather's office. When she slipped into the leather chair, she saw everything neatly placed on the desk blotter. She picked up the will and read it slowly. It was straightforward. There weren't even any charitable bequests—everything went to Elizabeth. Next to the will was the inventory that had been made a little over three weeks before his death. There were $211,347 in liquid assets, mainly certificates of deposits, treasury bills, and a few blue-chip stocks. Nothing in the portfolio was even remotely risky. There were eighteen mortgage notes that he held, totaling $96,112, representing money her grandfather had lent to various property owners in Craven County, none of whose names she recognized. There was a 178-acre farm that her grandfather had valued at $89,000. The house on Beauregard Street was valued at $65,000. With his Buick and household effects thrown in, the estate was valued at just under $500,000. The principal in her trust was over three times that amount, so it was not as if she needed the money.

Satisfied that she had a handle on the estate inventory, Elizabeth began going through the desk drawers. She felt a little guilty doing so, but she kept telling herself this was her property now. She found paperclips, bank statements, and a loaded thirty-eight pistol. Must be for unruly clients, she thought. There were stacks of letters held together by rubber bands. She knew that they were legally hers, but she couldn't bear to invade her grandfather's privacy, even if he was dead. At least this is what she thought until she recognized her handwriting on one of the stacks.

The letters were written in the flowery hand of a teenager, with circles for the dots of her *i*s and occasional smiley faces and hearts. The last one was postmarked the year she turned eighteen, and she opened it slowly. It was written the summer before she left for Wellesley, when she had been too busy to come down for her annual trip. She wrote of going to college with typical schoolgirl excitement. The envelope was dog-eared and slightly dirty. The folds in the letter had almost worn through the paper. It was a letter that had been read and reread many, many times. Suddenly Elizabeth realized that this was the last letter she had written her grandfather. The tears tickled her cheeks before she realized they were there. She hadn't known how much she had meant to him and how abruptly she had cut him off. This had to be particularly painful after her grandmother died. Elizabeth usually called at Christmas, but that was about the extent of her contact with them in the last few years. Grandmother had been faithful in writing, but when Elizabeth started her career, she just didn't have time to write or phone.

She found a handkerchief in her purse, composed herself, and started the inventory again. The rest of the drawers contained mundane legal documents, newspaper articles, and other insignificant mementos. She started to throw some of it away but was afraid Inez would think she was uncaring.

She heard a knock on the open door and saw Hamilton looking

at her. "I've got a closing over at the Savings and Loan in a few minutes that will probably take the rest of the morning. Do you have any questions?"

"Just a few, if you have a couple of minutes."

"Sure," he said and walked over to sit down opposite the desk. "No problems with the will, I hope?"

Elizabeth smiled at him before she answered. "I'm certainly not a probate lawyer, but it looks very simple to me."

"Couldn't be any simpler," he said, smiling back.

"I do have a few questions about South Carolina law. How long before I can close the estate?"

"It'll take about ten months to a year. You may owe a little bit of estate tax but not much."

"Will I have a problem liquidating everything within that timeframe?"

"You want to sell everything?"

"Yes, I have no need for any of it."

"The farm should be no problem. You can probably move that in thirty days after the claims period expires. The house may take a little longer, but it should sell within the year. Young people around here are starting to get interested in old houses, if you can believe that."

"Will there be any interest in the furniture, silver, that kind of stuff?"

Hamilton sat upright in his chair. "You want to sell your grandparents' personal belongings?"

"Why not? It will be very expensive to move them to Boston, and I certainly don't have room for that stuff in my apartment."

"Those things were very dear to your grandparents. A lot of it was passed down from your great-grandparents. On both sides," he added.

Elizabeth leaned forward in her grandfather's chair. "Mr. Hamilton, I know you think I'm insensitive and ungrateful, but I have no need for those things. They mean nothing to me because I didn't grow up with them. They're just objects."

"Your mother grew up with them," he said softly.

Elizabeth shrugged and held her arms out, palms up. "I'm sorry." There was an awkward silence for a few seconds. "Can we do most of the paperwork by mail, Mr. Hamilton?"

"Sure. Once we get everything filed and set up. When do you plan to fly back?"

"In four or five days."

"That quick, huh?"

"I'm very busy."

"We can do it, but it will half-kill Inez. She likes to work at her own pace, you know. Any other questions?"

"I understand from Rebecca there will be a big crowd at the house after the funeral."

"Yeah, I guess so," Hamilton replied.

"This town appears to enjoy a funeral."

"It is somewhat of a social occasion," Hamilton said, leaning back in his chair. "You have to remember, there isn't a whole lot going on in a small town like this."

"From what I've seen, I'd have to agree with you."

Hamilton looked at his watch and jumped up quickly. "I'm already late. If I don't get back here before lunch, I'll see you at the funeral." With a wave of his hand he was gone.

Elizabeth went back to her work. In a corner was a filing cabinet, and on the tabs of the files she saw that her grandfather had handled almost every type of case imaginable. There were land partitions, criminal cases with varying degrees of seriousness, and even a few divorces thrown in. One of the divorce actions had the largest file—two expandable folders—and she pulled it out when her curiosity got the best of her. She was skimming a deposition that contained some juicy accusations of adultery when she heard the front door slam.

She closed the file quickly, not wanting Robert Hamilton to see how nosy she was, and walked to the hall. When she looked toward the front door, she froze in her tracks. Not ten feet away stood one of the vilest-looking creatures she had ever seen.

Staring back at her was a short, white man who looked to be in his sixties. He wore a white shirt and blue trousers that appeared to be some type of uniform, though they clearly did not match. The shirt was grimy, and there were half-moons of perspiration under his arms. His body odor was nauseating, even at this distance. One of his cheeks bulged grotesquely with a thick chew of tobacco, and there was dried tobacco juice on both sides of his mouth. Two or three days of gray stubble grew on his round face, and one of his eyes looked as if it had been somehow plucked from his face, leaving behind a red socket. On his head, propped at a rakish angle, was some type of fireman or policeman's cap.

"What do you want?" she demanded.

"Who you?" the man shot back.

"John Snowden's granddaughter. Elizabeth Chase," she said sternly, putting her hands on her hips. "Who are you?"

"Me James."

"Me James?" Elizabeth repeated.

"Me James Cooper," the man said slowly, in a childlike voice.

Elizabeth realized that he was very slow, and she softened her tone. "What can I do for you, Mr. Cooper?"

"Call me James."

"Okay, James. How can I help you?"

His one eye stared at her a few seconds, and then he bowed his head as if he were praying. When his head started bobbing, Elizabeth realized he was crying. In a few seconds James regained his composure and looked at Elizabeth.

"Yo' granddaddy, he my friend."

"I'm glad, James. I'm sure he liked having you for a friend."

The man smiled, showing his rotten teeth. "Me worked for your granddaddy," he said slowly.

"What did you do, James?"

"Pick up trash in the yard," he said importantly.

"Well, I'm sure you were a big help to him."

"He pay me, too."

"That's fine. I'm sure you earned it."

"You want me to pick up trash for you?"

"No, James. I won't be staying here very long. I won't need you."

"Why? Me work good." The smile was gone now, and he looked close to tears again.

"Can you excuse me now, James? I've got a lot of work to do before the funeral."

"Me not going to funeral. Don't like funerals," he said. "Funerals scare me," he added, shaking his head as he started for the door. He carried on an animated conversation with himself as he walked down the hall, but Elizabeth couldn't understand a word he said. Even after the door shut behind him, his body odor hung in the air.

CHAPTER 4

John Snowden's funeral was held in the old United Methodist Church, with its grand Doric columns and ornate brickwork. The service wasn't even fifteen minutes long, much to Elizabeth's relief. The sanctuary was almost full, and most of those in attendance looked to be either in their sixties or seventies. A very young and very nervous minister conducted the service. He admittedly had never met John Snowden since he had been transferred to Weenee only several weeks earlier, and he recited few biographical details in his eulogy. The passages of Scripture the minister read were the same ones Elizabeth had heard at practically every funeral she had ever attended.

As expected, the crowd at the house following the service was much larger than the night before. The same bartender was there, food was everywhere you turned, and another hog had met the same fate as the one they had feasted on the night before. To Elizabeth's surprise, the people did not stay as long nor drink as much as they had at the wake. She stayed away from the bar because it was still early in the day, and she didn't know whether it was acceptable for a family member to have a drink after the funeral.

She was saying goodbye to a blue-haired great-grandmother who had at least two pictures of all of her descendants when she felt someone at her side. She turned and saw Jim Howard. It took several minutes more to get rid of the woman, and then she looked at the doctor.

"Hi," she said.

"You have a lot of patience with people," he commented.

"This is a piece of cake compared to the people I have to work with in Boston. Most of my clients aren't very nice."

"I can imagine," he answered. "Can I get you a drink?"

"No, not right now, thanks. Go ahead, though."

"No, I can't. I've got a waiting room full of patients back at the office so I'm heading out. How long did you say you would be staying?"

"Three or four more days. It depends on how quickly I can get moving on the estate."

"Would you care to have dinner Wednesday night?"

"That sounds good—if this is the last of the parties?" she said, looking around the room and rolling her eyes.

"I believe it is," he replied, grinning. "Will you be in your grandfather's office tomorrow?"

"Either there or here."

"I might call you tomorrow. Bye-bye."

Before she could respond, another old lady was tugging at her arm. After she walked the last guests to the front door, Elizabeth began taking food from the dining room to the kitchen.

"What you gonna do with all this food, Miss Elizabeth?" Rebecca asked.

"Why, I haven't even thought about that. There's no way we can eat it all. You take it home, Rebecca."

"I couldn't do that, Miss Elizabeth."

"Sure you can. I'll help you wrap it. Just leave enough for my dinner."

"You mean supper?"

"Yes, I mean supper."

After they had used almost a roll of aluminum foil and a number of paper plates wrapping the leftover food, Elizabeth plopped down at the kitchen table. "Sit down and talk to me, Rebecca," she said, pointing to a chair. Rebecca looked at Elizabeth and the empty chair. "Come on, I'm not eating." Rebecca smiled shyly and slipped into the chair. "See," Elizabeth said as she reached over and patted Rebecca's hand. "The roof didn't fall in. Nothing bad happened. Okay?" Rebecca nodded but remained silent. "I just want to talk with you, that's all."

"What you want to talk 'bout, Miss Elizabeth?"

"Well, the first thing I want to talk about is your calling me Miss Elizabeth."

"You want me to call you Miss Chase? I know you a grown woman now. A pretty grown woman," she added.

"No, I'd like for you to call me Elizabeth."

"I don't think I can do that, Miss Elizabeth."
"Why not?"
"You a white lady and I'm colored, that why."
"What difference does that make?"
"A lot of difference."
"It doesn't make any difference to me," Elizabeth said, raising her voice to emphasize her point.
"I know it don't, but you don't live here."
"What difference does that make?"
"Things is just done differently here from the way things is done up North. I been up there, Miss Elizabeth. I know what you're trying to say. But you really ain't never lived down here 'cept as a child, and a child can't understand the ways between white people and colored people."
"You may be right, Rebecca. Maybe I won't ever understand Southern ways. I'm not sure I want to understand them," she added. Elizabeth reached her hand across the table again and grabbed Rebecca's worn, callused hand. "Will you please try to call me Elizabeth?" she asked.
Rebecca smiled. "I promise I'll try, Miss Elizabeth." Elizabeth returned the smile, knowing she had done little to alter Rebecca's sense of Southern protocol. "That all you want to talk about?"
"No, I want to hear more about Princess."
"She doing fine. She in Rochester like most of my children. Her husband's a supervisor at the Kodak plant. Makes almost as much money in a month as I make in a whole year," she added, shaking her head.
"I would love to see her. Does she ever come home?"
"Yeah, they comes home every summer for the Fourth and a week around Christmas."
"How many children does she have?"
"She got three head and another one on the way."
"My God, that makes me feel old," Elizabeth said as she rolled her head back and stared at the ceiling. "Do you remember the time Princess and I climbed that big oak tree in the backyard, and we couldn't get down? You called Granddaddy, and he called the fire department."
"'Course I remember. Shoulda took a switch to both of you.

Princess would always mind me until she got 'round you." Rebecca pressed her lips together and made a weak attempt at looking scornful. Then she giggled and shook her head slowly.

"That was so embarrassing, and Granddaddy thought it was so funny. He picked at me about that for years. How old were we then, Rebecca?"

"Eleven years old," she said, not even stopping to think.

"Did she move right after high school?"

"No, she went up there her last year in school. Things was kinda rough around here then. That was during integration, you know. She stayed with my sister."

"Are things better here now?"

"Yeah, they is. The colored people are still poor people, though. I don't know when that's gonna change. We got a lot more rights now than we had before, but rights don't put no food on the table."

"Then black people really aren't any better off than they were fifty years ago, are they?"

"Well, we can sit in the downstairs at the theater, and we can sit down in the drugstore and order a sandwich."

"Rebecca, those are things you should have been able to do years and years ago. What about jobs? Are your people getting the jobs they should be getting?"

"I don't know, Miss Elizabeth," she said as her eyes wandered out the window. "I'm 'most sixty years old. I let the young people worry 'bout them kinda things."

"Well, you should be worried about them, too."

"Why? What good is it going to do for me to worry? It won't change nothing."

Elizabeth could tell by the look on Rebecca's face that she wasn't about to change her mind, so she changed the subject. "Rebecca, what do you know about Dr. Howard?"

Rebecca cut her eyes quickly at Elizabeth. "What you wanna know for?"

"Just curious, that's all."

"You got your eyes on a man that quick?" she asked.

"No, of course not. He just seems friendly and kind of nice."

"Don't know much about him. Know he makes a lot of money

and drives a fancy car. Never heard anybody talk about a wife or a girlfriend. He ax you out?"

"Not exactly. We're going to have a drink or two and maybe dinner, that's all."

"You mean to say that you ain't never been out with a man before and you gonna go drink with him?"

"It's not what you think, Rebecca."

"I hope not," she replied, shaking her head. "Who else you meet up with these last two days?"

"I met a Mrs. Middleton and her daughter Estelle."

"They's nice ladies. They use to come see your granddaddy a good bit. They like to drink liquor, too." Elizabeth did not miss the disdainful tone in her voice. "They always so dressed up. Like they was always getting ready to go to church."

"Then there was an awful-looking man who came into Granddaddy's office. James something. I can't remember his last name."

"What's so awful 'bout James? He ain't never hurt nobody."

"He just looks so bad— that eye—and he smells bad."

"James is all right. People can be mean to him but he ain't as dumb as everybody thinks he is."

"You have some unusual people in this town," Elizabeth said, shaking her head. "I'll help you finish cleaning up so you can go home."

There was no resistance from Rebecca.

CHAPTER 5

Sheriff Jack Carter found it difficult to concentrate on the report he was reading from the State Law Enforcement Division because he had eaten too much dinner at Holmes Diner. He needed to stay away from Beulah Holmes' fried fish and red rice in the middle of the day if he was to get any paperwork done in the afternoon. He was startled out of his sleepy state when his chief deputy Joe McKenzie barreled into his office.

"Sheriff, the dispatcher just got a call from Wilson. He was on Frenchie's place. Says it looks like something terrible has happened down there. The place is torn to hell and there is blood everywhere. No sign of nobody, though."

"Let's go," the sheriff said, jumping out of his chair. "We'd better take two cars. Tell Rita to get us some back up."

Sheriff Carter climbed into his patrol car, a powder-blue Lincoln Continental. It had been confiscated in a moonshine bust the previous year and had been hand-lettered in bold blocks by one of the sheriff's most talented trustees. It wasn't your typical law-enforcement cruiser, but Black Jack Carter wasn't your typical Southern county sheriff. The most obvious difference was Black Jack's skin, which was as dark as midnight. Ironically, his nickname was not derived from the color of his skin but originated from his early days on the force at the Weenee Police Department.

When he retired from a distinguished career in the military police, he was the first black hired as a Weenee policeman. Whenever there was the slightest hint of trouble, he wielded his blackjack indiscriminately, although most of the beneficiaries of its blows were his black brethren. Gradually, he gained the respect of both races, and he rose through the ranks of the force rapidly. When he announced his candidacy for Craven County sheriff, he was the assistant chief of the Weenee Police Department, and his filing surprised no one.

His opponent, Harold Parnell, was the incumbent and had held the office for over thirty years. Parnell was sixty-nine years old and looked and acted ten years older. He ran his office the same as he did in the fifties, and if he got one black vote it was because of a mismarked ballot.

Like anywhere else in the South in the sixties, Craven County had been in a state of upheaval. In the early seventies, the black people had begun to flex their political muscles. Weenee wasn't as bad as many places, because there were no riots or murdered freedom riders. The town was even peaceful when Dr. Martin Luther King, Jr., came for a march down Lee Street, Weenee's main thoroughfare.

The sixties were dominated by voter-registration drives, and the seventies saw the fruits of those labors as blacks were elected to countywide offices for the first time since Reconstruction. With the Craven County black voters turning out in record numbers, Black Jack easily beat the incumbent. In the same election, another black man, Isaiah Anderson, was elected county treasurer.

After he was sworn in, both whites and blacks were convinced that Black Jack was a natural for the job. His sense of fairness was unwavering, and he was hard on all criminals regardless of the color of their skin, who their families were, or how much money they had in the bank. His first two years in office had gone well, and there was even some talk of him running for higher office.

Once the sheriff moved his Continental into traffic, he flicked on his blue light and began driving aggressively out of town and onto River Road. This case had some bad possibilities, he thought as he eased up to seventy on the highway. It was hard for the sheriff to believe that anyone in Craven County would want to kill the old Frenchman, even though he could be very aggravating at times. No one knew much about him except that his name was Ovid Gilbert, he was French, and he appeared to be in his midseventies.

He got off of the train one day about five years ago carrying all of his worldly possessions in an old black valise. Reportedly, he was on the way to Florida, but for reasons known to no one, he never got back on the train. He rented a tenant house from a farmer not far from the banks of the Weenee River about ten miles out of town. He made a modest living repairing clocks and watches and selling vegetables from the large garden he planted between his house and the river. He was always a strange sight with his drooping gray mustache and black clothes as he sold his produce from the loading dock at the back of the depot. The people of Weenee liked him although he loved to argue and haggle over prices. His heavily accented English was a constant communication problem with the citizens of Weenee, whose thick low-country brogue was all but unintelligible to outsiders.

When Black Jack pulled into the yard of Frenchie's house, he could see Sergeant Wilson standing nervously near his cruiser with his service revolver in his hand. Sgt. Clarence Wilson was a holdover from Sheriff Parnell's years, but he was so close to retirement that Black Jack didn't have the heart to fire him. He usually assigned him to traffic duty at funerals or other low-profile jobs that he couldn't foul up.

The sheriff pulled into the yard as close as he could get to the other cruiser and jumped out. "Find anyone, Sergeant?"

"No sir." So much perspiration had soaked through the shirt of his uniform that Wilson looked as if he had been caught in a downpour. Black Jack thought this was the first serious case he had worked in years.

"Then put your weapon away," he ordered, pointing to the gun in Wilson's hand.

"Yes sir," he replied, looking down at the gun as if he had forgotten he was holding it.

"What have you found, Sergeant?" the sheriff asked, looking out toward the river as he shielded the afternoon sun from his eyes.

"Blood. It's . . . it's out near the garden. It's everywhere, and Frenchie's dog is back there dead. He looks like a butchered hog. And the garden is tore up, really funny like some kinda animal has been through there."

"Let's go have a look. Lead the way."

As they approached the garden, Black Jack could see that his sergeant was right. There was a wide swath cut randomly through the rows, and one section of the trellis that held the pole beans had been pulled over.

"It's a shame," the sheriff remarked. "That's about as nice a garden as I've ever seen in Craven County—at least it was before whatever came through here."

"The blood and the dog is over here, Sheriff." Wilson led him to an area just downriver from the garden, and Wilson was right again. There was blood everywhere. The sheriff took five minutes examining every splatter of blood on the ground, squatting at each sample to get a closer look but careful not to taint the evidence. Finally, when he had finished his inspection, he stood up, folded his arms, and stared at the river, deep in thought.

"You want me to do anything, Sheriff?" Wilson asked.

"Get some tape and secure the area. Then call Rita and tell her to get SLED down here ASAP. Tell 'em it's a probable homicide."

"Yes sir," Wilson replied. His hands began to shake, and the sheriff couldn't tell if it was from fear or excitement.

"What do you think, Joe?" the sheriff said, turning toward his chief deputy.

"Somebody's either dead or hurt real bad," he answered, shaking his head.

"I'm afraid you're right. Let's check out the house. Come on."

The sheriff and his chief deputy walked over to the tenant house and surveyed the front porch and steps. The front door was closed, so Black Jack pulled out his handkerchief and slowly turned the rusted metal knob. As the door squeaked open, the sheriff removed his service revolver from his holster and peered into the room.

"Frenchie!" he shouted. There was no answer. "Frenchie!" he called even louder, and again there was only silence.

Black Jack was surprised at how neat the room appeared. It was as if Frenchie had a wife or housekeeper, but he was always alone. The kitchen was just as spotless. There were a number of pots hanging from a rack suspended from the ceiling that reminded Black Jack of a restaurant kitchen he had seen overseas when he was in the service. The modest bedroom and the storage room revealed no sign of the missing Frenchman.

Finally the two officers gave up their search and went back outside. Sergeant Wilson was standing in the yard talking with another deputy who had pulled up while the sheriff was inside.

"Rita said the SLED people wouldn't be here before dark," the sergeant reported. Black Jack looked up at the sun and couldn't argue the point, as they were almost two hours from Columbia.

"Joe," he said, turning to his chief deputy, "after you make sure the crime scene is secure, I want you to check with the neighbors—anybody that might know something about Frenchie, his habits, his friends if he had any, anything that might help us. We have to treat this as a homicide."

Deputy Jimmy Watford didn't mind dragging the river. He was always assigned that duty, and it didn't come up too often because most people in Craven County loved the Weenee River too much to throw dead bodies in it. It was one of the best blackwater fishing rivers in the South, or in the country as far as Jimmy Watford was concerned. He just didn't like dragging in the river when it was right. The river was right, the locals claimed, when it was at a perfect level in the late spring for bream and redbreast fishing. There was always much discussion and argument in town this time of year as to exactly what depth made the fish feed so ravenously. Most townsfolk watched the U.S. Weather Service's depth marker on the Lee Street bridge the way investors watched the stock market. Because the river was either rising or falling this time of year, there was never enough time to confirm any one's opinions. As this opportunistic fishing frenzy lasted only a few days, oftentimes businesses closed unexpectedly and grown men would call in sick at work like hooky-playing schoolkids.

Watford hated to mess up the fishing in this stretch of the river, but he had no choice. He recognized some of his friends as they nervously gunned their outboards and sped on downriver at the sight of him. He had been on the river in the hot sun for over two hours. He kept his mind occupied by watching for birds in the stately cypress trees that guarded the banks, the ubiquitous water moccasins, and the occasional alligator that patrolled the river. Maybe they'll give up the search in a few minutes, he thought, and then he'd have a little time left for some real fishing. SLED, or the State Law Enforcement Division, had combed every inch of dirt within a mile of Frenchie's house and found nothing, so he sure didn't expect to find anything in the river.

Suddenly he felt a tug on the grappling hook, like a good-size catfish or maybe a big mudfish. The object pulled free from the bottom, and Watford reached down and yanked on the rope, realizing that whatever it was, was still on the line. Probably somebody's bait bucket that fell overboard, he thought as he began dragging the line into the boat. The hook was underneath the boat, and the deputy was pulling the rope straight up. When the hook neared the surface, he leaned over to shake the object free and realized he was staring into the face of Ovid Gilbert. It was the eyes in the severed head that Jimmy Watford would always remember, open and alert, staring angrily at a world the Frenchman had now left behind.

CHAPTER 6

Elizabeth sat alone at the kitchen table staring at the last two bites of pecan pie on the plate in front of her, trying to summon the willpower to stop eating the decadent dessert. Rebecca had left her supper on the stove at five when she left. As Elizabeth reviewed the day's events, she was thankful that things were getting back to a normal routine. She had met with the probate judge that morning, and he had assured her the probate would go smoothly and all of the estate filings could be handled by mail. The judge had given her the names of three individuals who would act as appraisers for the estate. She was able to contact them all by midafternoon and was pleased that everything seemed to be falling into place. She and Robert, as he insisted on being called, both agreed that she should be able to leave the day after tomorrow.

As she was putting her dishes in the sink, Elizabeth heard the ring of her grandfather's ancient telephone in the hall. Picking up the receiver, she wondered who would know she was there. "Hello?"

"Elizabeth? Jim Howard."

"Oh, hi, Jim."

"You sound surprised to hear from me."

"I forgot you said you might call."

Jim tried to mask his disappointment. "Are we still on for dinner tomorrow night?"

"You mean supper?"

"Are you making fun of us?" This time he did not try to hide the irritation in his voice.

Elizabeth laughed. "No. Don't be so serious, Doctor. Dinner sounds good. I can't stay out too late, though. I've got a lot to do tomorrow if I'm leaving Thursday."

"That quick, huh?"

"I've got a job, remember? I'm not a doctor. I can't take off when I please."

"Yeah sure. I'd like for you and any of your lawyer friends to follow me around for a couple of days. I'd show you what real work is."

"Just kidding. Can you find a decent meal around here at night?"

"You can. But no cocktails. You look like you enjoy your scotch, so I've made reservations for us at the beach."

"The beach. I was serious about getting home early. How far is it?"

"It's only an hour away and, believe me, it's worth the drive. Where we're going has the best food south of the Big Apple."

"Dr. Howard, you exaggerate."

"You just wait," he promised.

"You can pick me up here, Jim. What time?"

"About seven. See you then."

"Bye," she said as she hung up.

After Elizabeth finished the dishes, she went to the den and cut on the television. After forty-five minutes, she became bored and searched her grandfather's library until she found a recent copy of *TIME* magazine. She tucked the magazine under her arm and began turning off the downstairs lights, except for the hall light. As she climbed the steps, she remembered the cast-iron, footed tub in her grandmother's bathroom. They had modernized all the bathrooms, but apparently her grandmother couldn't bear to part with this late-nineteenth-century antique. She did her best thinking in there, Elizabeth remembered her saying. As Elizabeth was drawing her bath, she heard the telephone again in the hall.

It took her a minute to find it in the dark upstairs hall. "Hello," she said when she picked up the cold metal receiver. This telephone must be forty years old, she thought as she waited for the voice on the other end.

"Hello, Elizabeth!" a woman shouted.

"Yes, this is Elizabeth."

"This is Ida Pearl."

"Excuse me. Who did you say you were?"

"Ida Pearl Middleton. We met at your grandfather's the other day."

"Yes, of course. I'm sorry. I've met so many people these last few days."

"Don't worry about it, child. I know exactly what you mean. Estelle and I would like for you to come over for a drink late tomorrow afternoon. You can come about five thirty. Bye."

It took Elizabeth a few seconds to realize the line was dead. She was infuriated this woman didn't even give her time to respond to her invitation. She wanted to call her back and tell her that no, she didn't have time to come by for a drink.

It took her a minute to find the hall light, and she grew angrier when she couldn't locate a phonebook. She finally decided to wait until morning when she suddenly realized that she had left the tub running. She dashed into the bathroom, and a smile creased her cheeks when she saw that the old tub was two-thirds full—just perfect, she told herself. Finally something went right. She let her robe drop to the floor and eased into the hot water. When she sat down in the water, she lay her head back on the white enamel edge and stretched her legs without touching the other end of the tub. She had reclined there a full ten minutes, in a half-sleep, when she heard someone beating furiously on the backdoor. She dried herself quickly and pulled her robe back on. She hurried down the steps, not knowing what to make of the racket. If it was someone trying to harm her, surely they would not be making all this noise.

She cut on the kitchen light and the rapping stopped. When she flipped on the back-porch light, she saw a black woman and three children through the glass panels.

Elizabeth moved closer to the door. "What do you want?" she yelled.

"I need to talk to you, please, ma'am," the woman answered, her face contorted grotesquely. She could see that the youngest child, holding his mother's hand, had been crying. Elizabeth looked at the sad faces of the other two children and decided to let them in. She turned the key in the old lock and swung the door open.

"Come in," Elizabeth said, stepping back.

"We hate to bother you, ma'am, but we need yo' help."

"What kind of help?" she asked, studying the faces of the children but seeing only the same fear that was reflected in their mother's face.

"The high sheriff come and got Willie. Took him to jail," she added, her eyes filling up with tears. She tried to start again, but she broke out in sobs. The two younger children began to cry too.

Elizabeth looked at the oldest child, a boy who couldn't be over fourteen.

"They say my daddy killed Mr. Frenchie," the boy blurted out.

"What are you talking about?" Elizabeth asked, looking back at the woman.

"Somebody murdered Mr. Frenchie. He lives next to us. They wanna say my Willie done it. But he couldn't kill nobody. I know it. Will you help us?"

"No, I don't think I can help you," Elizabeth said, shaking her head.

"You got to," the woman pleaded.

"Why are you asking me? You don't know who I am."

"Yes we do. That's why we here. You's Mr. John's granddaughter."

"You knew my grandfather?"

"'Course we did. He was our lawyer. He was my daddy's lawyer way before I was born."

"Well, what makes you think I can help you?"

"They say you's a lawyer. And if you's Mr. John's grand, then you's a good lawyer."

"You have no way of knowing that." Elizabeth was a little put off by the woman's persistence.

"Excuse me, ma'am, for cutting cross you, but I do. And you got to help us."

"What exactly do you want me to do?"

"Represent Willie in court. Be his lawyer. He didn't kill nobody."

"I'm not even admitted to practice in this state." From the look on the woman's face, Elizabeth could tell that she had no idea what she was talking about. "Listen, why don't you meet me in the office around nine in the morning, and we can talk with Mr. Hamilton, and if he can't help you, maybe he can find someone who can, okay?"

"Okay," she said. "We'll be there at nine, but don't forget we want you to be Willie's lawyer."

"I'll see you in the morning then," Elizabeth said, grabbing the door.

"'Night," the woman said over her shoulder as she herded her three children down the back steps.

After Elizabeth cut off the downstairs lights, she trudged up the wide staircase and headed back to her bath. The water was lukewarm now, and she let out a sigh as she pulled the plug. As Elizabeth put on her nightgown, she thought about the poor woman and her three pitiful children. She promised herself to find them a good lawyer before she returned to Boston. Her travel clock on the bedside table indicated that it was after ten, too late to call Robert Hamilton.

CHAPTER 7

Elizabeth was relieved to see Hamilton's Pontiac parked on the curb in front of his office just before nine the next morning. She would feel much better, she thought, if her grandfather's partner was able to help the woman who had visited her last night.

The receptionist was not at her desk, so Elizabeth headed straight to Hamilton's office. He was sitting at his desk reading the Charleston paper. [POST & COURIER]

"Good morning, Robert."

The paper shook as his face appeared above the front page. "Whew, you scared me, Elizabeth. I didn't hear you come in. Guess the murder has me a little shook up."

"Tell me what you know about it."

"When did you hear?"

"Last night. From a woman who said her husband has already been charged."

"You talked to Willie Fulton's wife? Where?"

"She came to the house late. Do you know her?"

"Sure, she and Willie have been in this office a hundred times through the years to see your grandfather. John represented him about ten or fifteen years ago for stealing a hog, and he won an acquittal. After that, they thought he could walk on water."

"No wonder she was so insistent."

"Insistent on what?"

"You're going to laugh, but she wanted me to represent her husband."

"Well, I thought you told me you were a criminal lawyer. Haven't you handled murder cases before?" he added with mock seriousness.

"Yes, lots of them. But not in South Carolina."

"The South Carolina Bar will admit you to try a case here. It's not a problem, believe me. You would have to have a South Carolina lawyer to assist you with procedural and evidentiary matters. If you want to do it, I can sit with you."

"You're serious, aren't you?"

"Why not?"

"Well, thanks for your vote of confidence. You flatter me, but I've got a real job I've got to get back to." She paused. "They seem to be such desperate people. Will they set a bond for him?"

"Under our law, they don't have to, but they probably will. If the judge determines that Willie is a flight risk or a danger to the community, then he can refuse to set a bond."

"If he sets a bond, how high do you think it will be?"

"Probably in the neighborhood of fifty thousand dollars."

"Why so high?"

"For one thing, the victim was a white man."

"Why should that make a difference?"

"You figure it out. You're the one with the Ivy League education."

Elizabeth looked at him for more explanation, but he said nothing.

"Anyway, it may take a while to set bond," Hamilton continued. "On a murder case, a circuit judge will have to set it. Judge Lawson is out of the circuit this week and won't be back until next week."

"Will you represent Mr. Fulton?" she asked.

"No, it wouldn't be fair to me or Willie. I haven't tried a criminal case in ten years. I'm too old for the courtroom."

"They'll be here in a few minutes. Should I send them to the public defender's office?"

"Not unless you've got a burning desire to see Willie Fulton spend the rest of his life in the penitentiary."

"He's that bad?"

"What makes you think the Craven County public defender is a man?"

"Oh, come on, Robert. When I tell people around this town I'm a lawyer, they look at me as if I'm some kind of freak."

"I know," Hamilton replied, smiling broadly. "You're probably the first woman lawyer they've ever seen. And yes, Elbert Graham is a man. And yes, he's pretty bad. Elbert's a nice enough fellow. He's only a couple of years from retirement. It's a part-time job, and Elbert wouldn't have been able to make ends meet in his law practice without the public defender position. He never spent a whole lot of time preparing his cases for trial, and he's gotten so hard of hearing he can't hear thunder."

"Can't the Fultons hire someone in Weenee from the private bar?"

"No, not really. Your grandfather was one of the best criminal lawyers in South Carolina. Consequently, if anybody here in Craven County got into any kind of big trouble, they would turn to John. He always worked with them on the fee. If they had a lot of money, he would charge them an arm and a leg. If they didn't have much, he would take that into consideration."

"Would he have represented Willie Fulton in this case?"

"Oh sure. That's why you found all of those mortgages in the estate. Sometimes it would take people years to pay him, but he didn't mind. I really hadn't thought about it before, but since he's gone now, there's not anybody around to take care of the Willie Fultons of Craven County." He paused. "John and I tried a lot of big cases together. I always did the research, prepared the motions, investigated the jury panel. He tried the cases and I always took the second chair. That's why I offered to help you."

"I'm afraid it would be out of the question for me to represent Mr. Fulton. I really have to get back to Boston."

"I know," Hamilton said softly, "but I certainly like the idea of trying a murder case with John Snowden's beautiful granddaughter. That would be a great way to end my long legal career."

"Are you thinking of retiring?"

"Yes, I am," he said quickly, letting out a long sigh. "I don't plan on working until I die, like John. This profession is changing too quickly for me. I'll have a lot to keep me busy."

They both stopped and listened when they heard the front door open and, seconds later, slam shut.

"Your new clients?" Hamilton asked with a grin.

Elizabeth gave him a long look and inquired, "Do you have time to meet with us and explain the bail process to them?"

"Certainly. I'll bring them on back," he said, starting for the front.

Pearlie Mae Fulton had four children with her this time, and only two of them had been with her the night before. How many children does this poor woman have? Elizabeth asked herself, trying to do the math quickly in her head. They all looked under ten, two boys and two girls, all barefoot, and one, judging by his nose, was suffering from a horrible summer cold. Willie Fulton's wife had on a faded cotton dress, and she wore flip-flops. Her black hair was pulled back in a bun that was so tight it made her bloodshot eyes appear ready to bulge out of her head.

"Morning," she said, nodding at Elizabeth.

"How are you, Mrs. Fulton?" Elizabeth asked.

"I'll feel much better when we get Willie outta the jail. You call me Pearlie Mae—everyone else does."

"Okay, if you call me Elizabeth."

Pearlie Mae looked at her as if she was speaking Chinese but didn't say anything.

Elizabeth and Pearlie Mae settled into two comfortable, worn leather chairs opposite Hamilton's desk. Hamilton moved behind his desk as the youngest child crawled into her mother's lap. The other three children stood at their mother's side, staring at Hamilton with a forlorn look on their faces, as if he was some magician who could make their father suddenly reappear. Before anyone could speak, the younger boy reached for a carved bird on Hamilton's desk. The older boy quickly slapped the hand, which was instantly retracted. Pearlie Mae gave the older boy an approving nod.

"Can you get Willie out this morning?" Pearlie Mae asked, turning in her chair to look at Elizabeth.

"I'm not familiar with the bonding procedure here," she answered, looking to Hamilton for help.

"It's a little more complicated, Pearlie Mae, with a murder charge."

"What you mean?"

"A circuit judge has to set the bond."

"You mean a big court judge?"

"Yes, I do."

"Why can't the magistrate do it like he done them other times Willie got in trouble?"

"Because our law says that when a person is charged with murder, only a circuit judge can set the bond."

"Can't he do that this morning?"

"No, he can't. Judge Lawson is out of the circuit and won't be back until next week. I'm afraid Willie will have to stay in jail until then."

"Why he got to stay in jail 'til next week when he ain't killed nobody? You can't call the judge and get him back here this week?"

Hamilton smiled and held his hands together so that all of his fingertips were touching. "I'm afraid it doesn't work that way, Pearlie Mae. I must also tell you that the judge may not set a bond for Willie."

"What?" she said, sitting upright in her chair. "He's always had a bond and he ain't never run yet. You and Miss Elizabeth gonna tell the judge that?" She looked at Elizabeth for an answer.

"Of course, we will," she replied, again glancing at Hamilton for help.

"That will be a factor that will be in Willie's favor," Hamilton said. "The fact that he never jumped bond will be one thing the judge will consider, along with the fact that he has a lot of ties to the community, including his wife and his children. But if the judge decides that Willie is a danger to the community, he may refuse to set a bond."

"Willie ain't a danger to nobody," she said, shaking her head slowly.

"I know that, Pearlie Mae, but he is charged with a brutal murder. I've been practicing law for over fifty years here in Craven County, and I've never seen a killing like this. The only thing they've found so far is Frenchie's head."

"You're gonna help Willie?" she asked, staring straight at Elizabeth. Elizabeth became unnerved when she realized that the three older children were staring too. She stole a glance at Hamilton, but he also had her fixed in his gaze, and he offered no help.

"I tell you what I will do. I'll go to the jail and speak with your husband, explain his rights to him, and make sure he talks to no one about his case. And then Mr. Hamilton and I will try to find him a lawyer from this area who can represent him. Okay?"

"I 'preciate that. But I want you to help him all the way through the case."

"I don't think I can do that, Pearlie Mae. I've got a job with the public defender's office in Boston I've got to get back to."

"Miss Elizabeth, I didn't hardly sleep last night 'cause I was steady praying you'd help Willie."

Elizabeth looked at the woman and saw nothing but panic. "I told you what I can do. I'm not leaving until tomorrow. I'll go to the jail as soon as I can and speak with your husband. Then Mr.

Hamilton and I will try to find someone to represent Mr. Fulton. How much of a retainer do you think you can pay?"

"What's a retainer?"

Elizabeth stole a glance at Hamilton. "Money," she answered. "How much can you pay?"

"We ain't got no money," Pearlie Mae answered, looking at her hands folded in her lap. "Your granddaddy, he always told us to pay what we could, 'long and 'long. Willie would help him out in the yard, paddle him in the river, things like that."

Elizabeth let out a long sigh. "Let me talk to Mr. Fulton," she said, rising from her chair.

After Pearlie Mae had guided her children out the front door, Elizabeth slumped back into her chair. "What are those poor people going to do?" she asked Hamilton, almost shouting.

"We could get this case up for trial at the next term of General Sessions, which is in six weeks."

"What do you mean, 'we'?"

Hamilton pointed to Elizabeth and then himself and smiled sheepishly.

"You're serious, aren't you?"

"What else can they do? They can't hire anybody, much less a decent criminal lawyer. With Elbert Graham as their lawyer, about the best they could hope for would be manslaughter, and that carries up to thirty years."

"What am I going to do about my job?" she asked.

"Get a leave of absence for a couple of months. I don't know how to put this without it sounding like I'm some sort of a busybody, but your grandfather made it known to me that you were very secure financially—not counting what you have just inherited."

"I can well afford to help the Fultons is what you're saying."

Hamilton shrugged.

"I can't do it," she said, slapping the armrest with her hand. "It's impossible."

"Well then, it looks like Elbert Graham just got another case."

Elizabeth stared at Hamilton but said nothing. She looked out the window. "Can I get in to see Mr. Fulton now?" she asked, turning back to Hamilton.

"Sure. Do you want me to go with you?"

Elizabeth was ready to say no when she thought of all of the newspaper articles and film footage from the sixties about Southern lawmen and their views on Northern agitators. "Do you mind?"

"No, not at all. Just let me make one phone call, and I'll meet you in the front."

CHAPTER 8

The Craven County jail was located one block behind the courthouse in a long, low, flat-roofed, red-brick building. Constructed in the 1930s with New Deal money, its design was completely devoid of symmetry or scale. The side and rear yards were encircled by an eight-foot fence, topped by new, shiny, razor-sharp concertina wire that belied the sleepy appearance of the rest of the facility.

As the jail was also one block from Hamilton's office, the two lawyers walked. Crossing the neatly trimmed lawn, they spotted two men in orange uniforms washing a patrol car. Both stopped their work to leer at Elizabeth, but neither said anything. When one smiled, showing a mouth full of bad teeth, Elizabeth dropped her head quickly.

They entered the building, and to the right were signs pointing to the sheriff's office and various other administrative offices. Hamilton took Elizabeth's elbow and guided her down a hall to the jail area. Herman Baylor, the jailer, was standing behind his gray, metal military-surplus desk. Herman was in his late fifties, bald and with a gut so large that he seemed to be leaning forward at the waist. Elizabeth was afraid to get too close to him for fear he might topple over on her. Like James, he had tobacco stains on both corners of his mouth, but his cheeks showed no signs of the telltale bulge of Red Man.

"What can I do for you, Mr. Hamilton?" Baylor asked, looking at him for a second and then fixing his gaze on Elizabeth.

"Herman, we want to see Willie Fulton, please."

"You gonna take his case?" Baylor asked, his mouth dropping open.

"We might. We just want to talk with him first. Excuse me, Herman, this is Elizabeth Chase, an attorney from Boston."

Baylor's eyes opened wide. "You one of them lady lawyers? I've heard about 'em, but you're the first one I ever seen." Baylor inspected her from head to toe as if she were an expensive shotgun in a hardware-store display case. Elizabeth found the man revolting and wondered what he might have said to her if she had come alone. "Listen," Baylor said, lowering his voice, "I don't care how many lawyers they bring in here for this case, they got this nigger cold."

Elizabeth felt the blood rush to her cheeks. "Just what do you mean, Mr. Baylor?" she asked, trying to suppress the edge in her voice.

"They found the ax he killed Frenchie with out in his hog parlor," he said gleefully. Hamilton and Elizabeth exchanged glances. "There ain't a lawyer in this country that can beat a murder charge with evidence like that. No siree," he went on, shaking his head. "I'll be glad to bring him right up, though, and give you all the time you need. You can use our interrogation room right over there," Baylor said, pointing to a smaller room toward the rear of the building. "It'll take a few minutes. He's back in the bullpen."

As Elizabeth expected, the interrogation room was furnished very sparsely. There was a long table with metal legs and a Formica top and eight straight black chairs tucked underneath it. The only wall ornamentation was a calendar with a farm scene compliments of the Weenee Feed and Seed. At least she didn't see any high-intensity lights or blackjacks, Elizabeth reassured herself. The chairs made a loud scraping sound on the concrete floor when they pulled them back to sit down.

"It already looks bad, doesn't it?" Hamilton commented.

"Yes, it does. And it sounds as if that man would love to pull the switch if they put him in the electric chair. That's what you have here in South Carolina, isn't it?"

"Yes."

"Well, thank God for *Furman v. Georgia*. Has this state enacted any type of death-penalty statute to challenge *Furman?*"

"Elizabeth, you need to refresh my memory on *Furman,*" Hamilton responded.

"It was the case in which the United States Supreme Court in 1972 enacted the moratorium on capital punishment in this country."

"Yes, of course. Well, to answer your question, no new death-penalty legislation has been enacted."

"So there is no way they can turn this into a capital case?"

"Willie Fulton is safe from the electric chair, I assure you."

"That's a relief."

"Sounds like you've already convicted Willie Fulton in your mind."

"No, I haven't. But you'll agree with me that if they found the murder weapon on his property and the blood matches, he doesn't have much of a chance. Particularly if your juries here are made up of people like that jailer."

"Not everybody here is like Herman Baylor." Hamilton heard footsteps down the hall and stopped talking.

Willie Fulton walked into the room, followed very closely by Baylor. Willie's eyes were half-shut, as if he had been sleeping. He was dressed in the same orange uniform that the two inmates outside were wearing. His gait was unnatural, and Elizabeth looked at his feet when she heard the rattle of the leg irons on the floor. Fulton smiled when he saw Hamilton and extended his hand quickly.

"Real glad to see you, Mr. Hamilton, real glad," he said excitedly as the two shook hands.

"Willie, this is Elizabeth Chase, John Snowden's granddaughter."

"Oh, I done heard about you, ma'am," he said, bowing his head slightly.

"It's a pleasure to meet you, Mr. Fulton," Elizabeth replied, offering her hand.

"Just holler when you're through with him," Baylor said over his shoulder as he walked out of the room. The metal door reverberated shut.

"Sit down, Willie," Hamilton said, pointing to a chair.

As he took a seat, Elizabeth studied the man. It was hard to guess his age, but judging by the ages of his children, he had to be at least in his midthirties, she thought. His eyes were deep-set in his coal-black face that was dominated by a broad nose. His hairline was receding slightly, and his hair was cut close to the scalp. One of his front teeth was framed with a gold cap.

"You okay?" Hamilton asked.

"Yes sir, I'm fine. Just hard to get any sleep back there in the bullpen," he said, pointing over his shoulder. "You the lady lawyer, right?"

"Yes, I'm a lawyer, Mr. Fulton."

"Call me Willie, okay? Everybody calls me Willie. Has Pearlie Mae talked to you about taking my case?"

"Yes, we've had a couple of conversations. But I haven't made any commitments to her, Mr. Fulton, er, Willie. You see, I practice in Boston."

"You must be good there."

Elizabeth shrugged. "Let's talk about your case a minute."

"They ain't got a thing on me. They can't hold me 'cause they ain't got no evidence. I didn't kill nobody."

Elizabeth looked to Hamilton for help.

"Willie, I'd always heard there was bad blood between you and Frenchie," he said.

"Yeah, they was. If ever I was gonna kill somebody, he woulda been the first."

"Why? You were neighbors."

"He always call me names," he replied, his eyes widening as he looked at Hamilton.

"Like what?"

"Like 'nigger,' 'cept he always said it funny like. It didn't sound quite right. Other names, I can't remember. My hogs and chickens would get out and rummage through his garden. One time he caught my hog over there," he said chuckling. "Boy, that little man was mad."

"And now he's dead," Hamilton said.

"Yeah, he's dead, but I didn't kill him."

"Tell me about the ax."

"What ax?"

"The ax they found in your hog parlor, covered with blood."

"What are you talking 'bout, Mr. Hamilton?" Willie Fulton shot back, sitting straight up in his chair. "There wasn't no bloody ax anywhere near my house."

"So you're saying it wasn't yours?"

"Yeah, I got a ax. 'Course I got a ax. How I'm gonna chop wood with no ax? But I don't know nothing 'bout how any blood coulda got on my ax."

"I'm sure it's on the way to Columbia to be analyzed in the SLED lab. If the report comes back indicating that was Frenchie's blood on it, you'll have a hard job convincing a jury that you didn't do it."

"It wasn't me—you gotta believe me," Fulton said, dropping his head into his hands, his elbows resting on the table. "When can I get outta here?" he asked, looking up at Hamilton and Elizabeth. "I wanna see my family."

"We can move next week to have a bond set in front of Judge Lawson," Hamilton said.

"You mean I gotta stay in here 'til next week?"

"I'm afraid so. We're doing all we can. Will Pearlie Mae and the children be okay?" Hamilton asked.

"Yeah, her folks will look after them, I reckon."

"We'll try to get back over here before the bond hearing. Just make sure you don't talk to anyone about your case, you understand?" Hamilton instructed.

"Yes sir," Fulton replied weakly as Hamilton got up to call for the jailer.

Elizabeth waited until they got out of the jail and out of earshot of the two inmates washing the patrol car before she said anything. "You made it sound like I had agreed to stay and defend Willie Fulton."

"I guess I did convey that impression to Willie, but it was unintentional, I assure you. I'm not trying to put pressure on you to do something you don't want to do. It's your call."

"I want to talk with my boss to see if I can get another week. I'd like to do a little investigation on my own, talk to the sheriff, and see if we can arrange competent representation for Willie."

"That sounds reasonable. What can I do to help?"

Elizabeth suddenly remembered the call she received the night before. "I know what you can do. Get me out of going to Ida Pearl Middleton's house for drinks at five thirty."

"Why would I want to do that? You'll have a delightful time."

"Why do you think so?"

"I know you think those two ladies are a little eccentric, and so does almost everyone else in this town. But they're nice people."

"I'm sure they are, and I doubt I can get out of it now," she said, climbing the front steps of the law office.

After several hours of working with Inez on the probate filings, Elizabeth was confident she could leave the next day. The estate couldn't be closed until six months after the statutory notice to creditors ran in the local newspaper. After the initial filings, and with the appraisers already lined up, there would be little left to do for about seven months. Thank God for Inez, Elizabeth thought; she was really a whiz.

After her two o'clock meeting with the probate judge, Elizabeth decided to go back to her grandfather's office and check in with her office in Boston. Harry Hirsch, her boss, answered on the second ring. They talked a few minutes about the funeral, and Harry asked several polite questions about how she was getting along. She felt a hint of regret when he told her that there were no emergencies as far as her files were concerned and the office had everything covered for her.

"When are you coming back?" he asked.

"I have plane reservations for tomorrow morning. I think I have everything with the estate set up pretty well."

"So we'll see you in the office day after tomorrow?"

"Harry, can I ask you something?"

"Sure, go ahead."

"Do you mind if I take a few more days off?"

"No, not at all. I know you'll probably need a few days to get your head screwed on straight when you get back. No problem. I've got a couple of extra tickets for the Red Sox's game on Wednesday night if you feel like going."

"I think I'm going to stay here for a few days."

"I thought you said you had everything lined up. Why on earth would you want to stay in South Carolina, of all places? Are you going to take a few days off in Hilton Head?"

"No, I'm going to stay here in Weenee."

"What on earth for?" Hirsch replied, his voice rising.

"Do you mind? If so, please tell me if it's a problem."

"No, there's no problem. You take all the time you need. What's wrong?"

Elizabeth told him every detail she knew about Frenchie's murder and Willie Fulton. Harry Hirsch was tough to work for at times, but he was an excellent trial lawyer and Elizabeth wanted to see if he had any ideas. She told him about Fulton's problems retaining adequate counsel.

"That sounds pretty grim, Elizabeth, but there's not a whole lot you can do to help him, is there?"

"Well, I can try to find him a decent lawyer."

"Good luck with that one. Just don't forget where you are and who you're trying to help."

"Believe me, it's hard to forget. I'll call you in a few days. Bye, Harry."

"Elizabeth, be careful. If Willie Fulton didn't kill that Frenchman, someone else did."

As soon as she put the phone down, Inez buzzed her on the intercom.

"You have a call on line two. It's Dr. Howard," she added with a certain amount of importance.

"Hi," Elizabeth said when she picked up the receiver.

"We agreed on seven, right?" he asked.

In the excitement of the murder, Elizabeth had completely forgotten about their dinner engagement. "I . . . I . . ."

"You're not trying to back out on me, are you?" There was a bit of an edge to his voice.

"No, no. It's just been a very long day, that's all."

"Is seven still okay? It'll take us an hour to get to the beach."

"You better make it seven thirty. I'm supposed to join Ida Pearl Middleton for a drink at five thirty."

"Oh. That'll be interesting. And you're right, you'll be lucky to get out of there by seven thirty."

"What do you mean by that?"

"Oh, nothing. Those two ladies just love to talk, that's all. Seven thirty it is. See you then."

Over lunch, Rebecca had presented Elizabeth with the keys to her grandfather's Buick, so she decided to take a little tour of the town before going to the Middleton house. As she got behind the wheel, it occurred to her that she was now the owner of this big, gas-guzzling tank. As she circled the four-block area that was the downtown, she saw several landmarks she used to know as a child, such as Helen's café on Lee Street, where her grandfather would take her for ice cream, and Goldberg's Department Store, where her grandmother would take her to buy Sunday dresses. Across the street from Goldberg's was the town square, and on its benches were several sleepy-looking senior citizens. Keeping watch over them was the soldier who stood at attention atop the granite obelisk that memorialized Craven County's Confederate dead. A few feet away was the bronze statue of Henry Durant, a Weenee hero who had died on the beaches of Normandy. Next to him stood the newest addition to the town square family, a life-sized marble likeness of Dr. Martin Luther King, Jr.

Elizabeth made a left on Beauregard Street, where many of the antebellum homes had been in the same family for generations. Most of the dwellings were well maintained, but several looked abandoned. Elizabeth circled back to Lee Street and headed west across the Seaboard Coast Line tracks. As she crossed the railroad, she saw dozens of black people congregated around the depot, many with their luggage at their sides. Elizabeth was surprised at the number of passengers and made a mental note to ask someone what was going on. Two blocks past the tracks, the business section ended and she was in an area of town that she couldn't recall seeing before. She turned left and drove for a few blocks before taking two more lefts to head back to Lee Street. Most of the houses she saw were neat but deteriorating. Once she crossed the tracks again, she was amazed at how the railroad divided the town into two different communities.

Elizabeth decided that it might be a good idea to dress for dinner before she went to the Middletons'. As she pulled into the driveway, she immediately noticed that the backdoor was shut tight, and when she got out and tried the screen door, it was latched, which was unusual. She walked around to the front of the house and saw that the door there was also shut. Elizabeth turned the heavy doorknob but the door did not budge. She was alarmed because Rebecca didn't leave until five, so she rapped twice with the brass lion's-head doorknocker. She stood still and listened but, hearing nothing, rapped again. Suddenly she saw Rebecca's face in the sidelight next to the door, almost pressing against the handblown glass. The face disappeared, she heard a click, and the massive door swung open.

"Rebecca, I was worried. Why on earth do you have the house locked?" Elizabeth asked as she walked across the threshold into the hall.

"You ain't heard? There was a killing yesterday."

"Yes, I've heard. But they've arrested someone already."

"Yeah, I heard, Willie Fulton. But I don't know for sure if he done it."

"So, you think the real killer is going to come looking for you?"

"Well, you can't never tell," she said, shutting the door quickly. Rebecca turned and walked toward the kitchen, and Elizabeth followed her.

When they reached the kitchen, Elizabeth pointed to a chair and said, "Sit down and talk to me."

"I got to be getting home."

"What's wrong, Rebecca? You look frightened."

"I am."

"Sit down for just a minute, okay?"

"All right," she said, pulling a chair back. "But just for a minute."

"Don't worry. I can drive you home if you don't have your car."

"I don't own a car," she said matter-of-factly.

"Then how do you get around?"

"I walk."

"Everywhere?"

"No, I take the train when I go to Rochester."

Elizabeth laughed and Rebecca let out a chuckle.

"What do you know about the Frenchman and Willie Fulton?"

"I know that Willie didn't like Frenchie, and from what I heard, Frenchie didn't like Willie much neither."

"Why?"

Rebecca folded her arms across her chest and glared at Elizabeth for a few seconds. "Miss Elizabeth, I ain't getting into they business. There's evil in that business. It's the work of the devil, and it ain't gonna serve no purpose to talk 'bout it."

"What kind of evil?"

"I don't know," Rebecca answered, looking out the window. "Can you take me home now?"

Elizabeth drove Rebecca across the same railroad crossing she had been over earlier and, after following Rebecca's directions, let her out in front of a small house with a tin roof. The sides were covered in tarpaper that had been embossed and colored so that it would resemble brick veneer. After Rebecca thanked her and got out, Elizabeth calculated that the distance back to her grandfather's house was well over a mile.

CHAPTER 9

Ida Pearl Middleton's house was only two blocks down Beauregard Street, so Elizabeth decided to walk. The sun was still high in the sky at five thirty, but the street was shaded by an allée of live oaks so thick she could hardly see the sun. Most of the homes were built in the Greek Revival style popular just before the Civil War, with a few Victorian houses sprinkled in. Several residences looked forlorn and abandoned, although they appeared to be in decent shape. The Middleton house was much grander in scale with its massive fluted columns but was in desperate need of several coats of paint. It had a brick walk that led to a porch almost ten feet off the ground. Elizabeth rang the bell and was greeted immediately by a black man in a well-worn dark suit. It was as if he had been waiting by the door for her arrival, she thought.

"'Evening," the man said as he pushed open the screen door. "Come on in. Mrs. Middleton has been looking for you." The man was slender with a full head of gray hair and stooped shoulders. Elizabeth guessed he must be at least seventy-five. "They're right here in the front parlor," he said, pointing to a room to their left.

Elizabeth glanced down the dark hall that bisected the house. Several large mahogany pieces of furniture hugged the walls, and a threadbare Kazak rug stretched from the front door all the way to another door at the far end. The faces of long-deceased ancestors stared from oil canvases that lined both walls, as if they were participants in some type of receiving line of the dead.

Elizabeth walked into the parlor and saw Ida Pearl first, perched like a setting hen on an ornately carved Victorian sofa that was covered in a faded red damask. Estelle was sitting on the other end of the sofa at an angle facing her mother. Both women were dressed as if they were going to another cocktail party, Estelle in a sequined top and Ida Pearl in a linen dress. Again neither woman had skimped in her application of makeup, and it made Elizabeth wonder about the size of their monthly cosmetic bill. Sitting between them on a satin pillow was a white Pekinese, staring at Elizabeth with contempt. Ida Pearl had one hand on the dog, and the other hand was holding her drink. She put the drink down quickly and extended her hand.

"So glad you could make it, Elizabeth. Please sit down."

"Thank you," Elizabeth said, taking the woman's hand.

Estelle smiled at her and nodded. Elizabeth smiled and nodded back. She slipped into an armchair by the sofa.

"Tell us, have you gotten John's estate settled yet?" Ida Pearl asked.

"Excuse me?" Elizabeth inquired, not knowing whether the woman was being sarcastic or just ignorant. "I can't settle the estate for six months under South Carolina law."

"Oh, I know that," Ida Pearl said, waving a hand at her. "I was just kidding you."

Elizabeth realized there was someone standing over her, and she turned to see the elderly black man holding a silver tray with a drink on it.

"Your drink, ma'am," he said.

"Thank you," she responded, reaching for the glass. Once she had the drink firmly in her hand, he handed her a napkin.

"Scotch on the rocks," Ida Pearl said, raising her glass.

"You have a good memory."

"Not that many women around here drink scotch. And certainly not as much as you do," Ida Pearl said with a chuckle.

They must really have me under a microscope in this little town, Elizabeth thought. She took a sip of her drink and looked around the room. There was a wonderful Federal secretary against the wall opposite the sofa, and the rest of the room contained an impressive mixture of styles from Chippendale to Victorian. The rug was a faded and well-worn Oushak. A large portrait of a man in a Confederate uniform hung over a gouge-carved cypress mantel. Judging by the look on his face, the man either suffered from chronic constipation or the Union cavalry was beating on the door when he was sitting for the portrait.

"Grandpa," Ida Pearl said proudly when she saw Elizabeth studying the canvas. "He commanded a brigade at Cold Harbor."

"Was that good?" Elizabeth asked matter-of-factly.

"What do you mean?" Ida Pearl inquired, arching her eyebrows.

Elizabeth shrugged. "I don't know anything about Cold Harbor."

"I thought you went to Wellesley. What did you study there?"

"My degree is in art history."

"Art history? Oh, you probably had to go to law school just to find a job," Ida Pearl said with a chuckle.

Elizabeth was not amused. "I was offered a position with Sotheby Park Bernet when I graduated."

"Well, for your information, Grant lost about seven thousand men in forty-five minutes at Cold Harbor." Ida Pearl said the words slowly, emphasizing the numbers.

"You say that like it was some wonderful feat," Elizabeth replied a little testily.

"Well, it was for the Confederate army," Ida Pearl countered, raising her voice slightly.

"Thousands of people were slaughtered, and you make it sound romantic," Elizabeth responded.

"I didn't make it sound romantic. It is just a wonderful testament to our side's expert marksmanship, that's all." Ida Pearl put her drink down before she looked to Elizabeth for an answer.

"Our side, Mrs. Middleton? That horrible, senseless war ended well over a hundred years ago. Do you people down here still consider there to be two sides?" Elizabeth always prided herself in keeping her composure during the heat of a courtroom battle, but this woman, who was obviously still living in the nineteenth century, was getting on her nerves very quickly.

"I'll agree with you that it was a horrible war, child, but it certainly wasn't a senseless one."

Throughout the exchange Estelle watched in silence, her eyes moving from one woman to the other as they spoke.

"How can you say it wasn't senseless?" Elizabeth asked, leaning forward in her chair. She was almost screaming now at the old woman, and she didn't care. "You people bought thousands of black people. You enslaved them, and then you killed hundreds of thousands of Americans trying to protect that right, and you don't think that's senseless?"

"The War Between the States was not fought over slavery; it

was fought over states' rights," Ida Pearl said slowly, her eyes narrowing and unblinking.

"That's a bunch of crap!" Elizabeth screamed as she slammed her drink down on the coffee table in front of her.

"How dare you use that kind of language in my home!" Ida Pearl shrieked.

Estelle grabbed her mother's arm and patted her hand. "Mama, please, remember your heart."

"I think I should leave," Elizabeth said, jumping to her feet.

"I'll show you to the door." Estelle rose from the sofa.

"I can find my way out, thank you. Don't bother," Elizabeth said as she started for the front door and didn't look back.

Elizabeth regretted asking Jim Howard to wait until seven thirty to pick her up, but there was no way she could have known her appointment with the Middletons would be so brief. To make matters worse, he didn't pull into her driveway until seven forty. She didn't wait for him to come to the front door, and she already had it locked and was crossing the porch when their eyes met.

"You don't have to lock your door in this town," he said when he stopped on the top step.

She hadn't noticed before, but she now realized that behind that boyish grin was a nice-looking man. "Just habit," she said, holding her hands out to her side.

"You look nice," he remarked, "for a lawyer."

"Wow, thanks," she said as they walked to his car. "You look okay, too, for a doctor."

"I don't guess you want to hear my repertoire of lawyer jokes?" he asked as he backed out of the driveway.

"No, not tonight. It's been a long day," she said, rubbing her temples with her fingertips.

"All that estate business getting you down?"

"No, not really. That's coming together very nicely thanks to Robert Hamilton and Inez. Robert Hamilton is a real gentleman."

"No question about it."

"My day just seemed to deteriorate very quickly, that's all. I was invited to the Middletons for a drink. I think I told you as much. When I got there, I got into an argument with Ida Pearl."

"About what?" Jim asked, glancing quickly over at Elizabeth.

"The Civil War."

"You're kidding me."

"No, I'm not. Why?"

"That is the one thing you don't argue with her about."

"Why not?"

"Well, for one thing she has been the president of the UDC for as long as anyone can remember."

"What is the UDC?"

"Where did you go to college? You've never heard of the UDC?" he asked with mock seriousness.

"That's the second time I've been asked that question today. Tell me, what is the UDC?"

"The United Daughters of the Confederacy."

Elizabeth squealed. "You mean they still have something called the United Daughters of the Confederacy, over a hundred years after that war ended?"

"Not 'that' war—'the' war."

"Oh, my God," she said, shaking her head.

"What were you arguing about?"

"Oh, not much, just that little institution you guys had down here, slavery."

"Ooh! I wish I could have been a fly on the wall for that one. Do you know how many slaves her grandfather owned?"

"Oh, yeah, Jim, I had it right on the tip of my tongue, but I can't remember now."

"Somewhere over 150," he said, ignoring her sarcasm.

"So, I was really stepping on her toes, then. Serves her right. People shouldn't be proud of something like that; they should be ashamed of it."

"You aren't going to pull me into your little debate, Miss Lawyer," Jim said with a chuckle. "That's about all Ida Pearl has left."

"What do you mean?"

"All she has is her memories. The money's gone, the slaves are gone, and the plantation's gone."

"And you're telling me I'm supposed to feel sorry for her."

"She hasn't had an easy life."

"She certainly has a nice house and nice furniture."

"Yes, that's true. But she lost her only son in World War II, and her husband barely scraped out a living, and then there is Estelle."

"What about Estelle? She's a little strange, isn't she?"

"Yes, she has what I would call a psychoneurotic fixation on her mother."

"She never married."

"She got married right after she graduated from college. The marriage apparently didn't work out, and she moved back to Weenee a few months later. She has been right there at her mother's side ever since."

"She never worked?"

"Oh, yes, she's worked in the courthouse for years. She has to; they need the money. Estelle spends the rest of her time seeing after her mother. Other than going to work, she never goes anywhere without Ida Pearl."

"She has no social life of her own?"

"None whatsoever."

"That's pitiful," Elizabeth said, sighing as she looked out the window. They were out of the city limits now, passing wide fields with long rows of corn, soybeans, and tobacco. "There aren't many normal people in Weenee, are there?" she asked, still looking out her window.

Jim Howard chuckled and shook his head. "No, not really. Why, who else have you met?"

"I met James. He wandered into the office. You know the older man with one eye?"

Jim laughed again. "You have met some of the cream of the crop, all right."

Elizabeth looked out the window again, and she saw a mixture of older farmhouses and mobile homes. "Are we anywhere near the River Road?" she asked.

"We're on the River Road. What do you know about the River Road?" he asked, looking at Elizabeth.

"I was just curious. Doesn't Willie Fulton live out this way?"

"How do you know Willie Fulton?" he asked, turning again to look at her.

"He wants me to represent him."

"On his murder charge? You gotta be kidding me," he said, almost in a whisper. Jim Howard stared at her for an answer so long that his front wheel dropped off the highway, and he had to jerk the car back onto the road.

"Be careful," she said, as if she were speaking to a child. "You drive as if you're still in Boston. I didn't say I was going to represent him. He asked me to represent him. There's a big difference."

"Are you thinking about it?"

"To be honest, yes."

"What about your job?"

"I think I can get time off if I need it."

"Elizabeth, those people can't pay you any kind of fee. It would be a waste of your time."

"It wouldn't be a waste of time if I could get an acquittal."

"That might be very difficult from what I hear. The talk around town is that they've got Willie Fulton cold and that he'll be spending the rest of his life in the state penitentiary in Columbia."

"Do you think he can get a fair trial in Craven County?"

"Oh, yeah, he'll get a fair trial, all right. Justice will be done, and he'll be convicted, as he should be."

"I'm serious. Will a jury here listen to his side, or will they convict him just because he's black?"

"Obviously, you've never been inside the Craven County Courthouse when it's in session."

"Why do you say that?"

"This county is two-thirds black. So the juries are predominately black. From what I hear, most of the white people with any pull get out of jury duty when they're called."

"That's interesting," Elizabeth said, folding her arms.

"Tell me, why would you consider representing a man like Willie Fulton when you know in all probability that he is guilty?"

"Guilt or innocence has absolutely nothing to do with it," Elizabeth said casually, turning to look at a herd of cows standing knee-deep in a shallow farm pond. "What are those cows doing?"

"What do you think? Keeping cool, Miss Big City Girl," he said with a grin.

Elizabeth laughed at herself for missing the obvious.

"What do you mean by saying guilt or innocence doesn't matter? Would you really represent someone that you knew was guilty?" he asked.

"Not if they admitted their guilt to me, but very few do unless they want me to plea bargain for them. Otherwise, it's not my call."

"What do you mean? I still don't follow you."

"It's simply not my decision as to whether someone is guilty or not guilty. Remember, a jury is instructed to return a verdict of either guilty or not guilty. They don't really determine innocence. A person can be guilty as anything, but if the Commonwealth, or here, the State, doesn't prove someone guilty, then a jury is required by law to return a verdict of not guilty. Are you with me now?"

"I think so."

"Juries make decisions. Lawyers don't."

"Okay, I think I see. But why represent Willie Fulton? I'm sure there are hundreds of criminals waiting in the Boston Detention Center to be represented by the beautiful Elizabeth Chase."

Elizabeth smiled and nodded to acknowledge the compliment. "I just have a feeling that Willie Fulton is not going to be properly represented, that's all. From what I hear, the public defender in this county is not the greatest trial lawyer in South Carolina."

"No, I guess not. Do you have any idea how long it will be before the case comes up for trial?"

"Six to eight weeks at a minimum, according to Robert Hamilton. I would probably go back to Boston for a while and then come back for the trial."

"Well, it would be nice to have you around for a bit," he said, turning to smile at her.

They rode for a few minutes in silence as Elizabeth watched the passing countryside fly by. The sun was announcing its departure for the day by brilliantly bathing the woods and fields with an orange glow.

"Oh, there's the river," Elizabeth said pointing to the right, where the Weenee River snaked its way out of a dense stand of longleaf pines. The river straightened itself up like a drunk going home to his wife and followed the road for almost a mile before resuming its tortuous course, disappearing again into the woods. "It's beautiful," she said. "What are those trees growing out of the water?"

"Cypress. They're strange and wonderful trees."

"Why do you say they're strange?"

"Well, for one thing, they look funny with their obese trunks.

And they grow knees that come up out of the water—they've confounded scientists for centuries."

"The water is so black. It all looks surreal. Where does the river flow to?"

"To Georgetown and into Winyah Bay. You'll see. This road follows the river all the way to the coast. You'll see it peeping back at you for the next thirty miles. This road has been in constant use for over 250 years. The Weenee Indians started using it first."

Elizabeth watched the countryside more closely as they passed a number of landmarks, from rundown trailers to elegant entrances to plantations. "Who owns the plantations?" she asked finally.

"Mostly Yankees. A lot of them came down here in the thirties and forties when they could buy land for next to nothing. They come down in the fall and winter for hunting season."

"I bet they're real popular around here."

"Oh, they get along fine with everyone. They spend a lot of money in the county."

In a few minutes they were passing through the city of Georgetown, located strategically on Winyah Bay.

"I'll take you by the waterfront; it's only a couple of blocks off the highway," Jim said, taking a quick right down a residential street.

Elizabeth thought they were under a storm cloud until she realized the street was guarded on both sides by grand live oaks that formed an almost impenetrable canopy. Judging by the age of the houses, the town appeared to be ancient. They turned left on Front Street, and Elizabeth could see the river to their right, running parallel to the town's main street. Old stores, most of them constructed of Carolina gray brick or stucco, backed up to the river on one side.

"It's beautiful," Elizabeth said. "That river keeps spying on us every way we turn."

"It's not through yet," Jim said, taking a left and following another oak-lined street back out to Highway 17.

They traveled several minutes more on the highway, and Elizabeth saw a huge bridge rise up before them. As they made their ascent she saw the river in its final glory, stretching out its marsh-rimmed banks to embrace Winyah Bay and the Atlantic Ocean. Looking out over the horizon, Elizabeth could see thousands of acres of marsh, the spartina glistening in the late-afternoon sun like a green wheat field.

"Over there is Hobcaw Barony. Used to be home to Bernard Baruch, one of the richest men in America during his time. Roosevelt used to come here during the war to get away."

"How large is it?"

"Seventeen thousand acres."

"Wow. Who owns it now?"

"The University of South Carolina. They use it for a marine biology lab. One more shortcut and we'll eat. Okay?"

"Sure. Where are we going now?"

"Hold on, I'll show you." They drove for several more miles, and Jim turned right into a well-landscaped plantation entrance that bore no signs but had a guard gate. Jim slowed, and when the attendant recognized him, he waved him through. Soon they were in deep woods of palmettos, gums, and oaks. The road was dual laned but dirt packed.

"Where are we going?"

"I want to show you my beach house."

"We're going to the beach?"

"Yep. It's not much further."

"Watch out, Jim—there's a dog in the road!" Elizabeth screamed, pointing.

Jim was not going fast, and he quickly stopped dead in the road when he slammed on his brakes. A seven-foot alligator scampered to a lagoon just off the road to their left.

"Is that what I thought it was?"

Jim looked at her and nodded.

"I thought we were in South Carolina, not South Africa."

"There are a lot of similarities between the two, I'm told," he said as he began accelerating again.

Several minutes later they crossed a causeway across a salt creek, and a line of huge oceanfront houses came into view. The road led behind the houses and parallel to the beach. Elizabeth rolled down her window so she could hear the gentle rolling of the surf.

"These houses are tremendous. You own one of these?" she asked as she pointed to a pink stuccoed Bermuda-style home.

"Three-fourths of one," Jim answered. "It's still under construction. It's just up a-ways."

"This is so secluded."

"Exactly what I wanted. That's the clubhouse," he said, pointing to a Georgian-style building that backed up to the Atlantic.

"These are castles. I thought you said you had a beach house. I'm impressed. You must do well in such a small town."

"Here it is," he declared, turning left into a driveway already surrounded by a high, brick wall.

"Wow," Elizabeth said, louder than she intended. She estimated that the house had at least four thousand square feet in it, and it reminded her of one of those Addison Mizener houses she had seen in Palm Beach when she visited a college friend a few years before. The house was brown stucco with a tile roof, and it had a distinctive Mediterranean look to it.

"Come on. We've got time to let you have a quick look," Jim said, putting the car in park.

They walked from room to room, with Jim explaining various architectural details and room layouts. Elizabeth stopped dead in her tracks when she saw the view of the ocean from the main living area.

"Nice, huh?" he asked.

"I'm impressed. And I'm also hungry," she added.

Harold's was only a ten-minute drive from Jim's beach house. Elizabeth had been expecting a fried-seafood house based upon her limited knowledge of Southern cooking, but she was pleasantly surprised when she walked into the reception area to the left of a bar. It was devoid of the obligatory fishing nets and chandeliers fashioned from ship's wheels, and instead there were several nineteenth-century marine oils hanging on the mahogany-paneled walls. The bar was packed even though it was a weeknight, and they had to wade through the crowd to an empty table at the far wall. After Jim ordered drinks, they both scanned the noisy crowd. Elizabeth saw that the other diners were well dressed, although some of the women looked overdressed for the beach.

"I think you'll like the food here," Jim said.

"What's the specialty, fried catfish and hushpuppies?" Elizabeth asked, trying unsuccessfully to sound serious.

"Very funny, Miss Snotnose." Jim tried to sound offended but finally broke into a grin waiting for Elizabeth's response. "Actually the grouper is very good, and so is the salmon."

"You mean they catch salmon down here?" Elizabeth asked with mock seriousness again.

"As a matter of fact, they come up the Weenee River to spawn every spring. If you had looked hard when you rode over the bridge you could have seen the last stragglers."

Soon after their drinks came, they were led to their table in a dining area about twice the size of the bar. The room had scattered oriental rugs on the floor and there were more oil paintings on the walls, mostly Hudson River landscapes.

"Tell me what to order," Elizabeth said once they were seated.

"You do like fish, other than that tasteless stuff like cod, don't you?"

"What do you recommend?" Elizabeth asked, arching her eyebrows as she picked up her menu.

"The pan-fried grouper."

Elizabeth studied her menu for several minutes before putting it down. "The grouper it will be. I'm starved."

"Let me order an appetizer for you."

"Okay."

"Would you like wine?"

"That's fine, but nothing too sweet," Elizabeth answered.

After Jim ordered for both of them, he rested his elbows on the edge of the table. "It sounds as though you've decided to represent Willie Fulton."

"I think you're right."

Jim pursed his lips but remained silent.

When the wine came, they talked of Boston, and Jim asked about a number of his old haunts. They finished their bottle of a good California Chardonnay before dessert. Elizabeth was quite impressed with the grouper and the restaurant, and several times during the course of the meal she told Jim and the waiter how much she liked it.

After Jim paid, they again had to weave through the sea of people overflowing from the bar. They had almost made their way to the door when a well-dressed man a little younger than Jim spoke to him. Jim didn't hear the man, and as he walked past him, the man grabbed Jim by the arm a little too forcefully. The man was unsteady on his feet and looked glassy eyed. "How ya doing, Doc?" he asked.

"Do I know you?" Jim inquired, jerking his arm away.

"Sure you do. I'm one of your patients." The man laughed wildly.

"Good to see you," Jim said quickly as he placed his hand on Elizabeth's back and guided her to the door.

"Hey, Doc!" the man called out. "I'm gonna be needing some more of your medicine pretty soon, okay?" The man laughed again and waved as Jim and Elizabeth left the restaurant.

"What was that about?" Elizabeth asked when they got in the car.

"I don't have the slightest idea. Obviously he mistook me for someone else."

"Well, it would have to have been another doctor," Elizabeth answered, still puzzled.

It was a sleepy ride back to Weenee along the River Road. A quarter-moon hung in the night sky, and the moonlight reflected off the water, making the river look like a long, dark mirror. It was well after midnight when Jim pulled his Porsche into Elizabeth's driveway. Before she could say anything, Jim popped out of the car and opened her door.

"Ever the Southern gentleman," she remarked as she got out. "You don't have to see me to the door."

"My mama would never forgive me if I didn't," he replied, gently clasping her forearm.

At the front door, she turned to face him. "Thanks for a wonderful evening," she said, looking into his eyes.

"My pleasure."

"I'd ask you in for one last drink, but it's been a long day."

He bent forward and pecked her on the cheek. "That's okay—I understand. I'll check with you in a day or two."

He was gone with a wave over his shoulder before she could say anything else.

CHAPTER 10

Elizabeth was glad to see Robert Hamilton at the coffeemaker when she walked in the office just after nine.

"Good morning," he said in a chipper voice.

"Good morning. Do you think you can spare a few minutes to talk about the Fulton case this morning?" she asked, reaching for a cup.

"Sure. Do you want to do it now?"

"That would be great."

Elizabeth had to move the morning's mail out of one of the leather chairs across from Hamilton's desk in order to sit down. The other three chairs were stacked with files of varying thickness. His desk wasn't in any better shape, and once Hamilton sank into his low chair, Elizabeth had to sit up straight to see his face. Hamilton waited for her to speak first.

"Okay. Where do we go from here?"

"The bond hearing and then the preliminary hearing."

"How soon will the district attorney schedule them?"

"To begin with, Elizabeth, we don't call them district attorneys in South Carolina. We call them solicitors."

"Solicitor? That sounds archaic."

"Well, I guess it does, but it doesn't matter. They perform the same function as a DA, and we have to find a judge who will hear the bond motion and then coordinate it with the solicitor's office. We have it tentatively scheduled for ten o'clock next Monday before Judge Lawson." He paused. "I assume you were able to get next week off."

"At least," Elizabeth responded casually. "I'm worried about the Fulton family coming up with bond money, assuming the judge even sets a bond."

"You would be surprised at what people can do when they get

in a jam like this. Besides, it will be a surety bond, meaning that they can put up land to secure the bond."

"Do they have any?"

"Not much, but there are always relatives and church members who will come to the aid of their people in these situations."

"It would be a lot easier getting this case ready for trial if Mr. Fulton were out of jail. That jail gives me the creeps."

"You are right about that, but the jail doesn't bother me as much as all those jailhouse lawyers over there dispensing bad advice to Willie."

"How about the preliminary hearing? Do we get to put up any of our case?"

"We?" Hamilton asked. "Do you plan to stay beyond next week?"

"I haven't made up my mind yet. Although my boss wasn't too upset about me asking for the week off, particularly when I told him a little bit about this case."

"To answer your question, no, we cannot put up any evidence at all."

"Then what's the purpose of it?" Elizabeth asked, shrugging.

"Only to determine if there is probable cause that the accused committed the crime. It's usually very quick and a rubberstamp for the solicitor's office."

"What are the chances of us getting the charges dismissed at the preliminary hearing?"

"With the bloody ax, we have no chance of it getting it thrown out at the preliminary, short of a written confession from someone else."

"I see. Then where do we go from there?"

"There will be a coroner's inquest."

"I'm scared to ask what that is."

"Our coroners are, I suppose, like your medical examiners in Massachusetts. Except they have no medical training."

"How in the world can they perform a medical examiner's function without a medical background?"

"They use the assistance of a coroner's jury."

"You are confusing me now. Exactly what is a coroner?"

"He is an elected official whose duty is to determine the cause of death. To accomplish that purpose he can summon a six-man jury to make that determination."

"Won't the second trial, then, if there is one, result in double jeopardy?"

"Jeopardy doesn't attach in the first trial because it's not a criminal proceeding."

"Then what is the purpose of having it in the first place?" Elizabeth asked, throwing her hands up in the air.

"It's pretty much a formality in a murder case, but we can get some information on the State's case and a copy of the autopsy report."

"Well, that's discoverable anyway."

"We don't have criminal discovery in this state," Hamilton said.

"Boy, this is going to be an interesting case to try," Elizabeth remarked, shaking her head. "You have no discovery, and you have a coroner and his own little jury left over from the eighteenth century."

"You didn't take any legal-history courses at that fancy law school you went to?"

"As a matter of fact, I did, and I don't remember reading about coroners. They must be the creation of the brilliant legal scholars of this wonderful state."

"From what I've read, they have been around since the Middle Ages, although the coroner's powers were somewhat abridged by the Magna Carta. You did study that document, I hope?" Hamilton asked as he peered over his glasses at Elizabeth, waiting for her to answer.

Elizabeth was caught off guard by Hamilton's quick retort. "I'm sorry. I guess I was being a little too hard on you guys," she said. This was her first glimpse of the very quick mind hidden behind a façade of grandfatherly gentility. Her eyes then wandered above his head, and she saw his law-school diploma on the wall behind his desk. At least it looked like a diploma, but all of the writing was in Latin. Next to it was a framed certificate from the *Georgetown Law Journal*.

"I'm impressed," she said, pointing to the diploma. "Georgetown has a very good law school. I almost went there."

"I'm more proud of the other one."

Elizabeth looked over Hamilton's other shoulder and saw a diploma from The Citadel, the Military College of South Carolina. Elizabeth leaned back in her chair and exhaled. "Do you still think we can get this case tried in six weeks?"

"I've spoken with Clarence Phillips, the solicitor, and he is real anxious to go ahead and try this case. He's up for reelection in the fall and he views this as a high-profile case. So to answer your question, it's a go unless we feel like we need more time."

"Do you think we can get this case ready by then?"

"I don't see why not, unless something turns up at the last minute."

"Tell me about the solicitor. What can we expect from him?"

"He's a mediocre trial lawyer, but he wouldn't hesitate to put up the perjured testimony of his mother to get a conviction in a shoplifting case."

"That bad, huh?"

"That bad. They say he wants to be either the attorney general or the governor, or maybe both."

"I know a few of those types in Massachusetts. Believe me, they are not just indigenous to South Carolina," Elizabeth said, shaking her head in disgust.

"It sounds like you have decided to come on board for this trial?" Hamilton asked, folding his arms across his chest.

"Probably so," Elizabeth said, leaning forward in her chair. "I think I can work it out with my boss. Once we get our case in place, I'll probably go back for a couple of weeks. Do you think that'll work?"

"Yes, I do," Hamilton replied as he placed his fingertips together.

"I do want to speak with the sheriff before I make my final decision."

"Do you want me to go with you?"

"No, I don't think that will be necessary, do you?"

"Not really. It may be better if I don't go."

"Why is that?"

"You'll probably get more out of him than I will, that's all."

"Thanks for your time," Elizabeth said, getting out of her chair. "I'll let you know how our meeting goes." She started for the door and then stopped. "What can you tell me about the sheriff?"

"Black Jack? His is an interesting story." Hamilton went on to tell her about how he came home after his retirement from the military and how he rose through the ranks of law enforcement in Craven County.

"What kind of sheriff is he?"

"By the book, and from what I can tell, he's straight as six o'clock."

"He doesn't sound like your stereotypical Southern sheriff."

"No, and he certainly isn't," Hamilton said, shaking his head and grinning. "No siree, not by a long shot!"

"One more thing and I'll let you get to your mail. I need your advice on something else. I may have stepped on some toes at Mrs. Middleton's last night. We had an argument."

"About what?"

"We kinda restarted the Civil War."

Hamilton nodded knowingly. "Ida Pearl is real good about that."

"What should I do? I feel terrible."

"Just stop by around the cocktail hour. She loves company, especially when she is having a drink. One thing about her, and I've known her about fifty years—she never carries a grudge. Don't worry. Just pretend it never happened."

"I might just do that. Thanks again," she said over her shoulder as she headed for her grandfather's office.

CHAPTER 11

Elizabeth called the jail to make an appointment with the sheriff, and the receptionist put her on hold after she gave her name. Several minutes later the woman told her the sheriff would be available in a half-hour.

Upon her arrival, she was ushered into his office and shown a seat opposite a large oak desk. It was expensive looking and not something she had expected to see in a county office. She was told that the sheriff was in the jail and would be with her shortly. Elizabeth spent the time examining the many framed diplomas and certificates that filled the wall behind his desk. Black Jack had managed to display everything except his birth certificate and driver's license. He was a graduate of North Carolina A&T University and had even been awarded a certificate of outstanding citizenship from the Weenee Rotary Club.

"I beg your pardon, Miss Chase." The deep voice behind her made Elizabeth jump.

She turned in her seat and saw a much younger looking man than she was expecting. He appeared to be in his early forties, was dark skinned, and had closely cut hair with a razor part on the left side of his scalp. She could see the tiny outline of a thin mustache. What most stood out to Elizabeth was his muscular frame.

"I'm Jack Carter," he said, bowing slightly. "I'm sorry you had to wait but there was a little disturbance back in the bullpen."

"Hi, I'm Elizabeth Chase," she said, extending her hand.

"The lady lawyer. I've heard about you," the sheriff replied as he sat down behind his desk.

"People say that around here like I'm some exotic bird or something."

"It's just that we don't see many lady lawyers around here, that's all." Carter then leaned forward, his arms resting on his desk, waiting for Elizabeth to speak.

"I'm here about the Fulton case. What can you tell me about it?"

"Okay, I'll give it to you straight. I don't play games with lawyers, and I don't like it when they play games with me." Elizabeth nodded but didn't say anything. "We have a very tight case against Mr. Fulton," Carter continued as he folded his hands together. "It is common knowledge that your client and the deceased had a longstanding feud going."

"About what?"

"It started a number of years ago over some of Fulton's hogs."

"Hogs?"

"Yeah. He always keeps forty or fifty, and they were always getting out. When they did, they usually headed next door to the Frenchman's garden. Probably every one of my deputies has been out there at one time or another."

"Have there ever been any violent confrontations between those two?"

"None other than the hog Frenchie murdered several years ago."

"Murdered?"

"I'm just kidding," Carter said, chuckling. "Frenchie shot one of Fulton's hogs on his property. They settled that one in Magistrate's Court. To answer your question, though, there have never been any violent confrontations between the defendant and the deceased that I know of."

"I see."

"But I think you will agree that this history of bad blood will make it much easier to prove the State's case. And then there's the ax."

"Tell me about that if you would, please."

"It was buried under some hay in his hog parlor."

"It doesn't sound like the crime of the century."

"Your client is not known for his great intellect."

"But he would have to be stupid to think he wouldn't be a suspect. He would have known to dispose of the ax. If he put it there," she added.

"Oh, he hid it there, all right. I'm sure his prints will show up all over the handle. We'll know something from SLED in a few days."

"Isn't the river close by?"

"About 150 yards."

"Then why didn't he just throw the ax in the river?"

"Like I said, Fulton's not too smart."

"Do you have anything else?"

"Do you really think we need anything else?" Carter asked, extending his arms toward her, palms upward.

"I'm just trying to get an assessment of the State's case, Sheriff," Elizabeth replied.

"That's basically our case," Carter answered, with a small measure of conciliation in his voice. "Of course, our investigation is ongoing, and we are still talking to people who live in the area."

"If anything else turns up, would you mind having someone in the DA's office give me a call?"

"The DA's office?"

"Oh, excuse me, the solicitor's office."

"Do you mind if I ask you something, Miss Chase?"

"It's not Miss, its Ms., and no I don't mind."

"The talk around town is that you are going to stay down here to try this case. Is that true?"

"I'm seriously considering it. Why?"

"It's just a little strange, that's all."

Elizabeth started to ask him what he meant but then decided not to. Rising from her chair, she extended her hand. "Thank you for agreeing to meet me on such short notice, Sheriff. I appreciate your openness. It was a pleasure meeting you."

"My pleasure as well," he said as he took her hand. "My pleasure. Anytime you want to talk about a plea, my door is always open."

"A plea?"

"You lawyers do plea bargain in Massachusetts, don't you?"

Elizabeth shook her head ever so slightly. "I don't think Mr. Fulton is considering any type of plea in this case," she said a little more forcefully than she wanted to. "Good day."

Halfway through the short walk back to the office, Elizabeth felt beads of sweat popping out on her forehead. Boy, if it's this hot in June, what are July and August going to be like? she asked herself. She knew now this was a case she was going to try, and she started mentally juggling her own trial schedule. She realized it really was a good time for her, with nothing big coming up until the fall. It was the sheriff's smugness that really convinced her to stay.

Elizabeth spent the balance of the morning working with Inez on her grandfather's estate. She couldn't believe how organized his files were and how easy her task was going to be in administering the estate.

When she returned to her grandfather's house for lunch, she could tell that Rebecca was cooking up a storm. The exhaust fan in the kitchen looked as if it had been installed on the day the house was wired for electricity. Most of the smoke emanating from the stove stayed in the kitchen.

"Rebecca, it looks like the house is on fire."

"Just frying fish, child. That's all."

"What kinda fish?"

"Redbreast."

"What?"

"Redbreast. Out the river."

Elizabeth walked over to the stove and stood by Rebecca. Perspiration was streaming down her face, which she kept wiping with her apron as she continually flipped battered fish about the size of a man's hand.

"They're a funny shape for a fish. How did you get them?"

"Cleveland Tomlinson brought them by."

"Who's that?"

"He's a man your granddaddy got out of a heap of trouble a few years back."

"What kinda trouble?"

"He kill a man over a woman."

My God, Elizabeth thought. This town isn't quite as sleepy as it looks. "What did they do to this Mr. Tomlinson?"

"Didn't do nothing. Your granddaddy got him off."

"Got him off?"

"Yeah, the jury said it was self-defense. Yo' granddaddy was a good lawyer, you know."

"And that's why Mr. Tomlinson brought these fish?"

"Cleveland been bringing fish over here ever since the trial. He fish all the time in the river. He used to bring shad in March. My, how Mr. Snowden loved that shad roe. He used to make me scramble it up with eggs. Cleveland said he heard you was in town and he had fresh redbreast. So here I am cooking them for yo' dinner."

"Rebecca, I can't eat like this in the middle of the day."

"Really, I got to tell the truth, Miss Elizabeth. I'm being kinda selfish."

"What are you talking about, Rebecca? You're not making sense."

"Redbreast is my favorite. I haven't had any yet this year," she said sheepishly.

"Rebecca," Elizabeth replied firmly, stepping back and placing her hands on her hips. Rebecca looked up from the frying pan but didn't say a word. "We're going to sit down and eat us some fish, okay?"

Rebecca made a funny noise deep in her throat and then laughed. "I thought you was mad wid me."

Elizabeth moved closer to Rebecca and put one arm around her damp shoulder. "Show me how you're cooking these redbreast."

The two women sat quietly in the kitchen eating the fried fish along with red rice, hushpuppies, and collard greens. The white flaky fish had a sweetness to it that Elizabeth hadn't tasted before in a fish, and she could see why it was Rebecca's favorite.

"I got a pecan pie under that towel over there," Rebecca said when Elizabeth pushed her empty plate to the center of the table.

"Oh, heavens no," Elizabeth replied, clutching her stomach with both hands. "I'm about to die now. It was wonderful." Elizabeth looked at Rebecca's plate and saw that Rebecca had done a much better job of extracting the meat from the backbone of her fish. "What's the talk around town about the murder?"

"They's a lot of talk."

"What are people saying?"

"That Willie killed Frenchie."

"Do you believe that Willie killed Frenchie?"

"Don't know what to think. I leave that for other people. I don't want to get mix up in no murder."

"Is Willie Fulton the kind of man that could kill someone?"

"That's hard to say. Depends on the situation. He's a churchgoing man, I know that."

"Did you ever know him to hurt anyone?"

"Not real bad."

"Not real bad? What do you mean by that?"

"Well, like a lot of men, he get in he share of scrapes in them juke joints on the weekends. That's what happens to people when they get to drinking that liquor."

"But has he ever been violent?"

"What do you call violent?" Rebecca asked, raising her eyebrows.

"Has he ever really hurt someone badly? Like when he was mad?"

"He cut Bennie Player one time pretty bad but that was a long time ago."

"Oh, I see," Elizabeth said, pursing her lips.

"Like most men around here, he'd be all right if he stayed away from that bottle."

"You don't approve of alcohol, do you?"

"No, I don't," she said quietly. "You ask me so I got to tell the truth." She looked at her hands folded in her lap and was quiet a few seconds. "I don't think the Lord like it either."

"Well, where I come from, people don't think it's wrong to drink, if you don't drink too much."

"I wasn't trying to say nothing bad about you, Miss Elizabeth," Rebecca said in a barely audible voice.

Elizabeth reached across the table and grabbed the older woman's hand. "I didn't take offense at what you said, Rebecca. Just forget it."

"Then you mind if I ask you a question? They's something bothering me."

"Sure, go ahead. Ask me anything."

"Do you ever go to church?"

Elizabeth was surprised at the question. "Why, no, not much. I go for a wedding or a funeral every now and then but that's about it."

"You don't belong to no church?"

"No, I don't."

"Don't you believe in God?"

"Yes, Rebecca. I believe in God."

"I just wanted to know, that's all. Maybe you go to church with me some time?"

"Sure, Rebecca, I would like that," she said, patting her hand. "Guess who I met today?" Elizabeth asked, changing the subject.

"Who?"

"Sheriff Carter."

"You met Black Jack?" Rebecca asked, pulling her hand away from Elizabeth's.

"Yes, and he seems like a very nice man."

Rebecca gave Elizabeth a cold stare but didn't say anything.

"What's wrong—you don't like the sheriff? You should be proud of him."

"I don't think he goes to church either. And they say he got a lot of girlfriends around and him married. I just don't trust people like him, that's all."

"He's a very impressive man, professionally."

"What'd he say?"

"Well, most of the things he told me I can't discuss. Let's just say he was very helpful."

"He thinks Willie done it, don't he?"

"Well, yes, he does, but that's his job to make those kinds of decisions."

"You gonna be Willie's lawyer, ain't you?"

"Yes, I am. Mr. Hamilton is going to be one of his lawyers too."

"Why you wanna stay down here and get mix up in something like that?"

"Because I'm a criminal lawyer. It's my job."

"But why don't you go back to Boston and do your lawyering up there?" Rebecca asked, a scowl on her face.

"Why, Rebecca, I didn't think you'd be so anxious to get rid of me."

"That's not it," Rebecca said, shaking her head. "They's all kinda things going on down here that you just don't understand."

"Criminal law is basically the same all over the country. We play by the same set of rules. It's called the Constitution."

"I ain't talking 'bout the law. I understand 'bout that part. It's just that the people down here is different."

The loud ring of the old phone made them both jump in their seats. Elizabeth picked up the receiver on the second ring. "Hello," she said.

"Glad I caught you. I've been a step behind you all day." It was Jim. "I called earlier and the secretary said you were at the jail. How's your client?"

"Actually I didn't see my client. I had a conference with the sheriff."

"Black Jack? I bet that was interesting."

"Not necessarily interesting, but informative."

"How does it look for your client?"

"You don't discuss your patients, do you?"

"No, why?"

"Because I don't discuss my clients' cases."

"I'm sorry. I didn't mean it like that."

"That's okay."

"Do you want to try another restaurant with me tonight?"

"I don't know. I may never be hungry again."

"What do you mean?"

Elizabeth described her dinner of redbreast to him.

"It makes me hungry and sleepy at the same time. I'll pick you up late, then, about eight thirty."

"Where are we going?"

"Let's just say it's a little different than last night. Gotta run—I've got a waiting room full of patients."

Elizabeth made a pot of coffee with Inez's assistance when she returned to the office. Halfway through the second cup, she felt her nervous system return to normal. If I ate like that every day, I'd never get anything done, she told herself.

She spent the rest of the afternoon in the library. For a small firm they had a respectable library: two full sets of the *Southeastern Reporter,* two sets of *ALR,* various treatises and hornbooks, and about every edition of the South Carolina code dating far back into the nineteenth century when they were bound in leather. She was fascinated by a number of early volumes of South Carolina cases, some having been decided just after the Revolution. It was obvious to Elizabeth after thumbing through several musty volumes that murder, land disputes, and runaway slaves certainly kept the antebellum bar very busy.

By quarter to five she was confident she had a pretty good handle on South Carolina homicide law and was relieved to see that the State's criminal-procedure rules were few in number and appeared to be easy to follow. Barring the unforeseen, she felt that the Fulton case wouldn't be difficult to try, but although she had only spoken to him briefly, she doubted if he had much of an alibi. She gathered her notes, put them in a file, and dropped it on her grandfather's desk.

Elizabeth knew all afternoon that she would take Hamilton's advice and head for the Middletons' house after work. The black man in the suit opened the door just a few seconds after she knocked. He bowed slightly as he opened the screen door and gestured for her to come in with a sweep of his arm.

"Evening, Miss Chase. The ladies are in the parlor. They's looking for you. I told them when you drove up."

"Thank you," Elizabeth said as she walked toward the parlor door, snubbing Ida Pearl's family hanging on the walls. As soon as she looked into the room, she knew that Hamilton was right. Ida Pearl did not carry a grudge. Ida Pearl, with the dog and Estelle at her side, waved her into the room with a broad smile on her face.

"Elizabeth! We're so glad you stopped by. Come! Sit down," she commanded.

Estelle gave her a weak smile that looked forced. The dog frowned at her, as he had at her first visit. He was no doubt of Southern pedigree, Elizabeth told herself as she sat down in the same chair she had so briefly occupied last night.

"I know I should have called first," Elizabeth said, shifting in her seat.

"Nonsense," Ida Pearl replied, waving her hand at Elizabeth. "Nobody in this town ever calls before they come over."

"I want to apologize for my behavior last night. I know we don't agree on a lot of things, but I shouldn't have gotten angry and made such a poor choice of words."

There was another wave of the hand by Ida Pearl and another smile. "Forget it, child. I've forgotten it, and Estelle has forgotten it." Estelle nodded but didn't change expressions. "And I admire your spirit. I think Willie Fulton has himself one fine lawyer." After a pause, she asked, "You are representing him, aren't you?"

"Yes, I am. I made my decision today. I'm surprised you've already heard."

"Young lady, don't be surprised by how fast news travels in this town."

Elizabeth noticed Ida Pearl look to her left and, turning, saw a Dewar's on the rocks almost in her face. "Thank you," she said, taking the drink and then the napkin. Elizabeth took a long swallow and felt some of her tension drain down her throat with the whiskey.

"Tell me, have you ever tried a murder case?" Ida Pearl asked.

Elizabeth looked at the two women before she answered. They were well dressed and, of course, well made up, but at least their clothes didn't look as though they were going to a cocktail party.

"I've tried seventeen, to be exact."

"My," Estelle said, the first word to come out of her mouth.

"How many have you won?" Ida Pearl asked.

"Well, it depends on what you consider a victory. Six were found guilty of first-degree murder, five were acquitted, and the rest were convicted of lesser included offenses. So it's a record I'm not ashamed of."

"Have you ever gotten someone off that was guilty?" Estelle asked, suddenly taking a keen interest in the criminal-justice system.

"I don't know. Unless someone confesses to me that they've committed a murder, which they've never done, I don't really know if they are guilty or not. That's why we have juries."

"And you have to go into jailhouses to see these people?" Estelle asked, leaning forward. The dog gave her a quizzical look, as if he, too, was interested.

"Most of them, the ones that can't make bail."

"That must be awful," Estelle continued.

"You get used to it. I had to do it yesterday."

"You went to our county jail?" Ida Pearl asked before she took a long pull on her drink.

"Yes, that's the only way I could see my newest client."

"Do you think he did it?" Estelle asked. She hadn't touched her drink on the coffee table in front of her.

Ida Pearl turned to face her daughter. "Baby, she can't answer a question like that."

"Oh, I'm sorry, Elizabeth," Estelle said, embarrassed by the rebuke.

Elizabeth laughed. "That's all right. I get asked that question all the time. I did get to meet your sheriff. He's an impressive man."

"What's so impressive about him?" Ida Pearl asked calmly.

"Well, for one thing, he's not the type of sheriff I was expecting to see in South Carolina."

"What were you expecting?" Ida Pearl asked, raising her eyebrows.

Elizabeth paused for several seconds because she didn't want to get Ida Pearl going again. "I thought your sheriff was going to be white."

"And chew tobacco and have a potbelly?" Ida Pearl smiled slightly as she spoke, and Elizabeth nodded. "He probably would be," Ida Pearl continued, "but things are really changing around here."

"What do you mean?"

Ida Pearl shook her head before she spoke. "The Negroes are trying to take over everything." She pronounced the word "Negroes" in such a way that the first syllable sounded as though she was referring to the joint between the hip and the ankle. "And they're doing a good job of it, too."

"What do you mean by taking over? How can they just take over?" Elizabeth asked.

"The Negroes make up over 66 percent of the population of Craven County, and the NAACP is registering them to vote so fast that Lucille Hanna down at the Registration Board has had to hire extra help. Now whenever there is an election, they all meet at the churches, and the NAACP hires drivers, and they haul their people to the polls."

"There's nothing wrong with voting, is there?" Elizabeth thought it was a harmless question.

"No, I guess not," Ida Pearl said, shaking her head slowly. "It's just that they block vote, and they've already elected that Black Jack and another Negro as treasurer." She paused as she reached for her drink. "You never did tell me why you think he's impressive."

"He just seems to be very bright and very straightforward. I don't see those qualities too often in law-enforcement officers. You don't think he's impressive?"

"Well, he is pretty smart for a Negro," she answered. "It's just that I don't particularly like him, and they say he bought a $60,000 house and paid cash for it. Where's he get that kind of money?"

Elizabeth could feel the blood rushing to her head, and she wondered if her cheeks were getting flushed. "Could it be that it's because he's the chief law-enforcement officer for the county?"

"I don't know what it is about that man, dear," she replied, taking a long pull on her drink. Elizabeth was relieved to detect no irritation in her voice.

"Who else have you met in our little town?" Estelle asked, apparently trying to change the subject.

"Some horrible-looking creature with one eye named James.

He barged into my grandfather's office the other day and I had to run him off."

"Why did you do that?" Ida Pearl asked.

"He wanted to do some work. He said he had worked for my grandfather picking up trash."

Ida Pearl chuckled.

"What's so funny?" Elizabeth asked.

"John would pay him a dollar a day to pick up trash around the yard and he would help him out with food and things like that. James would have laid out in the middle of Highway 52 if your grandfather had asked him to. The man worshipped John."

"No wonder he was so emotional. He broke down and cried in the office."

"You must have talked kinda rough to him when you made him leave."

"No, not really. He started crying as soon as he came in the office. But maybe I was a little abrupt with him."

"You really don't have to worry about him, Elizabeth; he's harmless. Are you ready for another?" Ida Pearl asked, pointing to Elizabeth's glass.

"No, no, I'm fine," Elizabeth answered.

"Henry," Ida Pearl said in a lilting voice. "Henry."

"Yes ma'am," the old man said when he appeared in the doorway.

"Get Estelle and me another drink. And bring us something to nibble on, please. I'm getting hungry."

"I really need to be going," Elizabeth said, edging forward in her seat.

"Nonsense," Ida Pearl replied, waving her off. "We don't eat supper until half past seven around here."

The women waited in silence until Henry brought their cocktails. After he served the drinks, he retreated to the kitchen and returned with a silver tray that had a starched, white linen cloth on it. Henry extended it to Elizabeth, and she took one of the crackers off the tray. It had two distinct flavors that were very familiar to her but she couldn't recognize them at first. On the second bite, she realized that she was eating a saltine with parmesan cheese on it that had been toasted.

"This is good," Elizabeth said, holding out the remnants of the cracker.

"It's an old family recipe from my husband's side of the family. Or an old trick, I guess I should say. They were land poor and house poor, if you know what I mean."

Elizabeth had no idea what the woman was talking about, and she made a mental note to ask Robert Hamilton about it.

Ida Pearl put her drink down, pulled out a handkerchief that had been balled up and stuck between the cushions of the sofa, and dabbed her eyes. "I guess I'm like James," she said, her voice cracking. "I already miss your grandfather more than I ever imagined."

"You must have been close friends," Elizabeth said.

Estelle looked straight at Elizabeth and gave her an exaggerated wink.

"We were always good friends through the years. My husband, Peter, and I used to see a lot of your grandparents. Then Peter got sick, and we just couldn't go anywhere."

"How long has your husband been dead?"

"Nine years."

"He was sick for a long time?"

"For about five years before that. The doctors said it was hardening of the arteries. His mind was completely gone when he died. He didn't know me or Estelle," she added, shaking her head.

"That must have been very hard on you both," Elizabeth said, glancing at Estelle.

"Oh, it was horrible seeing Daddy like that," Estelle agreed, her eyes narrowing. "He was like a child when he died."

"It took us a while, but we put our grieving behind us. We just like to remember the good times, don't we, Estelle?" Ida Pearl asked, stroking the dog's back.

"Yes, Mama, we sure do," Estelle replied quickly.

"Several years after your mother died, John and I kept our eye on each other. We talked quite often and he would come over for a drink several times a week. He would eat Sunday dinner with us about once a month and he would have Estelle and me over for dinner quite often. That Rebecca was some cook."

"She still is," Elizabeth said. "If I don't get back to Boston soon, I'll have to buy a new wardrobe."

"I don't think you've got anything to worry about yet," Ida Pearl said, sizing her up. "You're as skinny as a rail. Why is it you young girls feel like you have to be so thin?" Ida Pearl reached for another saltine, and the dog eyed it curiously. "When are you going back to Boston?"

"Probably in a week or two, as soon as we find out when the preliminary hearing is scheduled."

"And you'll come back just before the trial?"

"Oh no, I've got a lot of work to do here getting ready for the trial. I'll only be in Boston for a couple of weeks."

"Have you given any thought to staying down here and practicing with Robert Hamilton?"

Elizabeth laughed before she could catch herself. "Heavens, no," she said.

"I didn't mean to insult you, child," Ida Pearl remarked a little curtly.

"Oh, I didn't mean it like that, Mrs. Middleton. Believe me."

"Call me Ida Pearl."

Elizabeth nodded. She took the last swallow of her drink and then stood up. "I've got to go. I've got an engagement I have to get ready for."

"Tonight?" Ida Pearl asked, stealing a glance at Estelle.

"Yes," Elizabeth replied.

Ida Pearl looked at her daughter again, and when she looked back at Elizabeth, a smile creased her lips. "I know you think I'm real nosy, but is it with Jim Howard?"

My God, Elizabeth thought, how could they know? "Yes, as a matter of fact it is," she said, trying to mask her irritation. "How did you know?"

"You know how a small town is. There aren't many secrets here in Weenee."

"I can already see that," Elizabeth replied.

"He's a very handsome man," Estelle said, the tone in her voice suggesting that she'd given careful consideration to that opinion.

"He is nice looking, but this is no budding romance, ladies, I can assure you. We just have some things in common, that's all."

"You two would make a nice couple," Ida Pearl said. "You have always been pretty, Elizabeth, but you really ought to do something with that long frizzy hair."

Elizabeth chuckled and unconsciously shook her head. She had worn her hair long and curly since her days at Wellesley and had never given it a second thought. "Thank you, Ida Pearl, but I like it like this, and it's easy to keep. Thank you for the refreshments, ladies," she said as she started for the door.

"You must come back real soon, dear. We love company."

The old gentleman was holding the front door open when she walked into the hall.

STOPPED
12-11-11

CHAPTER 12

The scotch had drained the fatigue from Elizabeth's body or at least hid it. After a bath in the claw-footed cast-iron tub, she pulled on a sleeveless cotton jumper as a concession to the heat. She heard a knock on the door almost dead on eight thirty.

"Hi," she said when she saw Jim through the screen door. "You are a walking oxymoron," she added as she unlatched it.

"What in the world is that supposed to mean?" he asked as he walked into the front hall.

"A punctual doctor. I have never heard of one before."

"I'm always punctual when I'm going to see a good-looking woman."

"My, my. The doctor is such a flatterer. Do we have a reservation, or do you have time for a drink?" she asked.

"No, we don't have a reservation. In fact I don't think Mabel knows what one is."

"Who is Mabel?"

"She runs the place where we're going to eat. Rebecca told me you loved barbeque."

"Have you had me under surveillance?" she asked with mock seriousness.

"I don't have to," he answered with a laugh. "Everybody in this town has been watching you."

"Don't I know it. I feel as if I've been living in an aquarium lately."

"Listen, if Ida Pearl doesn't know it in this town, it's not worth knowing," he said with a grin. "And yes, I'll take that drink. Mabel's is about a ten-minute drive from here so put them in a 'go' cup."

Mabel's was about five miles west of town away from the beach, and they passed chest-high fields of green tobacco on the way. The restaurant, in the middle of a field, was in a low building of rough-cut lumber with a tin roof. A screen porch on three sides of the building held wooden tables and ladder-back chairs. The floors were unfinished, and it was stretching it a bit to call the place rustic. The restaurant was crowded with mostly older men and women who looked as if they had come straight from the surrounding tobacco fields. The women appeared tired and hungry, and the men, most of whom still wore their fertilizer caps, were overfed. Jim and Elizabeth were led to their table by a young woman whose nametag indicated she was Denise. As they followed Denise across the room, all eyes were on the couple, particularly Elizabeth. She kept her eyes on Denise's back.

"Enjoy yourself," she told them as she plopped two greasy, laminated menus on the table. "Your waitress will be right with you."

Jim pulled out the wooden chair and seated Elizabeth, and the man at the next table in jeans and a dirty T-shirt looked at Jim as if he had just stepped on the Confederate flag.

"I think I see some of the same people we saw at Harold's last night," Elizabeth said, glancing around.

"Yeah, right," Jim replied, rolling his eyes.

"Wonder what the specials are?" Elizabeth asked, picking up her menu very carefully and holding it by the edges.

"Barbeque, barbeque, and barbeque. That's all they serve," Jim said.

"Then why do they have a menu?"

"Oh, you can get a hamburger steak, if you want one."

"No, I happen to like your barbeque down here."

"So I've heard."

"Who told you?"

"One of my informers."

"Well, I'm not surprised. Does anybody in this town have any secrets?"

"Oh yeah, there are a lot of them."

"Hey, Dr. Howard, I didn't see you come in. How y'all doing tonight?"

Elizabeth looked up and saw a broad-shouldered, heavyset woman in her fifties in a white cotton uniform, smiling down at Jim. A yellow pencil stuck out of the bun on top of her head, and she was wearing earbobs that were half as big as her ears.

"Hi, how's my favorite patient?"

"Real good, Dr. Howard, real good. I bet you call all your patients that," she said with a chuckle, patting his shoulder. "What can I bring you two?"

Jim looked at Elizabeth.

"I think I'll have the barbeque dinner," she said.

"You want skin wid it, honey?"

"Excuse me?" Elizabeth asked, leaning her head forward.

"You want some skin on the side wid your barbeque?"

Elizabeth looked at Jim for help.

"Yeah, bring her a little skin, Ramona, and I'll have the same."

"What you want to drink wid that, sweet tea?"

"No, I think I'll have a Budweiser," Jim said. "How about you, Elizabeth?"

"Dewar's on the rocks, please."

"What?" the waitress asked.

"Dewar's on the rocks," she repeated.

"You mean a liquor drink?"

Elizabeth nodded.

"We don't serve no liquor here. This here's a family restaurant. I can get you 'bout any kind of beer you want, though, honey."

Elizabeth's face dropped. "I don't drink beer," she answered, twisting her lips.

Jim held up his hands and shrugged. "I'm sorry, I didn't realize you don't drink beer."

"Tea will be fine," Elizabeth said to the woman.

"Got you covered," Ramona replied, scrawling on her pad. "It'll be here in a minute."

Elizabeth put her elbow on the table, rested her chin on her palm, and stared at the doctor. "It's been a long day," she said, "and I have to sit here and drink iced tea."

"I'm sorry. Is it going to ruin your night?"

"No," she said, a disgusted look on her face. The look was still there several minutes later when Ramona brought the beer and the tea.

"Ramona, is Sonny Boy in the kitchen?" Jim asked.

"Sure. You think we'd be lucky enough to get rid of him for even one night?"

"I'll be right back," he said, rising from his chair. The two women watched him disappear behind a swinging door.

"You're that lady lawyer from up North, ain't you?"

"Yes, I am. I'm Elizabeth Chase," she said, nodding.

"Pleased to meet you," Ramona responded pleasantly, folding her arms across her huge breasts. She glanced back at the kitchen door and then said, "You got your work cut out for you."

"What do you mean?"

"Every single woman in about three counties has been trying to catch that man for a husband. A man that good looking making the kinda money a doctor makes. Too much, too much," she said, rolling her eyes and then smiling at Elizabeth.

"I found you a little something," Jim said, putting down a large Styrofoam cup in front of Elizabeth. "You're not going to tell on me, are you, Ramona?"

"Sonny Boy probably give it to you. He's always sipping on that stuff back in the kitchen, and this being a family restaurant and all." She turned and walked away, shaking her head.

Elizabeth brought the gold liquid to her nose as Jim sat down. "What is this?"

"Taste it."

Elizabeth took a small sip. Then she took a larger one. "It's not bad. It's not scotch, but it beats the hell out of sweet tea." She noticed that the liquor left a faint, pleasant after-burn in her throat. "Was I not hearing that woman correctly? Was she saying 'skin'? She has such an accent. I can barely understand her."

"They are saying the same about you around town. You were hearing her right. It's the skin off the hog, that's all."

"And you ordered some for me?"

"Just wait—you might like it." Jim took a long swallow of his beer. "How is the Fulton case coming along?"

"No new developments. The bond hearing is Monday morning."

"Do you think he'll get out?"

"Mr. Hamilton seems to think so. I don't know. I met the sheriff today."

"What do you think of him?"

"Well, I thought he was impressive, but when I told Ida Pearl Middleton that, she jumped down my throat."

"That's just Ida Pearl. You have to realize that she's from the old school."

"The very old school, that's for sure."

"From all accounts, Black Jack does a very good job. The white people and the blacks both like him. He feeds everybody out of the same spoon," Jim said.

"From what he told me, they've got a pretty strong case."

"Is there any chance Fulton will plead guilty?"

"I don't think so."

"Do you think they have the right man?"

"I don't know. Sometimes the lawyer never knows."

"I heard Fulton and Frenchie had been feuding for quite some time."

"That's what I hear. Let me ask you something."

"Okay."

"Can I believe what the sheriff tells me?"

"What do you mean?"

"A lot of police officers don't exactly tell the truth, or the whole truth, if it can help put a defendant behind bars."

"If Black Jack Carter tells you something," he said, pausing as he put his beer down, "you can take it to the bank. And you know enough about human nature, I hope, to realize that he's not going to railroad one of his own people."

"I see," she said, taking a long sip of her drink. "That makes my job a little easier."

"Well, let me put it this way, and I don't know much about the law, but if Black Jack tells you he has a strong case, he has a strong case. That's all there is to it."

"You said you thought Mr. Fulton can get a fair trial in this county."

"Yes, I do. But it will be very hard for the jury to give him too much of the benefit of a doubt. What kind of doubt do you lawyers call it?"

"Reasonable doubt?"

"Yeah, reasonable doubt. Don't you think it's going to be tough proving reasonable doubt in Fulton's case?"

"We don't have to prove reasonable doubt, Jim. The State of South Carolina has to prove Mr. Fulton guilty beyond a reasonable doubt. We don't have to prove anything, and that's a big difference."

"Well, I still think you've got a tough row to hoe."

"Excuse me?"

"A tough job."

"Yeah, I'll agree with that. It seems that in homicide cases, at least to me, juries are less likely to give a defendant any breaks."

"Hope you people is hungry." It was Ramona, plopping down two full plates of barbeque, the steam rising from the pork and into their eyes. "Your drinks okay?" she asked, pointing to the beer can and the Styrofoam cup. Elizabeth picked hers up and rattled the ice.

"I'll take another Budweiser," Jim said. "You sound like you're ready, too," he added, reaching for Elizabeth's cup.

"Yeah, I guess so," she said, looking down into the cup. Jim grabbed it and quickly disappeared again behind the kitchen door.

"You need to be lettin' him drink that stuff, honey, and you drink the beer. He'd be a lot easier, that's all."

"What do you mean?"

"Figure it out for yourself, honey. That's pretty strong stuff you drinking. Enjoy yourselves," she said when Jim returned, giving him a hungry look as she walked off.

The two of them ate quietly, and the food more than made up for the lack of ambiance in the restaurant. Elizabeth pushed what had to be the skin to one side and enjoyed the sweet potatoes, rice, and coleslaw as much as she did the barbeque. The pepper in the pork and the gravy had her mouth on fire after a couple of bites, and the only way she could get any relief was to take long pulls on Sonny Boy's gold drink. Halfway through the meal, Jim had to refill her cup once again.

As soon as they finished, Ramona swooped down and grabbed their plates like a buzzard after fresh road kill. "What kinda dessert you want?" she asked, first looking at Elizabeth and then at Jim. "We got some wonderful 'nana puddin'."

The question almost gave Elizabeth heartburn and she thrust her hand out as if to repel any further mention of food. "I couldn't eat another thing, Ramona, thanks."

"Me either, Ramona. Just the check, please."

"Okay," Ramona said, jamming her pad down into one of her apron pockets as if she took it as a personal affront to the cooking skills of the kitchen staff. "I'll get your check." She soon returned and slapped the bill onto the wooden tabletop. "Thanks, and hurry back," she said. "Nice meeting you, Elizabeth. Good luck," she said with a surreptitious wink. She gave Jim one final pat on the shoulder, and she was finally gone.

Jim followed Elizabeth out of the now half-filled dining area.

One man with a long, scraggly, red beard and bib overalls sitting near the door followed her lustfully with his eyes. Jim reached for her arm when she seemed to lose her balance as they walked out the door, and Elizabeth pulled it back quickly in embarrassment.

"I'm okay, Jim," she said firmly.

It was a little past eleven when Jim's Porsche pulled into Elizabeth's driveway. "Would you like to come in for a nightcap?" she asked, slurring her words a bit.

"Sure, I can have one, but only one. I've got to make rounds early in the morning at the hospital. I've got one patient in pretty bad shape, and I don't know if he's going to make it."

Elizabeth made the drinks quickly, and they settled into the leather sofa in the library. "It's good to taste scotch again," she said as she slipped her flats off and pulled her feet underneath her body. "What was that you gave me to drink back at the restaurant? It was pretty strong."

"Just a little homebrew," Jim said.

"What does that mean?"

"Nothing. Don't worry about it. Would you look a gift horse in the mouth?"

"No, I guess I should be thankful. It was just strong, that's all. I think I'm a little dizzy," she said, putting her drink down.

"It might be a good idea if you leave that last one off," he suggested, pointing to her glass.

"I guess you're right," she said with a thick tongue.

"You need to get some rest, and so do I," he declared, leaning over and patting her leg. Then he stood up, took both drinks to the kitchen, and poured them out.

"I'll be out of town this weekend," he said as they walked down the hall to the front door.

"I'm sorry to hear that, since you are my only source of entertainment in this town."

"Are you okay? You look a little pale." he said, placing his hand on her cheek.

"I'm just a little tipsy," she replied, grabbing his forearm tightly before she pulled him to her. Their lips met and quickly parted, and before Elizabeth realized it, her tongue was in his mouth, pushing against his tongue. The last thing she remembered before the room started spinning was his body pressing against hers.

Elizabeth could see the first shadows of dawn on her bedroom wall when she opened her eyes. In a few seconds she realized where she was, but she had no idea why her head was in such excruciating pain. Then she remembered and moaned. "My God," she said loudly. She noticed the room had a peculiar smell to it, like disinfectant. She sat up in bed when she heard footsteps in the hall. She knew it was too early for Rebecca, and her heart was pounding.

"How's my newest patient?" Jim asked from the doorway.

"You scared the hell out of me," she said, flopping back on her pillow. "What are you doing here?" She noticed that he was wearing the clothes that he had on the night before, and he hadn't shaved.

"I stayed here with you." Elizabeth turned her head to the left and then quickly to the right, examining the covers and the pillows. "Don't worry. I was in the next bedroom. You were a very ill woman last night."

"What do you mean 'were'? I still am," she said, resting her forearm on her forehead. "What do I have?"

"Just a hangover, now. You did have rather serious nausea and vomiting."

"I threw up?" she asked, twisting her mouth and then inhaling.

"Off and on for about an hour. Then you started dry heaving," he said, sitting next to her on the bed.

"Nothing like that has happened to me before. I've always been able to hold my liquor pretty well. What did I have, four, maybe five drinks?"

"It wasn't the number of drinks. It was what you were drinking."

"What was it?" Elizabeth asked, turning her head to look directly at Jim.

"Moonshine. I am afraid you got into a bad batch."

"Is moonshine what I think it is?"

Jim nodded. "Homemade liquor."

"Who made that crap?"

"Normally I wouldn't tell you, since it's illegal. But I think you have a right to know. Sonny Boy has a little still in the woods behind his restaurant."

"I can't believe you gave me moonshine," Elizabeth said, closing her eyes.

"I'm sorry, Elizabeth, but I've never known anyone to get sick from Sonny Boy's liquor. He's always real careful, uses only copper tubing, and has his own oak barrels that he chars it in."

"When will I start feeling better?"

"I think you're over the worst of it, but you need to stay in bed today and drink plenty of fluids. I'll call in a prescription for you. You'll feel a lot better tomorrow."

"You stayed here all night with me?"

"I felt responsible," he said, standing up. He reached over and felt her forehead. "When someone gets as sick as you were, there is a real danger of ingesting the vomit, and that in turn could cause asphyxiation." He paused to let the words sink in. "I've got to be going," he said. "Will Rebecca be coming in today?"

"Yes, I think so."

"I'll check back with you later on in the day."

Elizabeth listened as he descended the wooden stairway, wondering what went on the night before in those time periods that were completely blank in her mind.

It was about midafternoon before Elizabeth could keep anything in her stomach. Rebecca worked all day downstairs, and Elizabeth could hear the faint words to unrecognizable hymns floating up the stairway. Rebecca checked on her on the hour and always returned with a small bowl of ice and Canada Dry ginger ale to replenish her glass on the bedside table.

Elizabeth drifted off to sleep around five and was startled awake around seven thirty by the sound of the back screen door closing. "Rebecca, is that you?" she called out. Several seconds later she heard her soft footsteps on the stairway.

"Miss Elizabeth," she said when she walked into the bedroom, "you must be feeling better. Your voice sound stronger."

"I do feel better," Elizabeth said, shifting her body and sitting up. "I think I'm going to make it," she added, smiling for the first time all day. "What are you doing here this late? You need to go home. Look what time it is."

Rebecca dismissed her with the wave of her hand. "Got nothing to go home to, child. I'm gonna stay here wid you tonight. I gotta make sure you okay."

"Don't be silly, Rebecca. Go home."

"I done made my bed up out back. I'm not leaving you sick like this."

"Where did you say you were going to sleep?"

"Don't worry. I'll be in that little house in the backyard. I stayed many a night back there through the years. It's kinda like home."

"Sit down, Rebecca," Elizabeth said, patting the mattress beside her. Rebecca did as she was asked. "Listen," Elizabeth said, almost whispering. "I'm fine. Please go home."

"Not 'til I see you walking around tomorrow," Rebecca said, folding her arms across her chest.

From the expression on Rebecca's face, Elizabeth knew she would not be able to talk her out of it. Elizabeth exhaled deeply and leaned back on the mahogany headboard. "Is something bothering you, Rebecca?" she asked finally.

"I don't like you being sick like this."

"Rebecca, everybody gets sick. It's unavoidable."

"Not like you been sick."

"What do you mean?"

"Dr. Howard, he called today and he told me how sick you been."

"Well, I'm over it now," Elizabeth said.

"I know, but it's the way you been sick, like somebody put something on you."

"What on earth are you talking about?"

"I believe it might have something to do with that case you working on," she said, turning to look at Elizabeth with narrowed eyes.

"You mean the Fulton case?"

"Yeah," she said, "that's the one."

"Rebecca, you're not making any sense at all. What are you talking about?"

"The only time I seen anybody sick like the doctor say you was, they had the root put on 'em."

"The root?"

"Yeah, the root," Rebecca said, her eyes almost closing when she said the word.

"What is the root?" Elizabeth asked calmly.

"I ain't talking 'bout it, 'cause if you do have it on you, they might keep it on you, and it could kill you."

Elizabeth could see that she was getting nowhere with her interrogation, so she dropped the subject.

"You just need to think about getting off of Willie Fulton's case, that's all."

"I can't do that, Rebecca."

"Just be real careful, then, real careful."

"I promise I will, Rebecca. Does that make you feel better?" Elizabeth asked, reaching for her hand.

"Yeah, it does, a little bit. But I won't feel good until all this mess is over wid."

"It will be, in a few weeks. I promise."

Rebecca stood up. "You need anything before I go to bed? Some more soup?"

"No, thank you. Are you going to bed now?"

"In a few minutes. Got to say my prayers first. Four thirty come early in the morning, you know."

"You get up at four thirty?" Elizabeth asked, shaking her head.

"Every day of my life. Goodnight, Miss Elizabeth," she said and was gone.

CHAPTER 13

The bond hearing was scheduled for ten o'clock Monday morning in the cavernous main courtroom of the Craven County Courthouse. The white stuccoed edifice had been designed in 1825 by Robert Mills, the first professionally trained architect born in America, when he was on the payroll of the State of South Carolina. Elizabeth was impressed with the symmetrical lines of the massive portico which was supported by four ionic columns.

Judge Charles Robert Lawson was holding Common Pleas Court, and he had promised to hear the bond motion after he sounded the civil roster. Since no one other than lawyers and litigants are remotely interested in wrecks and contract disputes, there were no spectators, just a bunch of bored-looking lawyers.

Solicitor Phillips had already positioned himself at one of the counsel tables along with his assistant, Jimmy Jacobs. Phillips was thirty-eight and like every other politician on the face of the earth, had aspirations for higher office. His abilities as a trial lawyer, according to Hamilton, were average at best, and he tended to take simple cases and turn them into difficult ones. His conviction rate was high, however, because he was not above circumventing the rules of evidence and the rules of fair play. Whenever he was caught crossing the line, the egregious behavior was blamed on Jimmy Jacobs. As Jacobs had passed the bar on his third and last try, he was grateful for his job and suffered the abuse without comment.

Elizabeth sat in the third row with Hamilton as the judge called out the cases to be tried, and most of the lawyers gave the same repetitious reasons why they were not ready to proceed to trial. Lawson honored most of their requests for continuances with an impatient grunt and a nod to the clerk of court, Shirley Barrineau.

Elizabeth let her eyes wander around the room with its mahogany paneled walls and its twenty-two foot ceilings. Behind the bench were three portraits of judges who studied the proceedings like some immortal appellate panel. There was a grand jury box on the right of the room with eighteen chairs and a petit jury box on the left with twelve chairs. The people sitting in the petit jury box would decide the fate of Willie Fulton.

Once Lawson completed the sounding of the roster, he announced to the lawyers that he would hear motions and pretry the first five cases set for trial after he heard their bond motions.

"Come on, that's us," Hamilton said, rising from the mahogany bench. Hamilton looked around for Pearlie Mae Fulton and spotted her along with eight or ten other black people sitting around her. Hamilton motioned for her to come forward.

As the three of them walked toward the bench, Willie Fulton was brought through a door from behind the bench. He was wearing a loose orange uniform and shower slides with white socks. He was handcuffed and wearing leg shackles. A deputy was pulling Willie by his elbow and closely behind these two men came Black Jack Carter. Philips and Jacobs moved toward the bench when they saw the officers bringing Fulton into the courtroom so that all of the participants formed a large semicircle around the long desk occupied by the clerk of court and the court reporter in front of the bench.

"Madam Clerk, tell us what case we have here, for the record," Lawson barked.

"This is the <u>State of South Carolina</u> v. Willie Fulton, who has been charged with murder," the clerk replied in a monotone.

"All right, Mr. Hamilton, I'll hear from you."

"Your honor, this is Elizabeth Chase of the Massachusetts Bar, and we represent Mr. Willie Fulton, who is standing to my left."

Lawson tilted his head forward and looked over the top of his glasses at Elizabeth for a few seconds. "Ms. Chase, have you been admitted to practice in this state?" he asked.

"Your Honor, we have filed a petition with the Supreme Court to have Ms. Chase admitted, and I have been assured by the clerk up there that it will not be a problem getting Ms. Chase admitted for this case."

"Very well, you may proceed," Lawson said.

"Your Honor," Hamilton continued, "Mr. Fulton has been

charged with the murder of Ovid Gilbert, and we would move to have a reasonable bond set on these charges."

"Tell me about this case, Solicitor," Lawson said, twisting in his chair so he could look at Phillips.

"Your Honor, this is the most gruesome murder I have ever prosecuted here in Craven County, and there is no doubt we have the man who did this horrible act," he said, pointing at Fulton and glaring at him with cold eyes.

"Don't try the case, Solicitor. You'll have plenty of time for that. Just tell me, does the State oppose bond in this case?"

"Yes sir, we do. I would like to point out that the victim was murdered with an ax. In fact his head was chopped off and thrown in the Weenee River. The head was the only thing we found. And not only can we prove that there was a long history of bad blood between the victim and the deceased, we also found the ax that was used hidden in his hog pen, and," he added, taking a long satisfied look at Elizabeth, "we now have the SLED lab report that confirms that not only was the deceased's blood on the ax, but that the defendant's fingerprints were all over it, too. Yes sir, we do oppose a bond," he said, glaring this time at Hamilton.

Lawson's facial muscles contorted when he heard the grisly details of the murder, and this did not go unnoticed by Pearlie Mae Fulton who was standing at her husband's side. Realizing that the prospects of her husband getting out on bond were weak, the tears came quickly, silently sliding down her cheeks.

Shirley Barrineau pulled a Kleenex out of a dispenser on her desk and offered it to Pearlie Mae. The woman reached for the tissue without looking at the clerk and wiped her tears with a series of quick jabs.

Lawson studied the woman momentarily and then looked at Hamilton. "All right, Mr. Hamilton, I'll be glad to hear from you."

"If it please the Court, Your Honor, I've known Willie Fulton ever since he was a boy. He was raised on the Gordon place where his family has farmed for the last three generations. He is thirty-six years old and stands here with his wife of eighteen years. They have seven children, all of whom are living with them. Other than some minor brushes with the law, he has never been in trouble."

"What do you call minor brushes, Mr. Hamilton?"

"Several drunk and disorderlys. He cut a man one time and got probation. That was eight or nine years ago, wasn't it, Willie?" he asked, turning to look at his client.

Willie Fulton looked at his lawyer with hollow, deep set eyes. "Yes sir, yes sir. Long time ago," he said.

"Go on," Lawson said, looking back at Hamilton.

"As I said, Your Honor, Willie Fulton has lived here all his life, and he is not a flight risk, I can assure you."

"He may not be a flight risk, but I can promise you he's a danger to the community, and that's enough of a reason to deny bond and keep him in the county jail until we can try this case," Phillips blurted out. "And another thing, Your Honor, Mr. Hamilton and I have been talking and we think we can get this case ready for trial at the August term, and that's less than six weeks away."

"Solicitor," Lawson said softly as he rested his arms on the bench and leaned forward. "I let you have your say, didn't I?"

"Yes sir, you did," Phillips said, dropping his head as he took a step backwards.

"Then let Mr. Hamilton finish, okay?"

"Yes sir, I'm sorry Your Honor."

"You may continue, Mr. Hamilton."

"Thank you, Your Honor. This man is not going anywhere, Your Honor. He has a wife and seven children to support. They'll starve to death if he has to stay in jail until this case is called for trial. And besides, he has nowhere to go. All of his people are here in Craven County. The only thing we ask is that the bond be reasonable."

"Anything else from the State?" Lawson asked, looking at Phillips, then at Jacobs.

"No sir, Your Honor, other than as I said, the State opposes any bond in this case."

Lawson nodded at Phillips and then picked up a pen and began writing on the back of the warrant. When he finished, he looked at Fulton and then at Pearlie Mae.

"Bond is hereby set at $15,000, surety. Mr. Fulton, I've taken into consideration the fact that you have a large family to support. The amount is not very high considering the charges against you. If you are convicted, you could spend the rest of your life in the penitentiary, do you understand that?"

"Yes sir, yes sir," Fulton said, standing up straighter when he spoke.

"If you don't show up for court, I'll issue a bench warrant for you and you can bet your last dollar Sheriff Carter will track you down, you understand," Lawson said, pointing his finger at Fulton.

"Yes sir, yes sir," he said again.

As soon as Elizabeth and the Fulton family reached the sidewalk, Pearlie Mae grabbed Elizabeth by the arm. "What the judge mean? I didn't understand him."

"Your husband's bond is set at $15,000. That's good, Mrs. Fulton," Elizabeth said.

"I don't think that's going to be a problem, Pearlie Mae," Hamilton interjected. "I've spoken with your pastor, and he has several people who will put up their land for the bond. Willie should be out in a couple of hours."

"Thank you, Jesus," she said, as she closed her eyes and held her hands together as if she was praying.

Willie Fulton was out on bond by lunchtime, and Inez set up a meeting with Elizabeth and Hamilton for ten o'clock the next morning. She and Hamilton talked briefly about scheduling her return to Boston, and they decided it would be best for her to go soon so that upon her return, her trial preparation would be uninterrupted. She booked a flight from Charleston for the following Friday and a return flight two weeks later. That would give her three weeks to wind up most of the estate and get the Fulton case ready for trial. The rest of the afternoon was spent with Inez on the estate, and she wondered to herself more than once over the course of the long afternoon how any lawyer could maintain his or her sanity doing estate work.

Rebecca was waiting for Elizabeth in the kitchen when she got home. "What are you doing here? Why haven't you gone home?" Elizabeth asked.

"They say he got out." Elizabeth didn't have to ask to whom Rebecca was referring. "Yes he did. The judge set a very reasonable bond. We're pleased."

"You's happy he got out? You don't think he killed Frenchie?"

Elizabeth decided to forego her constitutional arguments. "Yes, it makes it so much easier to prepare his defense, Rebecca. It's much harder to work with someone when they're in jail."

"Yeah, I guess you right about that. When they gonna try his case?"

"The first week in August."

"That quick, huh?"

"Yes, and I've got a lot to do by then. I'll be leaving for Boston Friday."

Rebecca's face dropped. "I thought you was staying here to be Willie's lawyer?"

"I am, but I've got to go back for a couple of weeks to take care of some things. I'll have plenty of time to prepare his defense."

"How you getting back to Boston?'

"I'm flying."

"I don't like them planes," she said, putting her hands on her hips. "I don't think God means for us to fly like a bird."

"Rebecca, it would take me two days to drive there, and two days to drive back. I don't have that much time."

"You could take the train. It stops here four times a day."

"Thanks, but I've already booked my flight."

"That doctor called here a few minutes ago looking for you. Said he was checking on you to make sure you was feeling okay. Said he would be out of town a couple of more days and to give you that message which I just did."

"Did he say where he was?"

"No, he didn't say."

Willie, Pearlie Mae, and four of their children were waiting on the sidewalk in front of the office when Elizabeth drove up just before nine the next morning.

"Good morning," she said as she approached the group. Two of the children were hanging perilously on the picket fence that surrounded the office. "We weren't expecting you until ten," Elizabeth said as she looked first at Willie and then at Pearlie Mae. Gone now from the woman's face was the anguish that had given her features a gargoyle-like appearance the day before. Willie's chiseled features had not changed since she had seen him in the courtroom the previous morning. Elizabeth couldn't begin to read his expression.

"We gets up early," Pearlie Mae said matter-of-factly, as if that explained their early arrival.

"I'm afraid you will have to wait awhile. Mr. Hamilton is not here yet," Elizabeth said, looking around for Robert's car. "And I've got to do a few things before we meet."

"That's all right," Pearlie Mae said. "We gots plenty of time."

"Come on in, please," Elizabeth said, motioning with her arm.

"No, we better stay out here wid these bad chilrun, 'til Mr. Hamilton come," she said, looking in disgust at the youngest of the four who seemed ready to impale himself on one of the pickets.

Elizabeth was going through the mail a few minutes later when Hamilton stuck his head in her door. "I see our client is already here," he said. "I can start whenever you're ready."

"I'm ready now. Where do you want to do it?"

"Let's go back to the library. I'll get Inez to get him."

Inez led Willie Fulton to the large room which stretched the width of the building across the back of the office. The musty smell of the old law reports permeated the room, giving the air an odor not unlike that of a cave. The finish had completely worn off the heart pine floors giving the boards a whitewashed look. The law books were all in glass-encased turn-of-the-century shelves, some of which were so dusty you could hardly make out the volume numbers.

Willie nodded at Hamilton and the two men shook hands when the couple entered the room. "How you doing, Willie?" Hamilton asked.

"Glad to get them handcuffs off me," he said, massaging his wrists. "They keep them things too tight. I sure do 'preciate both of you getting me out. I was about to starve to death in that place."

"Did Pearlie Mae cook you a good supper last night?" Hamilton asked.

Willie smiled for the first time. "Yes sir, she sure did. She fried up a mess of fish, and that was some of the best eating I done in a long time."

"Let's start from the beginning," Hamilton said, as everyone found a seat.

"Okay," Fulton said, nodding his head.

"Tell me what you know about the killing, Willie."

"Not a whole lot. I know a lot of people think I wanted to see him dead, and I probably did if I ever woulda given it any thought. But I didn't kill that Frenchman," he said, looking straight at Hamilton, then at Elizabeth.

"From what the law knows, they think he was killed sometime that afternoon. Do you remember where you were?"

"I was suckering tobacco."

"Whose tobacco?"

"It was mine. I got a little piece."

"How much?"

"I got an acre and three tenths. Almost three thousand pounds."

"Who was with you?"

"Nobody."

"How about Pearlie Mae and the kids?"

"They was down at the river fishing. Lord, that woman loves to fish."

"All of the children, too?"

"Yes sir. They love to fish, too. We try to keep 'em together as much as we can. They's always getting in more trouble," he said, shaking his head.

"Then no one was with you all afternoon?" Hamilton asked, looking at Elizabeth.

"No sir, not until about first dark when they all come back from the river."

"Then you don't have much of an alibi," Hamilton said, shaking his head several times. "Tell me about the ax."

"I heard they found my ax wid blood on it."

"Then it was your ax?"

"Well, I don't know for sure. But one of the deputies 'scribe it to me, and it sure sounds like my ax."

Hamilton looked at Elizabeth again and asked, "Do you know how the blood got on your ax?"

Willie shook his head. "No sir."

"When is the last time you and the Frenchman spoke to each other?"

"It been weeks, months ago. We try to stay out of each other's way."

"Tell me, did you ever threaten the deceased, Mr. Fulton?" Elizabeth asked, speaking for the first time.

"Everybody calls me Willie." He paused and then he began again. "Me and him had words before. Plenty of times. My hogs would get out, and we never did pay much attention to them until he moved into that old house. He was so particular about that garden and all them flowers."

"I understand," Elizabeth said, "but you didn't answer my question. Did you ever threaten Mr. Gilbert?"

"Probably so. I don't know. Maybe when I been drinking. He didn't like me, and I sure didn't like him."

"Do you recall if anyone heard you threaten him, or if you told someone else that you might harm him?" Elizabeth asked.

"I don't know," Fulton said, shrugging. "Could be, I don't remember." Elizabeth looked at Hamilton, who was making notes on a yellow legal pad. "You have been in a courtroom before haven't you, Willie?" she asked.

"Oh, yes ma'am. And I don't care nothing 'bout going back, neither."

"Well, you realize, don't you, that you have to go back."

"Yes ma'am. I guess so."

"Do you understand about a jury trial?" she asked softly, testing his knowledge of the judicial system.

"Yes ma'am," he answered, nodding vigorously.

"Do you understand what plea bargaining is?"

Willie looked at her with a blank expression. Finally, he spoke. "No ma'am."

Elizabeth breathed deeply and looked at Hamilton to see if he wanted to explain the process. He gave no indication of wanting to say anything.

"In a number of cases, the solicitor may want to offer you a plea bargain. If you are convicted of murder, the judge under South Carolina law has to sentence you to life in prison. You would not be eligible for parole until you served twenty years."

"I'd be an old man by then," he said under his breath. "If I lived that long," he added.

"Assuming the State has no witnesses, and since they have no confession, their case is purely circumstantial. As a result, they may offer you a lighter sentence if you agree to plead guilty. Say, something like manslaughter."

"No, I'm not pleading guilty. I didn't kill Frenchie. No way I'm gonna plead to something I didn't do," he repeated, louder this time.

"That's fine," Elizabeth said, extending her hand toward her client. "Believe me, the last thing we will do is try to get you to plead guilty to something you didn't do. Mr. Hamilton and I just have to make sure you understand how the legal system works, okay?"

"Okay," he said. "I understand."

"Now that we have that straight let's go over a few things. First, you don't talk to anyone about this case unless Mr. Hamilton or I am present. That's very important."

"Not even Pearlie Mae?"

"Pearlie Mae is all right only if there is no one else around. You understand?"

"Yes ma'am."

"And you need to think hard and try to remember if anybody saw you the afternoon Frenchie was killed."

"Okay," he said.

"Do you ever go out at night or on the weekends?"

"Sometime I go to the club and have a couple of beers."

"Well, you should stay home, and it might be a good idea to leave off the alcohol."

"What for?"

"If you go somewhere and get in a fight the solicitor could get your bond revoked, and you would have to stay in jail until the trial comes up," Hamilton said.

"You mean they could put me back in jail after they done put up the land?"

"They certainly can," Elizabeth said.

"She's right, Willie, and she has a good point," Hamilton said. "You need to keep your nose clean and stay out of trouble."

"You won't have to worry 'bout me. I can guarantee you that."

"Good," Hamilton said. "Now, can we answer any questions for you?"

"Y'all gonna get me out of this mess, ain't you?" he asked.

"We hope so," Hamilton said. "We hope so. Make sure Inez knows how to get in touch with you in a hurry. You do have a phone, don't you?"

"No sir, but Pearlie Mae's mama does, and she lives just down the road. You through with me now?" he asked, rising from his chair.

Elizabeth looked at Hamilton. "I think that's all we need to talk about right now," he said. "Why don't you check in with Inez at least once a week to see if we need you, okay?"

"Yes sir," he said. He left with an eagerness that bothered Elizabeth, but she didn't know why.

When they heard the front door slam, Hamilton turned to Elizabeth. "What do you think?"

"No real alibi. Strong circumstantial evidence. Motive. Unless we can pull a rabbit out of the hat, Willie Fulton may be looking at a lot of time."

"The judges in this state give a pretty strong charge on circumstantial evidence. And the bad blood between a defendant and the deceased is clearly admissible under our case law. Your assessment, unfortunately, is right on the money."

"Tell me about our worthy opponent, the solicitor. What can we expect out of him with a case like this?"

"This is about as high profile a case as he will get in this circuit. Phillips will keep it simple because he has the facts on his side. Juries in this county take murder cases very seriously. Burglaries and DUIs they're not as hard on."

"Do you think Phillips will offer us manslaughter?"

"Probably so. This is a crime obviously committed in the heat of passion, and he will recognize it as such. And he doesn't want to take a chance on losing a big case like this just before the election."

"Does he usually go with a set sentence if he goes with manslaughter? I know the max is thirty years from what I've read."

"No, but he will probably go with a recommendation of a sentence of not to exceed x number of years. In this state the solicitor can only make a recommendation to the court. The judge doesn't have to follow the recommendation."

"You mean a defendant can agree to plead to a charge based upon a recommended sentence, and the judge doesn't have to follow the recommendation?" Elizabeth asked as her eyes widened.

"That's right. But Lawson and most judges in this state will allow a defendant to withdraw his plea if he doesn't accept the recommendation."

"That makes it kinda tough on a defense attorney."

"And the defendant," he added.

"And the defendant, you're right. Where do we go from here?"

"When do you leave for Boston?"

"Friday."

"Well, there's not much we can do between now and then. I've got some contacts out in the River Road section, and I'll see what I can find out while you're gone."

"Do you have an investigator we can use?"

"Not really. There are a couple of retired police officers around here who call themselves private investigators. They do mostly surveillance work in divorce cases, insurance investigations, that kind of thing. Everybody out in that section knows who they are so I don't think anybody would give them any information."

"What are we going to do if we can't turn up a witness that can help us?"

"I don't know. It doesn't sound like Willie will consider any kind of plea."

"There may come a time when we have to lean on him," Elizabeth said.

"You mean try to get him to plead guilty?"

"No, not really. If he's guilty he may come around. If he doesn't, then we'll try to give it our best shot with the jury."

"I guess you're right."

"Are you sure there's nothing I can do before I leave?"

"No, not really."

"How about the preliminary or the coroner's inquest?"

"I think I can get them to wait to hold them until you get back."

"If you're sure, then I might try to change my flight to tomorrow. Inez says we've done all we need to do on the estate until the appraisers make their return in thirty days."

"She's right; go ahead. Just don't stay up there and not come back," Hamilton said with a grin. "I can't handle this case by myself."

"I won't desert you, I promise. Just give me two weeks, and I'll be back, ready to go. I'll be checking with you in case we need to talk about anything."

"Do you feel comfortable with three weeks to prepare for trial?"

"Heavens, yes. I tried a murder case once with only four days notice. Public defenders are used to working under pressure. This one doesn't sound very complicated."

"No, not really."

"What kind of witness do you think Willie will make?"

"A pretty good one, I think. He's always been honest with me, and although he has been in his share of scrapes, I think most people around here believe he's honest. Now whether that will outweigh the state's strong case, I don't know."

"What do you make of the ax?"

"Could be Willie's, and he could have used it to kill the Frenchman. Maybe he thought no one would search as closely as they did. Or the only other explanation is that someone planted it."

"Wait a minute. Did the Sheriff's Department have a search warrant?"

"I'm afraid so."

Elizabeth screwed up her face. "I guess it was too much to hope for, that they would be that stupid."

"Inez is working on getting us a copy. I'll go over it with a fine-tooth comb while you're gone."

Elizabeth nodded but didn't say anything. She stared out the window for a few seconds and then said, "This case is too clean, too cut and dried. Don't you think?"

This time Hamilton nodded.

"There must be something out there that we can hang our hats on. Something to create reasonable doubt."

Elizabeth had been able to get a seven-thirty connecting flight out of Charleston the next morning so she calculated that she'd have to leave Weenee by five a.m. Rebecca was upset by the change of plans, but Elizabeth calmed her down after a few minutes. The older woman left after giving Elizabeth a long embrace, as if she was afraid that she would never see her again. After eating a supper of meatloaf and mashed potatoes that Rebecca had left on the stove, she tried to call Jim Howard, but there was no one at his office and his home number was unlisted. She tried to page him at the Craven County Memorial Hospital, but there was no answer there, either. She cleaned up the kitchen, packed her bags, and, after a long bath in the old claw-footed tub, set the alarm for four a.m.

CHAPTER 14

On Elizabeth's first day back on the job, her coworkers appeared to have genuinely missed her. About nine thirty, Harry Hirsch sent word that he wanted to see her immediately. Elizabeth went straight to his office, knocked twice, and walked in. Hirsch was leaning back in his desk chair with a big smile on his face.

"Well, if it isn't Scarlett, come to pay us a little old visit," he said in an exaggerated attempt at a Southern drawl. "And do tell me why we are so honored," he continued, rising from his chair and bowing at the waist. "Sit down, please, Miss Scarlett. Can I get James to fetch you a mint julep?"

Elizabeth plopped down in the nearest chair. "You better stick to practicing law, Harry. That's the worst Rhett Butler imitation I think I've ever heard," she said, rolling her eyes.

"Oh, come on, Elizabeth," Hirsch retorted as he sat down behind his desk again. "It's good to have you back," he added, dropping the contrived accent.

"It's good to be back. How have things been here?"

"Not too bad. Everybody missed our star attorney, that's all. Including me," he said, pointing to his chest with his thumb.

"Thanks," she responded. "My schedule doesn't seem to be in too bad a shape."

"I think you're okay. We were able to get Judge Lodge to postpone the Mazurkiewitz case until the fall. We told him you would be trying a murder case down in South Carolina, and he went nuts. After we calmed him down, he was most interested in your case. He wants you to call him when you get a chance."

"It's a relief not having to worry about that case until this fall. I saw your note on the Allen file. The DA is going to recommend probation after all?"

"Yep. Can you believe it? After all the whining and posturing Oliver went through. That prick."

"Yeah, I can believe it. Deep down I still feel he's afraid to try any case he thinks he has any chance of losing."

"Believe me, any file he has his hands on, he has a good chance of losing. How long do you think you'll be down there, max?"

"Four weeks, maybe a little more."

"You've got that much vacation coming. You ought to take a few days off while you're down there. It's a nice place."

"Nice? We're talking about South Carolina, Harry. Have you ever been there?"

"Yeah, sure. I spent a week on Hilton Head a couple of years ago. I loved it. It's kinda pricey, but it's beautiful. The course at Harbour Town is one of my all-time favorites. I shot a seventy-nine there, I might add."

"Harry, we're not talking about Hilton Head. We're not even talking about Charleston, which is beautiful from what I saw of it. We're talking about Weenee, South Carolina, with a population of about three thousand people. It's about forty miles from the coast in the middle of a bunch of swamps, doublewide trailers, and the spookiest-looking oak trees you've ever seen. Once you leave Charleston, it looks as if you're going into some kind of time warp."

Hirsch shrugged. "How are you coming with your grandfather's estate?" he asked.

"Fine. My grandfather has a secretary who should be practicing probate law. She's been at it thirty years and probably knows more than most lawyers in her field. It's not nearly as complicated as I thought it would be, thanks to Inez."

"I'm glad to hear that," Hirsch said, sounding sincere for the first time. "Is your murder case winnable?"

"I don't know. It was a brutal murder, and there is some evidence that my client and the deceased were not too fond of each other."

"Do they have any kind of statement?"

"No, my client steadfastly maintains his innocence. Says he doesn't know anything about the murder although he and the deceased were practically next-door neighbors."

"Does the State have any witnesses that can put him at the scene of the crime?"

"No, not that I know of."

"Then it sounds like your man may be home free."

"There is one piece of evidence that may give us a problem."

"What is that?" Hirsch asked, leaning back in his chair and putting his hands behind his head.

"They found the ax that was used to decapitate the deceased buried in my client's hog parlor."

"Oh, Christ," Hirsch said rolling his eyes.

"And it had Willie Fulton's fingerprints all over the handle, according to the solicitor."

"Excuse me—according to whom?"

"The solicitor. That's what they call the DA down there."

Hirsch grinned as he folded his arms across his chest. "Do all of the lawyers and the judges wear powdered wigs?"

Elizabeth laughed out loud. "No, but it is different. The old courthouse is beautiful. It looks like something on a movie set. Just what you would expect in a small Southern town. White columns overlooking a square with a Confederate monument. It's very quaint."

"Do the locals sit on their porches late in the afternoon drinking mint juleps?"

"No, but, Lord, they drink their share of liquor."

"Sounds interesting, but I think I'll stay here. Those rednecks might want to lynch this Yankee Jew boy," he said, grinning. "I'll let you get to work. I just wanted to make sure everything was okay with you."

Elizabeth stood up. "Harry, I do appreciate you letting me do this."

"Do what?"

"Take this time off. This means a lot to me."

"What do you mean?"

"Willie Fulton won't get a fair trial unless I go back down there and represent him."

"Don't worry about it," he said. "Besides, I know you'd do it even if you didn't have my permission." He hesitated and then said with a wave of his hand, "Go to work."

Elizabeth worked twelve hours a day the following week. She had a burglary case that was scheduled for trial the next week, but that didn't bother her because she could try most burglary cases, including this one, in her sleep. She was about to call it a week at five thirty on Friday when the phone rang. Even her criminal clients didn't bother her this late, so she wondered who it was.

"Hello," she said.

"Elizabeth?"

She could not place the voice. "Yes, this is Elizabeth Chase. Who is this?"

"Jim Howard," the voice said coldly.

"Oh, I'm sorry—you caught me by surprise, Jim. How are you?"

"Fine, fine. You are a hard person to run down."

"I'm sorry. I left Weenee sooner than I had planned. I should have left you a number. I just didn't think about it."

"I didn't find out until a few days ago that you had left town. Did you decide not to represent Willie Fulton?"

"No, I'll be back down there after next week. I realized I had done all I could do for now on my grandfather's estate, so I came back here to catch up."

"Oh, I see. Nobody seemed to know what your plans were, or at least nobody wanted to tell me. I had to pry your number out of Inez. For some reason they are very protective of you. Are you feeling okay now?" he asked, changing the subject.

"Yes, I'm fine. Thanks."

"You were a sick woman."

"I know, please don't remind me."

"I just like to keep up with my patients, that's all."

"Jim, I did try to reach you at your office to thank you for what you did."

"Oh, I didn't know that. I was just concerned when you disappeared like you did."

"Tell you what I'll do. I'll cook dinner for you one night when I get back to Weenee. In payment for your services."

"Are you serious?"

"Of course, I'm serious. I'll call you when I get in."

"Sounds wonderful," he said. "I'll be waiting."

The following week was a whirlwind of activity for Elizabeth.

She was fairly comfortable with her trial schedule for the weeks immediately after her return from the Fulton trial, because most of the judges in Boston headed for the shore in August. September would be hell, because she already had three trials scheduled, including another murder case.

Her flight to Atlanta Sunday afternoon was crowded and suffocating. To her relief, there were only a dozen or so passengers on her connecting flight to Charleston, so she got some much-needed sleep. It was almost eleven when Elizabeth turned into her grandfather's drive. She took a long look at the old iron tub and decided she was too tired to get in.

The coroner's inquest and the preliminary hearing had both been held while Elizabeth was in Boston. Hamilton briefed her in detail, and she found two memos he had dictated for the file. Phillips, sensing a tactical advantage, refused to agree to postpone the hearings until Elizabeth returned. Apparently she hadn't missed much, and there were no new disclosures of any real damaging evidence. As Elizabeth was leafing through the file in Hamilton's office, the transcript of the coroner's inquest caught her eye.

"Did the coroner's jury actually reach a verdict? Did they deliberate?"

"For about five minutes. Their verdict was that the deceased died at the hand of another."

"That's all?"

"They recommended that the case be referred to the grand jury."

"I thought that was the purpose of the preliminary hearing. You told me to assume that the magistrate at the preliminary was going to send the case on up to the grand jury. Isn't that what he did?"

"Yes, the magistrate sent it up."

Elizabeth shook her head slowly. "Then why have a coroner's inquest?"

Hamilton shrugged. "As I told you a few weeks ago, it's been around for centuries. Things don't change real fast in this state, I guess."

"I'll say," Elizabeth said, plunging back into the file. "There are two things I want to do this week, if possible. I want to view the crime scene, and I also want to meet with the solicitor."

"Why do you want to talk with Phillips?"

"I want to see if he'll lay his cards on the table—tell me what his best offer is."

"It won't hurt, although he hasn't been known for thinking that far ahead."

"You're kidding."

"No, I'm not," Hamilton said, holding up his right hand as if he were about to swear an oath. "You talk to Phillips alone. You'll get more out of him than I will. I better go with you to the crime scene, though. When do you want to go?"

"The quicker, the better. Can you go tomorrow?"

"I think so. I'll check with Inez. I'll tell her to get a hold of Willie," Hamilton said, picking up the phone.

Elizabeth thought a minute. "Let's hold off on Willie right now. We can take him back there if we need to."

After her meeting with Hamilton, Elizabeth called the solicitor's office and learned that Phillips was in court in another county. His secretary scheduled a meeting for Friday afternoon and said she would call back if he got hung up with the jury on the case he was trying. Elizabeth was about to leave for lunch when Inez buzzed her on the intercom.

"Mrs. Ida Pearl Middleton is here to see you," she said.

What on earth for? she wondered. "You can send her on back, Inez."

Ida Pearl was dressed, as usual, as if she was getting ready to attend a meeting of the state garden club in Columbia, but her eyelids were swollen and her face was somber. Two steps behind her was Estelle, also inappropriately dressed for a sweltering summer day in the South Carolina low country.

"Come in, ladies. This is a wonderful surprise. Please sit down."

When the women were seated, Elizabeth waited for Ida Pearl to speak. She noticed the older woman's right hand was clutching a linen handkerchief, and it was shaking.

"How was your trip to Boston?" Ida Pearl asked, in a voice barely above a whisper.

"It was hectic, but I got a lot done while I was there."

Ida Pearl looked down at her hands for a few seconds, and then she said, "I'm afraid I owe you an apology."

"I really don't think you do," Elizabeth responded, recalling their argument at Ida Pearl's home. "I've completely forgotten that afternoon, and I hope you have too."

"I'm not talking about that," she said, looking up at Elizabeth. "While you were gone, I'm afraid I was guilty of being a little loose with my tongue."

"What on earth are you talking about?" Elizabeth asked, leaning forward across the desk.

"I said some things about you and Dr. Howard that were not true. That he spent the night with you in John's house."

"You did what?" Elizabeth almost shouted.

Ida Pearl looked down again and quickly covered her face with her hands. She let out three low sobs and wiped her eyes with the handkerchief. "I'm so sorry, Elizabeth. I shouldn't have listened to street talk. Jim called me, and he was very angry. I've never had a man talk to me like that, but I can't say I blame him. He told me exactly what happened," she said, and the sobs started again.

Elizabeth waited until the woman composed herself before she spoke. "You found out that I was really sick that night?" she asked.

Ida Pearl nodded as she wiped her nose.

"So it's all over town that Jim Howard and I slept together?"

"It was, but believe me, I've called everybody in town to tell them I was wrong."

"She did, I promise you," Estelle said, looking at her mother.

"You mean to tell me that you and the rest of the people in this little backwater town would think I would jump into bed with a man I've known for just a few days and been out with twice?"

This time Ida Pearl shook her head three times very quickly as she dabbed her handkerchief at her nose.

Elizabeth studied the two women before she spoke. "What the people of this town think of me doesn't bother me nearly as much as the fact that neither one of you ladies warned me when I came to town."

"Warned you?" Ida Pearl asked. "About what?"

"About how strong the moonshine is around here." Elizabeth stared hard at the two women for several seconds, and then a big smile creased her face.

Ida Pearl was caught off guard by the remark. When she

realized that Elizabeth was not serious, she chuckled, and both women laughed loudly with relief. "Then you're not mad?" Ida Pearl asked.

Elizabeth waved her hand at both women. "Don't worry about it. Is Jim okay with it now?"

"Yes, I think so," Ida Pearl said. "It's just different for a man."

"I'll talk to him."

"Anything you can do to smooth over this little bit of unpleasantness we will deeply appreciate," Ida Pearl said, rising from her chair. "We've taken enough of your time. Let's go, Estelle." When she reached the door, Ida Pearl turned and asked, "Are you sure you aren't angry?"

"Positive," Elizabeth said, and then she watched the two women shuffle down the hall.

Rebecca had lunch waiting for Elizabeth, and the older woman hugged her as if she had been gone for a year. Elizabeth ate in the kitchen and Rebecca continued her work but peppered Elizabeth with questions about her trip and what she did in Boston. When Elizabeth finished her lunch, she slid her plate to the center of the table and pushed her chair back. "Rebecca, did you hear any rumors about Jim Howard and me while I was gone?" she asked.

Rebecca stopped drying a pot and turned to face Elizabeth. Rebecca frowned. "What you say?"

"I understand some people were talking about the doctor and me being together."

"That's white folk's talk, Miss Elizabeth. Why you think I'd be hearing that?"

Elizabeth shrugged. "I don't know. I was just curious."

"I know one thing. He's a good-looking man. If you start to look around for a man down here, he'd be a good place to start at."

"I'll keep that in mind, Rebecca. Let me ask you something. Where's the best place to shop for groceries around here?"

"At the Pig."

"Excuse me?"

"The Piggly Wiggly."

"What is that?"

"It's a grocery store. Ain't that what you ask me about?"

"You have a grocery store called the Piggly Wiggly?" Elizabeth inquired, shaking her head slowly.

"It's the best we got. If you can't find it at the Pig, you don't need it. What you want to know for? I takes care of all the grocery shopping for this house."

It suddenly dawned on Elizabeth that she hadn't paid a penny for the groceries she had been eating since she first arrived. "Oh, my God, what have I been thinking, Rebecca? I've let you buy all the groceries. Why didn't you say something?"

"What do you mean? Mr. Williams, the head man at the store, lets me charge everything, and he sends it to Miss Inez, and she pays for it at the end of the month."

"I need to get straight with Inez, then."

"Reckon so," Rebecca said, swatting at a passing fly. "You still ain't told me why you want to know about the Piggly Wiggly."

"I told Dr. Howard that I would cook dinner for him. I was thinking about doing it tomorrow, and I have to get some things."

"You know how to cook?"

"A few things. I enjoy it."

"What you like to cook?" Rebecca asked in a serious tone.

"Veal parmigiana, things like that."

"What's that?"

"Veal and cheese and a few other ingredients."

"They got cheese at the Pig, but I ain't never seen any veal there. You want me to go with you in the morning and help you shop?"

"Well, I may need a little help. If we could go early, yes, I'd like your help."

Over Rebecca's protests, Elizabeth lent a hand with the lunch dishes, and the two women made an appointment to go shopping at eight the next morning.

There was a note on Elizabeth's desk when she got back after lunch to call Jim Howard. She returned the call and was put on hold by a surly receptionist for five minutes before Jim picked up and said, "This is Dr. Howard."

"You must be busy today."

"Elizabeth, I'm sorry to keep you waiting. I was giving an eleven-year-old a tetanus shot, and he kept getting away from his mother and me. How was your trip back?"

"Fine. I already feel like I never left."

"Did you get a lot done while you were up there?'

"Yes, I did. Things worked out pretty well."

"I'm glad," he said. "But I'm also glad you're back."

"I'm not so sure I'm glad to be back."

"What do you mean?"

"Ida Pearl and Estelle paid me a visit at the office today."

"What was that all about?"

"They came to apologize."

"Apologize for what?"

"I think you know, Dr. Howard. For spreading talk about you and me around town."

Elizabeth heard him exhale. "I was hoping you wouldn't find out about that. It seems the people in this town thrive on gossip."

"You must have really laid her out. She was teary eyed and very sorry."

Jim laughed. "As a matter of fact I did. I'm glad she went to see you. That's better than hearing it on the street, I guess. I'm just real sorry that I'm the reason they dragged your name through the mud."

"It doesn't bother me. I'll be out of here as soon as the Fulton trial is over. It's you who would suffer." Elizabeth hesitated for a couple of seconds. "Are you free tomorrow night?"

"Yes, why?"

"I meant what I said about cooking for you. Eating barbeque all the time isn't good for you. You ought to know that; you're a doctor."

"I thought you had forgotten about your promise. That sounds wonderful. What are we having?"

"It's a surprise. Rebecca and I have a date to go shopping early in the morning. To the Pig, I might add."

"Wow. This is going to be a real treat, I know. I've got to run an errand when I get out of here tomorrow afternoon. Will around eight be okay?"

"That sounds good. See you then."

Rebecca was dressed and waiting in the kitchen for Elizabeth when she walked downstairs at seven thirty the next morning.

Elizabeth noticed a faded green umbrella by the backdoor and was puzzled when she looked out the window and saw bright sunshine. "Is it supposed to rain today?" she asked.

"No, but the weatherman calling for it to be real hot."

"Then what's the umbrella for?"

"Umbrellas ain't just for keepin' the rain off your head, child."

"What do you mean?"

"Sometimes that old hot sun is worse'n the rain."

"Oh, I see," Elizabeth said. "I never thought about that. Let me get a quick bowl of cereal, and I'll be ready to go." Ten minutes later the two women got into the Buick to head downtown to the Piggly Wiggly.

"You never drive, Rebecca?" Elizabeth asked as she backed out of the driveway.

"Never no need to."

"Surely there were times when you needed to drive a car."

"You don't need to when you ain't got no car."

"You've never owned a car in your life." Rebecca shook her head. "Well, what do you do in case of an emergency?"

"Call the preacher, and he'll get somebody in the church to take me where I need to go."

"You and the other church members are pretty close, aren't you?"

"We all depend on each other. But that's the way it's supposed to be." Rebecca looked out the window at the big old houses they were passing and turned to look at Elizabeth. "That's another reason why you ought to go to church. I know your granddaddy would want you to. He probably looking down at you right now thinking that very same thing."

"Rebecca, do you think people in heaven can look down and see us?"

"Sure, I do. You don't?" Rebecca asked, staring at Elizabeth with wide eyes.

"To be honest, I've never given it much thought."

"Well, 'scuse me for saying this, Miss Elizabeth. I know you got a whole lot of education, and you being a lawyer and all that, and me, I ain't got no education at all. What I'm trying to say is for you to be such a smart woman, there sure is a whole lot of important things that you don't think about hardly a-tall."

Elizabeth bit her lip but not in time to stop her grin. "You're exactly right, Rebecca. Exactly right."

"There's the store right there," Rebecca said, pointing.

After they entered the building, Elizabeth looked around the large store and heard Rebecca behind her, already pushing a grocery cart.

"Tell me what you need," Rebecca said as she stopped the cart beside Elizabeth. "I can shop in this place with my eyes closed. What kinda meat you say you wanna cook for the doctor?"

"Veal," Elizabeth said.

"The meat counter is in the back," Rebecca told her. "Let's go."

Elizabeth saw that the Piggly Wiggly didn't have any veal. She studied a number of strange-looking meats before she picked one up. "Is this what I think it is, Rebecca?"

"Pig's feet. They's easy to cook, if you think that's what Dr. Howard likes. I'll be glad to show you."

Elizabeth put the package down quickly. "I don't think the doctor is too keen on pig's feet." She eyed another odd-looking meat and pointed to it. "What is that?"

"Beef tongue," Rebecca said matter-of-factly.

"People really eat a tongue?"

"All the time," Rebecca said.

Elizabeth shook her head and kept looking. The steaks looked good, but she couldn't think of any way special to cook them. Finally she decided to try a recipe for chicken divan that was pretty simple, so she put two packages of chicken breasts in the cart.

"You gonna fry 'em?" Rebecca asked.

"No, I'm going to make chicken divan."

Rebecca arched her eyebrows but didn't say anything. Elizabeth found the rest of the items on her list, including fresh broccoli and green beans, with Rebecca's help. It occurred to Elizabeth when they were checking out that Rebecca was probably right. She could find what she was looking for in the Piggly Wiggly with her eyes closed.

CHAPTER 15

Elizabeth and Hamilton started out for Frenchie's place shortly after nine. It was a cloudless July morning and the coolness of the night had long burned off.

"It's going to be a hot one," Hamilton commented as they passed the courthouse square.

"I think you're right," Elizabeth said, thankful for the air conditioning in Hamilton's Pontiac.

"April to June is almost perfect here. July to September, this county can be an inferno."

"How do the people stand it?"

"Those of us that can go to Pawleys Island. The rest are used to it and they just sweat it out."

They had left town and passed tobacco fields full of people in straw hats cropping the long green leaves by hand. "Why are there so many people in the fields?" she asked.

"Tobacco is a very labor intensive crop. A lot of times entire families, down to the small children, lend a hand."

"Is that what the Fulton family does?"

"Yeah."

"Can they make a living growing tobacco?"

"They do okay. They'll never get rich, but they can all eat."

Elizabeth recognized the highway as the road she and Jim had taken the night they drove to the beach. "This is the River Road, isn't it?"

"Yes. How did you know that?"

"Jim Howard took me to the beach one night for dinner, and we came this way."

"Oh, I see," he said, not taking his eyes off the road.

"Have you been talking to Ida Pearl too?" she asked.

Hamilton chuckled. "No, not me. I was glad to see her in the office yesterday, though."

"Did you hear what she was spreading around town?"

"I did, but it went in one ear and out the other. She called after that and said that Jim Howard had blessed her out. She was very embarrassed."

"Well, I'm glad you gave me the benefit of the doubt. That woman is something."

"She's really okay. Don't be too hard on her. Those two just love to have something to talk about."

"I guess we're kinda even when you consider my temper tantrum when we first met. Robert, tell me what you know about Jim Howard."

"He and his mother had it real tough when he was growing up."

"He told me about his dad deserting them."

"Yeah, everybody felt real sorry for them. Mona Howard had to work two jobs just to make ends meet. Jim must have started bagging groceries when he was twelve."

"It was just the two of them?"

"Yes," Hamilton answered, stealing a glance at Elizabeth.

"Why do you suppose he came back to Weenee, Robert? Please don't take any offense at this, but this town isn't exactly the hub of Western civilization."

Hamilton grinned. "You're right, and no, I'm not offended. I think he did it for several reasons. One, he wanted to take care of his mother, which he has done. He built her a four-bedroom home in the nicest subdivision in town, and other than doing a little bookwork for Jim, she has taken an early retirement."

"That's very commendable," Elizabeth replied. "What were the other reasons?"

"He said he wanted to give back to this community, and he has really done so in a big way. Even with Medicare and Medicaid, a lot of people around here fall through the cracks and have no way of paying for medical treatment. Jim Howard treats everybody who walks into his clinic, regardless of whether they can pay or not."

"I'm relieved to hear that."

"Why?" Hamilton asked.

"There's something about him I can't put my finger on. It seems he's always checking on me."

"He's probably already gotten attached to you, Elizabeth. You're a beautiful woman."

"Thanks for the compliment, but he seems to be overdoing it."

"It's probably some of those lingering childhood insecurities, don't you think?"

Elizabeth smiled at Hamilton. "Not only do you have a keen legal mind, you're also pretty good at psychoanalysis. It does appear, though, that most people Jim treats can afford to pay and pay well."

"What do you mean by that?"

Elizabeth told Hamilton about her tour of Jim's beach house under construction.

Hamilton whistled softly. "The lots alone on the front beach sell for at least $150,000. I have a client who owns over 2,000 acres with no mortgages, and he was looking at one his wife was about to die for. Finally, he told his wife he couldn't afford it."

Hamilton slowed down and made a sharp right turn onto a dirt road. As they passed more fields of beans, corn, and tobacco, the car kicked up clouds of brown dust that could be seen for miles. After driving for a while down this road, Hamilton made a left. The road narrowed to a grassy lane with two ruts just wider than the car's wheels. The trees on each side were mostly hardwoods growing close together like infantrymen closing ranks to fend off an enemy counterattack. Underneath the canopy, scrub palmettos and vines grew in every direction.

"I'm glad you insisted on coming," Elizabeth said. "I never would have found this place."

"We're almost there," Hamilton said, slowing down to ease across a small pond in the middle of the road. The large car almost stopped in the mud hole and then lurched forward as Hamilton gave it more gas.

"And I'm glad you're driving."

"Nothing to it," Hamilton said as they came into a large clearing. "There it is." He pointed to a small house.

"It's not much to look at," Elizabeth said when she saw what was little more than a shack. The wood-frame structure was covered in a tan tarpaper manufactured to resemble brick. The material had torn away in a number of places, exposing gray, weathered German siding underneath. The tin roof had turned a rusty brown from its decades of exposure to the sun and the rain.

They got out, and Hamilton headed for the front steps. They were rickety, and Elizabeth waited until Hamilton was safely on the porch before she tried them. Hamilton pressed on the batten door, and it opened with a creak. What served as the living room was in complete disarray. Newspapers and bags of old, dirty clothing were thrown all over the room. The kitchen and bedroom were no better, as their contents had been tossed about in every direction. Each room contained dozens of old umbrellas in various colors and states of disrepair.

"Do you think law enforcement is responsible for all of this?" Elizabeth asked.

"No, probably not. Some of it maybe. Everyone knew the old man didn't have any money. Some people around here will take anything that's not nailed down, though."

When they walked outside again they saw that the Frenchman's garden had fared no better. It had been picked clean of vegetables.

"How far is the river from here?" Elizabeth asked, looking around.

"Not far. Come on, I'll show you."

Elizabeth followed Hamilton across a grassy field 'til the river came into view. As they approached the edge, Elizabeth could see they were on a bluff, the water about thirty feet below, lapping against the bank. The far bank was about a hundred yards away.

"It's a beautiful river," she said. "Is this where they found the head?"

"No, it was downriver, past that bend," Hamilton said, pointing to his left. "They found it in about thirty feet of water."

"No other body parts have turned up?"

"Nothing. Not a trace."

"How far is Willie Fulton's place from here?"

Hamilton turned and looked downriver again. "You see that smoke over there? That's his place."

"Why would someone have a fire in this heat?"

"Probably burning trash. Have you seen enough?"

"Yes, I suppose so. There wasn't much to see, was there?"

"No, not really. But you know, I lost a case many years ago because I didn't go out and take a look at where it happened. It was a simple little wreck case. I never made that mistake again. The Chinese were right about the value of a picture, weren't they?"

"Yes, they were," she replied. As they turned around to walk back to the car, Elizabeth thought that Robert Hamilton was probably a much better trial lawyer than he led her to believe. They had taken several steps when they heard a loud roar coming from the river. They turned to see a Boston whaler with a center console glide by on the smooth water. Just above the waterline on the side of the boat were the letters *CCSD*. The driver was wearing a brown uniform and he waved at them as he passed by.

"Who's that?" Elizabeth asked.

"One of Black Jack's deputies."

"What's he doing in that boat?"

"He's on patrol. What you see there is one of many new programs the sheriff introduced to Craven County after his election. He says his deputies can respond to calls around the river much quicker by boat than they can by car."

"Well, if the rest of the roads around the river are half as bad as the one we came in on, then I think that's an excellent idea."

"And they help the game wardens keep an eye out for poachers and night hunters."

"Why would people hunt at night? How could you see anything?"

"People hunt deer with a bright light. The deer freeze when they look at the lights, and they're sitting ducks."

"That's awful. Why would anyone do anything so cruel, so unsportsmanlike?"

"Mainly for the meat."

"You mean people eat deer meat?"

Hamilton looked at her as if she had just landed from Neptune. "Sure, they eat deer meat. I don't know three people in this county who don't eat venison. I'm going to have to cook you some before you go back to Boston, young lady."

"I'll take you up on the home-cooked meal anytime, but I'm not going to eat any part of Bambi," she said.

Hamilton smiled. They watched the boat disappear around a bend upriver. "Are you ready to go, now?" he asked.

"How can we get to Willie's house from here? Do we have to go back to the other road?"

"I'm not sure. I think I saw a path about halfway between the house and the river. Let's take a look."

Elizabeth followed Hamilton diagonally across the field, and at the edge of the woods, they found a well-worn path that led to another clearing and a house, almost the same size as Frenchie's. The Fultons' house had tarpaper on the roof and was sitting on a foundation of stumps. A massive, twisted chinaberry tree seemed to be the only living thing in the clearing, until a mangy, brown, mongrel dog scurried out from under the house. The animal bared his teeth as he snarled, and they froze in their tracks. It stopped and stared, before suddenly charging them at full speed. Both Hamilton and Elizabeth made a run for the path. They heard a flop and turned around to see that the dog was attached to a long chain and had simply run out of freedom. They stopped, looked at each other, and burst out laughing.

"That was close," Elizabeth said, the short dash already causing beads of sweat to form on her forehead.

"He looks like he could tear your leg off if he got a hold of you," Hamilton remarked as he tried to catch his breath.

"You move pretty well, Robert, for your age."

"Isn't it amazing what fright can do to a person?" he asked, pulling a handkerchief out of his back pocket and patting his face. "I don't guess anyone is home except our friend here. They must be in a tobacco field somewhere. "Hello!" he shouted. "Anybody home?"

"I think you're right," Elizabeth said, staring at the house.

"What are you looking at, Elizabeth?"

She continued to look at the house before she answered. "Why would anybody paint over the door and windows like that and nowhere else? Particularly that awful-looking blue paint."

"Oh that," Hamilton said. "That particular shade of paint is known as haint blue."

"Haint blue? What are you talking about?"

"You see it from time to time here in the country. Some black families believe that shade of paint keeps out haints and other evil spirits."

"Robert, you're going to have to help me here. We don't have haints in Boston."

"Oh, yes, you do. You just know them by other names. They're ghosts," he said.

"You are kidding me," Elizabeth responded, barely above a whisper.

The dog had recovered from his fall and his lost dignity and was now back on his feet, snarling and testing the strength of his chain.

"Are you ready now?" Hamilton asked.

"Yeah, let's go, before Rover figures out how to stretch that chain."

Elizabeth went home for lunch and could hear Rebecca in the kitchen singing "Must Jesus Bear the Cross Alone?" as she fried something on the stove.

"What are you cooking, Rebecca?" Elizabeth asked as she walked over and stood near her, just out of range of the popping grease. "That looks like my chicken," Elizabeth said, leaning over to get a closer look.

"Some of it is," Rebecca replied, pulling up her apron to wipe her forehead.

"What do you mean, some of it?" Elizabeth could feel the blood rising in her cheeks.

"I got to thinking with you working so hard on Willie Fulton's case that you ain't really got no time to cook supper for the doctor, and when I unloaded that grocery bag and see what little bit of chicken you picked out, I walked back to the Piggly Wiggly and got you a whole chicken."

"But I was going to make chicken divan."

"All you had was white meat. You know what part of the chicken the doctor likes?"

"I assume the breast, Rebecca. Everybody likes chicken breasts."

"Can't never know for sure," Rebecca said, shaking her head.

Elizabeth eyed a pot at the back of the stove. "What's that?" she asked.

Rebecca reached over and pulled off the lid. "Your butterbeans."

Elizabeth leaned closer and saw a large piece of whitish meat with dark red strips running through it. "What on earth is that meat in there?" she asked, curling her lips in disgust.

"Fatback."

"Rebecca, what have you done to those beautiful beans?"

"Cooking them, that's all."

"In fatback?" Elizabeth raised her voice.

"That's how you suppose to cook 'em," Rebecca said meekly.

Elizabeth thought she noticed Rebecca's lips quiver, so she reached over and put her hand on the older woman's shoulder. "I'm sorry," she said softly. "I appreciate your helping me with supper tonight. I'm sure Jim will be a lot happier when he finds out you did the cooking."

Elizabeth was right. Jim Howard was delighted when he learned that Rebecca had cooked supper, and he asked Elizabeth to give her his compliments. Elizabeth rolled her eyes when he reached for a drumstick, and she told him the story of Rebecca's return to the Piggly Wiggly for more chicken. Jim ate two drumsticks and the back before he started in on the white meat. Rebecca also made a steamer of rice and brown gravy, which was wonderful, and Elizabeth had to admit that the butterbeans cooked in the fatback were not bad either. Rebecca topped the meal off with cheese biscuits, and when they had finished eating, Jim had Elizabeth wrap a half-dozen of them in aluminum foil for his breakfast the next morning.

Elizabeth had located a bottle of Sterling Vineyards Chardonnay on a dusty shelf in Gamble's liquor store, and they took what was left into the library after they put the dishes in the sink. They both sat on the worn, tufted leather sofa, and Elizabeth leaned her head back and put her feet on the walnut blanket chest that served as a coffee table.

"Why do you suppose Rebecca didn't want me cooking supper for you?"

"Maybe because she thinks cooking is her job."

"Or maybe she didn't want me messing up her kitchen," Elizabeth said.

"It could be a territorial thing with her, I don't know. All I do know is I'm stuffed."

"Me too. Would you rather have some brandy? My grandfather has some in his liquor closet."

"No, this is fine," he said, raising his glass. "Tell me, how is the Fulton case coming?"

"I don't know."

"You don't know, or you don't want to say?"

"No, I really don't know. It looks as if it's going to boil down to a question of credibility. If the jury believes Fulton, then he will go home after the trial. If they don't, then he goes to prison for a very long time."

"Then he is going to take the stand."

"He'll have to. With the bloody ax and his fingerprints all over it, he's going to have to tell the jury that he didn't do it, and he's going to have to be very convincing when he does it. Otherwise, he's history."

"Can Fulton be convincing?"

"I don't know. That's what I'll work on."

"How can you work on credibility? I would think that a person either has it or he doesn't."

"That's true to a point, Jim, but a good trial lawyer really works with a client, prepares him for the unexpected. Makes him believable to the jury. Tries to make him say the right things to the jury."

"And all of this is ethical?"

"The English don't think it is, but we do. And it really is ethical, in my opinion. It's just helping your client put his best face on for the jury. You've seen people before, haven't you, who are telling the truth but aren't very believable?"

"Yes, I have," he answered. "When you think about it, our criminal justice system can be a little scary."

"You're damned right it is. It scares me all the time."

"I'm glad you're the lawyer and not me," he said with a grin.

"Now it's my turn to ask the questions."

"About what?"

"About you."

"What for?"

"I don't know a thing about you," she said, "and you know all about me."

"Not much to know, and it's all boring," he replied, shrugging as he took a sip of his wine.

"I do know you grew up here."

"All my life right here. Weenee High School, class of '67."

"Are your parents still living?"

"I think so."

"What do you mean, you think so?"

"We haven't seen or heard directly from my father since he left when I was fifteen."

"Not a word?"

"Nothing. Oh, every now and then my uncle Charlie, his brother, tells us something. He's supposed to be up in Winston-Salem working in the tobacco market."

"He never sent your mother any money?"

"Not a dime."

"Your mother never took him to court?"

"She tried to, but they never could get the papers served on him. He has some buddies in law enforcement, and we've always felt that they just trashed the papers."

"That's too bad. Do you have any brothers or sisters?"

"No, it's just Mama and me."

"Did she work?"

"No, we had a little printing press in the kitchen. Every time we needed money we just printed up another batch," he said with a detached look in his eyes. Finally he stated, "Yeah, she worked two jobs."

"That must have been tough on her," Elizabeth said.

"It was, I'm sure, looking back now, but she never complained. And she was never too tired to take me to church and Sunday school every Sunday morning."

"She must be a wonderful person."

"She is. Now, I carried my share of the load when I started bagging groceries in the eighth grade. In college I worked on power-line construction crews during the summer. The pay was a lot better, but the work almost killed me."

"Is she still working?"

"No, I retired her. I built her a home, and she's on my payroll now. She does a little bookwork for me every now and then to keep her busy, but that's it."

"You're certainly sweet to do that," Elizabeth said, patting him on the shoulder.

"It's the least I could do for her," he replied.

"Where did you go to college?"

"Sewanee. It's a little Episcopal school in Tennessee. Most people have never heard of it."

"Oh, I have. I had a friend in law school who had a brother who went there."

"What was his name?"

"Harrison Franklin."

"I didn't know any Franklins."

"How about medical school?"

"The Medical University in Charleston."

"Did you like medical school?"

"Are you kidding? All I did was study and work. It wasn't much fun."

"Oh, I bet you had those Charleston belles chasing you all over town."

"I didn't have the time to do much socializing," he said, a grin forming on his lips.

"Did you like Charleston?"

"Yes, I did very much. I would have loved to have set up a practice there."

"Why did you come back, then?"

"That's a good question. Number one, it's home, and Mama's here. But it's really more than that. There are a lot of very poor people here in Craven County who have never received proper medical care. I wanted to change that, if only in some small way."

"That's inspiring," Elizabeth said softly. "Have you ever regretted that decision?"

"Not yet," he said, sitting up and reaching for the wine bottle. There were a couple of ounces left, and he tried to pour an equal amount in both glasses. "To a very impressive cross examination," he said, raising his glass in a toast and then downing the remainder of his wine. "I only hope you do half that well in the courtroom."

"Thank you," Elizabeth replied, raising her glass in the air. "But that was not a cross examination. Blood really flies when I get going on cross."

"Well, it's been a long day, and I've got to do rounds in the morning," Jim said as he rose to his feet.

A thought came to Elizabeth, and she laughed out loud.

"What's so funny?"

"I think you're more worried about your reputation than you are about your sleep."

"What are you talking about?"

Elizabeth stood up and faced him, still grinning. "You're more worried about Ida Pearl and all those old ladies who like to spread gossip all over this little town."

"That's not true," he said, folding his arms across his chest. "I do have to be going. Your supper, even though you didn't cook it, was wonderful. And I've got to go by Gamble's to see if they have any more of that Chardonnay."

"I got the last two bottles."

"Maybe Fred will order us a case."

"See what you can do," she said. "I'm going to need all the fortification I can get for this trial."

"Are you going to be around this weekend?" he asked as they stopped at the front door.

"Where would I go?" she asked, holding her hands out from her sides. Before she realized it, Jim grabbed her hands and pulled her to him. He kissed her quickly but very firmly.

"I'll call. Let's do something."

Before she could answer, he was out the door. "Good night," she called out to him as he bounced down the steps. Studying the back of his head, she had the strangest feeling that this wasn't the first time she had kissed Jim Howard.

CHAPTER 16

A secretary in the solicitor's office called Thursday morning to change Elizabeth's meeting with Clarence Phillips to eleven o'clock Friday. The judge holding court had a meeting in Columbia, so court had been cancelled for the entire day. Phillips' office was in a wing constructed around the turn of the century behind the main courtroom, and it was obvious to Elizabeth that little, if any, money had been allocated in the county budget for its maintenance since it was built. The wooden stairs, whose treads had been worn down to the bare grain, creaked as she climbed to the third floor, where Phillips' office was located.

The secretary, a brunette in her thirties, was chatting on the phone and filing her nails when Elizabeth walked into Phillips' office. The woman could have been attractive if she hadn't had on so much makeup and gold costume jewelry. Elizabeth thought the Avon lady must make a killing in Weenee.

"May I help you?" the secretary asked.

"Yes, I'm Elizabeth Chase. I have an appointment with Mr. Phillips."

"I thought that's who you were—the lady lawyer. Clarence is on the phone. He'll be with you in a minute. If you want, you can have a seat over there," the woman said, pointing to a sofa against the far wall.

Elizabeth sat down and looked at the magazines on the coffee table. There was a *Progressive Farmer,* some type of outdoors magazine with the cover torn off, and a catalogue for hunting supplies.

The woman studied Elizabeth. "I'm afraid there's not too much to read over there. I've got a *Cosmopolitan* here in the desk somewhere," she said, opening a drawer.

"Oh, don't bother. I'm fine."

"You mind if I ask you something?"

"No, not at all."

"What's it like being a lawyer and being a woman at the same time?"

Elizabeth had to pause before she answered to keep from chuckling at the question. "I don't know," she said. "I really don't know how to answer that."

"I guess it's kinda a silly question."

"No, not really. I don't suppose there are many women lawyers here in South Carolina."

"They got 'em in Columbia and Charleston, I hear. But we've never had a woman criminal lawyer in this circuit before."

Elizabeth could hear Phillips talking and laughing behind the door to his office. "Old Clarence is in a good mood this morning," the woman said, tilting her head toward the other office. "He won a big murder case over in Lee County this week."

"He must be a good trial lawyer," Elizabeth said.

"Oh, he's one of the best."

"Do you like working for him?"

"Yeah, I guess so. It's just real quiet around here when we're not having court."

"Have you always worked in this office?"

"No, I used to fix hair until this job come open."

"Did you like that job better than this one?"

"There was a lot more people to talk to, you know what I mean. It was a lot easier to keep up with the gossip, only it was a lot harder on your feet."

"I guess so," Elizabeth said.

"But the benefits are so much better with this job. At the Cut and Curl you didn't have none."

Both women turned when Phillips jerked his door open. "Miss Chase, sorry to keep you waiting. I was on the phone," he said, bowing slightly at the waist. "I see you've met Wanda, my very competent secretary."

"Yes, I have. It was nice talking to you, Wanda," Elizabeth said as she stood up.

"Pleased to meet you, Elizabeth," Wanda replied, in a voice that struck Elizabeth as genuine.

"Come on in," Phillips said with a wave of his arm.

"Oh, I forgot my manners," Wanda declared. "Can I get you some coffee?"

"No, I'm fine," Elizabeth said, walking toward Phillips' office. "It was nice meeting you, too, Wanda." Elizabeth walked into the office ahead of Phillips and took a seat in one of the two county-issued metal chairs opposite his desk. The windowless wall behind the desk was covered with framed certificates and citations, which ranged in degree of importance from his two-year, Sunday-school, perfect-attendance award to a citation from the governor. Elizabeth also saw that Phillips had been honored as the Craven County Jaycee of the Year and had been president of the Weenee Rotary Club. "Very impressive," she said, pointing to the wall.

"Not really," Phillips replied modestly. "I just like to give back to the community." After he slid into his desk chair, he looked at Elizabeth. "Since the Fulton case is the only one you have on my docket, may I assume that is what you're here for?"

"Yes, you may, Mr. Phillips," Elizabeth said.

"Oh, call me Clarence, please. No one calls me Mr. Phillips, not even the defendants."

"Okay, Clarence. I'll get right to the point. I haven't even discussed a possible plea with my client yet. Before I did that, I wanted to see if you were going to put anything on the table."

"To begin with, I believe you're aware that we have a strong case against your client."

"I will concede that you have some evidence that could possibly be considered incriminating."

"We have the ax, of course, with Frenchie's blood on it and Fulton's fingerprints. We know that one of Fulton's hogs tore up Frenchie's garden a while back."

"Did the hog confess?"

"Very funny," Phillips said, but he didn't smile. "There were hog prints leading from Fulton's house to Frenchie's house."

"Oh, come on, Clarence. I've been out there. There are animal prints all over the place."

"That's just another piece of the puzzle," he said defensively. "I didn't say that was one of our strongest points."

"Okay, go on, please."

"We have your client's reputation for violence in the community."

"Are you kidding? He has one disorderly conduct conviction and a public drunkenness on his record. That's all. I've already checked."

"Let me point out one little rule of evidence that we have here in South Carolina that you are probably unaware of. If a person has a reputation for violence within his, quote, community, then that reputation is admissible. Not specific prior acts of violence, mind you, just his reputation for being a violent person. In this case, we already have at least one person within the community who will testify that Fulton has a reputation for violence." Phillips concluded his evidence lecture, leaned back in his chair, folded his arms across his chest, and puffed out his lips smugly.

"It sounds as if you are ready to go to trial," Elizabeth said.

"I could try this case after lunch."

"Then you don't want to discuss any type of plea bargain?"

"Oh, I didn't say that," he said, leaning forward in his chair and resting his arms on his blotter.

"What's the best you can do, then?" she asked, trying not to sound too eager. She knew that if Phillips thought she was anxious to let Fulton plead, he wouldn't come off the maximum sentence very much.

"I'll let him plead straight up to manslaughter. His maximum exposure is only thirty years."

"Only thirty years," Elizabeth shot back. "That's a long time for a man Fulton's age."

"Lawson will never give him that if he pleads. Remember, if the jury brings back a guilty verdict on murder, Lawson's got to give him life. That carries a minimum service of twenty years before he becomes eligible for parole. He'll be an old man then."

"What do you think Lawson would give him in a straight-up plea?"

Phillips shrugged. "Probably twenty years. Is Fulton going to plead?"

"I don't know. I just wanted to find out what his options are."

"You'd better plead your man."

"Why do you say that?"

"With the evidence we have, a jury would stay out long enough to smoke a cigarette, go to the bathroom, and then bring back a guilty verdict. About ten minutes, I estimate."

"You're pretty confident, aren't you?"

"Been at it a long time. I know these people around here a lot better than you do," he said, pulling a cigarette out of a pack on his desk. He held up the pack and Elizabeth shook her head. "This ain't the North, where you got a bunch of bleeding hearts and flaming liberals. People around here don't take too kindly to murder."

"So you think Mr. Fulton is guilty?"

"Sure I do, and we've got the evidence to prove it. Who do you think chopped his head off like that, the tooth fairy?"

Elizabeth glared at Phillips. "I don't know who killed Mr. Gilbert. That's why we draw juries."

"You and Mr. Fulton do what you want to—I don't care. It's no big deal to me. If I don't have to try this case, I'll be trying some other one." Phillips leaned back in his chair and put his feet up on the desk. "Let me ask you something, if you don't mind."

"Sure, go ahead."

"Have you ever tried a murder case before?"

"Yes, I have. Why?"

"Well, I don't know how it is up North in New York or wherever you're from."

"Boston," she said.

"Right. I'm a real gentlemen to everybody outside the courtroom, coloreds and whites, men and women. But in the courtroom, when I'm trying a case, I don't take any prisoners, so to speak. I can't give you any special treatment, so I don't want you to get your feelings hurt. And I can tell you another thing while we're on the subject," he said, pointing his finger at Elizabeth. "Don't expect Judge Lawson to take a recess if you get upset or start crying."

Elizabeth folded her hands together to keep them from shaking. "Thanks for the trial pointers, Clarence. I'll certainly keep them in mind if we have to try this case. Thank you for your time," Elizabeth said, rising from her chair. "I will, of course, pass along your offer to my client. Good day."

Phillips lit his cigarette but didn't get up out of his chair. "Let's get together one night for a beer," he said as he took a long drag. He removed the cigarette from his mouth, and Elizabeth could see the sunlight reflecting off his gold wedding band.

Hamilton was waiting in his office when Elizabeth returned. She told him about the plea negotiation, and his expression didn't change. "That's exactly what I expected," he said.

"Then my visit was for nothing?"

"No, not at all. It was important for you to go. So he could size you up."

"Why do you say that?"

"I hear Clarence has been talking around town. He says if he lets a woman beat him in court, he won't run for reelection."

"That's pretty big talk."

Hamilton grinned. "Yeah, I know. He always was a big talker, ever since he was a boy."

"You wouldn't believe how he talked to me. Like I was just out of law school. He even asked me if I had ever tried a murder case before."

"That's Clarence, all right."

"Where do we go from here?"

"Let's sit down and talk to Willie again. Put a little pressure on him."

CHAPTER 17

As usual, Rebecca was singing in the kitchen when Elizabeth got home just after five.

"What is all this food doing here?" Elizabeth asked, walking into the kitchen.

Rebecca was sitting at the table, polishing silver. "Homecoming Sunday at the church."

"Oh, I see."

"We fed over two hundred people last year. They's looking for more than that this year."

"I'm disappointed that it's all going to your church," Elizabeth said, looking at the pies and casserole dishes lined up on the table.

"Oh, I'm leaving you plenty for the weekend. Even left enough for the doctor, if he wants to come over," Rebecca said, cutting her eyes at Elizabeth.

"He's supposed to be in town, so I may see him."

"Did he like the supper I left for him?"

"He ate like he hadn't eaten in a week. And you know what?"

"What?"

"He likes dark meat, just as I told you."

Rebecca started to say something and realized Elizabeth was teasing her.

"I'm not going to ask you how you knew," Elizabeth said.

"I don't tell my secrets no way," Rebecca replied, continuing with her work.

Elizabeth needed a drink. She thought about waiting until Rebecca, with her reproachful looks, had gone home, but she couldn't wait any longer. The July humidity had sapped every bit of energy out of her, and she had to have something to recharge herself.

Rebecca watched in silence as Elizabeth poured her scotch.

"Fix something cold to drink and come sit out on the back porch with me, Rebecca. It should be cool back there now."

"I need to be getting home," Rebecca said.

"Come on—just for a few minutes," she persisted. "You don't have anywhere to go tonight, do you?"

"I got prayer meeting at eight."

"You spend half your life going to church, Rebecca."

"Half yo' life is a lot better than not going a-tall."

"I was just teasing you. Come on," Elizabeth said, motioning with her glass. She walked down the hall, pushed the screen door open, and stepped out onto the screened porch. She settled down on the wobbly wicker settee and leaned back as it creaked loudly. She was right. It was much cooler back here on the east side of the house, away from the afternoon sun. Since her return, she hadn't been on this porch, and she couldn't remember the last time she had sat down back here. She surveyed the magnolias and azaleas that framed the yard. And she spotted the camellias her grandfather had loved so dearly. Their flowers were gone now for the year, but she could see their waxy green leaves giving off a shine that made them look as though they had been individually polished. Elizabeth remembered how at Christmas her grandmother would arrange the blooms on silver platters in a bed of Spanish moss, and she used to think they were about the most beautiful things she had ever seen.

"Miss Elizabeth, you out there?"

"Out here, Rebecca." Elizabeth heard the screech of the screen door opening. Rebecca was carrying a tall glass of iced tea. "Come sit down by me," Elizabeth said, patting the faded cushion next to her.

Rebecca sat down gingerly, as if she didn't think the settee would accommodate the weight of both of them. "Don't know when it was the last time I sat down back here. It was probably when I was watching you and Princess."

"That's the same tree, isn't it?" Elizabeth asked, pointing to a massive live oak in a corner of the yard.

"Yeah, that's the one," Rebecca said with a chuckle. "Your granddaddy laughed about that day for years. Every time Princess would come 'round here he would pick on her 'bout climbing so high you and her couldn't get out the tree."

"I thought he just teased me about that."

"No, your granddaddy loved to tease eve'ybody. There wasn't hardly a day that went by that he didn't pick on me 'bout something." She paused, deep in thought. "Lord, I miss that man," she said finally with a sigh.

"I do too, Rebecca. Sometimes I can feel him down at that office."

"That's funny you say that. I can feel he spirit sometime here in this house, too."

"So you believe there are spirits among us?" Elizabeth asked.

"'Course I do."

"Evil spirits, too?"

"Yeah, they's probably more evil spirits than any other kind 'round here."

"Do you believe in haints, Rebecca?"

Rebecca turned her head quickly and stared at Elizabeth. "What you know 'bout haints?" she asked.

"We went out to the Fultons' house earlier this week. They had blue paint over the windows and doorway. Mr. Hamilton said people do that to ward off haints."

"That's what it's suppose' to do."

"And a haint is an evil spirit?"

Rebecca nodded but remained silent.

Elizabeth got the distinct impression that she didn't want to discuss it any further. "Didn't you tell me earlier that Princess comes down during the summer?" she asked, changing the subject. "I'd love to see her."

"She came down right before the Fourth, while you were back up the road."

"Oh, I'm sorry I missed her. How is she doing?"

"Fine. Those children are growing up so fast, though."

"When is her baby due?"

"October. She asked me a million questions about you. She was sorry she missed you, too."

"Have you ever thought about moving up to Rochester with her?"

"Why I wanna go and do that?"

"Don't you think you could have a better life up there? Where people would treat you with more dignity?"

"Everybody treat me okay here. 'Sides, my people and my

church are here. Here is my home. I'm too old to be picking up and moving anywhere."

The women finished their drinks as Rebecca talked about her eleven grandchildren. Elizabeth just listened as she watched the shadows lengthen over the big yard until they melted into the darkness.

Jim called at eight fifteen, and Elizabeth asked him to come over to eat. She told him what Rebecca had left in the refrigerator and on the back of the stove. He didn't need much convincing, and they were eating at the kitchen table by eight thirty. Jim had made good on his promise to stop by the liquor store, and he brought four bottles of Chardonnay for the refrigerator, which went well with the pork chops. They talked mostly about Boston. Jim was genuinely shocked when Elizabeth told him she was a diehard Red Sox fan, but he wasn't convinced until she named the starting lineup of their 1967 American League championship team. After pecan pie, they moved to the library, this time with coffee cups in hand, trying to stay awake.

"I don't know why I'm so tired," Elizabeth said, putting her feet up on the coffee table.

"It's the heat. It does it to everybody, not just you Yankees."

"That and I had a very busy day."

"The Fulton case?"

"Mostly."

"What's going on now? Getting ready for the trial?"

"That and a meeting today with Clarence Phillips."

"What was that all about?"

"I'd better not say, Jim."

"You can trust me, Elizabeth."

"Why are you so interested in this trial?"

"I guess because everybody is talking about it."

"I know, but it's just something I can't discuss. Maybe later. The paper said there was an old Peter Sellers movie coming on at ten."

Jim got up and found the channel, went to the kitchen, dumped out his coffee, and poured himself another glass of wine.

"I'm not much better off than you," he said. "My day started at 5:15 at the hospital. Heart attack."

The movie came on, and Elizabeth could hardly keep her eyes open. "Did you slip me more of that moonshine?"

Jim laughed. "No, I didn't. Lean your head on my shoulder and make yourself comfortable."

"Okay," she said, sliding over, and she was asleep within seconds. When Elizabeth woke up, she didn't know how long she had been sleeping, and it took her a moment to realize where she was. Jim was up and she could hear him talking on the phone in the hall. She looked at the steeple clock on the mantel and saw that it was almost twelve thirty. Elizabeth tried to identify who Jim was talking to, but he was mainly listening to the caller. In a couple of minutes he hung up, and she could hear his footsteps in the hall.

"That was Robert Hamilton," he said, spotting Elizabeth sitting up on the sofa. "I'm afraid he had some bad news."

"What is it?" Elizabeth asked.

"Rebecca's son is dead."

"What happened?"

"He was murdered. Up in Durham. They found him in a ditch sometime tonight. Robert thought you would want to know."

"Oh, my God," Elizabeth said, covering her face with her hands. "This will kill poor Rebecca."

"Can I get you anything?" Jim asked, sitting down beside her.

"No, thanks," she said, shaking her head. "I slept for over two hours, didn't I?"

"Yeah, and you were sleeping hard. I lasted until about eleven and then my lights went out, too."

"Should I try to call her?"

"Not now. It's late."

"That poor woman. Do you know any of the details?"

Jim shook his head. "I really need to be going, if you're okay."

"I'm okay," she said, standing up. Elizabeth was a little wobbly on her feet as they walked to the front door.

Jim stopped there and asked, "Are you sure you're all right?"

Elizabeth nodded.

"I'll call you later," he said, and he was gone.

Elizabeth waited until nine before she called Robert. A woman with a sweet voice, who had to be Mrs. Hamilton, answered. It took him a while to pick up the receiver.

"I hope I'm not calling too early on a Saturday, Robert. I got your message last night. I had fallen asleep on the sofa watching TV with Jim."

"No, no," he assured her with a laugh. "I've been in my garden since six thirty. In this heat you have to get your work done early."

"Have you heard any more about Rebecca's son?" Elizabeth realized she didn't know his name.

"No, not really, other than it's just another senseless murder."

"How is Rebecca?"

"I've only talked with her sister. She was the one who called last night. As you would expect, she was taking it pretty hard."

"Poor thing."

"Do you know when the funeral will be?"

"It'll be a few days, with the family scattered all around. They take a few more days than we do to bury their dead."

"Should I try to see her today?"

"I'd probably wait a day or two. Let me see what I can find out. Will you be around all weekend?"

"Yes, I'll be right here."

Jim called later that morning to check on her and tell her that he would be at the beach working on his house for the rest of the weekend. She didn't hear anything from Robert until early Sunday afternoon. He had finally spoken with Rebecca, and they would be receiving visitors at the funeral home that night. Elizabeth said she wanted to go, and Hamilton told her he'd pick her up at seven.

The parking lot of the Nesmith-Pressley Funeral Home was filled with cars and pickups, many of them so old it was difficult to distinguish their make. The turn-of-the-century clapboard structure was across the tracks, on the edge of town. In an awkward attempt at modernization, its owners had brick-veneered the old building, and it looked like an aging fat man in a suit that fit too tightly.

Hamilton guided Elizabeth up the steps and across the cement porch crowded with men in dark suits quietly smoking cigarettes. They all nodded or bowed slightly in the direction of Hamilton, and several spoke.

"Good evening," Hamilton said as he opened the wide old wooden door. They walked in, and Elizabeth spotted Rebecca in a far corner of the large room, surrounded by a number of people. Looking around, Elizabeth realized she and Hamilton were the only white people there. The only furniture in the room was one sofa and about two dozen straight-back chairs, all pushed against the faded green walls. Over the mantel was a large, velvet picture of the Last Supper. Several of the mourners came over to speak to Hamilton, and he introduced Elizabeth. They all knew who she was and greeted her warmly. Hamilton took Elizabeth's arm, and they joined a loosely organized line that slowly moved in the direction of Rebecca. They reached her, and when she saw Elizabeth, she threw her arms around Elizabeth's neck.

"Thank you for coming, Miss Elizabeth," Rebecca said, barely above a whisper, as she held on to Elizabeth's neck. After a few seconds, the older woman pulled away.

"Oh Rebecca, I'm so sorry. What can I do?"

"Just pray for us, child, that's all. Pray hard for us. You can do that, can't you?"

"Yes, I can and I will, I promise."

Rebecca grabbed Elizabeth's hands and squeezed them tightly. "I'm not going to be at work until after the funeral, if that's okay?"

Elizabeth was mortified that Rebecca felt that she had to ask off from work. "Sure, you take whatever time you need, Rebecca."

"When is the funeral, Rebecca?" Hamilton asked.

"Oh, I didn't mean to ignore you, Mr. Robert," Rebecca said, taking his hand in both of hers. "It's Wednesday. So many people got so far to come. I 'preciate you coming, you know that."

"Yes, I do, Rebecca. If there is anything I can do, will you let me know?"

"Yes sir, I will. Princess said to tell you she'd be here Tuesday, and she can't wait to see you," Rebecca said, turning back to face Elizabeth.

"And I can't wait to see her, either. Is she bringing the children?"

"She bringing everybody."

"Good. Are you okay, Rebecca? I know this is terribly hard on you."

"It's the most terrible thing I ever been through in my whole life, but it's the Lord's will, and that's what I got to keep telling myself," she said as tears welled up in her eyes.

"I know these other people are anxious to speak to you," Elizabeth commented, looking over her shoulder at the line behind her. "I'll talk with you before the funeral, I know."

"You don't want to go and look at my baby? My Alphonsa?" she asked, tilting her head toward the back of the building. "They got him fixed up so good. He looks so peaceful."

"Not right now—maybe later. I'm sure he does look good." Rebecca grabbed her around the neck again and whispered in her ear, "Rebecca will always love you. Don't ever forget that."

"I won't, I promise. Call me, Rebecca, if you need me."

"Are you going to the funeral?" Hamilton asked her as they were pulling out of the parking lot.

"I guess so," Elizabeth said, looking at Hamilton. "Are you?"

"I hadn't thought about it. Would you like to ride with me?"

"You don't have to go just because of me."

"I know. Rebecca is an old friend of mine, too."

"Yes, I would like a ride, please. I don't want to go by myself. Do you know if Inez has set up an appointment with Willie Fulton yet?" Elizabeth asked, changing the subject.

"He's supposed to be in at eleven in the morning. Inez told them to find a babysitter."

"I'm glad you thought to tell her that, so we can all concentrate."

Hamilton chuckled. "Hell, I didn't have to. Inez told them on her own. She said those children were driving her nuts."

Elizabeth shook her head. "I've got a lot of work to do in the next two weeks."

"I know. Just tell me what you need for me to do. I may be old and worn out, but I'll help you any way I can."

"Can you meet with us?"

"Sure. Any chance he'll plead?"

"I don't have any idea."

As Willie Fulton sat down opposite Elizabeth at the conference table in the library Monday morning, she thought that he either had no concept of the seriousness of the charges against him or he was the coolest man under pressure she had ever seen.

"Good morning, Willie."

"Morning," he answered with a sheepish grin.

Elizabeth was disappointed to learn that Pearlie Mae was not with Willie. She had had to stay with the children because they couldn't locate a babysitter. Elizabeth always liked to involve the spouse in a case like this, particularly when it involved a decision such as a possible plea. Hamilton was seated at the end of the table, with a mug of coffee in front of him.

"We were out at your house last week, but we didn't see you, just your dog," Elizabeth said.

"Sometimes that dog ain't too polite when company comes to calling. We musta been in the field," he added.

"I think you probably were. We were mainly looking at the layout of your place and Mr. Gilbert's."

"Oh, okay."

"It was helpful to us in preparing your case." Willie nodded. "Did you go over to Mr. Gilbert's very often?" Elizabeth asked.

"No ma'am. Like I told you before, me and him didn't get along too good."

"Did you see him at all on the day he was murdered?"

"Not that I can recollect."

"Have you thought of anyone who could verify your whereabouts the day he was killed?"

"Only Pearlie Mae and them children."

Elizabeth thought about what even a mediocre trial lawyer could do with the Fulton family on cross-examination, and it made her shudder. She looked at Hamilton, and the expression in his eyes told her he was thinking the same thing.

The two lawyers spent the next hour going over and over the events of the day of the murder and the circumstances behind their past arguments. To Elizabeth, it sounded as if the two men were neighbors who couldn't get along as opposed to them being involved in a running feud, but she was sure of one thing—Phillips would milk that situation for all it was worth. Another thing that bothered Elizabeth was when she asked a question, Fulton would stop and think, even if the question was of a routine nature. Finally, she put her pen down on her legal pad.

"Willie, there is something else we need to talk about this morning."

"Yes ma'am," he said, as if he knew what was coming.

"I met with the solicitor, Mr. Phillips, on Friday. He made an offer to us, to you," she said, gesturing toward Fulton with her hand.

"What kinda offer?" he asked.

"He said he would reduce the charges to manslaughter if you would plead guilty."

"Plead guilty? To what?" he asked, gripping the armrests of his chair tightly.

"To the killing of Ovid Gilbert."

"I thought you was here to help me, and here you are trying to get me to plead guilty to something I didn't do," he said, raising his voice.

"Now, wait a minute, Willie," she replied, holding up her hands. "I'm not trying to get you to plead guilty to anything. When the solicitor makes an offer, say to reduce the charges, I'm bound by our code of professional responsibility to relay it to you. To tell you what he is offering. Do you understand what I'm saying?"

"Yes ma'am, I think I do."

"And I have to make sure you understand. What he is offering to do is drop the maximum amount of time that you are facing down to thirty years," she said. "Okay?"

"I'm not sure I follow you."

"Let me put it this way. If we go to trial, and the jury convicts you of murder, the judge has to sentence you, by law, to life imprisonment, and you cannot be eligible for parole until you serve at least twenty years. Are you with me?"

"I'm with you so far," Willie said.

"And if you plead guilty to manslaughter, the most time the judge can give you is thirty years, and you would have to serve ten years before becoming eligible for parole. Assuming you got thirty years."

"That's still a lot of time," Willie said, shaking his head.

"But that doesn't mean Judge Lawson will give you the full thirty years if you plead. From what lawyers tell me about Judge Lawson, you are probably looking at twenty years, which means you would have to serve less than seven years before you would be eligible for parole."

Fulton stared at Elizabeth for a few seconds and then looked at Hamilton. "I ain't pleading guilty to nothing," he said finally, shaking his head several times as he spoke.

"Well, that settles the issue of any plea negotiations, doesn't it?" Elizabeth stated, looking at Hamilton. Hamilton shrugged, and Elizabeth knew it was time to move on.

Hamilton and Elizabeth spent another hour with Fulton, going over the jury-selection process, the trial proceedings, and his constitutional right against self-incrimination. He appeared to be listening intently, asking questions from time to time.

"Do you think you understand the process, Willie?" Elizabeth asked after she finished her briefing. "How it works, I mean."

"I think so," he said. "I been in court a few times watching. I was on jury duty one time, but they never picked me on one."

"Do you understand that you don't have to testify, if you don't want to? You cannot be made to testify under our Constitution."

"I got to testify."

"No, you don't. That's what I'm trying to make you understand."

"Yes, I do."

"No, you don't. I thought I was making it clear to you," Elizabeth said, sighing loudly.

"Wait a minute. Time out," Hamilton declared, leaning forward on his elbows with a trace of a grin forming on his lips. "I think Willie understands. What he's saying, I think, is that he feels it would be in his best interest to testify, to tell the jury that he didn't kill Frenchie. Isn't that what you're saying, Willie?"

"Yes sir, Mr. Hamilton, that's 'zactly what I'm saying."

"And you realize what Ms. Chase is saying, that if you didn't feel like it would help your case to testify, you wouldn't have to."

"There you go. That's my understanding 'zactly, Mr. Hamilton," Willie said.

Hamilton nodded at Elizabeth. "Is there anything else we need to go over, Elizabeth? It's well past lunchtime."

"No, I think that covers it for now," she said, pushing her chair back from the conference table.

CHAPTER 18

At quarter to three on Wednesday afternoon, Hamilton and Elizabeth left the office to attend the funeral service of Alphonsa Mayrant. There were still few details of his murder, and no one had been charged by the police in North Carolina, which Elizabeth was sure added to Rebecca's misery.

New Jerusalem African Methodist Episcopal Church was only four blocks away, so it took the two of them only a couple of minutes to drive there. The churchyard was jammed with cars, and a hearse was parked directly adjacent to the front doors of the church. Black people were standing everywhere, and again Elizabeth realized they would probably be the only white people in attendance.

After Hamilton eased his Pontiac into a parking space, they walked silently to the huge, plain wooden church. The building was located on Lee Street and was built on a high lot on the banks of the Weenee River, near the river bridge. On the other side of the river, the Weenee swamp stretched for several miles, and except for the highway bed that bisected it, it was an impenetrable morass. It made the early settlement easily defensible from the Weenee Indians and later from invading Yankees during the war.

The double front doors were flanked by twin turrets with hipped roofs that gave the old structure a medieval look with a Southern twist. The building wore a new coat of white paint proudly, as it glistened in the bright July sun. Elizabeth saw all of the open windows and groaned, realizing the inside would feel more like an oven than a church. They climbed the steps and were greeted by an elderly man on the porch near the front door who broke into a warm smile when he recognized Hamilton.

"Right this way, Mr. Hamilton. We have a place reserved for you and Miss Chase," the man said, bowing his head slightly when he said Elizabeth's name. Hamilton and Elizabeth exchanged bewildered glances and followed the man down the long aisle. It didn't appear to either of them that there was a single empty seat in the packed sanctuary.

The man pointed to two seats on the second row, where a sign on the end of the pew indicated that it was reserved for family members. He handed them a program as they entered the pew, and Elizabeth followed Hamilton to the far end before they sat down.

As soon as Elizabeth was in her seat, she looked down at the program and saw a photograph of Alphonsa Mayrant on the cover. He had Rebecca's eyes and that same forlorn look on his face. Opening the program, she saw a long list of speakers, preachers, and hymns to be sung. Hamilton watched her and leaned over to whisper in her ear.

"You'd better thank me that your name is not on that program," he said.

"What are you talking about?"

"Miss Nesmith, the funeral director, called and wanted to know if you would speak at the service."

"Are you kidding?"

"No, not at all. It's not unusual. I told her I didn't think you would want to because you were too upset. I hope you don't mind. I didn't think you would want to."

"No, the thought terrifies me," Elizabeth said, looking back over her shoulder at the crowd behind her.

"I thought you were a trial lawyer," Hamilton whispered in a teasing tone. "Crowds like this shouldn't bother you."

"The crowds in a courtroom are different. I have a thing about funerals, though."

Hamilton winked at her and turned back in his seat to face the front of the church. As Elizabeth waited, she stole another glance over her shoulder at the congregation behind her. The old sanctuary was beautiful in its simplicity. The newly freed slaves who built the church used the most readily available materials, longleaf pine and cypress dragged from the deep swamps by government-issued mules. Like the outside, the interior pine walls had been coated with a glossy white paint, almost concealing the crosscut saw marks etched into each board. The huge window sashes had been raised on both sides of the building, and a cool breeze blew off the river, which made Elizabeth forget about the lack of air conditioning. Scanning the faces behind her, Elizabeth realized that she had been right. They were the only white people at the service.

Although the river breeze continued to blow through the church, dozens of hand fans moved back and forth like windshield wipers in a traffic jam. Elizabeth turned around and saw a fan wedged into the hymnal rack in front of her. She picked it up and examined it carefully. On the front was a color picture of Dr. Martin Luther King, Jr., and on the back was an advertisement for Badger's Furniture Store, across the street from the church. "Down on the river and down on the price," Badger claimed.

Hamilton watched Elizabeth studying the fan, and he leaned over and whispered in her ear. "Badger sells freezers, too, you know?"

"So?" Elizabeth whispered back.

"I think he even ships them to Alaska. For the Eskimos," he added.

"I can believe that," she said, successfully suppressing a chuckle.

Elizabeth heard a commotion behind her and turned to see forty people slowly walking down the aisle. She recognized the grief-stricken face of Rebecca leading the procession. Walking along with her was a middle-aged lady in a nurse's uniform, the whiteness of the uniform contrasting sharply with the somber clothes of the other mourners. Slowly the family was all seated in the pews surrounding Elizabeth and Hamilton. Then a door at the front of the church opened and three men ascended the steps to the pulpit. The service began with a long prayer, led by the oldest man of the three. The congregation sang three hymns and listened to a half-dozen preachers, deacons, and elders extol the virtues of the deceased, offering words of comfort to Rebecca and her family. The service was punctuated from time to time by loud amens that resonated randomly from different corners of the sanctuary. At one point, Rebecca let out a low wail, and the nurse seated next to her put her arm around her and fanned her rapidly with one of Badger's fans.

Just before the benediction, a rotund woman with gray hair pulled back on her head stood up in the choir loft. She was wearing a burgundy robe with *NJAME* in white stitching across the front. By the time the woman started into the second verse of "What a Friend We Have in Jesus," her forehead was shining with perspiration. The strength and beauty of her voice hypnotized the congregation, and Elizabeth wondered if she had had formal voice training.

The last preacher to speak pronounced the benediction, and the pallbearers quickly filled the front of the church, removing the flowers surrounding the casket. They slowly wheeled the casket down the aisle, the pine floorboards creaking under the heavy weight. The family followed the casket out with Rebecca leading the way, her head held high and the nurse at her side.

After the family moved out of the church, everyone converged on the center aisle and all seemed to talk at once. As Hamilton and Elizabeth moved with the flow of the crowd toward the front door, Elizabeth noticed that everyone seemed to bunch up when they got near the door, slowing down their exit. The two of them inched to within ten feet of the double doors that led to the narthex, and Elizabeth was horrified at what was causing the bottleneck. Alphonsa Mayrant's casket had been opened and positioned in the doorway. Elizabeth grabbed Hamilton's arm and looked around the room.

"There's not another way out of here?" she asked frantically. "I've never seen a dead person."

"Not that I know of," Hamilton said, looking around. "Maybe through the back. I'm sorry, Elizabeth," Hamilton whispered. "I should have warned you."

"You mean you knew that they would do this?"

"Yes, it's their custom. Just keep your head down. I'll lead you through."

Before Hamilton's instructions could register in Elizabeth's brain, Alphonsa Mayrant, dressed in a new blue suit, came into view. Elizabeth's knees buckled, and the next thing she knew there was nothing but blackness.

Elizabeth woke up on the bed in the downstairs bedroom at her grandfather's house with Jim Howard leaning over her. Hamilton and Inez were behind him, anxiously looking over his shoulder.

"Elizabeth," Howard said softly, mopping her face with a wet washcloth. "Are you okay?"

She focused her eyes on him and closed them again. "What happened?"

"You got a little overheated," Jim replied. "How do you feel?"

"Weak. But I'm okay."

Jim touched both her cheeks with the back of his hand. "I think you're going to be all right. Just keep this on your face," he said, folding the washcloth and placing it on her forehead.

"Inez will stay with you until you're feeling better," Hamilton said, shuffling closer to the bed so Elizabeth could see him.

Elizabeth nodded as she remembered what had happened. "I must have created a real scene," she said, looking at Hamilton.

"Not really," Hamilton assured her. "Only a few people were left in the church. They were very kind in helping me with you," he added.

"I'll check on you after work," Jim said, patting her hand. "I've left something for you to take to help you rest a while."

The medication knocked Elizabeth out. When she woke up, she didn't realize where she was until she spotted Inez in a wingchair reading a *Ladies' Home Journal*.

"Oh, you're awake," Inez said, looking at her over the top of her glasses.

"You shouldn't have stayed so late, Inez. It must be eight o'clock," Elizabeth said, looking out the window.

"I didn't mind. I kinda enjoyed the peace and quiet here. With Ralph retired now, I don't get much quiet time at home. How are you feeling?"

"Much better, thanks," Elizabeth said, sitting up in the bed.

"Are you hungry?"

"No, not really." Elizabeth was starving, but she didn't want to put Inez out any further.

"Dr. Howard called a little while ago."

"Oh really?" Elizabeth responded, trying not to sound too anxious.

"Yes, he said he would stop by around nine to check on you. I can stay until then if you like."

"No, go home, please. Your husband must be getting hungry."

"Ralph," she said, waving her hand. "He's hungry every waking hour, and you know what? That man is sixty-eight years old and he can't even boil water."

"I can't thank you enough, Inez. I'll see you in the morning."

"Now don't you try getting up too soon, you hear? Mr. Hamilton said you hit that floor pretty hard in the church," she remarked as she walked over to the bed. She leaned over and patted Elizabeth on the knee. "You call me if you need me, okay?"

"I will. Good night."

"Good night," Inez said, stopping to pick up her magazine on the way out the door.

Elizabeth was in the kitchen searching for something to eat when she heard Jim call for her in the hall. "I'm back here!" she yelled.

Jim stopped in the kitchen door and leaned against the frame. He had on a white polo, khakis, and topsiders with no socks, quite a contrast from his starched cotton shirts and red bowties.

"Feeling better?" he asked.

Elizabeth still had on the linen dress from the funeral, and she realized she must look as though she had waltzed with a tornado. "Yes, much better," she said.

"You look gorgeous, even when you've been ill," he remarked, staring at her dress.

Elizabeth glanced down and wondered what her hair looked like. "Yeah right," she said, instinctively brushing her hair back with her right hand. "I must be a mess."

Jim put his hand on her cheek as he had done earlier, but he kept it there for a bit longer this time and looked into her eyes. "Your color has come back," he said.

"I really do feel much better."

"Do you think you'll feel well enough to take a little trip with me this weekend?" he asked, dropping his hand slowly.

"What kind of trip, Dr. Howard?"

"An orthopedist friend of mine, a guy I refer a lot of patients to, called and offered me his house on Pawleys Island for the weekend. A couple of guys I was in medical school with are coming with their wives."

"That will be getting pretty close to the trial," she said. "I've got a lot of work to do in the next ten days."

"I thought you told me that you could be ready to try this case in no time. Listen, I'll have you back here in Weenee by midday Sunday. That old house at the beach must have ten bedrooms," he added.

The last sentence hung in the air for a few seconds. "Okay," she said finally, "I think I can swing it."

"Now, you have to remember, Pawleys Island is a little more rustic than Seaside Plantation."

"What's it like?"

"Well, it's not really my kind of beach, but a lot of people like it. It's one of the oldest resorts on the East Coast. The island was used by the rice planters on Waccamaw Neck as a summer refuge from the malaria that was so prevalent on their plantations. There are a lot of very old houses still left on the beach. Bill's must be 150 years old. Don't expect too much, Elizabeth. We're talking wooden floors and walls. No air conditioning."

"No air conditioning? You're kidding."

"If you want to change your mind, you can."

"No, I guess I can stand anything for a weekend," she said, shrugging.

"I'll talk to you later on in the week. I've got to get back to the hospital—I've got a very sick patient that may not make it through the night." He kissed her quickly and was gone.

STOPPED 12-25-11

CHAPTER 19

Elizabeth was in the law office's library Thursday morning, pulling every case she could find on manslaughter and murder that had any relevance whatsoever to the Fulton case. One of their biggest dilemmas was that Fulton, of course, claimed he knew nothing about the killing, so it would be hard to argue the distinctions between murder and manslaughter under South Carolina law. To Elizabeth, it looked as if the jury would either find Fulton guilty of murder or not guilty. What bothered her was that Fulton could have killed Frenchie in the heat of passion, or even in self-defense, but since he might not understand these distinctions in the law, he couldn't take advantage of them.

Absorbed in her research, Elizabeth didn't hear Inez until she was standing over her.

"There's a young colored woman here to see you," said Inez.

"Do you know who she is?"

"No, I assume she's here about the Fulton case."

"Send her back then," Elizabeth said as she placed a yellow scrap of paper in the *South Carolina Reports* she was reading and put the book on one of several stacks in the middle of the table.

A large black woman appeared in the doorway and stopped. Although Princess had gained forty pounds since Elizabeth had last seen her, the added weight was not enough to conceal a smile Elizabeth would have recognized in any far corner of the planet.

"Princess!" Elizabeth yelled as she jumped to her feet and dashed toward the woman. They threw their arms around each other and danced around the room.

They pulled away from each other, and Princess said, "My, you grew up to be a good-looking woman. Mama told me you were prettier now than you ever have been."

"You look wonderful too," Elizabeth said, taking another step back.

"Oh, hush your lying. I'm big as a house, now. I guess that's what having children will do for you," she said, patting her stomach.

"Rebecca told me you were expecting again. That's wonderful."

"I've told my husband, this is it for me."

"Where are your children? I'd love to see them."

"They're with Mama."

"How is your mother doing?"

"She's doing all right. All of the grands being around helps her. She'll be okay."

"I sure am sorry about your brother, Princess. I hope you know that."

"I do," she replied softly.

"Sit down, please," Elizabeth said, moving in front of a chair.

"I know you're busy. They told me about that murder case you're handling."

"I've got plenty of time," Elizabeth said. "Sit down, Princess. We've got a lot of catching up to do."

"When are you going to try the murder case?" Princess asked, slipping carefully into one of the chairs on the opposite side of the table.

"A week from Monday."

"I wish I could stay for it. I'd love to see you perform."

"How long can you stay?"

"I'm catching the Friday-morning train back."

"That's not a very long stay for as far as you have come."

"I know, but I've got to get back. Do you mind if I ask you something about your case?"

"No, if I can answer it I'll be glad to. But you understand that some matters are privileged, and I can't talk about them?"

"I know that. It's really not so much about the case itself but about Mama, really."

"What do you mean, Princess?"

"Mama's all worried about this case, but mainly she's worried about you."

"For heaven's sakes, I don't know why. I've tried dozens of murder cases, rapes, violent assaults, you name it. You know how Boston is."

"Yes, I do. But I can't convince Mama of that. You know how she feels about you. Like you're one of her daughters. Mama's been talking so much about you on the phone lately I told her I was getting jealous."

The two women giggled. Elizabeth asked about Princess's children, and before either one knew it, they had spent the next two hours bridging the years since their last meeting. Only after Inez buzzed Elizabeth on the intercom to tell her she was leaving for lunch did the two of them realize what time it was.

"I've got to be going," Princess said, easing out of her chair. "I didn't realize I had taken up so much of your time. I'm so sorry."

"Don't be sorry," Elizabeth said. "This has been wonderful. I hope I'll get to see you before you leave Friday."

"I'll call you, Elizabeth," Princess said, walking around the conference table. "Give me one more hug, girl."

Elizabeth returned from lunch and found a telephone message on her desk from Ida Pearl Middleton, asking her to stop by after work for a drink. Although the Fulton case would be relatively easy to try, Elizabeth still wasn't very comfortable with the trial being just over ten days away. She was out of her element, and she knew she wanted a take on this case from another angle. Perhaps, she thought, Ida Pearl could give her a different perspective on the case. Surely Ida Pearl knew, as well as Hamilton, what jurors would think of the evidence against Willie Fulton. She asked Inez to tell Ida Pearl that she would be there right after five.

Elizabeth settled into her usual chair at the Middletons' and was glad to see that Ida Pearl was her old self again. Her remorse over her gossiping was gone. Estelle was not feeling well, Ida Pearl said, and was lying down in the bedroom that mother and daughter shared.

"Are you getting nervous?" Ida Pearl asked after Henry had brought Elizabeth's drink and replenished Ida Pearl's.

"Nervous about what?" Elizabeth inquired.

"The trial. Isn't it coming up soon?"

"Oh," Elizabeth said, reaching for a cracker on the coffee table. "Not really. We don't start until a week from Monday," she added.

"Standing up in front of all those strange people doesn't bother you?"

"No. I've done it too many times. You don't think about people watching you, except the jury, of course."

"I see," Ida Pearl responded, stirring her new drink with her index finger.

"Let me ask you something, if you don't mind," Elizabeth said, leaning forward and putting her forearms on her knees.

"Certainly," the older woman answered.
"What have you heard about this case?"
"You really want to know the truth?"
"Yes, I do."
"Everybody I've talked to thinks your client is guilty as hell."
"Do you?"

Ida Pearl shrugged. "I don't know. If what they say about the ax is true, with Willie's fingerprints all over it, I think it will be a tough case to win. Is that talk about the ax true?"

"I'm not at liberty to say. But the State does have some pretty incriminating evidence. Have you discussed the case with anyone else? I'm interested to know what the people on the street think."

"Well, you don't want any of those ladies down at the Cut and Curl on your jury, that's for sure."

"They think he's guilty?"

Ida Pearl nodded and then took a long drink of her bourbon. "Even Monica, who does my nails, thinks he's guilty, and she's a Yankee. You've got to remember that a lot of people around here liked that old Frenchman. I know he was eccentric, but he was friendly and he would stop and talk to anybody on the street that would listen to him, white or Negro."

"That does make our case a little more difficult," Elizabeth said.

"And then there is your problem with Black Jack."

"What do you mean?" Elizabeth asked.

"Every colored person I know thinks he's some kind of messiah around here," she said, dropping her voice to a stage whisper, apparently so Henry could not eavesdrop on their conversation.

"I don't understand," Elizabeth prodded.

"He's their emerging leader, or so they think. What with all this integration business, he's the first Negro politician to get elected to office in Craven County since Reconstruction. From what I hear," she said, stopping to look over her shoulder for the ubiquitous Henry, "the Negroes won't be satisfied until they take over every office in the courthouse."

Elizabeth bit her lip and counted to ten before she answered. "Well, what does that have to do with the Fulton case?" she asked, probing further.

"You tell me," Ida Pearl answered, a trace of a smile appearing on her lips.

"I don't know," Elizabeth said.

"I think you do, but I'll tell you anyway. You're going to have at least seven or eight Negroes on your jury, right?"

"From what Robert Hamilton tells me, I would have to agree with that," Elizabeth said.

"And you know Clarence Phillips is going to put Black Jack on the stand."

"Yes, I would think so."

"I would too," Ida Pearl said. "Clarence can be a little slow sometimes—I taught him in Sunday school. But he's not stupid."

Elizabeth thought that this matron sure knew a lot about her case, but then she remembered that the whole town was talking about it, probably analyzing every detail since there wasn't much else to talk about.

"If all these Negroes hold Black Jack in such high regard, don't you think they would believe him over Willie Fulton?" Ida Pearl asked, winking at Elizabeth.

Elizabeth decided to play the devil's advocate. "Do you think they would want to put one of their people in jail for life, just to make their sheriff look good?"

"If both sides were equal, I would say yes. The average person, white or Negro, doesn't care anything about the Willie Fultons of this world."

"I don't understand why you would say that."

"It's a matter of power, Elizabeth. I've watched them like a cat watching a blue jay ever since all this civil-rights mess started twenty years ago. They weren't content just to sit downstairs at the Ackerman Theatre," she said, chuckling.

"What's so funny?" Elizabeth asked, staring at her host.

"Nothing really. I just remembered about Emerson Ackerman. The government said he had to close the balcony in his theatre, so he had someone burn it down for him, and he collected over $75,000 in insurance. He was the only person I know of around here who made money off the civil-rights movement. What I mean," she said after pausing, "is that the colored people don't just want to be equal with us whites. They want to control everything; they want to be the boss now."

"Well, the shoe has been on the other foot for over two hundred years, hasn't it?"

"Yes, it has, but I don't think I can live here with things like that. I just wish things would go back to like they were in the old days. It was so much better then. Nobody can even afford household help anymore because the federal government says we have to pay them minimum wage. Can you believe that?"

"Well, I think everybody is entitled to the minimum wage, but that's not what I want to talk about today," Elizabeth said, smiling politely.

"I'm sorry, Elizabeth," Ida Pearl replied, waving her hand in front of her face. "You have to bear with this old lady. I get off to running rabbits sometimes. What were we talking about? Oh, the trial."

"Yes, and Black Jack."

"What I was saying is that he'll be tough to beat. And the white people around here seem to like him, too. I guess if we had to have a Negro sheriff, he is the best one for the job."

"I hadn't considered his popularity with the white jurors," Elizabeth said.

"They like him because he doesn't give any preferential treatment to his own people. He feeds everybody out of the same spoon, from what I hear."

"It's hard to argue with that kind of policy," Elizabeth commented, and she meant it. She leaned back in her chair, and as she thought about what Ida Pearl had said, she knew she was right. "You've been very helpful," she stated finally. "I need to be going."

"Don't leave yet. We haven't had much company lately. Tell me some news."

The request sounded almost like a plea, and it was hard to miss the loneliness in her voice. "I'm going to spend the weekend on Pawleys Island. Are you familiar with it?"

"Oh, my Lord, yes," Ida Pearl said, closing her eyes as she tilted her head back. "Peter proposed to me in the Hucks' house on the north end of the island in 1922."

"What's it like?"

"It's a wonderful place. How do you describe heaven? It's nothing fancy, mind you. A wonderful breeze, large old wooden houses, fresh crabs and shrimp. But then again it may not be fancy enough for you."

"It sounds as if I'll really like it. A number of my girlfriends and I rent an old rambling house on the Cape every summer."

"Peter and I rented the same house for two weeks every summer for over thirty years," Ida Pearl said wistfully.

"Jim took me to see his house at Seaside Plantation a few weeks ago and that place is just not my style."

"Jim Howard has a place at Seaside?" Ida Pearl asked, leaning forward.

"He's building one. It's just about finished."

"Probably on the front beach, I bet."

"Yes, it is. Why do you say that?"

Ida Pearl shook her head. "I know he's a doctor, but that man spends money like he's a millionaire. That expensive foreign car and now a house at Seaside. They say he flies all over the place, just for the weekend."

"I don't know about Jim's finances," Elizabeth said with a shrug. "He seems nice enough to me."

"Oh, here I go again, stepping on your toes. I didn't mean it, dear. Please forgive me."

"Don't worry about it," Elizabeth said. "But understand one thing, Ida Pearl, please."

The older woman put down her drink. "What is it?"

"I'm not sleeping with Jim. I don't see any problem with staying in the same house with him for one weekend. I'm a big girl now, and I can make my own decisions."

"I understand," Ida Pearl said quickly.

"And I would appreciate it if you didn't mention my plans to anyone, okay?"

"I won't even tell Estelle," she said, looking back over her shoulder at their bedroom. She turned back around, touched her finger to her puckered lips, and nodded at Elizabeth.

Hamilton had agreed to spend most of the next day helping Elizabeth get Willie ready for the trial. They began the session by going over the names of the ninety people drawn for the jury venire. Elizabeth and Hamilton were both surprised that Willie knew almost a third of the people drawn to serve on this one-week term of General Sessions Court. That had to be a plus on Willie's side of the case, Elizabeth told herself.

They went over his direct examination twice that morning, with Elizabeth questioning him first and then Hamilton. They also took turns cross-examining him so he would have some idea of what to expect from Phillips. They finished their work just before lunch, and as soon as Willie left, Elizabeth couldn't wait for Hamilton's reaction.

"What do you think?" she asked eagerly.

"I think he's going to make a good witness. What do you think?"

"That's exactly what I was thinking. He comes across to me as very credible, and he seems to be able to take care of himself on cross-examination, even when you bore down on his thin alibi defense. As we've said before, whether or not Willie Fulton walks depends solely on his credibility on that stand."

"He's even made a believer out of me this morning."

"You thought he was guilty?"

Hamilton nodded. "But now he's telling the truth."

"What do you think of the jury panel?"

"I think we've got a pretty good draw. Inez is making a few calls on some of the ones I don't know."

"Did it surprise you that he knew as many people as he did on the panel?"

Hamilton let out a low whistle. "Hell, yeah, it did. That rascal must get around."

"How do you feel about the composition of the panel?"

"It's pretty typical of this county. Thank God, we've got ten strikes. There are a few people on that panel who wouldn't hesitate to convict their mothers if they thought they might be guilty of something. And there are also a few people in there that would give Jack the Ripper the benefit of the doubt in a criminal case. All in all, unless we just get a bad pull out the box, we'll be okay."

Elizabeth related her conversation with Ida Pearl. "Do you agree with her assessment?" she asked.

Hamilton shrugged. "Not completely. To a point she might be right, but I think she is underestimating our colored friends. The large majority of them want to do the right thing. I will agree that the sheriff can be very convincing on the witness stand. If they believe Black Jack and the State's evidence, Willie Fulton is going to be eating beans in the state pen for a long time."

"That makes me feel a little better," Elizabeth said.

"What do you want me to do in the trial?" Hamilton asked.

"What do you want to do?"

"As little as possible. Take second chair and help you with the jury and the evidentiary rulings. As I told you when you talked me into this, I'm getting too old for the courtroom."

"You haven't fooled me. I think you can handle yourself pretty well in the courtroom."

Smiling at the compliment, Hamilton pointed to his ear and said, "Can't hear like I used to. You do all the talking, and I'll keep you on track, okay?"

"Fine," Elizabeth said. "What else do we need to do today?"

"Nothing that I know of. I've had Harrington, that investigator I've used from time to time, do a little poking around but he hasn't come up with anything concrete that could help us at trial."

"Who else do you think we should call besides Willie and Pearlie Mae?" Elizabeth asked.

"I'm scared to death of Pearlie Mae taking the stand. I've got her coming in here on Tuesday. Inez said you were free then."

"I'd say so," Elizabeth said with a laugh. "Inez and I have done everything we can do until the notice to creditors expires on the estate. So the Fulton case has my complete attention."

"We can work her over like we did Willie and see how she holds up under the pressure," Hamilton said.

"I think that would be a good idea. Who else do we have?"

"No one, really. Apparently no one saw Willie that day except his wife and children."

"That's kinda scary," Elizabeth said. "I'm used to a lot of witnesses in a case like this, unless I put up no defense at all."

"Have you thought about that?" Hamilton asked.

"Sure, every criminal lawyer does. I was debating it in my mind until I heard Willie. He's going to be okay on the stand, I think. I've won several murder cases in Boston where I didn't put up a defense, but in those cases the circumstantial evidence was not nearly as strong as it is in this case. What do you think, Robert?"

"I'm sitting here trying to think of one case that I've won where I didn't put up any defense, and I can't think of a single one."

"Have you tried it very often?"

"No, not really. Unless the State has a very weak case, and my client has a horrible record, I stay away from it. Juries in Craven County like to hear from a defendant. They want to hear him say under oath he didn't do it. It's as simple as that."

"So you're saying put him up."

Hamilton's chair was pulled back from the conference table, and he leaned forward and put his elbows on his knees. "We've got a client with no record, or at least nothing that will really hurt him with the jury," he said, ticking his statement off on his little finger. "We've got a client that looks like he will be pretty credible with the jury," he continued, tapping another finger. "And the jury will hear him say he didn't do it and was somewhere else," he added, touching a third finger. Hamilton sat up in his chair and stared at Elizabeth. "We'd be crazy not to put him on the stand."

"I think you're absolutely right," Elizabeth said, glad that Hamilton agreed with her assessment.

"With that bloody ax and Willie's prints all over it, if he doesn't take the stand, the jury will convict him in fifteen minutes."

CHAPTER 20

Jim and Elizabeth left for Pawleys Island just after five, as the orange July sun bore down on them relentlessly. As they rode past fields lining each side of the road, they could see the heat hanging in waves just above the tobacco plants, now head high, all standing at attention like battalions of soldiers clad in bright-green uniforms.

"How much taller will the tobacco plants grow?" Elizabeth asked.

"That's about it right there. They'll start cropping them any day now."

"How do they do that?"

"By hand, mostly."

"That must be a hot job," she said, shaking her head.

They passed the river on the right, and Elizabeth looked away from the water because the glare was almost blinding. When they crossed the two long bridges spanning the Intracoastal Waterway, Elizabeth could see that the marsh grass in the old rice fields lining the river had turned a bright green, like the tobacco plants, and it crowded both sides of the bank as far as the eye could see.

"You were just kidding about the house not being air conditioned, weren't you?" Elizabeth asked.

"You getting cold feet about this weekend?" Jim inquired, keeping his eyes on the road.

"Ida Pearl said it was kinda rustic."

"Oh? When did you talk with her about Pawleys Island?"

"Last night."

"I hope you didn't tell her you were coming with me. Boy, that's all I need."

"Are you ashamed of being seen with me?"

"No, of course not," Jim said, glancing over at her. "Are you ashamed of being seen with me?" he asked playfully.

"Wise guy," she said, looking out the window. "How much further?"

"Do you recognize that?" he asked, pointing to an attractive building.

"Oh, its Harold's. It was so dark the last time I almost didn't recognize it. Are we going to eat there?"

"Tomorrow night," he said, "if that's okay."

"Sure, I'm already looking forward to it," she replied. "Tell me about the other couples who will be here with us."

"There's Chip and Melissa. He's a urologist in Greenville. They have two children, but I made sure they left them at home."

"What's wrong? Don't you like children?"

"Yeah, I do, sometimes. But I see them every day in my practice, and I get tired of them."

"How about the other couple?"

"John and Virginia. He's an oncologist in Charleston. They have one child on the way."

"Did you tell them to leave it home, too?"

Jim looked at Elizabeth and broke into a grin. "Wise guy," he said.

Jim made a right turn off the highway, and in a few seconds they were crossing a narrow causeway that stretched across a wide salt creek. In the distance, they could see the island, its houses framed by late-afternoon shadows.

"It looks so small. Is the ocean on the other side of those houses?"

"Yep. You should be able to hear the roar of the surf in just a few minutes."

Jim turned right at the end of the causeway and headed south on a winding road that did its best to follow the edge of the marsh, but in some places it was unsuccessful, and the spartina sprouted on each side of the roadway. To her left, Elizabeth could see the rambling old houses, most of which were either standing or kneeling on stilts. The houses were sheathed in every imaginable material, from brick to asbestos siding, and even the bricks showed the telltale signs of constant exposure to the salt air. They passed several houses that seemed to be intentionally camouflaged by yaupons, cassina berries, palmettos, and oleander bushes filled with bright-red blossoms. Elizabeth leaned forward in her seat to get a better look when Jim slowed the car and turned into a driveway with a sign that read *Sand Dollar*.

"Well, what do you think?" he asked, stopping the car and gesturing toward the house.

Elizabeth stared at the cottage, turned, and looked at Jim. "Ida Pearl was right," she said finally.

"Rustic?" he asked.

"Very rustic," she said, looking back at the house, which was dark and foreboding. The heavy limbs of the large, gnarled live oaks in the yard swooned almost to the ground, giving the landscape a prehistoric look. The house showed faint remnants of a coat of white paint, most of which had been sandblasted off by the constant winds of the nearby Atlantic. A long porch stretched the width of the house, and the window shutters had been closed tight and bolted shut.

"Are you sure this is the right place, Jim?"

"Sure, I'm sure. Come on—let's unload the car."

"When are the other couples getting here?"

"They said it would be late," he answered.

The front-door lock was so badly corroded that it took Jim several minutes of twisting and shaking to get it open. The heavy batten door creaked open like a sound effect in a horror movie, so Elizabeth let Jim go in first. They entered a wide center hall that led to a large living area on the beach side of the house. The room looked out over another wide porch that in turn looked out over the ocean. It had well-worn pine floors with no finish on them, and the walls were rough-cut pine with no paint. There were framed family pictures everywhere, and as she walked around looking at them, Elizabeth felt almost as if she was attending a family reunion, although she recognized no one.

"I can stand anything for a weekend," Elizabeth said.

"I'll get some windows open," Jim stated. "It's stifling in here."

For the next hour, they unpacked and made up beds. The bedrooms were sparsely furnished with iron beds and secondhand furniture. Once the sun went down, Elizabeth's fears about the lack of air conditioning were allayed as the windows throughout the house were strategically placed so the ocean breeze could be enjoyed in almost every room. In the living area, the old, faded cotton curtains at times seemed as if they would fly off their rods.

Finally Elizabeth and Jim were able to settle into the oak

rockers on the porch with their drinks and watch the white foamy surf in the darkness. At nine o'clock they both became concerned about the others and debated whether Jim should call to check on them. They decided to wait a while longer, and shortly after nine thirty the phone rang. Jim got up to answer it and was gone for five minutes.

"I'm afraid I've got some bad news," he said when he returned. "They're not coming."

"What happened?" Elizabeth asked.

"The doctor covering for John is sick, and Chip and Melissa are having babysitter troubles."

"Why didn't you tell them to bring the children? I certainly don't mind."

"I did, but Chip sounded really angry. I think he and Melissa must have gotten into it. Do you want to go back to Weenee?" he asked, exhaling loudly.

"No, not unless you do."

"Well, I don't either, but you probably think this is some kind of charade to get you down here for the weekend." He stared out over the ocean for a few seconds and bit his lip. "I can't believe this."

"Just calm down. Sit back down," she said, reaching for his hand. Jim slumped back in his rocker and threw his feet up on the porch railing.

"You can't depend on anybody anymore. I was really looking forward to seeing those guys. It's been almost a year since we've gotten together."

"Don't be too hard on them. You've got to understand things are a little different when you have a wife and a family."

"Yeah, I guess you're right. Things have been a lot different since Chip and John tied the knot, that's for sure."

Elizabeth reached over and patted his hand. "I do have one question, though. What are we doing for dinner?"

"Well, we can't get into Harold's tonight without a reservation. There's a seafood house out on Highway 17 that's not too bad. Do you want to try it?"

"Sure, I'm starved. I didn't want to say anything while we were waiting for your friends."

"How long will it take you to get ready?"

"Give me five minutes," Elizabeth said, rising from her rocker and stretching.

The Shrimp Trawler Restaurant was good, greasy, and crowded. The shrimp nets and fake seashells Elizabeth had expected at Harold's adorned every wall, and the other patrons had been baked almost as much as the deviled crab on their seafood platters. They ate mounds of fried shrimp, fried flounder, fried potatoes, and hushpuppies. After washing her food down with three scotches, Elizabeth thought Jim would have to call an ambulance, she was so stuffed.

It was almost twelve when they trudged slowly up the wooden steps of the Sand Dollar, a full moon illuminating the way for them.

"Jim," she said as she slumped down on the creaky wicker sofa in the living room. "Why is it that I always seem to be sick when I'm around you?" She draped her arm over her forehead, and Jim could see a toothy grin below it.

"Are you ill?" he asked.

"I'm either nine months pregnant or I'm sick," she said.

"I'm kinda bloated, too. Like I might be sick. Do you want me to get some Pepto-Bismol or something? I could use some myself," he said weakly.

"Either that or some of Sonny Boy's moonshine. I'm about to die."

"There's a drugstore on the highway. I'll be back in ten minutes."

Jim returned from his errand to find Elizabeth in one of the upstairs bedrooms, sleeping soundly on top of the bedspread.

Elizabeth awakened just after eight the next morning to the smell of breakfast cooking downstairs. At first she thought it was Rebecca but then remembered where she was as she felt the ocean breeze against her face. She saw her bed was still made and smiled. She had slept well, and somehow her digestive system had processed all the fried food she had bombarded it with at the Shrimp Trawler. Stretching as she sat up, she realized she felt better than she had in weeks. Her body had not adjusted well to the oppressive humidity of the South Carolina low country, and she was dragging by midafternoon most days. Maybe she was like those antebellum rice planters, she thought, in that she also had to retreat to the coast for health reasons. She pulled on a robe and walked downstairs barefooted. The worn pine floors were gritty with tracked-in sand, and it gave her an unmistakable feeling of informality that felt good. She told herself she could get used to this place in a hurry as she looked across the porch at the ocean. It was as calm as a millpond, and Elizabeth saw dozens of brown pelicans floating on the surface like cabdrivers patiently waiting for fares at the airport.

"Jim?" she called.

Jim leaned across the counter that separated the kitchen from the living area. "Good morning," he said, smiling. He was dressed in a T-shirt, shorts, and topsiders.

"Good morning," she said. "Come here."

He walked around the counter and handed her a white mug full of coffee. "Watch out for that cup," he said. "I couldn't find a single one that wasn't chipped. The sugar and cream are on the counter. I don't know what you like in it."

"Black is fine," she said. "Check out all those pelicans!" Jim leaned down to get a better look through the window where she was pointing. "They're beautiful," she commented.

"They were once on the endangered species list, but they've come back strong in recent years. They're known around here as the Pawleys Island air force."

Elizabeth watched the birds, then turned and studied the room, which was so full of light it was almost blinding. "What are we doing today?" she asked.

"Nothing," Jim replied.

"Nothing? What do you mean, nothing?"

"Just what I said," Jim answered, shrugging. "Pack a cooler and sit on the beach all day. The weather is supposed to be perfect. That's my idea of how to spend a day at the beach. There's an old john boat tied up to the dock on the creek if you want to go crabbing or something."

"No. Let's sit on the beach. I think my system can stand a day of doing nothing."

Jim placed silverware on an old weathered table on the porch, and they ate out there overlooking the beach. Jim had gone out early and found some eggs, sausage, and vine-ripened tomatoes to go along with grits and the Charleston paper. It was almost eleven before they finished the pot of coffee and the newspaper. Elizabeth did the dishes while Jim made sandwiches and packed a cooler with sodas, beer, and a bottle of wine for Elizabeth. They found rusty, but serviceable, beach chairs downstairs in the old servants' quarters.

By noon they were draped across their chairs, nearly comatose from the huge breakfast and the monotonous drone of the surf. Elizabeth was surprised to see so few people on the beach, considering it was the end of July and the height of the tourist season. She noticed that the old houses were a considerable distance from each other, apparently to maximize the rice planters' privacy.

They spent the afternoon on the beach and in the water. After a sandwich and two glasses of wine, Elizabeth stretched out on a beach towel. When she woke up, she was covered with another towel, and she noticed that the sun was no longer high overhead.

Elizabeth rolled over slowly. "How long did I sleep?" she asked.

"Almost two hours," Jim answered after looking at his watch. "How do you feel?"

"Other than a little sleepy, I feel wonderful." She gently pinched her pink arm to test for sunburn and said, "I think I have enough sun for one day. Thanks for covering me up."

"I kept checking on you. I've nursed you enough lately," he added with a chuckle. "Would you like some more wine?"

"When I get out. I'm going for a wake-up swim," she said, getting to her feet. "I'll be right back."

They decided to sit on the other porch before supper, so they could watch the sun set on the other side of the creek. Jim found a blender and made a pitcher of margaritas while Elizabeth was in the shower. They rested their sunburned feet on the porch railing as they watched the sun, now finished with its work for the day, retreating behind the tall pines at the edge of the marsh on the mainland side. The rays of sunlight filtered through the old trees at curious angles, a supernatural light show taking place on the horizon.

"This is exactly the prescription I needed, Doctor," Elizabeth said, resting her head on the back of the rocker.

"Oh yeah?"

"Oh yeah," she said, mimicking him as she reached for his hand. "Did anyone ever tell you that you make a mean margarita?"

"Yes, as a matter of fact, they have. I had quite a reputation as a bartender in med school."

"Do you have a secret recipe?"

"Just a secret ingredient."

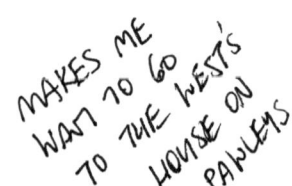
makes me want to go west to the west house on Pawleys

"What is it?"
"You won't tell?"
"Scout's honor," Elizabeth said, raising her right hand.
"It's Cointreau."
"It will be our secret," she said with mock seriousness.

They finished the last of the margaritas ten minutes before they were to claim their table at Harold's. It was fortunate they didn't have to take the highway to get to the restaurant, because they were both a little unsteady as they made their way to Jim's car.

Harold's was crowded and noisy, and they had to wait at the bar for a half-hour before their table was ready. They carried their drinks with them to their table, which luckily was tucked into a corner at the far end of the room where it was much quieter.

As soon as they ordered, Jim said, "Tell me about the trial."
"What do you want me to tell you?"
"Well, we haven't talked about it in a while. What is your prediction?"
"I don't really make predictions before a trial starts," she said, resting her elbow on the white tablecloth with her chin on her palm.
"Do you think you will win?"
"Do you mean do I think that Willie Fulton will be acquitted?"
Jim nodded.
Elizabeth shrugged. "I don't know," she said finally. "It depends."
"Depends on what?"
"On how good Mr. Fulton is on the stand."
"You mean it depends on how convincing he is to the jury?"
"Exactly."
"So, he is definitely taking the stand to testify."
"Oh, he has to. If he doesn't, then he doesn't have a prayer, in my opinion."
"He won't consider any type of plea bargain?"
"Not for a minute," she said quickly.
"Have you found anyone to back up his story?"
"No one, other than his wife, Pearlie Mae," Elizabeth said. "And I'm afraid she isn't going to be much help to us."
"Why?"
"Because she'll make a terrible witness, I think. Robert agrees with me. I think the woman is being truthful; it's just that she's not very calm."

"What exactly is Fulton going to say on the stand? What's his story?"

"It's very simple. That he was harvesting tobacco. That's not what everyone calls it. What's the term, Jim?"

"Cropping."

"Right, cropping tobacco in a field not very far from where Frenchie was murdered. There was no one with him that day."

"How will you explain the ax?"

Elizabeth shrugged. "I can always argue that someone planted it."

"Do you have any evidence to support that theory?"

Elizabeth shook her head. "No. But all I have to show is reasonable doubt."

"It sounds like it's going to be a pretty close case."

"Now do you see why I don't make predictions about cases before trial?"

"Spoken like a well-seasoned trial lawyer. Are you going to try the entire case, or is Robert going to help?"

"He's going to help with the research, the jury, the motions, that type of thing."

"I see," Jim said, taking a long sip of his drink.

Their dinner was even better than their first meal at Harold's. They both had the mahimahi, which was grilled to perfection, along with a bottle of chardonnay. When they left, Jim crept along the winding island road at a turtle's pace to keep from running into the marsh. They both held on to the stair railings as they climbed the wooden steps under the moon, high and small in the black sky. They paused on the top step, and Jim had to feel for the handle of the screen door in the darkness, as they had forgotten to turn on the porch light. He finally got both the screen door and front door open. As he slung the screen door wide, he dropped one foot back to catch it and pulled Elizabeth into his arms.

"Are you ready to go up?" he asked and kissed her.

Their lips parted and she leaned her forehead against his. "This has been such a wonderful day. I wish it didn't have to end."

"It doesn't have to end yet," he replied and kissed her again.

"I'm not ready yet," Elizabeth said softly and kissed him back. "Thanks for a great day."

Jim watched her walk up the stairs and shook his head in disgust.

CHAPTER 21

By the next Thursday, Elizabeth was getting impatient and was ready to draw a jury and start the trial. She and Hamilton had fine-tuned Willie's testimony, and they both felt he was ready to take the stand. They decided against calling Pearlie Mae because they thought there was a chance she could unwittingly hurt them on cross-examination. They agreed it simply wasn't worth the risk; they would let Willie tell his story, and that would be the last thing the jury heard unless the State called reply witnesses. If they kept their defense simple, the chances were good that the State would not have any testimony in rebuttal.

Elizabeth was glad to see that Robert and Inez had been very thorough in collecting background information on the jury panel. She still couldn't get over the fact that South Carolina law wouldn't allow defense lawyers the right to question prospective jurors, but there was nothing she could do but rely on Hamilton's information and instincts. They spent over an hour going over the panel, and Elizabeth pointed out that it seemed to be a pretty good cross section of Craven County's population.

"It won't be that representative on Monday morning, when we're staring them in the face," Hamilton said.

"Why not?" Elizabeth asked.

"Most of the professional people and just about all of the older white people call and beg off to Shirley."

"The clerk of court? You mean she can excuse them? On what grounds?"

"Vacations, sore throats, family reunions, you name it."

"That's ridiculous. I didn't see anything in your code that gave the clerk that kind of authority. Only a circuit judge can excuse a juror, from what I read."

"Well, Shirley does it every term."

"Then we should file a motion first thing Monday morning to stop her. The judge can send deputies for those jurors the clerk has already excused. Don't you agree? If nothing else, we should preserve the issue for appeal," Elizabeth added.

"Wait a minute," Hamilton said calmly, folding his arms across his chest. "We need to think this thing through. Number one, do we want anybody on our jury who has been picked up at their homes or offices by a deputy and brought down to the courthouse because of a motion made by Willie Fulton's lawyers? How sympathetic do you think they would be to our arguments? To Willie?"

"You're absolutely right," Elizabeth said, bouncing a clenched fist on her armrest. "It just irks me to no end for educated people to weasel out of jury duty. I see them trying to do the same thing in Boston, but the judges don't let them get away with it."

"It's human nature, I guess," Hamilton said with a shrug. "Number two, what Shirley does to the jury panel actually helps our case."

"What do you mean?" Elizabeth asked.

"Look who is getting out of serving." Elizabeth gave Hamilton a puzzled look. "Professional people, older people, white people."

"And?" Elizabeth asked.

"Do we want those people on our jury? I don't," Hamilton said, answering his own question. "Tell me if you disagree."

Elizabeth leaned back in the worn leather chair, and a smile formed on her lips. "You are absolutely right. They fit the profile of exactly who we would strike in Boston. There are exceptions to the rule, of course, but you're right. I was about to shoot both of us in the foot."

"And Willie," he added with a smile. "What else do we need to talk about?"

"My opening statement. Since this state has no rules of criminal procedure, I haven't been able to find much guidance. I've been meaning to ask you about it. Are there any restrictions on what you can say in the opening?"

"There are no written rules. It's up to the trial judge. Some judges don't even allow you to make an opening."

"You're kidding!" Elizabeth responded.

"No, but there are only two or three left on the bench who won't let you open. Most of them, like Lawson, will let you outline the evidence, but they won't let you argue your case."

"I certainly don't want to argue the facts, but I do want to lay out my case to the jury at the outset."

"Would you tell them everything you're going to try to prove?"

"Sure, why not?"

"It might be dangerous."

"In what way?" Elizabeth asked, sitting up and putting her elbows on the conference table.

"You may say too much."

"How could I do that? We know what the State is going to put up. And we also know that Lawson isn't going to buy our motion to suppress the evidence seized in the search. They did everything they were supposed to do, so we know the ax is going to come out, right? Don't forget Willie consented to the initial search, so that probably cures any potential defects in the warrant. Don't you think Phillips will mention it in his opening?"

"Probably not, as careful as he is. He won't take the slim chance that Lawson will keep it out."

"So that's all the more reason for us to bring it out. We need to beat him to the punch. If we tell the jury that Willie says he doesn't know anything about it right off the bat, then we'll have an immediate advantage."

"And what happens if Lawson keeps it out? Then we've convicted our client."

"What are the chances Lawson will throw it out? Have you ever seen him throw out evidence like this before?"

"No, I haven't. As a matter of fact, I've heard him many times tell lawyers in chambers that he would rather err on the side of the State in evidentiary matters because the Supreme Court will review his decision only if there is a conviction."

"Then I think we should withdraw our motion to suppress. I don't want the jury to think we're trying to hide anything."

"I think you're right," Hamilton said.

"I'll take care of the paperwork today. Let me ask you something, and be truthful with me, Robert."

"Okay."

"What do you think our chances of an acquittal are?"

"I don't know; it's hard to say. What do you think?"

"Everybody has been telling me this will be a very close case. What I'm thinking, Robert, is that I need to lay our whole case out for the jury in my opening statement. Why wait until they hear from Willie before they know what our case is about?"

"I think that's taking too big of a chance."

"Maybe in some cases you would be right. Here there are no question marks, are there?"

"There are question marks in every trial, Elizabeth. Sometimes we just don't see them until we get into the trial."

"I know that may be true sometimes, but trust me on this one. Everything I've ever read in trial journals or heard at seminars indicates that a large percentage of jurors make up their minds by the close of opening statements."

"Maybe so," Hamilton said, shifting in his seat, "maybe so."

CHAPTER 22

THE TRIAL [handwritten annotation]

Not only were there no seats left in the courtroom by nine forty-five Monday morning, but there also weren't any places left for spectators to stand. People were even sitting on the steps to the elevated seats, and the wide aisle down the center of the courtroom was filled shoulder to shoulder. The jurors, most with anxious looks on their faces, were sitting in a reserved area in the front of the courtroom behind the solicitor's desk.

Elizabeth and Hamilton, with Willie and Pearlie Mae trailing close behind them, entered the courtroom from one of the doors behind the bench a few minutes before ten. The last thing Hamilton had told Elizabeth on Friday afternoon was that they certainly didn't need to be in the courtroom early Monday morning because it would probably be after lunch before the trial started.

"What are all these people doing here?" she whispered in Hamilton's ear as they put their files down on the counsel table.

"A lot of them are defendants. You see the jury over there," he said, nodding in the direction of the panel. "The rest are spectators, here to watch the big trial."

"Why are all of these other defendants here if the Fulton case is to be tried this week?" she asked as she pointed Willie and Pearlie Mae to their chairs.

"Clarence loves to jerk people around. He'll keep fifty defendants in court all week if he thinks it'll help him squeeze one guilty plea. All of these people are here for roll call."

"You mean he makes people show up for court even if he knows their case won't be called this week?"

Hamilton nodded. "Yep."

"That's ridiculous," she said.

Suddenly, a voice shouted, "Order in the court! All rise."

There was the rustle of over two hundred people struggling

to get to their feet as Judge Charles Lawson descended a short stairway at the left of the courtroom and mounted the bench. He stopped behind the high-backed red leather chair and surveyed the crowd. Once he was satisfied that everyone was standing and paying proper deference to his position, he said, "Thank you. Please be seated."

Elizabeth considered what followed a huge waste of time for an awful lot of people. Phillips slowly went through his roll call of eighty-one indictments, ranging from murder, to driving under the influence, to one poor soul who meekly stood up amid a number of chuckles and answered to the charges of being a peeping tom. Elizabeth noticed that about 90 percent of the defendants were black, but she didn't know what inference to draw from that. When a defendant indicated that he wanted to plead guilty, Phillips ordered him down to the front and had him stand before the jury box like a schoolchild waiting to be dismissed.

As soon as Lawson realized that Phillips had finished with his roll call, he asked, "What are you going to do after I qualify this jury, Solicitor?"

"I've got enough guilty pleas to last until lunch. We can let the jury go after you qualify them, until two thirty. I have a murder case that I'm calling at that time," Phillips said.

"Very well, then. Madam Clerk, would you please call the names of the jurors."

Both Hamilton and Elizabeth turned their chairs around when Shirley Barrineau stood up with her jury list in hand. Hamilton had emphasized to Elizabeth that this was a critical phase of the jury selection because it was the only time a juror would speak in open court. The clerk, in an intimidating voice, ordered all the jurors to stand when their names were called and give their occupations, their spouses' occupations, and their mileage to the courthouse. Elizabeth was amazed at the number of people who either couldn't remember all of these basic instructions or were too nervous to follow them. How could they possibly follow the evidence and the judge's charge on the law? she wondered. This process took another forty-five minutes, and Elizabeth could see why Phillips wanted to wait until after lunch to select a jury.

Lawson called the lunch recess, and Hamilton and Elizabeth

I've always wondered how jury follow charges

went back to the office and sent Inez for sandwiches. Elizabeth took three bites and pushed the rest of her pimento-cheese sandwich to the center of the library table. She never ate much during a trial, but she couldn't remember being this nervous, even at her first trial.

She felt a little better once they started selecting a jury after lunch. Lawson had to excuse three jurors who said they had heard about the case, had already formed an opinion, and didn't feel they could be impartial. All three were white.

Elizabeth leaned over and whispered in Hamilton's ear. "Should we say anything, or object?"

"No, we don't want them anyway. They probably don't know anything more than the other jurors. That's just their way of getting out of serving."

They seated their jury in twenty minutes. Phillips used all but one of his ten strikes to strike black people, relying on local courthouse conventional wisdom that blacks tend to give a defendant the benefit of the doubt, regardless of the accused's race. Although Phillips was determined to keep as many blacks as he could off the jury, seven of the twelve chosen were black, and so were both alternates. Neither side expected the court to use either alternate, since it would be a fairly short trial. Four of the five white jurors were females. Hamilton had warned Elizabeth that they needed to stay away from most of the white males, particularly the older ones, as they more than likely would vote to convict. The one white male was Collards McGee, who ran a service station and was well respected by blacks and whites alike. According to Willie, a few years ago McGee had made him a loan of $100 when Willie was in a financial scrape and, thankfully, he had repaid the money. There was also a young woman in her late twenties who lived way out in the country that no one knew much about, a bookkeeper, a retired spinster schoolteacher, and the choir director of the Weenee First Baptist Church.

"Anything before I swear this jury, gentlemen?"

"Nothing from the State," Phillips barked out.

"Nothing from the Defendant," Elizabeth said calmly.

Lawson dropped his head suddenly and looked at Elizabeth. "You'll have to forgive me, Miss Chase," he said sheepishly when he looked up. "I think this is the first time I've had a female lawyer trying a case in my courtroom."

"That's quite all right, Your Honor," Elizabeth said.

Lawson read the indictment in a monotone, looked at Phillips, and instructed, "You may proceed, Solicitor."

Phillips rose from his chair and approached the bench with his right arm outstretched. Lawson handed the indictment to Phillips, and the judge looked at the jury with a very bored expression. Phillips walked over to a position in front of the jury box, stood ramrod straight, as he was trained to do in his National Guard unit, and said, "Good afternoon, ladies and gentlemen, I am Clarence Phillips, your solicitor for the Third Judicial Circuit in which Craven County is located." He made the unnecessary introduction in a solicitous manner, as if no one on the panel had been sitting in the courtroom all day and had enough sense to realize who he was. Phillips went on to thank the members of the jury for so unselfishly doing their civic duty, even though they had made the pilgrimage to the courthouse because of a jury summons that had been served on them by certified mail.

Phillips read the indictment once again in an animated voice. He closed his remarks by brashly stating that the State of South Carolina would offer overwhelming evidence that Willie Fulton was guilty beyond a reasonable doubt of murder. He turned and pointed at Willie and sat down.

"Miss Chase, do you wish to make a brief opening statement?" Lawson asked, peering over his glasses.

"Yes, I do, Your Honor," she replied as she stood up. "May it please the Court?"

"You may proceed."

"Thank you," she said, walking briskly to the same imaginary spot in front of the jury box. "Ladies and gentlemen, my name is Elizabeth Chase, and I, along with Robert Hamilton of the Craven County Bar, represent Willie Fulton, who has been charged, as you now know, with murder, by the State of South Carolina. Mr. Fulton, would you stand, please?"

Willie stood up quickly and looked straight at the jurors. Elizabeth had repeatedly emphasized to him that eye contact with the jury was extremely important to his credibility, and they had practiced this introduction to the jury at least half a dozen times. She introduced Pearlie Mae to show the jury that he had the support of a faithful wife, but Elizabeth instructed her to remain seated.

Elizabeth launched into a brief discussion of the presumption of innocence, the burden of proof, and reasonable doubt. Most of the jurors were politely attentive, although several had blank looks on their faces, as if Elizabeth were speaking Arabic.

She moved to the heart of her opening statement. She had gone over it word for word with Hamilton because she didn't want to get off on the wrong foot with Lawson by saying too much.

"Mr. Fulton stands before you pleading not guilty to the charge of murder. Under our system of jurisprudence, he doesn't have to take the stand to answer the charges against him, but he will because he wants you to hear his side, his version of the facts. He will tell you that he was working in a tobacco field when someone else so brutally murdered Ovid Gilbert, whom everyone knew as Frenchie. I simply ask you to listen very carefully to all of the evidence presented, not just the State's. If you do, then I submit to you that after you conclude your deliberations, you will render a verdict of not guilty."

As soon as Elizabeth turned to walk back to the counsel table, Lawson bellowed, "Call your first witness, Solicitor."

Phillips jumped to his feet. "The State calls Sgt. Clarence Wilson."

The sergeant was sitting at the solicitor's desk, and he wobbled toward Shirley Barrineau's desk. Wilson was wearing a starched khaki shirt with metal sergeant's stripes pinned to each collar. Although the courtroom was air conditioned, half-moons of perspiration stains reached almost halfway to his belt. Shirley instructed Wilson to raise his right hand and place his left hand on the Bible, and he did just the opposite. Elizabeth knew immediately that the State's first witness didn't like to testify in a courtroom. Shirley pointed out his mistake in a stage whisper, and the sergeant corrected himself with exaggerated movements. Once the clerk administered the oath, Wilson took the witness stand, looked up at Judge Lawson, and nodded. Lawson stared at the man until Phillips spoke to his witness.

"State your name and occupation, please."

"Sgt. Clarence Wilson. Deputy sheriff, Craven County Sheriff's Office."

"And Sergeant Wilson, how long have you been so employed?"

"October coming, it'll be twenty-nine years."

"Now, Sergeant, could you tell this jury if you were on duty June seventh of this year?"

"Yes sir, I was."

"Can you tell us what you were doing?"

"I was on routine patrol in the River Road area, and I decided to go check on the Frenchman."

"Who?" Phillips asked. He had also been over the sergeant's testimony a number of times, and he was more than a little disgusted that this almost retired officer had to be the one who stumbled onto the murder scene.

"Mr. Ovid Gilbert. Frenchie is what everybody called him."

"And how did you happen to go to his place off of River Road?"

"Me and him was kinda friends. We liked to talk. I ain't seen him in a while, so I thought I'd go check on him."

"And tell us, if you would, what you found when you got to Mr. Gilbert's place?"

"It was all tore up around his house. And they was blood. They was blood everywhere," he said, looking at the jury as if he were seeing them for the first time.

"What else did you see?"

"I found the dog. He was dead. Look like he'd been chopped up real bad with an ax."

"Objection, Your Honor," Elizabeth said in a firm voice as she rose to her feet. "I don't think the sergeant has been qualified as a forensic pathologist, and I don't remember seeing an autopsy report on the dog."

There were a few snickers from the spectators, and Lawson grabbed his gavel and slammed it on the bench. "We are going to have order in my court," he said, almost screaming. "If there are any more outbursts like that, I am going to have one of the deputies either put you in the street or in jail." Lawson looked at Elizabeth as if he was sizing her up and said in a normal voice, "Objection sustained."

Phillips glanced at Elizabeth, and she saw his cheeks flush. "Describe the dog for the jury, Sergeant," he said, looking back at his witness.

Sergeant Wilson looked at the judge to make sure it was all right to start again, and Lawson nodded for him to answer the question.

"He was chopped up real bad with something real sharp."

"Describe the garden."

"It was all tore up, like some animal had . . ."

Elizabeth rose from her seat again.

"Sergeant," Lawson said.

The deputy turned and looked at him. "Yes sir, Judge?"

"Just tell the jury what you saw. Don't tell them what you think happened there, okay? That is their job."

"Yes sir, Judge, I'm sorry," he said, turning back around in his seat to face Phillips.

"Go ahead, Sergeant, finish your answer," Phillips prompted.

"I forgot what the question was, Solicitor. Would you repeat it?"

"You were telling us what the garden looked like," Phillips replied, barely concealing his frustration.

"He had three or four rows of cucumbers, and they was all mashed down. And he had a row of Kentucky wonders, and part of the trellis was knocked down. It was all tore up, and Frenchie was so proud of that garden."

"Did you see any signs of Mr. Gilbert?"

"No, nothing but his blood and the dog's blood everywhere."

Elizabeth and Hamilton exchanged glances, but she decided not to object because she knew she could be more effective attacking his statements on cross-examination.

"What did you do next?"

"I radioed for backup like the sheriff always told us to do."

"How long was it before Sheriff Carter got there?"

"'Bout thirty minutes."

"What did you do until the sheriff got there?"

"I just waited."

"Thank you, Sergeant," Phillips said as he turned and walked to his seat. "Your witness," he remarked as he sat down.

Elizabeth stood up and walked slowly across the wide space between the counsel tables and the witness stand. She stopped about eight feet away from Wilson, with the jury just a few feet to her left.

"Sergeant, you've been in law enforcement how many years?"

"Almost twenty-nine years, ma'am."

"And how many times have you testified in a murder case, Sergeant Wilson?"

Hamilton couldn't recall ever seeing Wilson testify in any serious case, much less a murder case, and both lawyers had agreed that it wouldn't hurt to fish a little with this witness.

The sergeant leaned back in his chair, put his hand on his chin, and looked at the ceiling for a few seconds. "This might be my first one," he said finally.

"I see," Elizabeth responded. "And you just happened to decide to check on Mr. Gilbert?"

"Yes ma'am. That's what I said earlier."

"Isn't it true, Sergeant Wilson, that you used to go see Mr. Gilbert almost every day that you were on duty?"

"Not every day. But I went a lot to check on him. He was getting up in years, you know."

"And Mr. Gilbert loved wine, didn't he?" Wilson stared at her but didn't respond to the question. "Are you going to answer my question, Sergeant?"

"I know what you are getting at, miss, but I never drunk no wine with him when I was on duty. I was always off duty."

Four or five spectators laughed out loud, and before Elizabeth knew it, Lawson was banging his gavel on the bench again. "I mean it. Another outburst like that and I'll clear this courtroom. Bailiff, you bring me the next person who laughs out loud, you understand?" he barked, pointing his gavel at Hank Richardson, the bailiff guarding the front door.

Elizabeth noticed out of the corner of her eye that Phillips was standing at his table.

"What is it, Solicitor?" Lawson asked.

"I object to this line of questioning. It has absolutely no relevance."

"If the sergeant was drinking wine, and I have no way of knowing that, don't you think that it's possible that it may have affected this witness's perception and his credibility, Mr. Phillips?"

Phillips looked like a dog that had defecated on the kitchen floor and had just been whacked with a newspaper by his master. "I still don't think it's relevant, Your Honor," Phillips said weakly and sat back down.

"Objection overruled," Lawson declared, nodding to Elizabeth.
"Would you like for me to repeat the question, Sergeant Wilson?"
"Yes ma'am," he said.
"Mr. Gilbert loved wine, didn't he?"
"Yes ma'am. I guess so."
"And like a lot of Frenchmen, he drank a lot of wine?"
"Frenchie was the only Frenchman I ever knew, so I don't know how to answer that question, ma'am."
"Let me rephrase it for you, then. Didn't Mr. Gilbert drink a lot of wine?"
The sergeant thought for a few seconds and then nodded. "I'd say so, yes ma'am."
"And on occasion you would stop and have a glass of wine with him, wouldn't you?" The fact that Wilson and Gilbert were drinking buddies had been one of the few helpful pieces of information that Hamilton's investigator had uncovered. Elizabeth and Hamilton knew that it had little or no bearing on the ultimate issue of Fulton's guilt, but it could be useful nonetheless in making the State's case look wobbly.
Wilson slowly raised his finger as Elizabeth finished her question, like a schoolboy who wanted to answer his teacher but wasn't sure if he would be correct. "Only when I was off duty, ma'am."
Elizabeth was satisfied she had gotten her point across and decided to move on. "Now, Sergeant, would you say Mr. Gilbert was a good gardener? Did he work a lot in his garden?"
Wilson appeared to be relieved that Elizabeth had moved on to another subject. "Oh, yes ma'am. This time of year he worked in it every day. He really loved that garden. It looked like a pitcher in one of them seed catalogues."
"Now, Sergeant, you might have to help me with this question as I'm a city girl," Elizabeth said, smiling at the witness.
"Yes, ma'am, I will," Wilson replied, eagerly smiling back at her.
"What do you call the area of bare ground between the plants?"
"The row or the furrow is what we call it," Wilson said quickly.
"Okay, thank you, Sergeant. Now, had the rows been plowed recently, or were there weeds growing in this area?"
"Oh, Frenchie was always real particular about keeping them rows plowed."

"So there was nothing but bare earth or dirt between the rows of plants?"

"That's right."

"And the dirt would be loose because it had been recently plowed or hoed or whatever Mr. Gilbert would have done to keep the weeds out?"

"Oh, yes ma'am."

"Now, Sergeant Wilson, when you first inspected the garden, you would have seen the footprints of whoever or whatever tore up Mr. Gilbert's garden, wouldn't you?"

"Yes ma'am."

"And did you see any type of footprints?"

"Yes ma'am. They was all over that garden."

"Did you take any measurements, photographs, or plaster casts of these prints?"

"No ma'am. The investigators always handle that."

"I see. Now, Sergeant, on direct examination, you told the solicitor that you saw Mr. Gilbert's blood, and you saw the dog's blood everywhere, is that right?"

"Yes ma'am, I did."

"Sergeant, you don't have any training in blood analysis, do you?"

"Would you repeat that, please?"

"You didn't examine the blood in order to determine which blood was Mr. Gilbert's and which blood was the dog's, did you?"

"No ma'am."

"All you know is that you saw a lot of blood there, right?"

"Yes ma'am," he said weakly.

"Thank you, Sergeant," she concluded, nodding once at the witness. "No further questions."

"Any redirect, Solicitor?"

"No, Your Honor," Phillips said, barely rising from his chair.

"Very well. Call your next witness," Lawson instructed, looking at the clock on the back wall.

"The State calls Dr. Harvey Kerrison," Phillips said in a loud voice, apparently anxious to get his first witness off the stand.

Dr. Kerrison was chairman of the pathology department at the Medical University of South Carolina in Charleston. He had a thick head of gray hair that stuck out in various directions like a worn-out shoe brush, and he weighed close to three hundred pounds. Wearing a long white lab coat, he closely resembled a penguin as he waddled his way to the witness stand, and he let out a loud grunt when he sat down with no room to spare on either side of the chair. At the request of the Craven County coroner, Dr. Kerrison had performed an autopsy on the remains of Ovid Gilbert. After painstakingly qualifying the doctor as an expert witness, Phillips asked Kerrison to describe the autopsy. Elizabeth could see several female jurors flinch when the doctor described cutting open the head. Finally, Phillips got to the ultimate question, the cause of death.

"In my opinion, the deceased died as a result of his head being severed from the torso," the doctor responded pompously. Elizabeth looked over and, catching Hamilton's attention, rolled her eyes.

"And do you have an opinion as to what caused the deceased's head to be severed from his body?"

"In my opinion, to a reasonable degree of medical certainty, I would say that it was caused by a sharp heavy object such as an ax."

Phillips walked back to his table, picked up a manila envelope, and pulled out a number of photographs. He approached the defense table and dropped them on the table in front of Elizabeth. "We are going to offer these," he said.

Elizabeth looked down and quickly closed her eyes. She also realized that she cringed just before she did so and knew it was a reaction she didn't want the jury to see. In the top photograph, the head of Ovid Gilbert was sitting on a stainless-steel slab in the Medical University forensic pathology lab. Elizabeth felt a wave of nausea as she opened her eyes and looked at Lawson. She got to her feet without looking at the photographs again.

"Your Honor, may we approach the bench?" she asked, trying to sound as calm as she could.

"Okay," Lawson said, motioning with his hand for them to come forward. Both Phillips and his assistant, Jimmy Jacobs, wore smirks as the four lawyers converged at sidebar.

"What is it, Miss Chase?" Lawson asked impatiently.

"The solicitor is trying to introduce photographs of Mr. Gilbert's head. I think this is highly improper. I would ask that we take up the admissibility of these photographs outside the presence of the jury."

Lawson looked at Phillips, who shrugged and smiled.

"They're clearly admissible under our case law," the solicitor said.

"Well, I haven't even seen them yet. Let me send the jury out so we can put everything on the record." Lawson walked behind his chair and faced the jury. "Ladies and gentlemen, there is a matter of law which we have to take up outside your presence. It is time for our afternoon recess, anyway, so I am going to ask you to go to your jury room. I'm going to let the lawyers take a break after we get through with an evidentiary matter. Please keep in mind that you are not to discuss this case at all until I instruct you to do so at the conclusion of all of the evidence. The bailiff here will show you to your jury room."

As the judge sat down, the bailiff signaled to the twelve jurors and two alternates, who followed him up the steps that led to one of the rear doors. About a half-dozen spectators got up to leave at the same time, and Lawson quickly reached for his gavel and banged it loudly several times.

"You people sit down back there. Court is not in recess yet," he yelled, and the chastened offenders quickly retook their seats. Lawson waited until it was quiet in the courtroom before speaking again. "Let the record reflect that the jury has retired to the jury room. Miss Chase, I believe you had an objection you wanted to make outside the jury's presence."

"Yes sir, Your Honor," Elizabeth said. "The solicitor has handed me six eight-and-a-half-by-eleven color photographs of the deceased's head, which he intends to offer in evidence."

"Let the court reporter mark them for identification purposes only and then let me see them," Lawson said.

As the court reporter was marking exhibit tags to go on the photographs, Hamilton commented to Elizabeth, "Go ahead and state your objections, and maybe I can help you with the law."

Elizabeth nodded her assent. When the reporter had marked all the photographs, the bailiff handed them up to Lawson. The judge arched his eyebrows when he saw the first one, and he studied all six carefully.

"Okay, state your objection, Miss Chase."

"Your Honor, these photographs are so grotesque," she remarked and then looked at Hamilton.

"Your Honor, if I may say something?"

"Certainly, Mr. Hamilton. Go ahead."

"Thank you, Your Honor. It is not really in dispute that the deceased died as a result of decapitation. Therefore, these photographs are entirely unnecessary to substantiate the State's case. And our Supreme Court has long held that photographs are inadmissible when they can inflame the sympathies or prejudices of the jury. You've seen the photographs, Judge. They are the most gruesome ones I've seen in over fifty years of practicing law."

"I feel like Herod looking at the head of John the Baptist," Lawson replied. "They are pretty bad. Miss Chase, are you okay? You look a little pale."

"I'm all right, Judge, I think. Mr. Phillips caught me a little off guard," she said, looking at the solicitor. Phillips tried to maintain a serious demeanor, but it was clear to everyone in the courtroom that he was enjoying the moment.

"What do you say, Solicitor? Apparently there is no dispute about how the deceased died. You have to admit, they are pretty gory."

The smug look on Phillips' face immediately disappeared when he realized that Lawson might keep the photographs out by sustaining the objection. "Your Honor, they clearly show the manner in which the deceased met his very untimely death. The State can't help it if the photographs are gory. That's Willie Fulton's fault."

"I am unpersuaded by your argument, Solicitor," Lawson said. "You tried a murder case in front of me about a year ago, and you tried to get in photographs that weren't nearly this bad, remember? And I wouldn't admit those."

"But the facts were different in that case, Your Honor," Phillips said weakly.

"The facts are different in every case, Solicitor. Mr. Hamilton is correct in his statement of the law. Your objection is sustained, Miss Chase. We'll be in recess for fifteen minutes."

CHAPTER 23

When the trial resumed, Phillips stood up and said, "We have no further questions of Dr. Kerrison."

"Your witness, Miss Chase," Lawson stated.

"Thank you, Your Honor," Elizabeth said. "Good afternoon, Dr. Kerrison."

"Good afternoon," Dr. Kerrison replied, moving around in his chair, which took quite some effort.

"How long have you been a forensic pathologist, sir?"

"Thirty-three years."

"About how many autopsies would you say you have performed?"

The doctor smiled at Elizabeth, pursed his lips, and gazed out of one of the long windows in the courtroom. "Thousands," he said finally, looking back at Elizabeth.

"And how many autopsies have you performed when you had only the head to work with?"

He smiled at Elizabeth again. "I had a feeling that you were going to ask me that question. This is the only one that I can ever recall."

"And were you advised by the authorities here in Craven County prior to performing your autopsy that the deceased was believed to have been killed with an ax?"

"Yes, it was in their transmittal report, but that information didn't influence my findings in any way whatsoever."

"Not even subconsciously, Doctor?" Elizabeth shot back.

"Not even subconsciously," he said slowly. "I'm chairman of the pathology department, Miss Chase. I reached that position based upon my professional reputation. I earned that reputation based upon my work, not the work of others."

"Not having the body of the deceased to examine, you had no

way of knowing, did you, whether or not there were other wounds inflicted on the body?"

"The presence or absence of other wounds to the missing body would have no bearing on my ultimate opinion, Miss Chase. Are you suggesting to me that cutting a person's head off would not result in death?" He asked the question in a rapid, high-pitched voice as if he were lecturing a first-year medical student.

"Are you suggesting to me, Doctor, that it is not possible to cut a person's head off after they are dead?"

"Oh, I see what you are saying," he responded, the abrasiveness now gone from his voice. "Yes, it is possible to do so."

"For example, someone could have fatally shot Mr. Gilbert, severed his head, and then disposed of the body, isn't that correct?"

"No, you are mistaken, Miss Chase. The deceased would have to have been alive when his head was severed. The head was well preserved, because I specifically instructed the sheriff, Sheriff Carter, to put it on ice when he called me. Sheriff Carter did as he was instructed, and the head was delivered to me personally by the sheriff, iced down in a Styrofoam cooler. Since Sheriff Carter responded so quickly to my request, I can state, to a reasonable degree of medical certainty, that the deceased was alive when his head was severed."

"Well, let me ask you this, Dr. Kerrison. Couldn't the deceased have been unconscious when he was beheaded by this ax?"

"Yes, he could have."

"Then it would have been possible for someone to knock the deceased unconscious with a heavy object and then sever his head?"

"No, not in this case."

"Why not?" Elizabeth asked, walking toward the witness.

"Because there was absolutely no evidence of trauma to the head."

"Well, then the deceased could have been rendered unconscious by trauma to the body, such as a gunshot wound, couldn't he?"

"Yes, that's possible."

"And then someone could have decapitated him while he was still breathing, isn't that correct?"

"Yes," he answered.

"And you could state that to a reasonable degree of medical certainty, couldn't you?"

"I suppose I could," he answered.

"Okay, when the head was severed from Mr. Gilbert's body, wouldn't it be fair to assume that whoever did it would most probably have splattered blood on themselves?"

"On themselves, and everywhere else around them," he added, nodding.

"Now, Dr. Kerrison, you told Mr. Phillips on direct examination that in your opinion the head was severed by a sharp heavy object such as an ax."

"Yes, I did."

"But you can't state for certain that it was an ax, can you?"

"No, I can't, but I can't think of another instrument that would have severed the head other than an ax."

"The head could have been severed by some type of saw, couldn't it?"

"No, it couldn't have been severed by a saw. If I had my photographs, I could show you what I mean. The condition of the . . . "

"Your Honor, I move to strike that last statement concerning the photographs. Dr. Kerrison knows better than that." As Elizabeth made her objection, she stole a glance at Phillips, and the smirk had returned to his face.

"Ladies and gentlemen of the jury, please disregard that last statement by the witness." Lawson gave his instructions in a low monotone, as if he were reading the weather report out of a newspaper. "Don't mention the photographs anymore, Dr. Kerrison. Did you finish answering the question?"

"No, I didn't. The skin around the neck was not cut in a uniform pattern like a saw would do. There were dozens of random cuts that eventually caused the head to be separated from the body. I ruled out a saw entirely."

"But again, you cannot state to a reasonable degree of medical certainty that it was an ax, can you?"

"No, not completely."

Hamilton leaned forward in his chair and slid a scrap of yellow paper across the table to Elizabeth. She picked up the note and read it. "Move on to something else quick," it said.

Elizabeth walked over to the counsel table and leaned over close to Hamilton's face. "Can you think of anything else?" she asked.

"No, I'd leave him alone," Hamilton replied.

"That's all I have. Thank you, Dr. Kerrison." As she was sitting down, Elizabeth looked at Hamilton's anxious face.

Phillips stood up and reached for the pile of photographs that was sitting on the corner of his table. "Just a couple of questions, Your Honor," he said as he walked toward the witness stand, clutching the photographs in his left hand. "Dr. Kerrison, Miss Chase asked you several questions about what type of object was used to decapitate the deceased."

"Yes sir, she did."

"And you told her, I believe, that in your opinion it was an ax that was used by the assailant, based upon the way the skin on the deceased's neck had been cut?"

"Yes, I did."

"Did you or your staff take photographs of the head illustrating exactly what you are testifying about?"

"Yes, we did."

"And are these the photographs that you took, which have been marked as State's exhibit for identification one through six?" he asked, holding up the photographs.

"Your Honor, I object!" Elizabeth said, almost screaming. "You have already ruled that these photographs are inadmissible."

"Your Honor, I don't know how they try cases in Massachusetts, but in this state she has opened the barn door, and it is wide open. After Your Honor ruled that the photographs were inadmissible because they were unnecessary to substantiate the State's case, Miss Chase asked a series of questions about the manner in which the head was severed. The doctor has now testified that the photographs will, in essence, aid and illustrate his testimony."

"Miss Chase, I believe the solicitor is right. You have opened the door on this issue. I'm going to let the solicitor continue with this line of questioning."

"Thank you, Your Honor," Phillips said. The smirk had now turned into a twisted smile. "Dr. Kerrison, I think you told me a minute ago, before I was interrupted, that these photographs I hold in my hand were taken by you or your staff?"

"Yes, they were."

"And I hand you these photographs, which have been marked State's exhibit for identification one through six, and I ask you if you can identify them." Phillips passed the photographs to the doctor, folded his arms across his chest, and waited for an answer.

"Yes, I can. Those are the autopsy photographs showing the severed head of the deceased."

"And do the photographs reasonably and accurately depict the subject that was photographed?"

"Yes, they do."

"Dr. Kerrison, do these photographs in any way substantiate any of the opinions that you gave a few minutes earlier?"

"Yes, they do."

"In what way?"

"The photographs show the random cuts that caused the head to be severed from the body."

"Your Honor, we offer the photographs in evidence," Phillips said, taking the exhibits from the doctor.

Lawson looked at Elizabeth.

"May we have the Court's indulgence for a minute?" she asked. Lawson nodded. Elizabeth sat back down, leaned over, and whispered to Hamilton in a panicked voice, "I can't believe the judge is letting these photographs in now."

"Your Honor," Hamilton said, rising from his chair.

"Yes, Mr. Hamilton. I'm anxious to hear what you have to say on this issue."

"Even if Miss Chase opened the door, Your Honor, and we don't concede that she did, it's still a question of weighing the probative value of the photographs against their highly inflammatory nature. We still vigorously contend that these gory photographs are too inflammatory and should not be admitted into evidence."

"You have chosen your words well, Mr. Hamilton, but I'm going to overrule the objection."

"Is the judge right on this?" Elizabeth whispered to Hamilton as he sat down, trying to control her panic.

"It's a close call. Don't worry about it."

Phillips said, "Your Honor, we would like to pass the exhibits to the jurors and let them examine them at this time."

"You really want them to see them now?" Lawson asked.

"Yes sir, we do."

Lawson turned in his swivel chair to face the jury. "Ladies and gentlemen of the jury, in a minute you will have the opportunity to look at photographs of the deceased, or at least what was found of him. You do not have to look at them now if you don't want to. They have been admitted into evidence, so you will take them along with any other exhibits that may be introduced in this case to the jury room at the conclusion of the testimony, when you start your deliberations. You do not have to look at all of them if you don't want to. As a matter of fact, you don't have to look at any of them if you don't want to." Lawson then nodded at Phillips.

Phillips walked to the end of the jury box and handed the stack of photographs to Collards McGee. Hamilton told Elizabeth that Collards was a good person to start with, since he had served with the United States Marines in the South Pacific during the war and had probably seen some pretty gory things. All eyes in the courtroom were on him as he studied the top photograph for a few seconds and then quickly shuffled through the other five. When he finished, he turned to Marie Williams, a white retired schoolteacher, who grabbed the exhibits and passed them on to the black minister sitting next to her. He looked at the top picture and passed the stack as if he had been handed a water moccasin. The rest of the men on the panel looked at the top photograph and passed them over. Not a single female juror glanced at the photographs. Hamilton was thankful that the damage had been minimized for the moment, but he knew that the photographs would be discussed at length when the jury began their deliberations. When the exhibits came back to McGee, he put them on the rail in front of him, face down.

"I have no further questions," Phillips said, retreating to his seat with a skip in his step now.

"I'd leave him alone, Elizabeth," Hamilton counseled, grasping her arm. She nodded.

"We have no further questions of Dr. Kerrison."

"You may step down, Doctor," Lawson said. "Does the defense have any objections to excusing Dr. Kerrison so he can go back to work?"

Elizabeth looked at Hamilton, and he shook his head.

"No objections, Your Honor," Elizabeth said half-heartedly.

Lawson looked at his watch and turned to face the jury. "Ladies and gentlemen, it's almost five o'clock, and this is a good stopping point. We are going to break for the evening. Do not discuss this case tonight with anyone, including your spouse. Is that understood?"

The jurors nodded, almost in unison.

"Very well, then. Have a good night, and please be in the jury room promptly at nine thirty in the morning."

When they got back to the office, Elizabeth grabbed a Coke while Hamilton checked his messages. She was reading over her notes for the next day when he rejoined her.

"It was not such a good start," Elizabeth said, rubbing her neck.

"I thought, all in all, things went pretty well," Hamilton countered as he sat down.

"I screwed up, and everyone in that courtroom knows it, including Willie Fulton."

"The photographs didn't do as much damage as you think. They hardly looked at them, and there is no dispute about someone chopping off poor Frenchie's head," Hamilton said, trying to sound upbeat.

"But they will look at those pictures when they start deliberating, and they're awful. They literally made me sick to my stomach, Robert. I've seen some bad autopsy pictures, believe me, but nothing like these."

"Forget about the pictures, Elizabeth. I think we have a good jury. I could hardly be more pleased with who we drew."

"You do think we have a good jury?"

"Yes, I do. And you really hammered Sergeant Wilson."

"Yeah, but he really wasn't an important witness. He was sort of pitiful, if you ask me."

"The important thing is you started to sow the seeds of reasonable doubt and that's all we need, you know?"

"Kerrison really is a pompous jerk, isn't he?"

"He always has been," Hamilton said, shaking his head.

"Who do they have left to testify?"

"The lab man from SLED. We have those reports, so we know what he's going to say. Black Jack. Maybe a couple of witnesses to testify about the bad blood between Frenchie and Willie. Who else?"

"I can't think of anyone else that is remotely connected with the investigation," Elizabeth said, rubbing her temples with her fingertips.

"You look tired."

"I still get stressed out during trials, particularly when my client is looking at a very long jail sentence if we lose. And I guess it's this heat, too. Do we have a chance of Lawson directing a verdict?"

"Not really, in my opinion. They've got the ax, of course, and the matching blood. They've got evidence of bad blood, and Willie has no real alibi. That will be enough for Lawson to send it to the jury."

"We've got to put up Pearlie Mae, I think."

"I've been thinking about that, too, and I believe you're right. Let's sleep on it, okay?"

"When do you think the State will rest?"

"By lunch."

"That quickly?"

"Clarence is definitely not a detail man. It won't take him long tomorrow to wrap up his case. Why don't you go home and get some rest?"

"Do we need to go over anything tonight?"

"No, I don't think so. Willie is supposed to be here at eight in the morning, and we can go over his testimony one more time. If we decide to put up Pearlie Mae, we'll have time to go over her testimony, too."

CHAPTER 24

Pearlie Mae and Willie were standing on the sidewalk when Elizabeth pulled her grandfather's Buick up to the curb the next morning. She had slept poorly all night and was up by six o'clock, an hour before she usually got out of bed. A good strong scotch on the rocks would have made her sleep better, she thought, but she had a hard and fast rule of no alcohol during a trial.

"Good morning. You're both up early," Elizabeth said as she got out of the car.

"Miss Elizabeth, we got to talk," Willie told her.

"I know we do, Willie. We need to go over your testimony one more time and Pearlie Mae's in case we decide to call her as a witness. Mr. Hamilton will be here soon," she said, pushing against the old door as she turned the knob. "Come into the library," she instructed, walking ahead of them. "Would you like some coffee?" she asked over her shoulder.

"No ma'am" came the response in unison.

Elizabeth started the coffeepot, and Hamilton showed up several minutes later. "Did you sleep okay?" he asked as they stood waiting on the coffee to perk.

She looked at him and rolled her eyes. "Are you kidding? I never sleep well during a trial, and last night was no exception. How about you?"

"I slept like a baby until four this morning, and then I was wide awake, thinking about this case. I think we need to call Pearlie Mae," he said.

"I agree with you," Elizabeth replied, reaching for two mugs. "They're already in the library," she said, motioning with her head.

"We don't have much time," Hamilton remarked after he greeted the Fultons. "Pearlie Mae," he said softly, "we think it would help

Willie's case a lot if you told the jury where he was when Frenchie was killed."

"She ain't gonna testify, and I ain't gonna testify," Willie declared, sitting up in his chair.

"What are you saying, Willie? We've been over this dozens of times. You'll make good witnesses. You don't have to be afraid," Hamilton said in a calm voice.

"I ain't 'fraid of nothing, not even no jail. I just decided last night not to testify. I done a lot of praying last night, me and Pearlie Mae both. The Lord told me and her not to get on that stand. That everything gonna be all right like it is."

Elizabeth looked to Hamilton for help. She knew that this was a horrible dream and that she would wake up any second now.

"Willie, you and Pearlie Mae listen to me," Hamilton said, just above a whisper. "Maybe we can get by without you testifying, Pearlie Mae, but that jury needs to hear from Willie. They need to hear him say he didn't kill Frenchie."

"But they know I didn't kill him. They know I'm pleading not guilty. Miss Elizabeth already told 'em so."

It was Hamilton this time who looked to Elizabeth for help. She just shook her head slowly, her eyes wide with panic.

"What has made you change your mind like this at the last minute, Willie?" Hamilton asked. "We've planned your whole defense around your testimony. That's why we've worked so hard with you. It all boils down to your word against the evidence that the State has against you."

"They don't have enough evidence to convict me," Willie said firmly.

"We don't know that, Willie," Hamilton replied calmly. "This morning in court they are going to introduce into evidence an ax that they say was found . . ."

"That ain't my ax," Willie said angrily.

"Let me finish, please," Hamilton told him politely, holding up his hand.

"I'm sorry for cutting 'cross you, Mr. Hamilton. You go right ahead. I'm listening."

"They're going to show the jury an ax they said they found in your hog parlor, and they are going to say that the ax has blood on it. And they have a man coming from Columbia who tested the blood, and he is going to say that the blood came from Frenchie."

Hamilton saw no point in telling Willie that he and Elizabeth also had an expert analyze the blood samples and his report corroborated the findings of the SLED chemist. Willie and Pearlie Mae were both sitting back in their chairs, listening passively, looking at Hamilton like two people sitting on a bench waiting for a city bus. "It will take just a few minutes for you to get on the stand and tell that jury your story. Will you do that?"

"Miss Elizabeth done told that jury my side of the story. They already know what I'm gonna say."

"Willie, I've already told that jury that you would testify and tell your side of the story." Hamilton watched as she squeezed the edge of the table so hard her knuckles turned white. "How do you think they will react if you don't do what I told them you would do?"

Willie shrugged. "Ain't it up to me?"

"As to whether or not you testify?"

"Yes ma'am."

"Yes, it is," Elizabeth said. "We've explained all of that to you a number of times."

"But haven't you told me and Miss Chase a number of times when we were discussing your case that we were the lawyers, and you said you would do whatever we recommended?" Hamilton asked, his voice rising for the first time.

"Yes sir, but we decided last night that this was the one thing we would make up our own minds on, ain't that right, Pearlie Mae?" Willie asked, looking at his wife.

"That's right," Pearlie Mae said, staring at her hands folded in her lap.

"Willie, have you and Pearlie Mae been talking about your case with someone else?" Hamilton asked, looking first at Willie and then at Pearlie Mae for an answer.

"No sir," Willie said, shaking his head.

"Willie, do you understand that what I told the jury at the beginning of the case is not evidence?" Elizabeth asked.

"I'm not clear what you're saying," he answered.

Elizabeth thought for a moment, choosing her words carefully. "I was only telling the jury what evidence we were going to have on our side of the case. Now we are not going to have *any* evidence on our side, do you understand that?"

"I think so," he said, "but it ain't gonna matter."

Elizabeth and Hamilton exchanged glances. "Willie, Miss Chase and I need to talk a minute," Hamilton said. "Would you and Pearlie Mae mind waiting up front?"

"No sir," they said as they got up.

"We'll be with you in a few minutes," Hamilton promised as he closed the door behind them. "What do you think?" he asked after he sat down.

"You tell me. You know these people better than I do," Elizabeth shot back.

"I don't know if it's fear, or if they really think the Lord told them not to testify," Hamilton said. "But I don't believe that we're going to change their minds."

"Then what the hell are we going to do?" Elizabeth asked as she put her elbows on the conference table, grabbed her cheeks, and exhaled loudly.

"I don't know. We've kinda painted ourselves into a corner, haven't we?"

"What do you mean 'we,' Robert? You're being very gracious. You mean *I've* painted us into a corner. I was the one who insisted on laying out our whole case in the opening. This has never happened to me before," she added, closing her eyes. "Where do we go from here?"

"We'll just have to do the best we can with what we have."

"And what if it isn't good enough?" Elizabeth asked, leaning back in her chair.

"Elizabeth, all we can do is our best. Neither you nor I had any way of knowing that Willie was going to change his mind about testifying. But this is still a winnable case. All they really have is the ax. You've already punched some holes in their case, and we only need one good hole in it to win. Stop blaming yourself for everything that doesn't go just like we want it to, okay?"

"Okay," she said weakly.

CHAPTER 25

"All rise!" the bailiff cried, signaling the start of the trial.

"Thank you. You may be seated. Bailiff, do we have all of the jurors present?" Lawson asked.

"Yes sir," Hank Richardson replied.

"Bring the jury in, then."

Richardson, a World War I veteran, started slowly up the steps to summon the panel.

"What the hell?" Lawson asked, standing up again. "Bailiff, wait a minute." Lawson walked around the bench, never taking his eyes off the witness stand. "Shirley, look at this stuff," he said, pointing at the witness stand.

The clerk got up from her desk and walked quickly over to the witness stand. The chair that the witness sits in was blocked from view by a waist-high partition, and Shirley rested both arms on it as she looked down.

"Oh my God!" she cried. "What is that?"

On the floor in front of the chair was a semicircle of white powder about a half-inch wide. Phillips rushed to the front of the courtroom to see what they were looking at, and Elizabeth and Hamilton were quick to follow.

"Do any of you lawyers have any idea what this stuff is?" Lawson asked. Everyone shook their heads. "Shirley, get the janitor in here to clean this mess up."

"Go get Lawrence—he's down on the first floor in the boiler room," Shirley said to the bailiff.

Several minutes later, Lawrence DeWitt, a tall gangly black man in his early sixties, walked into the courtroom carrying a broom and a dustpan. Shirley motioned him over to where they were standing and pointed at the white powder on the floor. "The judge wants this cleaned up right away."

Lawrence leaned over the partition. When he saw the white powder, he dropped the broom and the dustpan at the same time and took a step back.

"No, I can't do that, Miss Shirley. I can't touch that, no ma'am." Elizabeth and Hamilton could see the man's hands shaking.

"I'm telling you, Mr. Janitor, I'm going to my chambers for five minutes, and when I get back, that white powder better be cleaned up, or I'm going to hold you in contempt and put you in jail. Do you understand me?" Lawson almost shouted the question as he pointed his finger at the man.

"Your Honor, please don't make me touch that powder," Lawrence pleaded. "I'll get somebody to clean it up, I promise."

"You're the janitor here, and it's your job to clean up that mess." He stormed off to his chambers.

As soon as Lawson left the courtroom, Shirley looked at Lawrence, who had now broken out in a sweat, and shook her head. "Just go on back downstairs, Lawrence, and finish what you were doing. Richardson and I'll get this up," she said, reaching for the broom.

"Thank you, Miss Shirley," he responded and immediately disappeared.

As the clerk and bailiff were working, Elizabeth walked over to their counsel table, where Willie and Pearlie Mae were sitting in silence. "Do you have any idea what all this is about?" she asked.

"Just a little protection, that's all," Willie said calmly.

"What did you say?" Elizabeth asked, putting her palms on the table and leaning over.

"All rise!" the bailiff shouted for the second time, and Lawson was back on the bench before she could get an answer from Willie.

The judge leaned over and examined the witness box before he sat down. "I'm glad to see the janitor came to his senses. I would have hated to put that man in jail for something that silly. Now, we're ready to bring the jury in," Lawson said, nodding at Hank Richardson.

"Good morning, ladies and gentlemen. I trust you all slept well and no one discussed this case with anyone," Lawson said once the jury was seated. "Solicitor, you may call your next witness."

"Thank you, Your Honor. If the Court pleases, the State calls Edward Wellingham."

A chubby man in his early forties got up from the front row and approached the clerk's desk to be sworn. Elizabeth and Hamilton recognized the name as the chemist from SLED headquarters in Columbia who had performed the blood analysis. Phillips spent ten minutes qualifying him and another twenty minutes going over his procedures and findings, on several occasions asking the witness the same question three times. After the chemist had been on the stand for half an hour, Elizabeth noticed that McGee and two of the black men on the jury had dozed off. As expected, Wellingham testified that the blood samples he examined all matched the blood of the deceased.

As their expert had confirmed the match, Elizabeth and Hamilton saw no point in questioning the procedures or findings of the State's expert. They had decided to argue later that the ax in evidence may have been used to kill Frenchie, but Willie didn't do it. When Elizabeth stood and advised the Court that the defense had no questions, Phillips looked surprised, as if he thought this would be a hotly contested issue.

"You may be excused," Lawson said, nodding to the witness. "Call your next witness, Solicitor."

The next two witnesses Phillips called were deputies who helped establish the chain of custody for the blood samples. In order for the samples and ax to be admitted into evidence, it was necessary for the State to account for the whereabouts of the evidence at all times. These officers had properly made all the necessary entries on the logbooks, and neither Elizabeth nor Hamilton saw any need to cross-examine these harmless witnesses. When Elizabeth stood up and said "no questions" for the third consecutive time, Phillips had a smug look on his face, as if he was on a roll.

"We call Caesar Shaw," Phillips said, motioning to one of the deputies near the back of the courtroom. The deputy left the courtroom, and Shaw appeared in the doorway. He was in his early thirties, about six two, and a very muscular black man. He wore jeans, a tight-fitting brown T-shirt, and flip-flops. His head was shaved, and around his neck were four gold chains that nicely complemented both of his gold-capped front teeth. He was sworn by the clerk and, after giving his name, slumped into the witness chair.

Phillips asked for Shaw's full name, then turned and pointed across the room at Willie. "Do you know the defendant, Willie Fulton, sitting over there by his lawyers?"

"Yeah, I know him," Shaw said.

"And how long have you known him?"

"Long time."

"Years?"

"Oh, yeah."

"How many years?" Phillips asked impatiently.

"Eight or ten. I dunno." Shaw said, shrugging.

"Where do you live, Caesar?"

"You mean where I stay at?"

"Yes, where do you sleep at night?" Phillips asked, folding his arms across his chest.

"Off the River Road, 'bout eight or ten miles from here."

"Caesar, did you know a man who lived out that way? His name was Ovid Gilbert, but everyone called him 'Frenchie.'"

"Yeah, I knew Frenchie."

"Do you know whether or not Frenchie knew Willie Fulton?"

"Yeah, they knew each other."

"How do you know that?"

"We used to play cards together. Gamble a little bit. One night I seen 'em get into a big argument."

"Your Honor, I object," Elizabeth said, jumping out of her seat like a rocket.

"On what basis, Miss Chase?" Lawson asked, looking over the top of his glasses.

"May we approach the bench, Your Honor?"

Lawson waved them up to the sidebar. "We don't even know what he's going to say, Elizabeth," Lawson said as they gathered by the bench. She was surprised that he used her first name, but she thought it was a good sign.

"I don't know either," Elizabeth said. "I anticipate that the solicitor will attempt to establish prior misconduct on the part of the defendant. I think we at least ought to send the jury to the jury room and hear what he has to say. If you don't, there is always the danger of a mistrial."

"I don't have any problem with that. Do you, Clarence?"

"No, I guess not, Your Honor," Phillips said halfheartedly.

Once the door closed behind the last juror, Lawson nodded to Phillips.

"Caesar, before I was interrupted, I had asked you whether or not Frenchie and the defendant knew each other, and you told me that they did. Tell us how you know that."

"I told you I seen 'em get in an argument one time," Caesar said.

"When was that?"

"Last summer sometime."

"How do you remember it as being last summer?"

"'Cause a couple of Willie's hogs got loose, and they was over in Frenchie's garden eating his tomatoes."

"Was the deceased angry?"

"Who?"

"Frenchie. Was he angry?"

"Shore he was mad. Anybody woulda been mad if somebody else's hogs was eating their tomatoes."

There were a few snickers from the spectators. Lawson banged his gavel several times, but he didn't erupt into one of his tirades.

"What did Frenchie say?"

"He say a lot of things. Most of it was in French talk, I guess. I did recognize a few cuss words. Then he get in Willie's face and point his finger."

"What did Willie do?"

"He slap his hand down. Then he told Frenchie that if he ever put he hand in his face again he would be sorry."

"He said he would be sorry?" Phillips asked dramatically, apparently forgetting that the jury wasn't in the courtroom. After a pause he stated, "Your Honor, that's basically what this witness knows, and every word of it is admissible."

"Miss Chase, what is your objection?"

Elizabeth and Hamilton knew that Phillips was going to offer some type of evidence about bad blood between Frenchie and Willie because Willie had admitted to it. As a result, Elizabeth had spent hours and hours of research in the library on the <u>South Carolina</u> case law on this point. In most cases like this, certain types of evidence were admissible, she had discovered to her disappointment.

"Your Honor, I have read most, if not all, of the <u>South Carolina</u>

Supreme Court cases on the issue of prior difficulties or bad blood between the deceased and the defendant. In most of the cases, prior misconduct is admissible. But here, we have no evidence of a defense of self-defense. For all we know, the deceased died in his sleep. We submit that evidence of prior misconduct or bad blood is admissible only when self-defense has been raised."

"What do you say about that, Mr. Phillips?"

Phillips swallowed hard. "Your Honor, you have always allowed evidence of prior aggression in."

"Yes, but I believe that they were all self-defense cases. We don't know if the defendant is going to raise the issue of self-defense, at least not now, do we?"

Phillips shrugged and looked at his assistant.

"Anything else, Miss Chase?" Lawson asked.

"One other thing, Your Honor. The defendant has done nothing to put his character at issue. As I read your case law, until a defendant does that, the State can offer no evidence of a defendant's character. What the State is trying to show through this witness is that Mr. Fulton is a violent gambler. And on that basis I also object."

"This is not character evidence, Your Honor. It simply shows the ill feelings between the deceased and the defendant." Phillips' voice was high pitched with emotion, as if he knew he was losing the most critical argument in the trial so far.

"Let's take a fifteen-minute break while the jury is out and let me think about it. Besides, I've got to make a phone call," Lawson said, looking at his watch.

When Lawson finally returned to the bench and sat down, he had a pensive look on his face. "I have spent the entire recess looking through my trial notebook. I didn't even get a chance to make my call," he said with a trace of a smile appearing on his lips. Hamilton had assured Elizabeth that they would get a fair shake on these issues from Lawson because he was a student of the law, and what he didn't know, he didn't mind looking up. You couldn't say the same for a lot of other judges in <u>South Carolina</u>.

"Miss Chase, you have made several convincing arguments. And let me say, I am impressed with your preparation. To be honest, I had grave doubts about a woman lawyer from Massachusetts trying a murder case in my court. You have shown me that my doubts were unfounded. As far as ruling on the admissibility of Mr. Shaw's testimony, I am going to let him testify concerning an altercation that the deceased had with the defendant over the defendant's hogs, under *State v. Lyle*. It goes, Miss Chase, to show the possible identity of the intruder in the garden. But I'm not going to let the witness go into any further details of this conversation, including this alleged threat. And I also agree with you, Miss Chase, that any testimony by this witness relative to the defendant's gambling habits is a reflection on the defendant's character, although from what I know about this county, most people would not consider gambling a character defect. When I bring the jury back in, I will instruct them to disregard any references to gambling. Now, do both of you understand my ruling?"

"Yes, Your Honor," Phillips replied.

"I understand, Your Honor," Elizabeth said. Although she was not pleased with the ruling, it was obviously the best she could expect under the circumstances. She had minimized the damage, but what bothered her was that at the break, Willie was adamant in saying that he had never played cards with Caesar Shaw and that Shaw was in jail, he believed, when he and Frenchie got into their argument last summer.

Once the jury was brought back into the courtroom, Lawson instructed them to disregard any reference to the defendant's alleged gambling and nodded to Phillips to proceed with his direct examination.

"Thank you, Your Honor. Now, Caesar, my last question to you before our break was how did you know that the defendant and Frenchie knew each other. Do you remember that?"

"Yeah, I remember," Caesar said.

"Now tell the jury how you know that." Phillips instructed as he looked at the jury.

"I already told you that I seen 'em argue."

"What were they arguing about?"

"Frenchie say . . ."

"Your Honor, I object. That is hearsay, and it is also contrary to your ruling," Elizabeth said.

"Sustained. On both grounds. Solicitor, you make sure your

witness testifies in accordance with my guidelines, or I'm not going to let him testify at all, you understand?"

"Yes sir, Your Honor. Now, Caesar, just tell us what they were arguing about," Phillips said, holding his arms out as if he could control his witness with them.

Shaw looked at the judge and then answered, "They was arguing about Willie's hogs eating Frenchie's tomatoes."

Phillips glanced at Lawson, then walked over and whispered in his assistant's ear. Jacobs nodded.

"That's all we have. Your witness."

As Elizabeth was about to get up, Hamilton grabbed her forearm. She leaned over so he could whisper in her ear. "Willie says he is sure Caesar was in jail last summer for selling marijuana when he and Frenchie got into an argument. He says Caesar was in there four or five months. Pearlie Mae verified it with her brother sitting behind us on the front row." Elizabeth turned around and spotted a man sitting directly behind Willie who had to be Pearlie Mae's brother, the resemblance was so marked. The man nodded at Elizabeth.

"That's fine, but how do we prove that?" Elizabeth whispered.

"We can subpoena the jail records," Hamilton said.

"It won't hurt to ask this witness, will it?" Elizabeth was referring to one of the Ten Commandments in the art of cross-examination: never ask a witness a question that you don't already know the answer to, because the witness may blow you out of the water with his reply.

"No, go fishing," Hamilton said, squeezing her arm.

Elizabeth got up and walked across the courtroom, stopping several feet from the witness. Shaw was still slumped back in his chair, but he never took his eyes off Elizabeth.

"Good morning, Mr. Shaw," she said pleasantly. Shaw said nothing. "Mr. Shaw, tell us, what kind of work do you do?"

"I'm not employed at the present."

"When was the last time you held a job?"

"I dunno."

"Was it over a year ago?"

"Yeah, it was over a year ago," he said with a sarcastic tone.

"Could it have been as much as two years ago?"

"Yeah, that's about right."

"What kind of work did you do about two years ago when you last worked?"

"Cut grass on a golf course at the beach," he said.

"Who do you live with? Are you married?"

"No, I ain't married. I stay with my girlfriend."

"Whose house do you stay in?"

"It's her house. She got a trailer house."

"Does she work?"

"No, she don't work. She used to."

"Where did she work?"

"At a sewing plant."

"When did she last work there?"

"'Bout six months ago."

"Do you have any children living with you?"

"Yeah, she got two head, but they ain't mine."

"Do you get any government assistance?"

"You mean a check?"

"Yes, a check."

"Yeah, she gets two hundred and some odd dollars a month."

"Do either of you have any other income on a monthly basis?"

"No."

"Is there a mortgage on the trailer?"

"What?"

"Is the trailer paid for?"

"No."

"How much is the payment?"

"The payment is about one hundred eighty something a month."

"It doesn't leave much to live on does it, Mr. Shaw?" Elizabeth asked in a deferential tone so as to not antagonize any jurors who might have to struggle to make ends meet.

"We get by all right. I do little odd jobs here and there to make ends meet."

"And who do you do these odd jobs for?"

"Different people," he said, shrugging. "I work in a club two or three times a month when they get shorthanded."

"And what is the name of this club, Mr. Shaw?"

"Up Jump the Devil."

"Excuse me?" Elizabeth asked, moving closer to the witness.

"The name of the club is Up Jump the Devil," Shaw said very slowly.

"Up Jump the Devil?"

"You got it," Shaw said.

"And how much would you say you earned on a monthly basis at Up Jump the Devil?"

Shaw rubbed his chin and thought for a few seconds. "Probably forty or fifty dollars a month," he said finally.

"Now, Mr. Shaw, you have told us that you saw an argument between Willie Fulton and Frenchie last summer?"

"Yeah, I did."

"Were you visiting Willie Fulton?"

"Yeah."

"A friendly visit?"

"Yeah. I've known Willie for a long time. Me and him was playing cards that night," Shaw said, looking over at Fulton.

"And then Frenchie came over, and he was angry?"

"Yeah, I told you he was mad about Willie's hogs getting into his garden and eating his tomatoes."

"And this was last summer, you're sure?"

Shaw leaned forward in his chair and stared at Elizabeth briefly. "Lady, if you was from 'round here, you woulda known it had to be in the summer, 'cause people here don't grow tomatoes in the wintertime."

There was a loud outburst of laughter from the spectators, and even Phillips and Jacobs were grinning at their witness's response. Lawson grabbed his gavel and slammed it down hard four times, pushing his chair back quickly to stand up.

"We are going to have order in this court!" he yelled in a voice that could be heard in the middle of Lee Street. "If I hear one more peep from you people, I'm going to clear this courtroom." Lawson's face was flushed, and a large vein was sticking out on the side of his neck. "Mr. Shaw," he said as he sat down again.

"Yes sir," Shaw answered.

"You just answer the questions put to you by these lawyers and say nothing else. If you get smart again, I'm going to hold you in contempt, and you will be a guest of Craven County tonight. Do you understand me?"

"Yes sir," Shaw said quickly, sitting up straight for the first time.

Elizabeth walked over to the defense table and pulled a thin file out of an expandable file folder. "May I have the Court's indulgence for a moment, Your Honor?"

"Certainly, Miss Chase," Lawson said.

Elizabeth studied the file before pulling out a single sheet of paper. She walked over to within six feet of the witness, holding the document in front of her, chest high. In her hand was a letter that had been written to Phillips weeks earlier about the SLED blood analysis, and it had absolutely nothing to do with this witness. She was trying to bluff Shaw into thinking that she had his rap sheet in her hand. It was a trick she had picked up from watching one of Boston's best trial lawyers.

"You got into some trouble with the law last year, didn't you?" she asked.

"We object, Your Honor," Phillips said as he stood up. "The defense has laid no foundation for this question."

"This is cross-examination, Solicitor. Objection overruled."

"You can answer my question now, Mr. Shaw."

Shaw looked at Phillips as if he wanted help. "Yeah, I got arrested for something I didn't do. If you wanna call that trouble."

Elizabeth walked back to the defense table, pulled another document out, read it for a few seconds, and walked back to where she had been standing.

"And what were you charged with, Mr. Shaw?"

"Your Honor, we object to this line of questioning," Phillips said as he quickly came around his table and walked over to Elizabeth. "Your Honor, Miss Chase obviously hasn't studied our rules of evidence as much as she has our case law. She is trying to impeach this witness by apparently trying to show that he was convicted of a crime of moral turpitude. And she can't do that because Mr. Shaw hasn't been convicted of anything. He has a spotless criminal record, so the question is highly improper."

"I'm going to overrule your objection, Solicitor. I think she can ask the witness questions concerning his whereabouts and what he was doing when he observed this alleged argument between the defendant and the victim. Go ahead—answer the question, Mr. Shaw."

"What was the question again?" Shaw asked, shifting in his seat.
"What were you charged with?" Mr. Shaw.
"They say I was selling marijuana."
"And you were in jail for quite some time on that charge, weren't you?"
"Well, I didn't have no choice. They set my bond so high. None of my people could bond me out."
"When did they lock you up?"
"They came and lock me up May twelfth. I remember it exactly because it was two days before my birthday."
"How long did you stay in jail, Mr. Shaw?"
"I got out right before Thanksgiving."
"Your family was able to post the bond?"
"No. The sheriff talked to the magistrate for me, and the magistrate changed it to a PR bond."
"A personal-recognizance bond?"
"Yeah."
"Isn't that where you sign your name stating that you will appear in court, and you don't have to put up any money?" Elizabeth knew what it meant but she wanted to make sure the jury did, too.
"That's right."
"Why did the sheriff do that?"
"I dunno," he said, shrugging.
"Have you ever been tried on these charges, Mr. Shaw?"
"Not yet. They still pending."
"Do you know when your case will come up?"
"No. Nobody has said nothing about it."
Elizabeth walked back to the defense table, turned around, and faced Shaw from across the courtroom. "Let me ask you one more question, Mr. Shaw. And you will have to help me with this because you are right, I am from up North, and I don't know anything about growing tomatoes. When do you start harvesting tomatoes? What month?"
"You mean, when do they start getting red so you can eat 'em?"
"Yes, that's what I mean."
"Around the fourth, I guess."
"The fourth of what?"

"The Fourth of July," Shaw said, cutting his head at her as if it was a trick question.

"And when do you plant them?"

"April or May, depending on the weather."

"Your Honor," Phillips said, "I know this is cross-examination, but this witness is not here for the sole purpose of instructing Miss Chase on how to grow tomatoes. I suggest she buy a *Farmer's Almanac* and quit wasting the Court's time."

"Objection overruled, Solicitor," Lawson said, motioning for Phillips to sit down.

"And when did you say you plant them?"

"April or May."

"And when do you first see tomatoes on the plants?"

"Around the first of June, I guess."

Elizabeth looked at Hamilton, and he nodded once. "That's all I have, Mr. Shaw. Thank you very much."

"Redirect, Solicitor?"

"Just a few questions, Your Honor," Phillips said, straightening his tie. "Now, Caesar, you can't really be certain about when you were locked up, can you?"

"Yes, I can. I'm telling you, if you was locked up two days before your birthday, wouldn't you remember it, too?"

Phillips glared at his witness for several seconds and sat down.

"You may step down," Lawson said to Shaw. "Call your next witness, Solicitor."

CHAPTER 26

"Your Honor, we call Sheriff Jack Carter."

"Come forward, Sheriff, and be sworn," Lawson said as Carter got up from his seat at the solicitor's table next to Jacobs.

Phillips elicited from Black Jack everything he had done in the military and in his law-enforcement career. Although many of the details were boring, Elizabeth saw that every member of the jury watched the sheriff very carefully. He sat ramrod straight in the witness chair, and when he answered Phillips' questions, he turned toward the jury before he gave his answer. Elizabeth had to admit he made an impressive witness.

Finally, Phillips moved to the facts of their case. "Now, Sheriff, were you performing your duties as the sheriff of Craven County on June seventh of this year?" Phillips' manner became very formal.

"Yes sir, I was."

"And did anything unusual happen on that date?"

"Yes sir, very unusual. We had a homicide here in the county on that date. We haven't had many here since I was elected sheriff."

"When did you learn of this homicide?"

"It was just after lunch when the call came through the dispatcher. I was reading a report from SLED. That's the State Law Enforcement Division," he added for the benefit of the jury.

"What did you do then?"

"I went to the crime scene with a backup team."

"And where was this crime scene?"

"Nine point two miles out the River Road and then down a dirt road for seven-tenths of a mile," he said with military precision.

"This crime scene that you located, was it a residence or a commercial establishment or what?"

"It was the residence of Mr. Ovid Gilbert."

"And who was this Ovid Gilbert?"

"He was a Frenchman who came here five or six years ago. He was a friendly, talkative sort of man. No one knew a whole lot about him, though, because he never talked about his past."

"How did Mr. Gilbert earn his living?"

"He repaired clocks, watches, umbrellas, things like that. In the summer he sold vegetables out of his garden. He couldn't have made a lot of money, but then again he didn't need much, the way he lived."

"He lived modestly?"

"Very modestly. He rented an old sharecropper's house from Warren Tisdale."

"Tell us what you found when you got to Mr. Gilbert's place."

"The first thing we noticed was the blood. There was blood everywhere." Black Jack described in great detail the scene and the physical evidence he and his officers had found. Elizabeth continued to watch the jury, and they seemed mesmerized by his testimony.

"At some point in your investigation, did you come up with any suspects?"

"I knew immediately after I surveyed the scene that I wanted to talk to Willie Fulton because he was the closest neighbor. I don't know if I would have considered him a suspect at that point in time, though."

"And this is the defendant you are speaking of?" Phillips asked, turning and pointing at Willie.

"Yes sir."

"And did you speak with the defendant?"

"Yes sir, I did."

"What did he say?"

"Well, before he said anything I read him his Miranda Rights. I did this even though this was not a custodial interrogation, and the Miranda warnings were not necessary under the law. I didn't want to take any chances."

"What rights did you advise the defendant of?"

Black Jack pulled a small card from his breast pocket. "I always read them," he said, holding the card up. "I advised Mr. Fulton that he had the right to remain silent, that anything that he said might be used against him in a court of law, that he had the right to the assistance of an attorney, and that if he could not afford an attorney, the court would appoint one for him."

"And did Mr. Fulton seem to understand his rights?"

"Yes sir, I believe he did."

"And did Mr. Fulton exercise his constitutional rights and remain silent?"

"No sir, he said he would be glad to talk to me."

"What did Mr. Fulton tell you?"

"I asked him if he had seen his neighbor, Mr. Gilbert, except that I referred to him as Frenchie since that is what everyone called him."

"And what was his response?"

"He said that he hadn't seen Frenchie in about a week. That he had been too busy with his tobacco."

"What else did you ask him?"

"I told him that I had just come from Frenchie's place, that someone had killed his dog and maybe Frenchie, too."

"What was his response?"

"He acted surprised. He said, 'Dear Jesus, God in Heaven.' Then I asked Mr. Fulton if he heard anything unusual that day and he told me no. And then I asked him if he knew anything about what happened at Frenchie's and he said no. So then I asked him if he would mind if some of my deputies looked around his place."

"What did he say?"

Elizabeth knew what the answer was so she didn't object. Willie had readily agreed to allow the deputies to search his place without a search warrant. As there was no trickery or coercion on the part of the law-enforcement officers, it was a valid waiver by Willie. Elizabeth and Hamilton both knew that Lawson was going to admit the ax into evidence, and Willie's willingness to allow the officers to search his place lent credibility to their contention that Willie knew nothing about the ax.

"He said, 'Go right ahead. I don't have anything to hide.'"

"And did your officers conduct a search of the Fulton place?"

"Yes sir, they did."

"And did you find any evidence that led you to believe that Willie Fulton was involved in the murder of Mr. Gilbert?"

"Yes sir, we did. Corporal Floyd came and got me about thirty minutes after they started the search. He took me to a hog parlor about a hundred yards behind Mr. Fulton's house. Corporal Floyd had pulled back some straw and an ax was lying on the ground. Actually it was lying in the muck in the pen."

"Would you describe the ax for us?"

"It was a regular ax but it had blood all over it."

Phillips walked behind his table and picked up the ax, walked over to the witness stand, and handed it to the sheriff. "I hand you what has been marked as State's exhibit number eight for identification and ask you if you can identify it."

"Yes sir, I can. That's the ax that we found in Mr. Fulton's hog pen."

"Your Honor, we offer this blood-stained ax into evidence."

"What say the defense?"

Elizabeth and Hamilton had spent a lot of time discussing the pros and cons of objecting to the admission of the ax into evidence. They knew Lawson was going to let it in because Phillips and Black Jack had done everything by the book. The only reason to object was to preserve the issue for appeal, but that consideration was outweighed by their fear that the jury might think they were hiding something from them if they objected. They had decided to keep quiet.

"No objection, Your Honor."

"Very well, admitted as State's exhibit number eight," Lawson said in a monotone.

"Now, Sheriff, did you confront Mr. Fulton with this very damaging piece of evidence?"

"Your Honor, we object to the Solicitor's characterization of the ax as being damaging," Elizabeth said.

"Don't get into your jury argument yet, Solicitor. Rephrase the question," Lawson said.

"Okay, Your Honor. Now, Sheriff, did you confront the defendant with this piece of evidence?"

"Yes sir, I did."

"What explanation did he give?"

"He got real upset, claimed he didn't know anything about it."

"What did you do then?"

"I placed him under arrest for the murder of Mr. Ovid Gilbert and took him to the county jail and booked him."

"Now, Sheriff Carter, to this day, has the defendant Willie

Fulton given you any explanation as to why this bloody ax was buried in his hog pen?" As Phillips asked the question, he picked up the ax and raised it high over his head.

"No sir," Black Jack answered in a resonant voice, staring at the jury. "Your witness."

Elizabeth stood up, and as she approached the sheriff, she could feel her stomach tighten. She knew she had to be careful in her cross-examination because Black Jack was like a coiled rattlesnake, ready to strike. Hamilton had warned her that he handled himself well on cross-examination, and if you gave him too much leeway with a question, or asked the wrong one, he could bury you and your client very quickly. Nor did she want to be too heavy-handed with him, for fear of alienating the black people on the jury.

"Good morning, Sheriff," she said, smiling briefly.

"Good morning, Counselor," he answered very politely.

Elizabeth asked Black Jack a number of benign questions about the investigation, but primarily she was trying to get a feel for the witness. He appeared to Elizabeth to be very deliberate, helpful, and forthright with his answers. Then she moved on to the points she wanted to focus upon.

"You told the solicitor that Willie Fulton was the first person you wanted to talk to?"

"Yes ma'am, I did."

"And when you asked Mr. Fulton to talk with you, he readily agreed?"

"Yes ma'am."

"And after you told Mr. Fulton what you had found at Mr. Gilbert's place, he acted surprised?"

"Yes, I would say he was surprised. And very upset."

"Wouldn't that have been a natural reaction from anyone who had just learned that their neighbor had probably been murdered?"

"Yes, I guess so."

"And when you asked if some of your officers could search his place, he readily agreed again, didn't he?"

"Yes ma'am."

"Wouldn't you agree with me, Sheriff Carter, that Willie Fulton, on the day that this murder was committed, certainly acted as if he had nothing to hide?"

"At least not at that time," the sheriff replied.

Elizabeth thought the snake was ready to strike as soon as an opening appeared. "Now, Sheriff, as far as the crime scene, you have described pretty much every detail of it for the jury, haven't you?"

"I think so, yes ma'am."

"And neither you nor any of your officers found any physical evidence at Mr. Gilbert's place that implicated Willie Fulton, did you?"

"We saw where the defendant's hogs tore up Mr. Gilbert's garden."

"Sheriff Carter, you can't even be sure that it was hogs that tore up Mr. Gilbert's garden, can you?"

"No, but I've seen what hogs can do to a garden and, in my opinion, that's what caused the damage."

"But you can't be sure, can you?"

"No, no one can be sure unless they saw them."

"And even if it were hogs that did the damage, you can't be sure it was Mr. Fulton's hogs, can you?"

"No, but he had the closest hog pen."

"Now, going back to my earlier question, you did not find any physical evidence placing Mr. Fulton at the scene of the murder, did you?"

"Not at the scene, but, of course, finding the ax was all we needed."

"Sheriff Carter, without the ax, you wouldn't have any evidence with which to charge Mr. Fulton with murder, and we wouldn't be here today, would we?"

"No, we wouldn't."

"And I think you told the jury earlier on direct examination that the ax was found in a hog pen about a hundred yards behind Mr. Fulton's house?"

"That is correct."

"And the river is back behind the hog pen?"

"Yes, it is."

"About how far?"

"I'd say about another 150 yards."

"And if someone wanted to plant that ax, they could have approached the pen from the river, couldn't they?"

"Yes, they could have, but we saw no evidence of that."

"And from what I've seen of the river, it flows down to Winyah Bay and out into the Atlantic Ocean?"

"That is correct."

"So anyone in a boat in the Atlantic Ocean could get as close as 150 yards of Willie Fulton's hog pen?"

"Well, it would take them quite a while, and the boat couldn't be very large."

"Did you and your men search Mr. Fulton's residence?" Elizabeth knew that after they found the ax, Black Jack went to a magistrate and got a search warrant to search the house. They ransacked the Fultons' meager possessions but found no incriminating evidence.

"Yes, we did, and we had a search warrant."

"And you didn't find any other evidence that incriminated Mr. Fulton, did you?"

"No, we didn't, but this was hours after the murder."

"You, of course, heard Dr. Kerrison's testimony, didn't you?"

"Yes, I did."

"And did you hear him say that decapitating someone with an ax would result in blood splattering in just about every direction?"

"Yes."

"And you found no blood-splattered clothes or anything that had blood on it in the Fulton house, did you?"

"No ma'am. Like I said, this was hours later."

Elizabeth walked over to the defense table, poured a cup of water, then took two sips as she gathered her thoughts.

"Sheriff Carter," she said as she put the cup down. "You remember Sergeant Wilson's testimony, don't you?"

"Yes, of course."

"And I believe that he said Mr. Gilbert was very meticulous about his garden?"

"Yes, he was, very meticulous."

"And he kept the rows plowed?"

"Yes, he did."

"And it was easy to see footprints and animal prints in the rows of the garden, wasn't it?"

"Not completely."

"The ground was soft, wasn't it?"

"Yes, that was the problem. The ground was so soft and dry the footprints didn't show up clearly."

"The truth is, neither you nor any of your officers, nor any

SLED agents, attempted to photograph or take plaster casts of the footprints, did you?"

"No ma'am, we didn't because the ground was too soft."

"You didn't even attempt to take any partial footprints, did you?"

"No, because I already told you we couldn't."

"How long had you known Mr. Gilbert?" she asked, changing directions.

"About five or six years, shortly after he first came here."

"Do you remember when you first met him?"

"Yes, I do. I was the assistant chief of police here in Weenee. I approached him down at the depot, where he was selling vegetables. It turned out he didn't have a business license."

"Did you arrest him?"

"Oh, no. I just sent him down to the town hall and made him buy a business license. He got mad as a hornet about it."

"Did he get angry often?"

"No. Really, that was the only time I ever saw him angry. Now, he was excitable, very excitable, but that was just his general nature. He loved to haggle over prices, that sort of thing."

"What did you learn about his past?"

"Not very much. Although we became friends and we often talked, he never revealed anything about his past. The only thing he ever mentioned about his earlier years was that he was a graduate of the Sorbonne."

"Did he ever leave town once he came here?"

"Not that I know of."

"Did he ever mention relatives?"

"If he had any family, I never saw them, and he never mentioned them."

"Didn't you find it strange, Sheriff Carter, that he would just get off the train in this small town and never leave?"

Black Jack shrugged and smiled. "I guess. He seemed to like it here."

"If Mr. Gilbert was running from his enemies, Craven County would be a good place to hide, wouldn't it?"

"It would be hard for a man who looked like Mr. Gilbert to hide anywhere for very long with that mustache and goatee and those black clothes he always wore."

"How far, approximately, was Mr. Gilbert's house from the river?"

"I'd say probably about two hundred yards."

"And whoever killed him used the river to dispose of the body or at least the head, didn't they?"

"Yes ma'am."

"And whoever killed him could have used the river to get there as well, couldn't they?"

"I suppose so," the sheriff said, dropping his voice for the first time.

"Could I have the Court's indulgence for a moment, Your Honor?" Elizabeth asked. She had covered every area she wanted to, but she wanted to check with Hamilton before she sat down. They had gone over everything in her cross-examination several times, but she wanted to make sure she covered all the bases. When she leaned over the table in front of Hamilton, he didn't wait for her to speak.

"That's it. I'd leave him alone," he said.

She turned around and looked at Black Jack. "That's all I have, Sheriff. Thank you."

"Any redirect?" Lawson asked.

"Nothing further, Your Honor," Phillips said, rising out of his seat. "Your Honor, that's the State's case," he added, looking over at Elizabeth for her reaction.

Lawson squinted at the clock on the back wall of the courtroom and checked his wristwatch. "It's almost one. Ladies and gentlemen of the jury, we're going to take our lunch recess at this time. I remind you all not to talk with anyone or each other about this case. Please be back in the jury room promptly at two thirty. You may be excused now." Lawson waited until the door shut behind the last juror before he looked at the lawyers. "Miss Chase, I assume you have some motions."

"Yes sir, we do."

"Very well, we will take them up at two thirty. After the motions, we can start right in on your case."

Elizabeth's heart sank, because she realized that Lawson was not going to grant her motion for a directed verdict of "not guilty" based on lack of evidence. Hamilton had warned her not to get her hopes up too high, because he knew that Lawson would give the State the benefit of the doubt in a murder case and let the jury decide the issue.

"Court is adjourned until two thirty," Lawson barked.

CHAPTER 27

"Willie, you and Pearlie Mae really need to reconsider your decision not to testify," Elizabeth said as soon as the four of them sat down at the conference table in the library. Inez had gone to Helen's Café for cheeseburgers and iced tea.

"I really don't see no need, Miss Elizabeth," Willie said, slowly shaking his head. He had a serene look on his face, as if he had just sold his tobacco crop for a huge profit. "You have done a fine job. I 'specially like the way you talked to the sheriff. I think that jury already knows I didn't kill Frenchie."

"Yes, but I think the jury needs to hear your story. You need to tell them yourself that you didn't kill Frenchie." Elizabeth spoke slowly so she could better control her emotions.

"No ma'am. I think we done proved enough, right, Pearlie Mae?" he asked, turning to look at his wife. Pearlie Mae simply nodded.

Elizabeth looked to Hamilton for help.

"Listen, Willie. You and I have known each other a long time, right?" Hamilton asked.

"Yes sir, that's right."

"And you understand that I agree with Miss Chase, that I think you ought to testify, too."

"Yes sir. I understand, and I don't mean no disrespect. I just don't agree with you, although I know you are both good lawyers. This is my case, and I done made up my mind. I ain't gonna testify, and that's all there is to it."

"Okay," Hamilton said as he stood up. "Inez will be back with the food in a minute. Miss Chase and I need to talk over a few legal matters in my office. You two go ahead and eat when she gets back."

"He's not going to budge," Hamilton said as he flopped down in the worn leather chair behind his desk.

"What has gotten into those people?" Elizabeth asked, putting her elbow on the armrest of her chair and resting her forehead in her hand. "You're right," she said finally, looking up. "And I'm not ready to argue this case this afternoon."

"At least you get to go last."

"What do you mean?"

"In this State, if the defense doesn't put up any evidence, they get the last argument."

"That helps some, but what am I going to tell that jury after I told them in my opening statement that they would hear from Willie?"

"Tell them at that point you didn't realize the State was going to put up such a flimsy case."

"Do you think Judge Lawson would let us wait until the morning to argue?"

"Probably so, if you explain to him that we were caught completely off guard. He's going to make us rest our case, though. After that, Willie can't change his mind, come hell or high water."

It was two fifty before Lawson went back on the bench. "I'm sorry to make you lawyers wait, but it looks like one of the jurors must have taken a nap after lunch. He wandered in a minute ago. Miss Chase, I believe you have some motions before we bring the jury back in?"

"Yes sir, Your Honor. On behalf of the defendant, we move for a directed verdict of 'not guilty.' The only shred of evidence the State has produced is a bloody ax that was found in a hog pen behind the defendant's house. The State is relying solely upon circumstantial evidence. As I understand the law of circumstantial evidence in <u>South Carolina,</u> it must constitute positive proof of facts and circumstances which reasonably tend to prove guilt and from which guilt may be fairly and logically deduced to the exclusion of any other reasonable hypothesis. In this case, there are a number of reasonable hypotheses as to who committed this murder. We simply believe that the State has failed to produce sufficient evidence that would exclude these other hypotheses."

"But isn't the issue of whether there is sufficient circumstantial evidence one for the jury to decide?"

"I don't think so, Your Honor," Elizabeth said.

"I am going to respectfully deny your motion, Miss Chase. Do you have any others?"

"Yes, Your Honor. We would move to reduce the charges to manslaughter. The only evidence offered by the State is that there may have been some bad blood between the defendant and the deceased. There has been no evidence whatsoever of malice aforethought, which is required to support a conviction for murder."

"Our law says that the use of a deadly weapon such as an ax can be a basis for implying malice," Lawson replied.

"I understand that, Your Honor, but there is no evidence that Willie Fulton used the ax. If the State could put the ax in the defendant's hand, I would concede your point. But they didn't, so there is no proof of malice."

"Again, it is a jury issue, and I am going to have to deny your motion. Is there anything else?"

"I have no other motions, Your Honor, but I do have one other matter that I would like to take up before the Court."

"Go ahead," Lawson said, looking at the clock behind Elizabeth.

"We were prepared to go forward with our case this afternoon, Your Honor, but Mr. Fulton advised Mr. Hamilton and me just before lunch that he was exercising his constitutional right not to testify, which has caught us completely off guard. He doesn't want us to put up any testimony at all. We would ask Your Honor to recess court until tomorrow morning, at which time we will be ready for final arguments."

"Solicitor?"

"Yes sir," Phillips said as he jumped up from his seat.

"Do you have any other cases for trial this week?"

"No sir, Your Honor. We expected this case to last at least until Thursday."

"If that's the case, then I am inclined to honor Miss Chase's request. Do you have any objections, Solicitor?"

"Well, Your Honor, we are prepared to go forward and conclude this case this afternoon. Yes sir, we do object," Phillips said, looking at Elizabeth.

"I am going to recess court until the morning since it will not prejudice either side. Miss Chase, you will have to rest your case now. I'm not going to let you ambush the solicitor if Mr. Fulton changes his mind tonight."

Elizabeth looked at Hamilton, and he nodded.

"Yes, Your Honor. The defense rests."

Phillips' smug expression returned as he looked back at his assistant.

"Mr. Fulton, stand up, please," Lawson said in a booming voice.

"Yes sir," Willie responded, almost leaping from his seat.

"Do you understand my ruling?"

Willie looked at Hamilton. "I think so," he said.

"Your lawyers tell me that you have decided not to testify. That no one will testify on your behalf, is that right?"

"Yes sir, that's right."

"And you know that you can testify if you want to?"

"Yes sir."

"And you are telling me you don't want to testify?"

"That's right."

"Now you understand that if you leave here, and tonight you change your mind, I'm not going to let you or anybody else testify. Do you understand that?"

"Yes sir."

"Okay. After I let the jury go, we'll be in recess until ten o'clock in the morning," Lawson said, nodding to the bailiff.

"You don't think both of us should argue this case to the jury?" Elizabeth asked Hamilton when they had returned to the office. They had sent Willie and Pearlie Mae home, since it was now in the hands of the lawyers.

"It's your case," Hamilton said.

"Yes, I know. But you know most of the jurors. And I botched things," she added.

"Nonsense," Hamilton said quickly. "You've done a fine job."

"Yeah, except for my opening statement and those horrible photographs," Elizabeth said, pursing her lips. "Do you think we have a chance with that jury?"

"I've been watching them closely," Hamilton said. "I think you have built up a lot of credibility with them."

"I don't know. I noticed Collards McGee dozing a couple of times. That worries me."

Hamilton chuckled.

"What's so funny?" Elizabeth asked.

"Just something Collards' wife told me one time when she was fussing about him sleeping in church. She said Collards would have slept through the Sermon on the Mount. He'll be all right; he's pretty bright. Elizabeth," he added after a pause, "I think we ought to have one closing argument."

"Then you make it," she said.

"No way. You're doing fine."

Elizabeth spent the rest of the afternoon working on her closing argument in the library. Hamilton and Inez were long gone when she realized she was famished. It was almost seven thirty and her cheeseburger from lunch, with the grease showing through the paper wrapper, was still on the phone table at the far end of the room. She remembered Rebecca had told her she would leave supper on the stove and had promised her best cooking for Elizabeth during the trial. Elizabeth was bone tired, so she decided to eat supper, take a bath, try to get some sleep, and then return to the office and her notes early the next morning when she was fresh.

She was on her second pork chop when the phone rang. She picked it up on the third ring.

"Elizabeth, how did it go today?"

"Jim?"

"You sound awful. Are you that tired?"

"Sorry, I wasn't sure it was you. I'm beat."

"You got time for a drink so you can tell me about the big trial?"

"Thanks, but I think I'll pass tonight. I'm just finishing supper, and I'm going to bed after I get my bath."

"How is the trial going?"

"I don't know. It's hard to say."

"I heard your client isn't going to take the stand. That he caught you and Robert by surprise."

"Where did you hear that?"

"I stopped at Collards' Exxon for gas. Collards was at home because he knew everybody at the station would be talking about the case. They say you were a buzz saw on cross-examination. The talk is you had all of the men on the jury hypnotized by your trial skills and by your beauty. Everybody's betting on an acquittal."

"That's interesting," Elizabeth said, not sure what to make of Jim's comments.

"Do you think the jury will find Willie not guilty?"

"I don't know, Jim. I personally think his chances would have been much better if he had decided to testify."

"Can he change his mind in the morning?"

"No. Judge Lawson made us rest our case. Even if Willie changes his mind, it would be too late."

"I see," Jim said. "You sure you won't change your mind about that drink?"

"No, not tonight."

"When will the trial be over?"

"The jury should get the case by late morning. Now, how long they will deliberate is anybody's guess."

"Well, when this is over, maybe I can have a big victory celebration for you."

"Maybe so, Jim," Elizabeth said wearily.

CHAPTER 28

"Good morning," Lawson said to the jury when they were seated just after ten o'clock the next morning. "I trust no one has tried to contact any of you to discuss this case since yesterday. If they have, please let me know right now." Lawson surveyed the jury but no one gave any indication that any attempts at jury tampering had been made. "Very well then. In just a minute the lawyers will have the opportunity to summarize or argue their respective cases to you. Please keep in mind that what the lawyers say to you is not evidence in this case." Lawson then turned and looked at the solicitor. "Is the State ready?" he asked.

"The State is ready, Your Honor," Phillips said pompously.

"Is the defense ready to proceed, also?"

"The defense is ready, Your Honor," Elizabeth said, looking over at the jury. Elizabeth was ready, she knew, but her heart rate was a little faster than normal. She had slept well until about four o'clock, and then she was wide awake and out of bed by four fifteen. After forcing herself to eat a bowl of cereal, she was in the library by six, going over her notes.

"You may proceed, Solicitor."

"Thank you, Your Honor," Phillips said as he walked briskly to a position in front of the jury box, indictment in hand. "Good morning, ladies and gentlemen of the jury. Before I get into the facts of this case as I see them, I want to thank all of you for serving on this jury panel this week. I have been watching you, and you've been very attentive in discharging your duties as jurors for this fine state. As you know, I am elected by you people, the voters, every four years to prosecute crimes here in this circuit, which, of course, includes Craven County. It is my job, and will continue to be my job if you reelect me in November, to put people like Willie Fulton behind bars for a long time." Phillips turned around and glared at Willie, then slowly raised his arm and pointed at him, as though he had a big buck locked in his gun sight at close range. "He is the man who so callously and cold bloodedly killed Ovid Gilbert by cutting his head off with an ax, which he then brazenly buried in his backyard."

All the jurors turned to look at Willie, and Elizabeth could feel her client flinch, but she dared not see for herself.

"His lawyer from Massachusetts, I am sure, will stand before you and tell you that the State of South Carolina has the burden of proving the defendant guilty beyond a reasonable doubt." He pronounced Massachusetts in a mocking tone, slowly stringing out the syllables. "But the facts that the State has proven from that witness stand," he said, pointing in the opposite direction, "should remove the slightest trace of doubt from your minds, if you ever harbored one, that Willie Fulton is guilty of the murder of Mr. Gilbert.

"Let's talk about poor old Mr. Gilbert for a minute. You heard our sheriff talk about what a fine man he was and how everyone in this peace-loving community loved him so much. How could he defend himself from an ax?" Phillips asked, his voice rising theatrically. "How could a man his age defend himself at all, against a strong farm worker like Willie Fulton? And this man, this animal, didn't even allow poor old Mr. Gilbert to have a decent burial. The Lord only knows where the rest of his body is. This is all we have left of the man everyone lovingly called Frenchie," he said, holding up one of the photographs of his head. "I'm sorry we had to bring these photographs in here, but Willie Fulton gave us no choice. When you jurors look at these photographs, particularly you ladies," he said, this time picking up all of the photographs, "don't blame us; blame the defendant. He is the one who is putting you through all of this," he continued, turning to glare again at Willie. Elizabeth was ready to object, but when she looked at Hamilton, he shook his head.

"And what has Mr. Fulton said about this ax? His lawyer from up North stood before you at the beginning of this trial and told you that you would hear Willie Fulton's side of the story."

"Your Honor, I object!" Elizabeth shouted in a voice so loud that it startled Lawson.

"What is the basis of your objection, Miss Chase? This is

closing argument." Hamilton had warned Elizabeth not to object to anything Phillips said in his closing argument unless he really crossed the line, for fear of alienating the jury by interrupting.

"It is highly improper. Opening statements are not evidence," she said. She had been poised, waiting for Phillips to exploit her initial mistake.

"Leave it alone, Solicitor. Move on to something else," Lawson said, looking at the clock on the back wall, sidestepping her objection.

"Certainly, Your Honor," Phillips replied smugly, knowing that the damage had already been done. He walked over and picked up the ax, which was sitting prominently on the corner of the clerk's desk, in full view of the jury. "You heard the pathologist, Dr. Kerrison from the Medical University, testify." Phillips had deftly changed his delivery to a conversational tone now, but he continued to hold the attention of the jurors. "He testified that, in his expert opinion, and mind you, he is a medical doctor who teaches other doctors, that Mr. Gilbert came to his death as a result of being decapitated with an ax.

"And you heard the testimony from the SLED chemist, who said that the blood on this ax matched completely the blood of Mr. Gilbert. Did you hear Miss Chase ask this expert one question? No you didn't," he said after a pause. "Why?" he asked, and again he paused to let the question sink in. "Because they can't dispute or contradict his findings, that's why. This is without question the ax that killed Frenchie," he said, his voice rising a little higher. "It has Frenchie's blood on it; look at it, ladies and gentlemen." Phillips pointed to a dark spot near the head of the ax. His voice was high-pitched now, and Phillips had a wild look in his eyes. "And where was it found? Buried in the hog parlor of that man!" he screamed as he turned and pointed at Willie Fulton once again.

Elizabeth felt uneasy at these theatrics, but she knew it was not objectionable. She could feel Willie squirming next to her.

"And did he take the stand and deny that this was his ax? Did he take the stand and deny that . . ."

"Your Honor, I object!" Elizabeth shouted from her seat, even before she stood up. "I move for a mistrial, Your Honor."

Lawson swiveled in his chair until he spotted the bailiff, then looked at the jury. "Ladies and gentlemen, I'm going to have to ask you to go to your jury room. It won't be but for a few minutes. There is a matter of law that I need to take up outside your presence."

As soon as the last juror filed out, Lawson turned to Elizabeth. "I'll hear your motion now, Miss Chase," he said tersely. Elizabeth noticed that the same vein was bulging in his neck again.

"Your Honor, we move for a mistrial. I don't know what they teach in the law schools down here, but where I practice law it is highly improper for the prosecutor to comment in any way on a defendant's assertion of his constitutional right not to testify. The last time I checked, Mr. Phillips, the United States Constitution applied here in <u>South Carolina</u>, too," Elizabeth said, pointing a finger at the solicitor. She quickly dropped her hand because it was shaking from her anger.

Lawson removed his glasses and glared at Phillips. His face was contorted, his neck was red, and the vein seemed to protrude even farther now. "Solicitor, I am real anxious to hear what argument you will present to justify what you just did. I'm like Miss Chase—I'm starting to wonder what law school you went to."

Phillips looked to his assistant for help, but Jacobs stared blankly back at his boss.

"Your Honor, I've made that same argument before other juries."

"It wasn't before me, Solicitor, was it?"

"No sir."

"And the other lawyers didn't object, did they?"

"No sir."

"And you just thought you could slip it by me and Miss Chase, didn't you?"

"Well, I didn't ever think about it that way, Your Honor."

"You want to tell me why you think it is proper to comment on a defendant's failure to take the witness stand or present any evidence?" Lawson asked, leaning forward in his chair and resting his forearms on the bench.

"I'll agree with Miss Chase that my comments would usually be improper. But in this case, she opened the door when she promised the jury that the defendant would testify."

Elizabeth folded her arms across her chest and rolled her eyes. "Your Honor," she said, staring now at Phillips, "this is the most ridiculous statement that I think I have ever heard a lawyer make in a courtroom. Nothing I say can waive Mr. Fulton's constitutional rights."

"And you want me to grant a mistrial, Miss Chase?" Lawson asked.

"Yes sir, I do."

"And you realize that we will have to start over from the beginning, with a new jury at the October term?"

"Yes sir, I do," she said, but she hadn't realized until then the implications of the judge granting her motion. Coming back in October to retry this case would be a nightmare, she told herself.

"Let's take a five-minute recess and let me think this over."

"Just one more thing, Judge," Phillips said, raising his finger in the air like a precocious third grader.

"What is it, Solicitor?"

"I'm not going to call this case for trial in October if you grant Miss Chase's motion."

"Why not?" Lawson asked as he stood up.

"Because I'm running for reelection in November, and I'm planning to take annual leave for most of October to campaign. It would have to be retried either in the December or February term."

"Next year?" Elizabeth shot back.

"Yeah, next year," Phillips sneered. "The last time I checked, Miss Chase, the solicitor still has control of the docket in this state."

"If I grant Miss Chase's motion, when this case is retried is not my immediate concern," Lawson said. "You talk to Mr. Hamilton and your client and let me know if you want to withdraw your motion, Miss Chase."

"All rise!" the bailiff shouted as Lawson headed for his chambers. Phillips walked over to his table, leaned over, and whispered something to Jacobs, and both men laughed.

Elizabeth, seeing the exchange, walked over, grabbed Phillips by the arm, and jerked it. "That was the biggest cheap shot that I've ever seen in a courtroom," she said under her breath, so only the two of them could hear. She felt a tug on her arm.

"Elizabeth, come on. We need to talk," Hamilton said calmly, putting his hand on her shoulder. "This won't do any of us any good."

"You're right about that, Robert," Phillips said and walked away.

Hamilton motioned for Willie and Pearlie Mae to follow and led them to a room used as a holding cell for prisoners awaiting pleas or trials. The four of them sat around a wooden table with dozens of names carved in it. The pale-green walls were covered with graffiti.

"Are you all right, Elizabeth?" Hamilton asked.

"Yeah, I'm okay. I hate it when I lose my cool like that. Phillips is such a jerk. I can't believe he would put off this case until next year," Elizabeth said, slamming her fist down hard on the table.

"Calm down, Elizabeth. You're going to have a heart attack," Hamilton said, reaching over to pat her forearm.

Elizabeth nodded, sighed loudly, and leaned back in her chair. "I hope you will forgive me for getting so mad in there, Willie," she said. "It's bad for a lawyer to get that mad in a courtroom. You lose your effectiveness."

"I like the way you's fighting for me out there in that courtroom. You might be a woman lawyer, but you sure ain't scared of no man lawyer."

"Amen," Pearlie Mae said softly.

"For a minute there, I thought she was gonna fight the solicitor, Mr. Hamilton," Willie remarked with a chuckle.

"Yeah, me too, Willie," Hamilton said. "Let's get back to your case for a minute. What Elizabeth did was ask for a mistrial. What that means is the judge may stop this case right now and dismiss this jury. Send them home. Then, at another term, either in December or February of next year, we would start over with a new jury."

Willie's eyes narrowed.

"We don't have any choice, Willie," Elizabeth said as calmly as she could. "The solicitor has poisoned the minds of the jurors. There is no way we can erase from their minds what Phillips said. If we went forward with this jury, the judge would tell them to disregard what the solicitor said, but it wouldn't help much, in my opinion."

"You mean the judge would tell the jury not to pay no attention to what the solicitor said about me not taking the stand?"

"That's right," Elizabeth replied, nodding.

"Then if the judge will tell them that, that's good enough for me."

"What are you saying?" Elizabeth asked, her voice rising.

"I like this jury, Miss Elizabeth, and as long as the judge will straighten this little mess out, I want to finish my case today."

Elizabeth looked at Hamilton but he just shrugged. "Look, Willie," she said. "I really think you ought to let the judge rule on my motion for a mistrial. To put it off. That way, if he denies my motion, and the jury convicts you, we will have grounds for an appeal."

"That jury ain't gonna convict me of nothing," Willie said, shaking his head.

"It's his case," Hamilton commented, looking at Elizabeth. Elizabeth pursed her lips and stared back at Hamilton, but she remained silent. Hamilton stood up and said, "I'll get Phillips and go tell the judge in chambers that we are withdrawing our motion. I'll make sure he agrees to give the jury a curative charge."

Phillips had his now-familiar smirk on his face when the bailiff brought the jury back into the courtroom to resume the trial. The jury was attentive as Lawson instructed them at length to disregard any references that the solicitor made to Willie's decision not to present any evidence or testify. The main problem with curative instructions, Elizabeth knew, was that they reminded the jury and emphasized to them what had previously been said by the offending party.

"You may proceed, Solicitor," Lawson said after finishing his instructions.

"Thank you, Your Honor," Phillips replied, with not a trace of remorse. He rattled on for the next twenty minutes, mainly about abstract principles of justice that didn't appear to interest the jury very much. He concluded with one more finger-pointing tirade directed at Willie and sat down. From the look on his face, it was clear that he was very pleased with his performance.

"Miss Chase?" Lawson asked.

"Thank you, Your Honor," Elizabeth said. "May it please the Court?" She walked briskly across the courtroom, maintaining eye contact with the jury and carrying a yellow legal pad with a two-page outline of her argument on it. In every trial, she either held a pad at her side or placed it on the rail of the jury box, more as a security blanket than anything else. She seldom referred to her pad, but it reassured her to know that it was there <u>if her mind went blank</u>.

"Good morning, ladies and gentlemen," she said. Her stomach contained a net full of butterflies that had been absent since the first year she started trying cases.

"Good morning," most of the jurors answered.

Elizabeth started, as she always did, by pointing out to the jurors the basic concepts of the burden of proof, the presumption of innocence, and reasonable doubt. She spent quite some time defining and explaining reasonable doubt and hammering home to them the idea that if they had reasonable doubts about the guilt of Willie Fulton, then their duty under the law was to find him not guilty. Elizabeth knew that if the jury didn't convict Willie, it would have to be because they had some reasonable doubts about his guilt.

"Ladies and gentlemen," she continued, "at the outset of this case, I got off on the wrong foot with you. I told you that you would hear from Willie Fulton in this trial, that he would tell you his side of the story. Well, I was mistaken. I was wrong to tell you that. It was my mistake, not Willie Fulton's," she said, turning to look at her client. "And I am asking you not to hold my mistake against Mr. Fulton. Please don't penalize him for something I said. After we got into the trial of this case, he chose not to testify, and that is his constitutional right. Not even Solicitor Phillips or the State of <u>South Carolina</u> can take that away from him." She paused and surveyed the jury for a few seconds before she began again. "And after listening to the testimony presented by the State," she said softly, "there is no need for Willie Fulton to testify. There is, quite simply, no evidence that Willie Fulton killed Ovid Gilbert. What evidence exactly has the State introduced against Mr. Fulton? The testimony of the State's first witness, Sergeant Wilson, merely set the scene of the crime. It told you that someone or some animal tore up Mr. Gilbert's garden, that someone killed his dog and probably murdered Mr. Gilbert there, also."

Elizabeth could have belittled Sergeant Wilson for his unprofessional investigation or for his wine drinking with Ovid Gilbert, but she knew it wouldn't help Willie's case. Sergeant Wilson was an honest, hardworking, well-liked deputy who wasn't very bright, and Elizabeth knew she would probably alienate some jurors if she attacked him directly.

"Did any of you hear any testimony from Sergeant Wilson that pointed to the guilt of Willie Fulton?" She paused to let the jurors consider the question. "I don't believe there was any, but you be the judge. Was there something in Sergeant Wilson's testimony that, if developed properly, could have assisted you jurors in determining who may have been in that garden and killed Mr. Gilbert? Do you remember when the sergeant was educating me about farming and gardening? He said Mr. Gilbert was very meticulous with his garden. The sergeant said it looked like a picture in a seed catalogue," she added, smiling at his simile. "Then he said, and this is the important part, that there were footprints all over that garden." Again she paused. "If that was the case, then why weren't measurements and photographs taken? Why weren't plaster casts made? Couldn't the investigators then determine whether or not these footprints matched Mr. Fulton's?" she asked as she turned and looked at her client. "Let me remind you, ladies and gentlemen, that it is the State of South Carolina that has the burden of proof, not Mr. Fulton. The State, through the officers of the Craven County Sheriff's Department, had a golden opportunity to develop some hard evidence against the killer but failed to do it. I am asking you to ask yourselves during your deliberations why this wasn't done.

"Next, you heard from Dr. Harvey Kerrison, the doctor who performed the autopsy on the deceased. He testified that in his opinion Mr. Gilbert died as a result of his head being cut off with an ax, although he did concede that other wounds could have been inflicted on the body prior to death. We don't know because we don't have the rest of poor Mr. Gilbert's body. We don't really contest that issue, ladies and gentlemen," Elizabeth said forcefully, holding her arms up from her sides. "Someone killed this Frenchman. Who that was, we still don't know. Does the testimony of Dr. Kerrison do anything to lift the presumption of innocence from the shoulders of Willie Fulton?" she asked, taking a long pause to look at her client. "I don't think so, but you be the judge of that.

"And when you consider the testimony of Dr. Kerrison, if you look at those awful photographs, please don't let them inflame your passions or prejudice your view of the evidence, because they are dreadful and really have no direct bearing on the guilt or innocence of my client. The photographs merely prove that a grisly murder has been perpetrated.

"I asked no questions of the State's next witness, Mr. Wellingham, the chemist from SLED, because we don't dispute his findings. The blood on that ax belongs to Mr. Gilbert," Elizabeth said, pointing to the exhibit on the end of Phillips' desk. "Again, I ask you, does that evidence or that witness shed any light on the guilt or innocence of Mr. Fulton?" Elizabeth gave the jurors a few seconds to think about her question before she moved on.

"The two deputies who testified after the chemist were merely satisfying the requirements of proving the chain of custody for the ax. Again, I did not hear the name of Willie Fulton mentioned by either witness.

"Then we heard from Mr. Caesar Shaw." Once again Elizabeth knew she had to be careful because Shaw was black, and so were most of the jurors. To her, he was not a very likeable person because of his hostility, which even seemed to be directed toward Phillips.

"Is this man credible?" she asked. "He lives with a woman and according to Mr. Shaw's testimony, they draw two hundred and some odd dollars every month in government assistance, and don't get me wrong, I'm not running down people who need government benefits to survive," she said diplomatically. "They have a house payment of approximately one hundred and eighty dollars per month. Mr. Shaw earns another forty or fifty dollars a month working at a club called Up Jump the Devil. I'm not sure I know what they do in a club with a name like that, and I'm not sure I want to know," she added with a grin. Three of the male jurors smiled back at her. "How does this man make ends meet?" she asked, shrugging.

"Then he goes on to tell us about an argument between Willie Fulton and the deceased that he witnessed last summer. He said the argument started after some of my client's hogs got loose in Mr. Gilbert's garden and ate some of his tomatoes. And Mr. Shaw has pretty well pinpointed the date of the argument for us. He tells us, and all of you probably already knew this long before you were called for jury duty this week, that tomatoes don't appear on tomato plants until sometime in June, and they don't get ripe until about the Fourth of July. But something is wrong here with Mr. Shaw's calendar. Something is wrong because he tells us that he was arrested for selling marijuana and locked up on May twelfth." Her voice rose slightly when she said the date, and she paused and looked over the twelve people facing her. The eyes of those jurors who had not realized the inconsistency of Shaw's testimony now lit up with amazement. "May twelfth, long before the first tomato appeared on any tomato plants here in Craven County. Now the solicitor, Mr. Phillips, realized the crucial mistake his witness made and tried to correct it, if you remember, but the damage had already been done. He tried to get Mr. Shaw to say that he could have been confused about the date, but what did Mr. Shaw tell him? He said, 'I was locked up two days before my birthday. Wouldn't you remember it, too?'" Several of the jurors nodded at Elizabeth as she recounted this portion of Caesar Shaw's testimony.

"It should be crystal clear to all you jurors that Caesar Shaw is not a credible witness, and for some reason he came into this courtroom and perjured himself. And you don't have to read a *Farmer's Almanac* to realize that," she said, not being able to resist the verbal jab at Phillips.

"Lastly, we heard from the sheriff of Craven County, an impressive man by anyone's standards." Elizabeth had realized long before the trial started that it could be disastrous to attack the sheriff with a frontal assault, so she had to choose her words carefully. "When the sheriff is confronted with a crime committed in this county, he has to conduct his investigation in a manner he deems appropriate. He has to develop the facts as he uncovers them and then present them to you, a jury, here in Craven County." Elizabeth was speaking now in a casual, conversational tone, using small hand movements to emphasize her points. She wanted to convey to the jury the impression that she respected the man, which she did, before attacking his theories and assumptions. "He has to play the cards he is dealt in each case, and in this case, unfortunately for him, he has been dealt a bad hand, because he has the wrong man.

"Even though Willie Fulton chose not to take the stand, you jurors can still judge his credibility," she said, glancing over at Willie. She was thankful that he had remembered his coaching, sitting up straight in his chair and looking directly at the jury. "How can you do that? Remember when the sheriff testified that Willie acted like he had nothing to hide when he first questioned him? Does that sound like a murderer to you? And what did Willie Fulton say when the sheriff asked him if he could search his place?" Elizabeth increased the volume of her delivery now, and she was gesturing with her hands. "He said go ahead." She swept her hand by her side as she turned sideways to the jury box. "Again, I ask you, are these the actions of a guilty man? I submit to you that Willie Fulton wouldn't have allowed the sheriff's deputies to search his place if he had known that the bloody ax was buried in his hog pen. And why didn't the murderer take the time to clean the blood off the ax? It wouldn't have taken but a few seconds. The murderer didn't do that because whoever it was wanted to make sure that Willie Fulton would be charged. And while we are on the subject of searches, please remember the search warrant that Sheriff Carter had issued. What did they find, bloody clothes?" Elizabeth stopped dead still and shook her head, making eye contact, ever so briefly, with every juror. "Nothing," she said finally, barely above a whisper. "You remember the testimony of Dr. Kerrison, I'm sure. He said that the blows from the ax would cause blood to splatter in all directions and, in all likelihood, on the assailant and his clothes. Where were the bloody clothes of Willie Fulton? They searched every inch of his house, I'm sure, and they found nothing.

"And while we are still on the subject of who buried the ax, consider if you will, when you start deliberating, that the hog pen was only 150 yards from the river, and Mr. Gilbert's house was only 200 yards from the same river. Anyone in Craven County, or Georgetown County for that matter, who had access to a boat could have killed Mr. Gilbert. Or better yet," she added, tapping her fist lightly on the rail of the jury box, "anyone who had access to the Atlantic Ocean had access to Mr. Fulton's hog pen and Mr. Gilbert's garden. Think about it," she said, lowering her voice again. The retired schoolteacher nodded ever so slightly, and Elizabeth could have reached across the rail and hugged her.

"What do we know about this man, Ovid Gilbert? Very little, I'm afraid, and whatever secrets he may have had died with him, unfortunately. We do know that he got off the train here, in Weenee, five or six years ago. Where he was coming from we don't know. He loved to talk and haggle with people, according to Sheriff Carter. Why did he stop here in this sleepy, pretty little town in the first place? Was he running from someone? His enemies? Had he been involved with organized crime? We don't know. We may never know. The one thing we do know is that there is no credible evidence to show that Willie Fulton had any motive to kill Ovid Gilbert. The only evidence the State offered regarding a motive was the testimony of Caesar Scott, and I have already told you why he is not believable.

"In closing, I would like to make one final observation to you, If the investigators with the State Law Enforcement Division had done their job properly and documented the footprints of Mr. Gilbert's assailant, you probably would not be sitting here today. These so-called professionals failed to do that," she said, pointing her finger in the air. "If SLED had done what it was supposed to do," she continued, "this evidence would have either pointed to Mr. Fulton's overwhelming guilt or excluded him as a suspect. And remember, ladies and gentlemen, it's Mr. Phillips and the State of South Carolina's job to prove Willie Fulton guilty beyond a reasonable doubt." She pointed to, but did not look at, the solicitor's table. She paused, studying the jurors. "And they haven't done it," she said calmly and softly. "Thank you."

As she sat down, Willie was beaming at her, obviously pleased with his lawyer's performance.

"Thank you, Miss Chase," Lawson said and turned to face the jury panel. "Ladies and gentlemen, we have now concluded the arguments of counsel. It is now time for me to charge you the law of the State of South Carolina as it applies to the charges in this case against the defendant, Willie Fulton. It will take me about twenty-five minutes to do so, and if any of you need to take a break before I start, please raise your hands." Lawson looked up and down the jury panel twice to make sure no one wanted to stop. "As I see no hands, I will proceed," he said, smiling at the panel.

Lawson must have given these same instructions to hundreds of juries during his long career because he finished in the promised twenty-five minutes. He explained in detail the presumption of innocence, the burden of proof, and, most importantly, reasonable doubt. He gave several examples of that principle, and Elizabeth was glad that the jurors seemed to take particular interest in this portion of the charge.

Hamilton and Elizabeth had filed a request to charge on manslaughter, and Elizabeth was pleased when he explained the elements of that charge after defining the elements of murder. Although she hoped it wouldn't be necessary in this case, juries often used lesser included offenses such as manslaughter as a way to compromise on a verdict. If they did so in this case, it would at least cap Willie's maximum sentence at thirty years, and he would be eligible for parole in ten years.

[margin note: THATS WHAT THEY DID TO MY CLIENT BRANDON RAY - HE GOT VOLUNTARY MANSLAUGHT- ER AS OPPOSED TO MURDER]

It was a little after noon when Lawson finished, and he took off his glasses, carefully placing them on his blotter. "This concludes my charge to you. I am now going to let you retire to your jury room, but please do not begin your deliberations until I send word for you to start. As soon as you leave, I am going to ask the lawyers if they have any additions or objections to my charges. Once you get the word to start, you are free to begin your deliberations. And when you get hungry, please tap on the door so the bailiff can take your order. You will be the guests of Craven County for lunch, but I'm afraid it will be nothing extravagant. The bailiff has the menu from Helen's Café," he said, smiling in a grandfatherly way.

"Any objections to my charges from the State?" Lawson asked as soon as the jury had been dispatched to their room.

"None whatsoever, Your Honor," Phillips said confidently.

"From the defense?" Lawson asked, turning to face Elizabeth.

"None, Your Honor," Elizabeth answered. Lawson had been fair to them on his charges so she had no complaints.

"Bailiff, you can tell the jury to begin its deliberations now. Sheriff, you are to place the defendant in custody until the jury reaches a verdict. We will be at ease until further notice."

"All rise!" the bailiff shouted as Lawson rose and headed for his chambers.

A tall, muscular black deputy reached over the railing and took Willie's arm, gently pulling him out of his chair. "Let's go, Willie," he said.

"Where we going? That jury ain't convicted me of nothing," he declared, trying to pull his arm free.

"You have to go with him, Willie," Hamilton said. "It's the law. It's only while the jury is deliberating."

"How long they gonna be?"

"We have no way of knowing that," Hamilton said, raising his hands from his sides.

"You're just going in one of those rooms up there," the deputy said, pointing to one of the rear doors.

Willie looked at Hamilton and Pearlie Mae. "Okay," he said.

CHAPTER 29

"What do you think?" Elizabeth asked Hamilton when they were seated at the conference table in the library. Inez had gone for sandwiches, and Elizabeth was hungry again now that most of the pressure of the trial was over.

"That was a beautiful closing. One of the best I've ever heard," he said.

"Oh, come on. Stop trying to flatter me," Elizabeth said as she leaned back in her chair and rubbed her temples with her fingertips.

"I'm serious. Your delivery is very polished. You had that jury hypnotized."

"Thanks, I really appreciate that, Robert. But do you think they'll acquit our client?"

"Through the years, I've been pretty good at reading juries. And I made it a habit to talk with as many of them as I could after a case was over. It was especially helpful in validating my opinion of a particular jury."

"What was your read on this jury, then?" Elizabeth asked quickly, leaning forward.

"I believe they'll turn him loose."

"I hope you're right," she said, pursing her lips. After a pause, she added, "Let me ask you something, Robert, that's been bothering me throughout the trial."

"What is it?"

"Have you noticed that older black gentleman sitting in the courtroom behind Willie's family? He was always wearing blue sunglasses, and he was constantly chewing on something. Do you know who he is?"

"I saw him, too. He does look strange, but I have no idea who he is."

Elizabeth headed back to the courthouse after she attacked a B.L.T. and a greasy order of fries. Hamilton had other work to do, and she promised to call Inez as soon as the jury reached a verdict. To her, waiting for a jury to return a verdict was the worst part about trial work. Her longest wait had been two and a half days, but that was a double murder with four defendants that had taken three weeks to try. When Hamilton told her the deputies watching Willie would let her sit with him, she knew where she wanted to endure the wait.

She spotted the same muscular deputy who had escorted Willie from the courtroom standing in front of a door with a large opaque panel of glass. "Is Mr. Fulton in there?" she asked, pointing over his shoulder to the door.

"Yes ma'am," the deputy replied. "Would you like to go in? There's plenty of chairs in there."

"Yes, I would. Have you seen Mrs. Fulton?"

"Oh, Pearlie Mae's in there with Willie," he answered as he turned the knob and opened the door. "You can go on in."

Willie and Pearlie Mae were sitting in folding chairs at the far wall. Pearlie Mae stared at Elizabeth, wild eyed, but Willie was sound asleep with his chin on his chest. Elizabeth wondered how a man whose entire future was being debated a few feet away could sleep at a time like this.

"Has the jury decided the case already?" Pearlie Mae asked as she shook Willie hard. He jumped as if he had backed into an electric fence.

"No, they haven't. I decided to come over and wait with you."

"Where's Mr. Robert?" she asked. Willie was awake now, but he kept quiet.

"He's back at the office. He had some other work to do."

"Ain't you got other work to do?"

"No, not really," Elizabeth said.

"Well, come sit down," Pearlie Mae urged, patting the chair next to her. Elizabeth eased into the chair, finding it just as uncomfortable as it looked. "How much longer you think they's gonna be?" Pearlie Mae asked in her rapid-fire delivery.

"It's hard to say," Elizabeth said, looking at the two of them. She was amazed to watch Willie go back to sleep, and he began to snore.

"Don't let that snoring worry you none. You get use to it after a while," said Pearlie Mae.

"I just don't see how he could sleep at a time like this," Elizabeth remarked, shaking her head slowly.

"Willie, he could sleep on a picket fence," she said, her broad smile showing a perfect set of teeth lined up like piano keys.

"He's not worried?"

"There ain't no need to," Pearlie Mae said matter-of-factly.

"How can you say that?"

"You ought to know. You's the lawyer. You sure did a beautiful job talking to that jury, Miss Elizabeth."

"What do you mean, I ought to know?"

"You ought to know that jury ain't gonna convict Willie."

"How can you be so sure?"

"We just know, that's all," Pearlie Mae said smugly, folding her arms across her chest.

The two women waited in silence after that, the only sounds being Willie's rhythmic snores, punctuated from time to time by a loud snort. After an hour, Elizabeth left the room and walked down the hall toward the jury room. The bailiff, Hank Richardson, was hunched over in a chair with his back to her, his right hand cupped to his ear and almost touching the opaque glass panel of the door. When he finally heard her footsteps, he jumped to an upright position like a sentry caught sleeping at his post.

"You scared me," he said, smiling sheepishly.

"Can you tell how they're coming in there?" she asked, pointing at the door.

"You really got that jury riled up, Miss Chase," he said, grinning again.

"What do you mean?"

"They's arguing and carrying on in there like I ain't heard in a long time."

"Can you tell which way they're leaning?"

"No ma'am," he said. "All I know is that they gonna be a while. They been raising sand like that ever since they finished dinner."

Elizabeth sighed and nodded. "If I'm not here in the courthouse when they reach a verdict, I'll be over in Mr. Hamilton's office."

"Yes ma'am," he said, bowing his head slightly and tipping an invisible hat.

As Elizabeth walked through the courtroom, she was surprised to see thirty-five or forty spectators lounging on the benches or, like Willie, catching up on their sleep. Outside, the wide, second-story porch of the old courthouse provided a bird's-eye view of the town square and its surrounding storefronts. Elizabeth walked over to the black wrought-iron railing and spent the next forty-five minutes watching the remaining spectators, the unemployed, and the retired lounging on the benches and grass of the square.

The Confederate monument, located dead in the middle of the common, had a graduated base built out of granite that formed a set of steps, and on the bottom row sat three elderly black men, smoking cigarettes and talking animatedly. To the right was a statue of a young man in military fatigues looking skyward, holding a grappling hook, and Elizabeth made a mental note to ask Robert about this strange monument. To the left of the Confederate monument was a life-size likeness of Dr. Martin Luther King, Jr., who appeared to be frozen forever in midsentence during one of his fiery orations. The local pigeons, Elizabeth noticed, seemed to be apolitical, as they appeared to distribute their droppings equally on all three statues.

Beginning to feel the strain of the trial on her body, she decided to head back to the office. As she walked by the jury room again on her way out of the courthouse, she noticed that the jury was quiet now, and Hank Richardson was nodding off in his chair by the door.

Inez looked up expectantly as Elizabeth walked in the front door. "Any word yet?" she asked quickly.

"No, not yet. Is Robert in his office?"

"Yes, and he doesn't have anybody with him."

"Let me know if you hear anything."

"Oh, I will," Inez replied.

Hamilton was behind his desk, reading the Charleston paper. "Have they got a verdict?" he asked, slapping the paper down on his desk.

"No, not yet," Elizabeth said, shaking her head.

"They've been out a good while," he observed.

"Earlier in the afternoon they were shouting at each other."

"How do you know that?"

"The bailiff and I could hear them out in the hall."

"Have a seat. It may be a while."

"I thought you said you had work to do."

"I can't ever concentrate on anything else when a jury is out. That's why I was reading the paper," he said, looking at the wad of newsprint on his desk.

"Is this a good sign or a bad sign?"

"Well, you know that usually if they convict, they do it pretty quickly, so I'd say it was a good sign," Hamilton said. "What are you going to do if it's a hung jury?"

Elizabeth leaned back in her chair and rolled her eyes. "I've tried not to think about that. Do you think Phillips would retry the case?"

"Sure he would. This is a high-profile case for this circuit."

"I guess I'd have to see this lovely town in the winter," Elizabeth said. "Let me ask you something, Robert."

"Okay."

"What was that business about the white powder around the witness stand yesterday?"

Hamilton leaned back in his chair and smiled. "Root," he said finally.

"Root? What on earth are you talking about?"

"It was root powder."

"Robert, you're talking in riddles," Elizabeth said with a sense of urgency in her voice.

"It's a part of the witchcraft or black arts that many of the black people here practice. It's something they brought over from the west coast of Africa."

"What is the purpose of the white powder?"

"It's supposed to have some type of magical effect."

"And people believe in this stuff?"

"Many of them do. A lot of them are very afraid of it. The powder is just one form. They have roots, potions, all kinds of things."

"So that's why the janitor wouldn't touch it?"

"Exactly."

"That poor man was scared to death. Did you notice his hands shaking?"

Hamilton nodded. "They believe that if they touch that powder, something very bad will happen to them."

"Who do you think put it there?" Elizabeth asked.

"Some root doctor."

"Mr. Hamilton!" Inez shrieked as she rushed into the room. "That was Betty from the clerk's office. They've got a verdict."

Hamilton and Elizabeth looked at each other as they stood at the same time. By the time they hit the sidewalk, Elizabeth could feel her heart rate going into overdrive.

Word of the jury's verdict must have spread quickly up and down Lee Street, because the courtroom was almost as crowded as it had been on Monday morning. Willie and Pearlie Mae had been brought in from their holding room and were back in their seats. Willie looked very calm, but Pearlie Mae appeared to be terrified. Phillips, Jacobs, and Black Jack were already at their table, all wearing somber expressions.

Elizabeth sat down, clenching her fists to keep her hands from shaking. She glanced at Willie and saw his forearms and hands resting motionless on the shiny tabletop. Receiving jury verdicts had always made her nervous, but never like this, she told herself.

"All rise!" Hank Richardson shouted, and the crowd snapped to its feet quickly. Lawson sat down and gazed at both sides of the courtroom to make sure all of the lawyers and the defendant were present.

"I understand the jury has reached a verdict," he said finally. "Let the record reflect that the defendant is present in the courtroom along with both of his attorneys. Let me say this, and I'm only going to say it one time." He looked out over the crowded spectator section. "I don't want any outbursts when the clerk publishes the verdict. I'm going to ask the bailiff and the deputies to move out into the aisle, and if they see anyone creating any disturbance, I want them brought forward so they can be taken directly to jail. Is that understood?" Lawson paused for several seconds so that the crowd could absorb his threat. The courtroom was so still all you could hear was the traffic on Lee Street.

"All right, bailiff, you can bring the jury in now," Lawson said, nodding to Hank Richardson. Slowly the twelve jurors filed into the jury box, their weariness from their long day showing on their faces. Elizabeth watched them carefully, not really sure what she was looking for. She knew that trial lawyers had long claimed, probably since the formation of the republic, that they could determine whether or not a jury had convicted a defendant by watching them entering the courtroom. The conventional wisdom was that if the jurors looked at a defendant, they had found him not guilty. With this jury, Elizabeth couldn't get any type of read, because some looked at Willie and others stared straight ahead, ready to get their ordeal over with.

As soon as they all were seated, Lawson said, "Mr. Foreman, I understand you have reached a verdict."

"Yes sir, Your Honor, we have," Collards McGee replied, standing as he spoke, with the indictment in one hand.

"And is it a unanimous verdict?" Lawson asked.

"Yes sir, it is," replied the foreman.

"Let me see it, please," Lawson said.

Shirley Barrineau got up from her seat quickly, took the indictment from the foreman, and handed it up to Lawson. The judge turned the document over and studied it for a few seconds, then glanced at the defense table before handing it to the clerk.

"The verdict appears to be in order. You may publish it, Madame Clerk."

Shirley Barrineau turned around after taking the indictment and cleared her throat. Elizabeth's heart was beating so rapidly she thought her blouse was shaking.

"The State of South Carolina versus Willie Fulton. We, the Jury, find Willie Fulton guilty of murder. Is that your verdict, so say you all?" she asked, turning to look at the jury. A number of heads nodded. *GUILTY*

"Does the defense waive polling of the jury?" Lawson asked, looking at Elizabeth.

Elizabeth stood up slowly, hoping her knees wouldn't buckle. "No, Your Honor. We request that the jury be polled," she said, certain that at least one juror would tell the court that this was not their verdict.

One by one, the clerk read each name and then asked each juror, "Is this your verdict?" Some nodded but most answered affirmatively. No one dissented from the decision. Shirley nodded to Lawson when she finished and sat down.

"Let the record reflect that the jury has been polled and that the verdict is unanimous. Ladies and gentlemen, let me thank you for your very fine service on this jury. I will say that your verdict is well within the evidence. Come forward for sentencing," Lawson said to Willie Fulton.

Elizabeth turned to look at Hamilton.

"I'll handle this part for you," he said. "Come forward with me, Willie," he instructed calmly, putting his hand on the man's shoulder.

"Where we going?" Willie asked, his eyes darting back and forth as though he was a caged animal.

"The judge is going to sentence you now. We have to walk up to the front of the bench. Miss Chase and I are going with you," Hamilton said.

Willie slowly shook his head, but that was his only response. Suddenly the big deputy who had been assigned to him walked around the rail, grabbed his left elbow, and jerked him to his feet. "Don't give me no trouble, Willie," the deputy said in a stage whisper and started walking him to the front of the courtroom. Pearlie Mae grabbed him by the other arm and held on with both hands. The deputy half-dragged Willie with Pearlie Mae in tow to a position in front of the clerk's desk. Hamilton and Elizabeth had no choice but to follow closely behind.

"Is there anything else from the State?" Lawson asked, turning to face Phillips and Jacobs, who were standing to his left, facing the jury across the clerk's desk. They were not doing a very good job of controlling their glee.

"Nothing from the State," Phillips replied, folding his arms across his chest and wearing his usual smirk.

"Is there anything else from the defendant before I impose sentencing?" Lawson asked, looking at Elizabeth and Hamilton.

"I don't think so, Your Honor," Hamilton said.

"Very well," Lawson replied. "It is the sentence of this Court that you, Willie Fulton, are hereby sentenced to the South Carolina Department of Corrections for the balance of your natural life."

As Elizabeth turned to look at Willie, she saw him falling backward out of the corner of her eye. He went down hard, like a pine being felled by a chainsaw. Almost as soon as he hit the floor, Pearlie Mae was on top of him, her face almost touching his. Then she put her head back and let out a high-pitched wail like a wounded animal deep in the woods.

"They's killed my husband!" she shrieked. "They's killed my husband!"

"Bailiff, call an ambulance!" Lawson yelled at Hank Richardson.

"Help me with her," Hamilton said to Elizabeth.

Elizabeth rushed over and put her hands on Pearlie Mae's shoulders, who was now sobbing uncontrollably. "Move, Pearlie Mae, so they can help Willie," she said as she pulled the woman to her feet.

An older deputy knelt over Willie and loosened his collar. "He's breathing," he said, glancing up at Lawson. Elizabeth looked down at Willie and saw him staring at the ceiling, blinking his eyes.

The kitchen lights were on when Elizabeth pulled into her grandfather's driveway, so she knew that Rebecca was still there. After she turned off the ignition, she gripped the steering wheel and quickly replayed the afternoon's nightmare one more time. At least Willie was all right, she told herself. The EMS personnel had checked him out in the courtroom and could find nothing wrong with him. He had only fainted, one of the paramedics told Lawson, and Willie was quickly pulled to his feet and unceremoniously hauled off to the Craven County Jail. Pearlie Mae didn't fare as well, collapsing twice as her relatives helped her out of the courtroom.

When Hamilton and Elizabeth had gotten back to the office, they could tell by the look on Inez's face that she had already heard the verdict.

"Can I get you anything?" she asked.

"I'm okay, Inez," Hamilton said. "We'll be in my office." Elizabeth just shook her head.

"Are you all right?" Hamilton asked when they sat down.

"I just can't get Pearlie Mae's screams out of my mind."

"You look exhausted. Go home. Get some rest. We'll talk about our next step in the morning."

CHAPTER 30

Rebecca pulled open the front door just as Elizabeth reached for the knob. The two women stared at each other for a moment before Rebecca grabbed her, and they embraced.

"You didn't have to wait on me, Rebecca," Elizabeth said as she pulled away.

"I heard what that jury did, so I knew you'd be upset. I got your supper ready if you hungry."

"Not right now. I just want to sit down and put my feet up. Come to the library with me."

"I'll be right there, Miss Elizabeth, in just a minute," Rebecca said and disappeared down the hallway.

Elizabeth fell on the sofa, leaned her head back, and closed her eyes as she put her feet on the coffee table.

"Here you go," Rebecca said, walking into the room holding a glass.

"What is that?"

"It's some of that liquor you like to drink."

Elizabeth couldn't suppress her smile. "I didn't think you approved of alcohol, Rebecca."

"I don't, 'cept when somebody needs it for medicine. And you look like you could use some now. No offense, Miss Elizabeth, but you look awful."

"Thanks," Elizabeth said, accepting the glass. She took a small sip, then a long swallow. "This is just what I need. Thank you. Sit down, Rebecca," she said, moving over to make room for her.

Rebecca sat down but didn't say anything. "Can you do anything else to help Willie?" she asked finally.

"We can file an appeal with the State Supreme Court."

"Will that do any good?"

For the first time since the jury came back with their guilty verdict, Elizabeth thought about the probability of Willie Fulton spending the next twenty years in prison. She heard the wail of poor Pearlie Mae again, ringing in her ears. What would she tell her children? How would she support that big family? Elizabeth leaned forward and put her head in her hands.

"Miss Elizabeth, you okay?"

The tears came slowly at first, tickling her cheeks and rolling off her hands and onto her legs. Rebecca had her arms around her before the first sobs, and she rocked her gently back and forth just as she had done when Elizabeth was a child. Finally, her crying stopped.

"You're gonna be okay," Rebecca said, still rocking.

"Would you get me a Kleenex, please?" Elizabeth asked, her voice muffled by Rebecca's shoulder.

"Sure, honey, I'll be right back." Elizabeth had regained her composure by the time Rebecca returned. "You okay?" Rebecca asked as she sat down beside Elizabeth.

Elizabeth nodded.

"It always makes you feel better when you talk 'bout trouble," Rebecca said.

Elizabeth nodded again. "I know," she said.

"You gotta realize, Miss Elizabeth, you can't put all them people's troubles on your shoulders."

"I know, but I feel as if it's my fault Willie's going to jail."

"Why you say that? That jury's done spoke, and they said he was guilty. You done done all you could do."

"I just don't feel that what I did was good enough," Elizabeth said slowly, her voice barely above a whisper. "If only Willie had testified, I think he could have convinced that jury that he didn't do it."

"You really think he didn't kill that man, don't you?"

"I don't think he did, Rebecca," she said, turning to look at her. "I don't," she repeated, her voice rising now. "Rebecca, will you answer one question for me?"

"Sure, I will if I can. What is it?"

"What do you know about root?"

Rebecca pulled her arms to her waist and sat up straight. "Who told you about the root?"

"Robert Hamilton. Someone spread white powder around the witness stand yesterday, and Robert said it was root powder. Who would have put it there, Rebecca?"

"I don't know nothing 'bout no root powder in no courtroom, you hear?" There was a sharp tone to Rebecca's voice that Elizabeth had never heard before.

"What is the powder supposed to do?"

"It suppose to work a spell."

"A spell?"

"Yeah, a spell."

"On whom?"

"On the people trying to work against Willie. It suppose to protect him, but in this case it ain't work too good."

"Do you believe in the root, Rebecca?"

"I ain't wanna say," Rebecca said, holding her hands out. "I don't want to talk 'bout that stuff no more, Miss Elizabeth." Rebecca squinted as if in pain, then stood up and said, "I gonna warm your supper."

"All right," Elizabeth responded as Rebecca quickly left the room.

Elizabeth finished her scotch before she followed Rebecca to the kitchen. There was a baked chicken in the oven and rice and gravy and butterbeans on the stove. After several minutes of insisting that she would be okay, Elizabeth cut everything on low and drove Rebecca home.

Elizabeth ate supper at the kitchen table. She was numb with fatigue as she put the dirty dishes in the sink, and when the phone rang, it startled her so much she almost dropped a plate.

"Are you okay?" Jim asked when she answered.

"Yeah, I guess so," she said weakly.

"You sound awful. I'm at the beach, or I would have stopped to check on you."

"What's going on there?"

"Just a little problem with the house, but it's no big deal. I've got it taken care of. I heard they convicted Willie Fulton."

"That's right," she said.

"I'm sorry," he told her.

"Yeah, so am I."

"When will you be heading back to Boston?"

"In a few days, I guess. I've still got to sort some things out in my head first."

"Like what?"

"I don't know. I know this sounds strange, but something just isn't right."

"I'll call you tomorrow when I get to town. Do you want to have dinner tomorrow night?"

"Yeah, I guess so."

"Why don't you take some of that medication I gave you last month to sleep."

"I think I will. I'll talk to you tomorrow."

Elizabeth took his advice about the sleeping pills, and she was asleep almost as soon as her head hit the pillow.

Elizabeth heard someone calling her name, and at first she thought it was a dream. When she opened her eyes, she saw Rebecca standing over her with both arms on her shoulders, shaking her. Rebecca had a contorted, agonized look on her face, and Elizabeth sat straight up in her bed when she realized that something must be dreadfully wrong.

"What is it, Rebecca?"

"I gotta talk to you, Miss Elizabeth. I'm so sorry for waking you up like this."

"For God's sake, what's wrong?"

"Why don't you put your housecoat on and come downstairs? We gotta talk."

"What time is it, Rebecca?" she asked, looking out the window. It was barely daylight.

"A little after six."

"Nobody died, did they?"

"No," she said. "We just gotta talk 'bout some things, that all. I'll make some coffee."

Elizabeth took several minutes to wash the sleep out of her eyes and brush her hair before she joined Rebecca in the kitchen.

"Why did you get here so early?" Elizabeth asked while Rebecca poured two cups of coffee.

"I ain't slept all night," Rebecca said as they sat down at the table.

"Well, tell me what's bothering you, then."

"It's something that ain't right."

"What isn't right?"

"I stayed up praying all night."

"About what, Rebecca?" Elizabeth asked.

"My people been talking. Been doing a lot of talking. I heard a lot at church last night."

"What did you hear?"

"Talking 'bout Willie's case."

"What about Willie's case?"

"They's talking about Willie and the root and Black Jack."

"What about Black Jack?" Elizabeth asked quickly, putting her coffee cup down.

"They's always been talk 'bout him, you know what I mean?"

"No, I don't, Rebecca," Elizabeth said patiently. Rebecca put her head down, and her hands were shaking. "Rebecca," Elizabeth said, reaching out for her hand, "you've got to tell me what's on your mind. Tell me what you know about the sheriff."

Rebecca bit her bottom lip and stared at Elizabeth. "They always say Black Jack is a root doctor," she said quickly, as if to get the words out before she lost her resolve.

"What is a root doctor?"

"You ain't never hear of a root doctor?"

"Robert mentioned it, but what do they do?"

"They got all kinda powers."

"What kind of powers?"

"They can put a spell on you."

"What sort of spell?"

"Make you sick. Make some people die."

"Let's get back to the sheriff. Do they say he uses powder when he's casting his spells?"

"Oh yeah, he use powder all right."

"And that was his powder that was used in the courtroom to protect Willie from harm?"

"Yeah, it was suppose to, but it don't look like it did any good to me."

"How would someone like Willie get the powder from the sheriff?"

"Oh, they pay him for it."

"I see. A root doctor makes money selling spells and powder and things."

"Oh yeah, they say they make a lot of money."

"So you think the sheriff was paid to try to help Willie with a spell."

Rebecca nodded.

"Rebecca, why didn't you tell me this about the sheriff before?" Rebecca shrugged. "If we can prove this, this may be enough to get Willie a new trial," Elizabeth said, banging her fist down on the table and causing the older woman to jump.

"Have you gotta bring what I'm telling you up in court?" Rebecca asked, arching her eyebrows.

"I sure do. I just don't know how I'm going to prove it yet."

"Please, Miss Elizabeth, don't say nothing in the courtroom 'bout what I said," Rebecca implored, reaching for Elizabeth's hands.

"You don't have anything to be frightened of."

"Oh yes, I do. I'm 'fraid of that root, Miss Elizabeth. I've seen it hurt and kill people. I've seen it drive people fool out they heads."

Elizabeth looked at Rebecca, not knowing what to say. She had to follow up on what Rebecca was telling her, because Lawson would have to grant Willie a new trial if she could prove this connection between Willie and the sheriff.

Rebecca leaned forward and put her head down. Elizabeth could see her tears hitting the linoleum floor in tiny splashes. "I just don't know what my people gonna do to me. Somehow, I knew you were gonna have to tell the judge what I'm telling you. I just don't know what they gonna do to me."

"Why would your people do anything to you, Rebecca?"

"It could get Black Jack in a heap of trouble, couldn't it?" she asked, raising her head.

"It could, but it could also keep Willie from spending twenty years in jail for a murder he didn't commit. Have you thought about that?"

"I thought 'bout everything. That's why I was up all night. I even called Princess and talked to her."

"You called Princess about this?"

"Uh huh," Rebecca said.

"What did she say?"

"She said, 'Mama, you already knew what to do before you called me.'"

"What did she mean by that?"

"She just say, 'Mama, what you always tell us? Right's right, and wrong's wrong.'" The older woman put her elbow on the table and rested her chin in her hand. "I knew all night long I had to talk to you."

"It's going to be all right, Rebecca."

Rebecca leaned back in her chair and looked at Elizabeth. "Miss Elizabeth, you jus' don't know my people. You might know white people, but they's a lot of colored people around here that's scared to death of that root. And they's a lot of people around here that's scared of Black Jack."

"Does he really have special powers?"

"He always has since he born."

"Since he was born?"

"Yeah, they say he was born with a caul over his body."

"What is a caul, Rebecca?"

"It's a special skin covering a baby. Anybody born with it has special magical powers. And they say he got the strongest powder you can get. Even stronger than what Dr. Buzzard has."

"Who is Dr. Buzzard?"

"He stay down near Beaufort. They say you got to get in a boat to get to him."

"Does Black Jack sell a lot of his magical powder?"

"They say he does."

"Is it always white?"

"Just as white as a cotton field in October," Rebecca said, nodding.

As soon as she could, Elizabeth went over every detail of Rebecca's story with Hamilton in the office library. "Don't you agree with me that we have an excellent chance of getting Willie a new trial if we can prove that there was contact between Willie and Black Jack during the trial?" she asked.

"I think we'll have to show some type of prejudice to the defense for Lawson to grant the motion. Mere contact and the possible sale of some harmless white powder to Willie may not be enough."

"Do you think that powder is harmless?" Elizabeth asked.

"You're not starting to believe in that root too, are you?"

"No, not in the root. But Rebecca told me Black Jack has the strongest powder anyone has ever seen."

"What are you getting at, Elizabeth?"

"I'm not sure. I need to think about this a bit more."

CHAPTER 31

Willie shuffled into the visitor's room, barely looking at either of his lawyers as he sat down in a metal chair. He was wearing an orange prison uniform that looked more like a pair of loud pajamas, and shower slides with white socks. His eyes were bloodshot, and it was obvious he hadn't had much sleep.

"Good morning, Willie. How are you?"

"Not so good," he answered, looking up slowly. "I forgot how much racket they make back in that bullpen. A man can't get no sleep."

"We need to ask you some questions," Hamilton said.

"I thought court is over with," he responded slowly.

"Maybe not," Hamilton answered.

"The fellows in the back said to make sure you filed an appeal," Willie stated, pointing over his shoulder.

"Oh, we'll file one all right," Hamilton said. "Now, listen to me carefully, Willie, because what I'm going to ask you is very important."

"All right."

"Did you talk to the sheriff during the trial?"

Willie's eyes widened. "'Bout what?"

"About anything concerning your case?"

"What me and the sheriff talked about didn't have nothing to do 'bout that killing."

"Well, what did you talk about?" Elizabeth asked. Willie didn't answer. "It was about the root, wasn't it?" Willie lowered his eyes but didn't say anything. "The sheriff is a root doctor, isn't he, Willie?"

"They say he is."

"Did you pay Black Jack to put a spell on that jury, Willie?" Hamilton asked in a calm voice.

"That ain't got nothing to do with my case. I don't want to spend the rest of my life in no stinking jail. Let's talk 'bout my 'peal."

"Don't you understand, Willie, that if we can show that Black

Jack and his powder somehow influenced this case, we may be able to get you a new trial?" Elizabeth asked, trying to sound upbeat.

"I don't want to talk any more about no powder or no root," Willie said firmly, staring intently at Elizabeth.

Elizabeth looked at Hamilton, and he shook his head slowly.

"What are we going to do now, Robert?" Elizabeth asked once they were back on the sidewalk.

"I'm not sure."

"Why wouldn't Willie talk to us?"

"He's scared out of his wits."

"You would think he would be very cooperative now that he's facing a life sentence."

"Well, you have to understand, Elizabeth, that a life sentence is a whole lot better than a death sentence."

"What do you mean?"

"I'm sure he thinks that Black Jack can put a death spell on him."

"And that's why he won't talk?"

"Probably so," Hamilton said.

"Then I've got to find Pearlie Mae."

"Are you going out to her house?"

"Just as quickly as I can get there."

"Then I'll go with you."

"I think I can find their place. Maybe she would open up more if it's just me," Elizabeth said.

"Are you sure you can find their place?" he asked.

"If you'll draw me a map, I can find it."

Elizabeth put the map on the seat beside her in the Buick and drove down Lee Street, making a right turn at the edge of town onto River Road. She watched the odometer carefully, as she recalled Black Jack's testimony that Frenchie's house was 9.2 miles out of town. She knew she had missed the turn when she had driven 11 miles, so she stopped at a country store and got more explicit directions. She was right; she had passed the turnoff to the Fulton place, and as she retraced her route, she drove much slower this time, watching carefully for the turn. The lane was marked by a beat-up mailbox, and this time she found the house easily.

The mean-looking dog was nowhere in sight this time, which alarmed Elizabeth as she crossed the hard-baked ground that served as the Fultons' front yard. She kept looking in all directions, thinking the mongrel was lying in wait for her, but he never showed his head. When she raised her hand to knock on the old batten door, it swung open, and a black woman appeared in the doorway. She looked just like Pearlie Mae except older, and Elizabeth knew that the woman had to be a sister.

"Is Pearlie Mae at home?" Elizabeth asked.

"You the lawyer, right?"

"Yes, I'm Elizabeth Chase, one of Mr. Fulton's lawyers. I was looking for Pearlie Mae."

"She here. Wait a minute. I'll get her," the woman said.

It was a good five minutes before Pearlie Mae stepped out onto the porch, wearing a tattered housecoat. "What you doing way out here?" she asked, her puffy eyes opening wide. "Is something wrong with Willie?"

"No, Willie's fine. I just left him at the county jail."

"What you want, then?"

"Pearlie Mae, we need to talk."

The woman looked into the house and then back at Elizabeth. "I'll get some chairs, and we can talk out here on the porch. It'll be cooler out here," she added as she walked back inside. She returned with two straight-back wooden chairs, which had most of their original varnish worn off.

"What you wanna talk 'bout?" Pearlie Mae asked as soon as she sat down.

"Mr. Hamilton and I think Willie was listening to somebody else about his case." Elizabeth had rehearsed her lines as she drove. She waited for a comment, but none was forthcoming.

"What you mean?" Pearlie Mae finally asked.

"Does Willie believe in the root?"

"What you know 'bout the root, you being a white woman?" she asked, her eyes narrowing.

"I've learned a lot in the last twenty-four hours," Elizabeth said, staring back at Pearlie Mae. The woman didn't respond, and she refused to make eye contact with Elizabeth. Elizabeth leaned forward and put her forearms on her knees. "Listen, Pearlie Mae. I'm trying to help Willie."

"How can you help Willie? It's done too late," she said, looking out over an open cornfield that had already turned brown in the broiling August sun.

"Not necessarily. If you give me some information, I may be able to get the judge to give him a new trial."

Pearlie Mae turned and looked Elizabeth square in the eyes for the first time. "What it is you need to know?"

"First, does Willie believe in the root?"

"Yeah, I reckon he does."

"Do you remember that powder in the courtroom during the trial?"

"Yeah, I remember."

"That had something to do with Willie's case, didn't it?" Pearlie Mae looked at Elizabeth but didn't answer. "I'm trying to help, Pearlie Mae, so tell me, please."

"It was suppose to help his case, but it don't look like it was too much help to me," Pearlie Mae said, folding her arms and resting them on her stomach.

"Willie paid somebody money to put that powder in the courtroom, didn't he?"

"Yeah, he did."

"Who did he pay?"

"I don't know who he give it to. I wasn't there."

"Was it the sheriff?"

"No, it wasn't the sheriff."

"But the sheriff is a root doctor, isn't he?" Again Pearlie Mae didn't answer. "Pearlie Mae, I've had other black people tell me that the sheriff is a root doctor, so you don't have anything to be afraid of."

"Yeah, he a root doctor," she said quickly.

"Could Willie have paid for a spell to somehow be put in the courtroom?"

"The spell was to be put on that jury, but like I said, it didn't work none too good."

"Could the man Willie gave the money to—could he have been working for the sheriff?"

"Yeah, he coulda been."

"How much did Willie pay the man?"

"Five hundred dollars."

"Did Willie's decision not to testify have something to do with the root?"

"I don't know. That same night he pay the man was the night he decide he ain't gonna testify."

"Did Willie tell you why he changed his mind about testifying?"

"No, he just say he changed his mind."

"Do you know the name of the man that Willie gave the money to?"

"Everybody call him Pokey."

"Think hard, Pearlie Mae. Have you ever known Pokey to work for the sheriff?"

"Just days work."

"What do you mean by that?"

"He would work a day here and a day there. Wash cars, things like that, for Black Jack."

"Does Black Jack sell a lot of his root powder?"

"They say he does, but I don't mess wid it."

"Can you think of anything else Willie did during the trial or anybody else that he talked to?"

Pearlie Mae thought for a few seconds, then shook her head. "No, not really," she said.

Hamilton listened carefully to what Elizabeth told him about her trip to the Fulton place as they sat in the library after lunch. When she finished, she waited for his reaction.

"Do you really think Black Jack has some involvement in Frenchie's murder?"

Elizabeth nodded. "I do."

"Why?"

"I think Black Jack has perhaps been involved in some type of illegal activity," Elizabeth said.

"What kind of illegal activity?"

"Cocaine. It's becoming more popular than marijuana. It provides a better high, apparently, and the so-called jet set loves it. In our office in Boston, we get a lot of cases for simple possession, and we also represent a lot of the street dealers. We don't see the big dealers because they can pay the enormous fees the private defense bar is charging."

"But how does Black Jack fit into all of this?"

"I think some of his root powder may be cocaine."

"Do you have any idea where he gets it?"

"Probably Winyah Bay or further out in the Atlantic. That's usually how the middlemen get their supply in New England and south Florida—by water."

"So how does Frenchie's murder fit into this?" Hamilton asked.

"I think Black Jack is using his patrol boats to pick up the cocaine. I think maybe Frenchie saw too much, and Black Jack had to kill him."

"What I can't figure out is how Willie got involved in all this," Hamilton said. "Maybe we can find out after someone talks to this fellow Pokey. I think I know Pokey. He hangs around the jail a good bit."

"Where do we go from here, Robert?" Elizabeth asked. "We can't turn to the sheriff's office for help, and I don't think Phillips and his staff will fall all over themselves to overturn the verdict."

"I'll call the chief," Hamilton said.

"Who is the chief?"

"J. D. Stevens. He's an old college classmate of mine from Carolina. He's the only head that SLED has had since it was organized almost thirty years ago."

"What can he do?"

"They have concurrent jurisdiction all over the state with local law enforcement. I'll see if he will send us a couple of agents to begin an investigation."

"Do you think he can do it quickly?"

"I'll call him right now," Hamilton said as he stood up to leave. It was a while before he returned to the library.

"You must have reached him," Elizabeth said.

"Yeah, I did," Hamilton replied with a grin. "It's been a while since J.D. and I talked, and he wanted to catch up on some of our friends. He always was a talker."

"Is he going to send help?"

"There will be two agents here at nine sharp in the morning," Hamilton said.

"Good. If we're through here, I think I'll dictate a detailed memo so Inez can have it ready for them when they get here in the morning," Elizabeth said as she gathered up the file spread out on the table in front of her. Taking the file into her grandfather's office, she saw a phone message from Jim on the blotter and remembered they were supposed to have dinner together. She dialed his office and was put on hold.

"Elizabeth," he said when he finally picked up. "Sorry to keep you waiting. I was stitching someone up and couldn't stop."

"That's okay."

"You still on for dinner?"

"I guess so."

"You don't sound real enthusiastic."

"I'm sorry, Jim. I guess I'm still numb from yesterday."

"Well, don't take the verdict personally."

"Jim, I take all of my cases, especially murder cases, personally," she snapped.

"I'm sorry. I didn't mean it like it sounded."

"That's okay. I just don't feel like going out."

"I didn't think you would, so I brought back some fish from the beach. I was going to grill it."

"That sounds good. What time?" Elizabeth asked.

"Is eight thirty too late? I've got a full waiting room, and I'm already an hour behind."

"That's fine. I'll see you then."

"You seem preoccupied," Jim said later, as he stirred his drink with his finger. He and Elizabeth were seated in the rear courtyard of Jim's townhouse in lawn chairs, facing a grill where the swordfish steaks were already sizzling. "Are you still thinking about your case?"

"I'm sorry," she said, not realizing she was staring at the sky. "Yes, I guess I am. I can't get those poor people off my mind."

"What will happen to Fulton? Won't he be out on parole in a few years?"

"No, the law here says he has to serve at least twenty years. He'll get that cut some for good behavior, but the shortest active sentence he can hope for is around eighteen years, from what I've been told."

"That's a long time."

"For a man his age, it's a very long time. And for Pearlie Mae, it's probably even longer. I don't know how she will take care of all of those children."

"I wouldn't worry about that, Elizabeth," he said as he carefully turned the fish with a spatula. "The government will take care of them, like they do most of the people in this county. You wouldn't believe the people I see in my office who are on the welfare rolls."

"But what kind of life will that be for Pearlie Mae and her children?"

"Probably better than they have now."

"Without a husband and a father?" Jim looked at her as he put down the spatula, but he didn't say anything. "Hopefully we won't have to answer that question," Elizabeth remarked.

"What do you mean by that?"

"I haven't given up on this case yet."

"You're going to file an appeal, then?"

"We are, but that's not what I meant."

"What did you mean, then?"

"I have uncovered some information since the trial which may be helpful in Willie's case."

"How can it be helpful now, after the jury has found him guilty?"

"It's called 'after discovered evidence.' If we can produce new evidence that shows Willie is not guilty, and we could not have discovered it prior to trial, then the judge can grant a defendant a new trial."

"I didn't know that," Jim said as he sat down by Elizabeth and reached for his drink. "What kind of evidence have you found?"

"Well, I really haven't found any concrete evidence yet, but we have some pretty good leads."

"Just how are you going to follow up on them, if I might ask?"

"This is serious, Jim. Maybe I can tell you the whole story in a few days."

Jim reached over and grabbed her arm. "I'm sorry. I was just kidding. I realize this is serious."

"It is," Elizabeth said, nodding.

"Tell me, please. I swear I won't breathe a word of it."

"You promise?"

"I promise."

"Robert is a close friend of the head of the State Law Enforcement Division. He's called him for help."

"What will they be investigating?"

"I can't tell you that."

"What do you think I'm going to do? Spread our conversation all over town like Ida Pearl? You don't think there is any trust in our relationship?" Jim's voice had an edge to it that Elizabeth hadn't heard before, so it was obvious she had offended him.

"I'm sorry. You're a professional, and you know about confidences," she said, reaching over and grabbing his hand. "We don't know much. Somehow, though, I think the sheriff knows something about this murder."

"Why do you say that?"

"Do you know what a root doctor is?"

"Oh heavens, yes," Jim said chuckling. "Of course I do. A lot of my black patients talk about their root treatments for their ailments. Some of them I ask in advance what else they are taking. I don't know who my competitors are, however, because they won't mention the root doctors by name."

"Have you ever heard that the sheriff is a root doctor?"

"Black Jack?"

"Yes, Black Jack."

Jim shook his head. "No, never," he said.

"That's the word I've gotten from more than one source."

"But what does a root doctor have to do with this case?"

"Apparently Willie paid a root doctor, probably through an intermediary, to put a spell on the jury."

"A spell for what?"

"A spell so the jury wouldn't find Willie guilty."

"Well, that's one spell that sure didn't work."

"I know, but that's how Black Jack comes into the picture."

"What do you mean?"

"I think Black Jack made Willie think the jury was going to decide in his favor."

"Well, if the spell didn't even work, what difference does it make?"

Elizabeth pointed her index finger at Jim and smiled. "You know, you might make a halfway decent lawyer yourself. You're right. We have to take it at least one step further."

"And how are you going to do that?"

"I think we might be able to show that Black Jack persuaded Willie not to testify."

"How could he do that? The man was on trial for his life. He's not stupid."

"Good point. But if Willie was convinced that the spell was

all he needed, then why take a chance by testifying?"

"I see," Jim said, leaning forward in his chair. "It's all very interesting, but can you prove it?"

"I don't know; that's why we are bringing in SLED to investigate."

"Why do you think Black Jack would want to see Willie Fulton convicted of murder? Isn't that what you are saying?"

"That's my theory."

"Then tell me why."

"Do you promise to keep quiet about this?"

"Absolutely," he answered, nodding.

"I think Black Jack is somehow involved in a cocaine ring."

"Good God, Elizabeth. This isn't the big city. What makes you think people around here are involved with cocaine?"

"You heard about the powder around the witness stand during the trial, didn't you?"

"Oh yes. It's been the talk of the town."

"It was snow white."

"And you think it was cocaine."

"I've seen enough cocaine to know what it looks like."

"Okay, but that doesn't prove that Black Jack is a dealer."

"I know that. Say, you're a pretty good cross-examiner too," Elizabeth said with mock seriousness.

"Well, what else do you have?"

"Not much. The story is that Black Jack sells magic powders."

"I think that's a pretty common product for all the root doctors in these parts."

"But from what I hear, Black Jack's powder has been a lot stronger these past few months."

"Who told you all this Elizabeth?" Jim asked, leaning back in his chair and running his fingers through his hair.

"Different people."

"Well, it sounds farfetched to me. You don't know how the black people look up to Black Jack around here. He's their hero, their leader. There's even talk about him running for the State Senate."

"Haven't you seen heroes with feet of clay before?"

"Yes, I have, but I don't think Black Jack is your man. I know him too well."

Jim made a cream sauce for the fish, which was grilled to

[margin note: IDA PEARL SAID THE DOCTOR WAD MONEY TO SPEND]

perfection. It was almost ten thirty before they finished the dishes and a bottle of wine.

"Have you had enough time, yet?" Jim asked as he punched the start button on the dishwasher.

"Time enough for what?"

"To size me up."

"Yes, I think I have," Elizabeth answered. The two of them were standing a foot apart. "I've been watching you closely, and I've been checking up on you," she added, grinning.

"Yeah?"

"Robert Hamilton thinks quite highly of you, you know."

Jim stepped forward and put his arms around her waist. "I have a lot of respect for Robert Hamilton, but I'm a lot more interested in your opinion of me. Why don't you stay over?"

"I've got a busy day tomorrow," Elizabeth said, yawning and stretching her arms.

Jim grabbed her before she could pull her arms back into her body and held her close to his face. "I'll have you up and back home before daybreak."

"Before Rebecca gets to the house?"

"Even before Rebecca is up," he added, drawing her mouth to his.

CHAPTER 32

The two agents from SLED were already in the library with Hamilton drinking coffee when Elizabeth arrived at the office a few minutes before nine. The two men stood politely as Hamilton made the introductions. The younger agent was in his mid-thirties, slim, with a closely cropped military-style haircut. The other man was in his early sixties, was short, and weighed about 240 pounds. He was introduced as Puddin Brown, and Elizabeth almost giggled when she heard his name. Both men wore short-sleeve shirts with clip-on ties.

After they all sat down, she and Hamilton made small talk with the men for several minutes. Then Hamilton nodded to Elizabeth, and she started from the beginning. From time to time the younger agent would interrupt her and ask questions, and he made a lot of notes on a legal pad as Elizabeth talked. The older agent sat back quietly, with his arms folded over his massive stomach.

Elizabeth's briefing took a little over an hour. When she finished, she stared across the table at Lieutenant Fields, the younger agent.

"Obviously, the first person we need to check out is this man Pokey," he said, putting his legal pad on the table in front of him. "The problem, of course, is how to conduct this investigation without tipping off the sheriff. We have to do this very delicately," he said, looking at Hamilton.

"You're right, Lieutenant. The sheriff is a very popular man in this county," Hamilton said.

"We are well aware of that, Mr. Hamilton," the lieutenant responded. "The chief and I had a long conference yesterday afternoon after your call. We are well aware that he's the first black sheriff in this state since Reconstruction. Normally, this is Agent Brown's jurisdiction, but the chief asked me to assist him on this case. If Miss Chase is wrong about the sheriff, this could blow up in our faces and become very embarrassing for our agency. The chief is going to retire next year, and he doesn't want the governor pushing him out the door if this investigation backfires. Do you know what I mean?"

"Certainly we do, Lieutenant. We fully understand your position," Hamilton said.

"And you understand this may take a while," Lieutenant Fields continued.

"How long?" Elizabeth asked.

"I don't know, Miss Chase," Fields said, shaking his head. "Weeks, months, I just can't tell this early in the investigation."

"Well, we've got an innocent man sitting in jail with a family of seven out there to feed," Elizabeth said.

"Miss Chase, we will check everything out, but you need to understand that these things take time. We just can't walk up to this man Pokey when we find him and start asking questions. We'll probably have to bring in a black undercover agent to help us. And you just told me a little while ago that the black people around here are very reluctant to discuss the root, as you call it."

"I understand," Elizabeth said calmly. "Just do it as fast as you can, please."

After showing the agents out, Elizabeth and Hamilton returned to the library.

"What do you think, Robert?" she asked before they sat down.

"They didn't seem real enthusiastic," he said.

"My God. I don't think there has ever been an ounce of enthusiasm in Agent Brown's body. Is his name really Puddin?"

"That's what everybody has called him for as long as I can remember."

"It sounds like this thing could take months," Elizabeth said, biting her lower lip.

"I'll talk to J.D. again. We have to realize we are asking one law-enforcement agency to investigate another law-enforcement agency. And we are asking their assistance in freeing a convicted murderer." Before Elizabeth could reply, she saw Inez standing in the doorway.

"Excuse me for interrupting," she said timidly, walking toward Elizabeth, "but I thought you might want this phone message right now." She handed her a slip of paper.

Elizabeth took the slip and looked at it. *Call Sheriff Carter as soon as possible,* it read.

"Miss Chase, thank you very much for returning my call so quickly," Black Jack said when Elizabeth identified herself. She was at her grandfather's desk, and Hamilton was seated across from her, watching her face closely.

"Glad to, Sheriff. I hope there is nothing wrong with my client?"

"No, Willie is fine. I checked on him first thing this morning."

"That's good."

"The reason I called, Miss Chase, is because there is a matter I would like to discuss with you."

"Do you want to discuss it over the phone, or would you like me to come to your office?"

"Can you hold a minute, Miss Chase? I need to close my office door." As Elizabeth waited, she could hear the sheriff get up and close the door. "You still there?" he asked when he picked up the phone again.

"Yes, I'm here."

"I need to discuss a development in your client's case," the sheriff said slowly, as if he was choosing his words carefully.

"Sheriff, I can be there in five minutes," Elizabeth offered, looking up at Hamilton.

"No, we can't discuss it here," the sheriff said, just above a whisper.

"Why not?"

"I would rather not say now, other than to tell you it may be of great benefit to Willie Fulton."

"Where do you want to meet, then?"

"At Frenchie's place."

"Frenchie's place?"

"That's correct."

"That will be fine, Sheriff. What time?"

"This evening if that's okay. I have to go to Columbia today for a meeting. Say seven o'clock. Can you find it okay?"

"Sure. Seven's fine."

"One more thing, Miss Chase."

"What's that?"

"Would you please come alone? What we will discuss could

be very embarrassing to my office if it gets out."

"Sure, I'll come alone. I'll see you at seven, Sheriff," Elizabeth said and put down the phone.

Hamilton's eyes were wide as he put his elbows on the old walnut desk. "You're not going alone, Elizabeth. That's completely out of the question. Don't even consider it, because I won't let you."

"Why not?"

"Why not?" Hamilton almost shouted. "Because if what you say is true about that man, he could be very dangerous."

"Even if he's a drug dealer, he would have better sense than to harm me, Robert. He's not your run-of-the-mill crook."

"I know that, but why would he want to meet you at Frenchie's place? Why couldn't he meet you in his office. Or come over here? We're only a block away."

"He said that what we will be discussing could be very embarrassing to his office."

"I have no idea what that could mean," Hamilton remarked, shaking his head. "I still can't let you go by yourself."

"We can talk to Lieutenant Fields or your friend the chief and arrange for some backup. They do it all the time with informants."

"But that still won't guarantee your safety."

"It will if they can arrange a wire."

"What is that?"

"It's fairly new. Undercover agents and informants are wired for sound with a voice transmitter. As long as I don't get out of range, the backup can hear every word that's said."

"I still don't like it." Hamilton rubbed his chin.

"Do me a favor, Robert, please. The lieutenant said they were heading back to Columbia. Can you talk to the chief and see if they can meet us back here late this afternoon? Tell him we're looking for backup and would also like to arrange a wire for me."

Hamilton stared at Elizabeth for a few seconds and then got up slowly. "I don't like this," he said finally.

"Go ahead, Robert. Everything will be fine. I'll be perfectly safe."

Hamilton did not return for thirty minutes, so Elizabeth assumed they were visiting on the phone again.

"I'm sorry that took so long," Hamilton said when he finally returned from his office.

"Oh, I figured you two were still catching up on the gossip."

"No, this was all business, Elizabeth. J.D. wanted to know every detail. He doesn't want this thing to blow up. And he agrees with you; he thinks the wire might be a good idea."

"Great."

"He wanted to know all about you, whether you could handle something like this."

"What did you tell him?"

"I had to tell him the truth. I just hope I don't live to regret it."

"What do you mean?"

"I told him that you were a crackerjack trial lawyer and that I thought you could handle yourself in just about any situation."

"Thanks, Robert," Elizabeth said, grinning. His gloomy expression did not change. "What time are they coming?"

"They'll be here around five. That will give them enough time to brief you. He's sending two other agents, much younger, to take Puddin's place."

"That's a relief," Elizabeth said. "I think that the only thing that man can get physical with is a refrigerator door."

"He said Fields is one of his top agents, and the other two are rising stars in the agency." Hamilton exhaled loudly and paused for a few seconds. "J.D. thinks you will be okay. He wanted to know all about the layout at Frenchie's place. As long as you and the sheriff stay near the house, they can position themselves in the woods close enough to be on top of the situation if anything goes wrong."

"Nothing will go wrong, Robert. Stop worrying."

Hamilton stared at Elizabeth for a few seconds and then said, "God, I hope not." After another pause, he asked, "What do you think the sheriff has up his sleeve?"

"I have no earthly idea," Elizabeth said, touching all of her fingertips together to form a steeple.

Elizabeth spent the rest of the day in the library researching the law on after discovered evidence in South Carolina. As she didn't know exactly what additional evidence they might uncover, she didn't know how helpful the cases were that she pored over. All of the decisions did expound on one central factor that was necessary to warrant a new trial: the discovered evidence had to affect the outcome of the case. She was about halfway through a rough draft of a memorandum on this issue when Inez interrupted her.

"It's Dr. Howard," she said. "I'm sorry to bother you, but I figured you would want to talk with him."

"Yes, I do, Inez. Thanks." She got up and walked quickly to her office. "Hello, Jim," she said when she picked up the phone.

"Hey, Elizabeth, how are you?"

"I'm better."

"Has there been some new development in the Fulton case?"

"No, not yet, but I may have a lead on something."

"Tell me what's going on."

"The sheriff called me this morning."

"Oh yeah? What did he say?"

"He wants to meet me tonight at seven o'clock."

"Did he say what he wanted to talk about?"

"No, he didn't."

"That's interesting. Is he coming to your office?"

"No, we're meeting somewhere else."

"Where?" he asked, his voice rising slightly.

"I'll tell you later. Maybe when I get back."

"What's the big secret?"

"He wants me to meet him alone, and I'm afraid you'll tell everybody in town about this. The sheriff was very secretive. I shouldn't even be telling you this."

"Alone, did you say?"

"Yes, alone."

"Where are you going to meet him, Elizabeth?" Jim asked very slowly and deliberately. "I don't know if I like this."

"You sound just like Robert. I'll be fine."

"Listen, they are calling me over at the emergency room. One of my patients is apparently going into cardiac arrest. I'll see you before six," he said and hung up.

The three SLED agents arrived at quarter to five wearing combat fatigues, and if they had been carrying M-16 rifles, they would have looked as if they just stepped out of the jungles of South Vietnam. Lieutenant Fields introduced the others as Agent Harrison and Agent Wall. They were lean and muscular, and Elizabeth guessed that they were about her age. They nodded as they shook Elizabeth's hand firmly.

"We've spent most of the afternoon reconnoitering the area around the rendezvous point," Fields said after the introduction.

"Excuse me?" Elizabeth said.

"We've checked out the area around Mr. Gilbert's house completely," Fields explained. "We don't anticipate any problems in keeping you under close surveillance. We won't have you under visual surveillance because that is too risky. It won't be dark yet."

"I understand," Elizabeth said.

"Now, about the wire," Fields continued and nodded to one of the other agents, who opened a briefcase and pulled out a small device with wires running out of it. "Fortunately, these transmitters work better with women."

"Why is that?" Elizabeth asked.

Fields grinned sheepishly. "Because it is worn on the chest, and a lot of times a man's shirt will rub against the transmitter when he is walking around, creating a noise that makes it harder to listen to the conversation."

"Oh, I see," Elizabeth said.

"But they are a little more difficult to install on a woman's body because the wire is run straight up the breastbone. The wire needs to be under . . ."

"Under my bra, Lieutenant?" Elizabeth asked.

"Yes, yes," he said, pointing. The younger agents grinned at Fields' awkwardness, and Elizabeth winked at them.

"Just tell me exactly how to strap it on. I'll get Inez to help me, and then we can test it."

"That is what I was going to suggest, Miss Chase," Fields said.

After fumbling with the device for a few minutes in the bathroom, Inez and Elizabeth got it in place under her bra. Still in the bathroom, Elizabeth spoke to the agents to test the transmitter, and upon her return to the library, they pronounced it to be working perfectly.

Fields then spent the next ten minutes briefing Elizabeth on exactly where they would be positioned, and he gave her a code word to use if she thought she was in any danger. They assured her that they could be on the scene within one to two minutes and that if she and the sheriff moved for any reason, the wire had a range of one-quarter to one-half mile.

They were gone by five thirty, and Elizabeth felt an empty feeling in her stomach that was more tension than fear, she told herself.

When she went back to her office, Inez was waiting for her. "I thought you left when we finished with the wire, Inez," she said.

"I could have left you a message, but I wanted to make sure you got it. Dr. Howard called, and he's on his way over here."

"Oh, my God. I forgot he said something about coming over here," Elizabeth said, twisting her lips. "Is it too late to call him, Inez?"

"I'm afraid so. He was leaving his office as soon as he hung up." Both women heard the front door and looked down the hall.

"Elizabeth," Jim called out. "I'm so glad I caught you." He walked quickly down the hall.

"How's your patient in the emergency room?" Elizabeth asked.

"Pretty bad, I'm afraid. I shipped him on over to Florence. I don't think he's going to make it."

Elizabeth looked at Inez and their eyes met. "I'll see you in the morning," Elizabeth said.

Inez reached over, took both of Elizabeth's hands in hers, and whispered in her ear, "Please be careful."

"I will. Don't worry," Elizabeth murmured back. Inez nodded at Jim and then looked at Elizabeth one more time before she left.

As soon as Inez shut the front door behind her, Jim asked, "Are you still going?"

"Yes, I am."

"Well, then, I'm going with you."

"No, you're not. I appreciate your concern, Jim, but I have to do this by myself."

"It's too dangerous."

"The sheriff is not going to harm me."

"How do you know that?"

"I just do. He's no fool."

"Just the same, I'm going with you."

"He made me agree to come alone. Listen, he may have a legitimate reason for wanting to meet me at Frenchie's place. He may have uncovered some evidence out there that he wants to show to me."

"Okay, but why would he want you to meet him out there alone?"

"Because maybe he doesn't want anybody to know he turned over evidence to me that can help my client. I can live with that.

In fact, I don't blame him. I'd probably do the same thing. Don't forget the sheriff is an elected official."

"You think you have it all figured out, don't you?"

"It's certainly a reasonable theory, don't you think?"

"Yeah, maybe, but I'm still going with you."

"Jim, listen. If he's trying to help me and my client, and he sees you riding with me, that's going to get him mad, don't you think?"

"I'll get down on the floorboard of the backseat where he can't see me."

"No, Jim, please don't do this to me."

"If you don't let me ride in the back, I'm going to follow you out there in my car," Jim said, folding his arms across his chest.

Elizabeth put her hands on her hips and stared at him intently for a few seconds before she realized he wasn't going to change his mind.

Elizabeth felt a little silly riding down River Road with Jim lying on the floorboard of the backseat. She watched her odometer and the side roads carefully, and she didn't have any difficulty finding the turnoff to Frenchie's place this time. She followed the ruts of the dirt road slowly because the grass was higher now, and it made swishing noises on the underside of the Buick.

"He's already here," Elizabeth said as soon as she saw the powder-blue Lincoln parked near the front steps of Frenchie's house. "Don't say another word," she added, sounding like a schoolteacher rebuking a disruptive student.

"Okay," Jim responded in a muffled voice.

Black Jack was leaning against the front grille of his car with his back to the sun, in full uniform, wearing a campaign hat. Elizabeth parked her car about fifteen feet away from Black Jack's and got out casually, not wanting to appear too anxious.

"Good evening, Sheriff," she said cheerfully.

Black Jack stood up ramrod straight and touched the brim of his hat. "Hello, Miss Chase," he said, then took several steps toward her. "I appreciate you coming out here to meet me. You did come alone?" he asked, looking over her shoulders.

"Of course," she said, turning to look back at the road and extending her hand. "You can see for yourself."

"Good," Black Jack said. "Do you mind if we talk here?"

"No, this is as good as anywhere," Elizabeth answered, relieved that the sheriff didn't want to change the site of their meeting. "What do you want to talk about?"

"Your client."

"What about Mr. Fulton?"

"I want you to know that I am in a position to help him."

"In what way?"

"By making the service of his sentence a lot easier."

"How can you do that?"

"My meeting in Columbia today was with the governor."

"I had heard that you were very well connected, Sheriff, so I'm not surprised," Elizabeth said.

"He signed an Order that I have in my car that allows Willie Fulton to serve his entire sentence in the Craven County Jail. Do you want me to get it?"

"No, I believe you."

"Usually a prisoner has to serve two or three years in Columbia before he's eligible to come back to his home county. If I don't want somebody back here, I don't have to take 'em."

"That was considerate of you, Sheriff. I'm sure the Fulton family will appreciate that very much."

"After he's here three months, I can put him on work release."

"Work release?"

"Yes, work release. That means I can let him go home during the day and return to the jail, say, around nine at night."

"Is this legal?"

"Most of it. Let's just say the rest is within my discretion as sheriff of this county. Besides, no one is going to check behind me anyway."

"Do you mind telling me, Sheriff, why you are being so helpful to a convicted murderer?"

"Willie Fulton is not a bad man. He just made one serious mistake."

"Was that mistake trusting you too much?"

Black Jack put his hands on his hips and winced. "Miss Chase, I'm trying to make life bearable for your client. So he can see his family every day and earn a living—and what do you do but make some slanderous accusations?"

"What do you want from me, Sheriff? You didn't drag me all the way out here just to tell me what a compassionate man you are."

Black Jack bit his lower lip and stared intently at Elizabeth for a few seconds. "What do I want from you?" he asked. "To go back to Boston, where you came from."

"Why are you so anxious to get rid of me?" Elizabeth shot back.

"Because I don't like you spreading nasty rumors about me, that's why. I'm cutting the best deal for Fulton that I can give you. If you don't shut your mouth and leave quietly, the deal's off, and your client stays in the state penitentiary for a long, long time."

"We are going to file his notice of intention to appeal this week. The Supreme Court could reverse his conviction."

"The solicitor and I had a long talk about that, and he says our investigation was clean and Fulton doesn't have a snowball's chance in hell of getting a new trial."

"I will concede that you are probably right about Mr. Fulton's chances of getting a new trial from the Supreme Court. I do think we have an excellent chance of Judge Lawson granting us a new trial, though."

"What are you talking about?" The bravado was gone from the sheriff's voice now.

"We think we can get a new trial based upon after discovered evidence."

"What kind of after discovered evidence?"

"Your involvement with Mr. Fulton's decision not to testify."

"You think I had something to do with Fulton not taking the stand?" the sheriff asked, pointing at his chest. "Oh, come on, Miss Chase, you're crazy," he said, forcing a chuckle.

"Am I, Sheriff?"

"You aren't going to take my offer to help Fulton, are you?" he asked slowly.

"Nope. And I suppose this ends our little meeting, doesn't it?" Elizabeth started walking toward her car.

In one motion, Black Jack grabbed her with his left arm and pulled out his service revolver with his other hand. "Not so fast, miss," the sheriff said as he pointed the gun at Elizabeth's face.

Hearing a noise, they both turned and saw the backdoor of the Buick spring open.

"What are you doing here, Doc?" Black Jack asked, loosening his grip on Elizabeth's arm slightly. Jim walked quickly toward them carrying a pistol at his side, pointed toward the ground.

"What are you doing, Black Jack? You promised me you wouldn't hurt her." Jim had a wild look in his eyes that Elizabeth had never seen before.

"What are you talking about, Jim?" Elizabeth shrieked, and the sheriff tightened his grip again.

"I tried, Doc, but she wouldn't listen," Black Jack said. "We don't have any choice now."

"What do you mean, we? What's he talking about, Jim? Tell me," she demanded.

"You didn't realize when you were spreading all that talk about my drug dealing that you were dragging the doc's name through the mud too, did you?" Black Jack asked.

"What is he saying, Jim?" Elizabeth pleaded.

"What I'm saying here is that the doc has been my partner all along. You think he makes all that money he spends delivering babies?"

Elizabeth stared at Jim for a denial, but he said nothing. She turned back to look at Black Jack, and his face was not more than eighteen inches from hers. "Then tell me one thing, Sheriff," Elizabeth said as calmly as she could, but she was unable to keep her voice from trembling.

"What's that?"

"What did Willie Fulton and Mr. Gilbert have to do with this so-called partnership?"

"They just got in the way. You see, Miss Nosy Lawyer, my boys meet the big boat in Winyah Bay. Then they bring our cocaine up the river and, once it gets in my county, load it into one of my patrol boats. The Frenchman was in the river one night fishing, and he saw my boys loading the stuff into our boat. Then the bastard tried to blackmail me."

"So you killed him and made it look like Willie Fulton did it," Elizabeth said with all the contempt she could muster.

"Exactly," Black Jack replied, grinning now.

"And you also convinced Willie Fulton that he didn't need to testify because you would put the root on the jury and protect him."

"My, my, Doc, it looks like your girlfriend here has finally figured it all out," Black Jack declared, looking at Jim. Jim's eyes narrowed as he stared at the sheriff, but he didn't say anything. "Now we've got to put plan B into effect," Black Jack continued, raising his revolver and placing it within two inches of Elizabeth's temple.

Elizabeth closed her eyes. The shot almost deafened her, and then she felt Black Jack release her arm. When she opened her eyes, she saw Black Jack on the ground, blood oozing out of his forehead. As soon as she realized what had happened, Elizabeth started shaking uncontrollably.

"Are you okay?" Jim asked as he threw his arms around her.

Elizabeth knew she was in shock, but she tried to compose herself. "Jim, you were in business with him?" she demanded, glancing down at Black Jack's body and shaking her head repeatedly.

"Yes, I was, but not anymore. I've got over a million in a bank in the Cayman Islands, and that's where I'm headed. I want you to go with me. Nobody else but you knows about my involvement with Black Jack. There's nobody to testify against me. This was in your self-defense," he said, pointing the gun again at Black Jack. "I know that much about the law."

"Jim, they know."

"Who is they?"

"SLED."

"What are you talking about?"

Elizabeth reached into her blouse and pulled up the wire transmitter so it was visible. "I'm wired."

Jim's eyes widened as he glared at Elizabeth. Slowly he raised his pistol.

"Freeze!" they both heard someone shout from the edge of the clearing. "Drop that gun. SLED." Elizabeth recognized one of the younger agents who was crouched and pointing a rifle with a scope.

Out of the corner of her eye, Elizabeth saw Jim's hand jerk. The pistol went off, and she immediately felt a sticky liquid on her face. The last thing she remembered was that she was screaming.

EPILOGUE

As Elizabeth's plane climbed through the cloudless sky, Charleston once again came into focus in miniature. Six days had passed before she felt well enough to travel, and it had given her enough time to finish most of the work on her grandfather's estate. Inez had assured her that the rest of the paperwork could be done by mail.

She knew it would take more than six days to get over Jim's suicide and his life of deception. Although the wire ultimately had ended Jim's life, it had saved another. As soon as Phillips heard the recording, he called to tell Elizabeth that he would not oppose her motion for a new trial. Lawson immediately granted the motion, Phillips dismissed the indictment, and Willie was a free man.

She knew she would miss Robert, Inez, Ida Pearl, and particularly Rebecca, and she promised them that she would stay in touch. Her reverie was interrupted by a blaring voice. "Good morning, ladies and gentlemen, this is your captain, Lane Elmore. As you can see, I have turned off the seatbelts sign, and you are free to move around in the cabin, if necessary. We are about sixty miles north of the airport now, and if you look out the right side of the aircraft, you can see Winyah Bay and the Atlantic Ocean in the distance."

Elizabeth looked out her window and she could see the ocean many miles away, reflecting the bright morning sun like a giant prism. Realizing that they were probably over Craven County, she looked down, and in a few seconds she spotted the serpentine black ribbon of the river, snaking its way through the pine forests to Winyah Bay as it had done for thousands, if not millions, of years.